Calling All Neighbours

by

Tara Ford

Is it compulsory to love your neighbour?

© Tara Ford 2016
All rights reserved

ISBN-13: **978-1534999480**

No part of this publication may be reproduced, stored in a retrieval system, or transmitted in any form or by any means, without the prior permission in writing of the author, nor be otherwise circulated in any form of binding or cover other than that in which it is published and without a similar condition including this condition being imposed on the subsequent purchaser.

Cover design by Jacqueline Arbromeit
http://www.goodcoverdesign.co.uk/

Other titles by Tara Ford

Calling All Services

Calling All Dentists

Calling All Customers

Acknowledgements

Thank you to everyone who has supported me and my writing along the way. Thanks to my family for putting up with me in those 'Deadline' moments when I can no longer hold a simple conversation with them and tend to mumble my way out of most things – including cooking the dinner.

Thank you to Reid, Suzi Hoskins and Pat Ford who put forward names for characters, it has been such fun to include them in my books – in the best possible way of course – I do hope.

Huge thanks, as always, to Jane Hessey. She does a great job and we have a lot of fun along the way too.

My biggest thank-you goes to those of you who have taken the time to leave a short review on Amazon, they are so important to me – I appreciate all of them (good or bad) as always.

Tara Ford
http://taraford.weebly.com/
Twitter: @rata2e
Facebook: Tara Ford - Author

For my dear friends

Clair F
&
The Downes

Chapter 1

Stepping away from the bay window, Tiffany turned her head and tried to shout in a whisper. "Joe." She turned her head to see where he was. "Joe – quick. Come here."

From the kitchen-diner, Joe's head appeared around the doorway. "What?"

"Ssh. She's there again." Tiffany gesticulated frantically at the window.

Joe frowned in puzzlement as he wound around the doorway idly and moved closer.

"The woman – there," said Tiffany, pointing a finger to the window and pursing her lips as she made an exaggerated shushing sound. "The one I told you about last week."

Joe moved closer still. "Where?"

"Shush – there," she replied, feeling a little frustrated that he hadn't guessed what she was talking about. "Remember? I told you about her last week." Beckoning to him to move closer still, Tiffany pulled him around by his shoulder and pointed a finger past his nose to the small bench in the front garden, underneath the study window. "See?"

Joe nodded his head nonchalantly. "Go out there and ask her what the hell she thinks she's doing then."

"No," said Tiffany, scowling, as she pulled Joe back by his arm. "No, we can't be nasty to her."

"I'm not saying be nasty to her. Just go and ask her what she's doing in our garden. Do it politely."

Tiffany drew in a deep breath and peered out of the window again. "I will," she replied, unconvincingly. "In a minute. You go back to your work. I just wanted you to see her, that's all. I didn't think you believed me before."

Joe huffed a deep sigh and turned to leave. "I did believe you babe. I just don't know why you won't go and ask her what she's doing. Are you sure you don't want me to talk to her?"

"No, I'll do it. I just wanted to show you, that's all. I'll go out there, in a minute."

Shrugging his shoulders, Joe returned to the kitchen-diner and plonked himself down at the small, oval, wooden table. Tiffany could see through the doorway that he was staring, long and hard, at the computer screen in front of him. He then proceeded to tap the keyboard at quite a speed, considering the size of his rugby-playing hands. She watched him for a moment before turning back to the window and peering out again.

The afternoon sun beamed down on the small front garden, creating little picket fence shadows around the perimeter. A small, tidy lawn lay on each side of the paved pathway leading to the front door. Underneath the living room's bay window was a border, containing an assortment of leafy plants, bursting with flower buds. These were mirrored on the other side, the exception being the tiny, wooden bench, situated centrally within the flower border, upon which the woman was sitting.

Easing herself up from the bench, the elderly woman brushed a white curl away from her cheek and took a deep breath. With difficulty, she leant over and picked up her brown satchel, pulling the long strap over her head and positioning the bag in front of her. Slowly, she waddled off down the garden path.

From the window, Tiffany watched her walk out of the front gate and proceed across the green. Then she disappeared around the corner of the end house on Sycamore Close and was gone.

Tiffany sighed. "Oh no, she's gone now," she called out, sheepishly. "I'll have to catch her next time she comes."

Joe said nothing but nodded his head briefly as he continued typing.

"What shall we have for tea?" Tiffany asked, entering the kitchen-diner.

Looking up from the screen, Joe stopped typing and smiled warmly. "Let me finish this and then we'll sort something out. Five minutes and I'll be done, I promise."

Tiffany smiled. "OK, I'll have a look at what we've got in the freezer. I need to do something quick for tea, as I want to wash my hair tonight and have a good soak in the bath."

Again, Joe nodded his head but this time a little more fervently like he was annoyed by the constant interruptions to his work.

"Oops – sorry. I'll leave you alone for five minutes," she added, holding her hands up in the air, submissively.

Discarding the idea of rummaging through the freezer to find something for their tea, Tiffany went out to the back garden. It was a peculiarly shaped garden but a good size and certainly big enough to accommodate a young family in the future, should that ever happen. The oddly shaped garden (which Joe had described to his parents as an upside-down, right-angled triangle with a bit missing) was mainly laid to lawn with muddy, empty borders all around. The two side fences adjoined neighbour's gardens on both sides, and the lower fence at the end of the garden, looked out on to a large field, lined with giant sycamore trees. Several well cared-for horses roamed around the field, munching at the grass and flicking their groomed tails to deter the constant barrage of flies hovering around them. In the distance, a sparkling river could be seen weaving a pathway through the countless meadows which seemed to go on forever. Just on the other side of the garden fence was a gravel pathway which appeared to go around the back of the houses and then off through the fields. Tiffany wondered if it would take her to the river if she followed it. Both her and Joe enjoyed walking and there was plenty of beautiful countryside all around them to do it.

The view from the back of the garden had been a selling point for both of them. Overlooked only by their neighbour on the right, Tiffany and Joe had made the decision to buy 4 Sycamore Close almost immediately. It was their dream, first home together and although they weren't married yet, or indeed, made any sort of commitment to each other, they hadn't been able to resist the opportunity to purchase the house when it appeared in their local estate agents some four months ago.

Sycamore Close was set back from the main road which ran into the small town of Bashfield. There were nine houses, set out in the shape of a square horseshoe. Numbers one, two and three were on the left side, then Tiffany and Joe's house was on one end of the back row, alongside numbers five and six. The right side had house numbers seven, eight and nine.

In the middle of the three-sided square was a small green, surrounded by an access path. Almost every house had a picket fence around its front garden and several of those were painted white. Tiffany and Joe had liked the look of the picket fences and agreed that their first job, when they moved in, was to paint theirs white to blend in with the majority.

The houses themselves were bigger than they first appeared. Joe and Tiffany assumed that, like theirs, each house consisted of three bedrooms (although the third bedroom was more of a box room, but with some careful planning it could most definitely be made into a small bedroom) and a good sized bathroom upstairs. Downstairs there was a spacious kitchen-diner at the back, a front lounge to the right of the front door and a study and utility room to the left.

They were ecstatic when their offer was accepted and spent the next four months, during the purchasing period, collecting bits and pieces of old furniture, cookware, curtains, rugs and anything else that family and friends were kind enough to donate or sell to them.

Strolling down the length of the garden, Tiffany reached the fence at the bottom and leant on it, resting her elbows on the top. The horses were over in the far distance, nearest the field's gate. Tiffany wondered whether it was tea time for them too and perhaps they did actually eat more than just grass all day. She knew nothing about horses. She hadn't seen anyone visit the field in the two weeks that she'd lived in the house, but it was obvious that someone was coming to tend to their needs as on two occasions, during wet spells, they had been wearing waterproof coats over their backs.

Turning round, Tiffany leant back on the fence and rested her arms on the top, absorbing the heat of the late afternoon sun. This was her house. Her garden. Joe was indoors. Her future husband – hopefully, one day. Life couldn't get any better right now. She was living her dream and even if there was an elderly woman coming into their front garden, goodness knows how often, and making herself comfortable on the small bench, it really didn't matter. Not at the moment anyway.

Snapping the lid of his laptop shut, Joe stood up and stretched, making a loud yawning noise as he did so. "I'm done," he said, squinting his eyes as he stepped out to the brightly lit garden. "And now I'm starving. Shall we?"

Tiffany grinned, pulled herself away from the fence and sauntered across the patchy grass. "Yes, let's go. Think we've got some battered chicken breasts in the freezer. Shouldn't take long to do. Fancy those?"

"Don't mind a bit of breast any day of the week." Joe greeted her with a smirk and a cheeky slap of her rear as she passed by him.

"Oi – get off," she giggled. "You're a rampant monster, Joe Frey. Oh, and while I think of it, the fence at the bottom needs sorting out. One of the panels looks like it's going to disintegrate at the slightest breeze – and very soon. I don't fancy going out there to hang the washing out one morning and coming face to face with one of those horses from the field."

"Another thing to add to the growing list of jobs to do."

"Uh-huh," Tiffany replied with a smirk on her face. "They'll keep you out of mischief won't they?"

"Mischief? Me?" Joe frowned. "Don't know what you're talking about. Come on, I'm hungry. Do your thing and get those breasts out babe."

They'd met two years previously at a rugby presentation evening in their local community centre, which Joe was presenting. He had fallen for Tiffany at first sight but she had to be wooed somewhat, for several weeks, before she agreed to go on a first date with him. Shy, reserved and placid, Tiffany, or Tiff as she preferred to be called, was, in her nature, a stark contrast to the large, loud and gregarious boyfriend she had managed to hook up with. When Joe Frey walked into a room, everyone knew it. Aside from his sturdy, muscular physique, his height and a perfect smile on his chiselled face, Joe's booming voice and humorous banter attracted both men and women to flock round him admiringly. He was a party animal. A social junky. A man with a motto to live for the moment. Yet, when alone with Tiff, he was the gentlest, kindest and most thoughtful man she could have wished for. He was an affable companion and a sensuous lover.

Joe's love of rugby stemmed from his childhood days of playing for his school. Battered and beaten, he had spent most of his senior school days with black eyes and bruises in every conceivable place. Upon leaving school, he had signed up for the college rugby team and continued to play for a further two years while he studied for his 'A' levels. But sadly, Joe's rugby career came to an abrupt end in his final season at the college, when a vicious tackle took him down to the ground. With all of his weight, he had landed on his twisted left leg, snapping the tibia and fibula in half.

So a career in the world of physical rugby was no longer an option. However, Joe's 'A' level qualifications and a further two-year apprenticeship in the leisure industry allowed him to build a career as a personal trainer and most recently, become the manager of a local leisure complex.

In his spare time, he coached a team of 14–16 year-old youths in rugby and helped to organise the county's under 18's league. As if this wasn't enough to do in his spare time, he had also volunteered to design and update a new website for the Hampshire Rugby League. The new website had taken up most of his time since he and Tiff had moved into their new home. He could only apologise profusely to her, about the time-consuming task he'd taken on, every time she walked past him and huffed or when she sighed exaggeratedly whilst working around him in the kitchen.

"I know. I'm sorry. I promised I'd get this done. How was I supposed to know that we would be moving into a new house when I offered to build a new website? It's crucial that I get this finished before the season starts. Bear with me babe."

How could anyone not 'bear' with him? Joe was so perfect in every way. He made Tiff laugh. He made her cry. On a number of occasions, he had surprised her with a romantic break or an unexpected gift, or flowers. Countless bouquets of beautiful flowers. He made her feel safe and secure. He cared for her and provided for her. He was the steadfast strength that she didn't have. Tiff's failings were Joe's substance. They worked well together and were made for each other. Except, now that they had bought their very own home together, there were still no signs of that ultimate gift, an engagement ring, let alone the peal of wedding bells.

Luckily, Tiff was a patient person. She was sure it would come. One day. After all, they'd made the first big step, hadn't they? Buying a home together had not been a decision made lightly. The hefty mortgage repayments would be tough to manage during the first few years while they re-vamped and furnished the old house. The only thing that Tiff had insisted upon was a new bed, when they moved in. She couldn't bear the thought of a second-hand bed.

"You just don't know who might have slept in a second-hand one. Or what they might have got up to. Ugh, no. We have to get a new one." She had said to him one day.

Joe had agreed entirely, although he playfully embellished on the idea of what other people might get up to in their beds. "I totally agree. There are people out there who quite enjoy partaking in the odd session of watersports you know."

"Watersports? What do you mean?" Tiff enquired, innocently.

"You haven't heard of it?"

"No, I haven't." She stared, puzzled. "In bed?"

"Don't worry about it." Joe laughed. "You wouldn't want to know. We'll definitely get a new bed babe. Without a doubt."

After that conversation, Tiff had curiously decided to *Google* 'Watersports in bed'. She hadn't wanted to pursue the subject further with Joe, fearing her naivety would have added ammunition to his jesting ways. To her horror, the words, 'Golden shower', along with numerous sexually explicit thumbnail images displayed on the *Google* search results, dawned on her and were enough to repel her away from the page instantly.

However, after two days of troubled thoughts and images churning around in her mind, Tiff had taken the brave step of confronting Joe with the subject again.

"Joe..." she whispered, as they lay in bed, one Sunday night. Nudging his broad shoulder gently, she called him again. "Joe. Can I ask you something? Don't go to sleep yet."

Joe turned over, sleepily. "Yeah?"

In the darkness it was easier to ask the all-important question. "I've been thinking..."

"Hmm," he mumbled from under the quilt cover.

"What you were saying the other day... about watersports."

Lifting his head from the pillow, Joe peered through the gloom. "What?"

The urgent tone in his voice startled Tiff and she pulled herself up and rested her elbows on the pillow. It was too late. She'd broached the subject. She had to follow it through. "Watersports. What you said the other day. I know all about it."

Propping himself up on a strong, muscular arm, Joe peered through the blackness worriedly. The whites of his eyes could be seen staring widely. He looked fearful in the gloom. "Tiff, I... err..." he stuttered. "No way. I'm sorry but there's no way I'm doing that."

"What?" Tiff shrieked at him. "No, I know. Neither am I. You've got it wrong." Clasping her hand to her chest, she continued. "I didn't mean that *I want* to do it."

"Thank God for that. What then? Why are you asking about it?"

"I was only going to ask you if *you'd* ever done anything like that before." Tiff cringed embarrassedly, and silently thanked the night time for its obscurity.

"No I have not – never," he grunted in horror.

The tone in Joe's voice suggested that he was aghast by her questioning. "Sorry, of course you wouldn't have. I'm being silly. Forget I mentioned it. Goodnight darling. Love you."

"Love you too." Lowering himself back on to the pillow, Joe stared up at the ceiling. "Can't believe that you'd ask me a question like that."

"Neither can I. Sorry."

"No, I mean it's ok to ask me. It's just that you've obviously been thinking about it since I mentioned it. Don't take everything so seriously babe."

Snuggling into his side, Tiff wrapped her arm across his firm stomach. "I'll try not to. Let's just forget that I said anything. Sorry Joe. Night, night." She cringed at her questions and was horrified to think that Joe thought she wanted to try out watersports with him.

She really was going to try not to take everything so seriously in the future.

Chapter 2

Peering through the window of the smallest, back bedroom, Tiff could just see the young woman who lived on the left side of the square at number 3 Sycamore Close. She was lounging on a recliner, in her back garden, soaking up the warm sunshine. The slim, well-proportioned woman reached under her chair and pulled a lever, allowing the backrest to recline further. She was wearing lime-green shorts and a lemon t-shirt. Her long blonde hair was tied up in a messy bun on the top of her head and over-sized, dark-rimmed sunglasses with silver arms concealed her small, attractive facial features. A rickety looking wooden table stood beside her and on the top, rested a paperback book and a tall glass of, what looked like, orange juice.

Tiff knew that there was also a large black dog living next door as, on occasion, she had seen the woman being whipped out of her house and dragged across the green by the frenetic pace of the unruly creature. Yet there appeared to be no sign of the animal in the garden today.

There was also a young girl who visited at the weekends. With long blonde hair, a pretty face and perfectly presented attire, Tiff assumed that she was the daughter of the woman. The young girl looked to be around seven or eight years old and although she hadn't been seen very often, she had certainly been heard. With the whining, screeching, and demanding coming through the walls each weekend, Tiff was sure the girl was a spoilt brat and got everything she wanted. Every Friday evening the girl would be delivered to the house and picked up again on the Monday morning by, Tiff could only guess, her father.

Stepping back from the window, Tiff continued to watch the woman as she removed the sunglasses from her face and placed them on the top of her head, just below her bun. She yawned and stretched her arms and legs. Taking a quick sip from her drink, she began to remove her t-shirt.

Tiff moved back another inch or so, not wanting to be seen spying on her new neighbour. Well she wasn't spying exactly but more intrigued as to where the little girl and the dog might be as there was no sign of either of them.

Pulling the t-shirt over her head the woman's ample, curved breasts plopped out on to her chest with a wobble. She was topless. Half naked. Revealing her womanly figure.

Tiff gasped and stared hard through the window. How could the woman be doing that in her garden? The neighbours might see her. More importantly and more worryingly – Joe might see her.

The woman's seductive figure could be appreciated and admired by either sex, but Tiff did not want Joe to discover his very own topless show right from the comfort of his own home. A jealous twinge trickled through Tiff's mind. How could she stop the woman from going topless in her own garden? Obviously, she couldn't. How could she stop Joe from ogling the woman's breasts, given the chance? She couldn't. Wouldn't any red-blooded, young man be mesmerised by the hot blonde baring all in her garden? Or any man, of any age, for that matter. Tiff decided the answer was most definitely, a big fat yes.

Sighing heavily, she continued to watch as the woman stretched her arms back behind her head and closed her eyes. As she did so, her large breasts lifted and pulled together slightly, creating a deeper, more provocative cleavage. Tiff tutted to herself. She knew she was being unreasonable by having envious thoughts. In comparison, she was a small-breasted woman with slightly too wide hips – a typical English pear-shape. The woman next door had the ultimate of figures, as far as Tiff was concerned. She had a perfectly proportioned hourglass shape. Basically, everything was in the right place and of the right size. Tiff frowned as an image of Joe in the bedroom, sat in an armchair with a pair of binoculars, entered her mind. Shaking her head, she took one last look at the woman, left the small bedroom and closed the door firmly behind her. Very firmly.

Week three and they still hadn't done anything productive to brighten up the tired décor in the house or start any of the other niggly little jobs that needed doing. Drippy taps, creaky floor boards, flaky paint, frayed carpets and draughty windows were just a few of those tiresome tasks, not to mention the weeds in the front and back gardens, broken fences and unwanted bushes.

Joe and Tiff had been fully aware of the amount of work they would need to do but somehow, since they'd moved in, not one thing had been done. It seemed that they'd moved into their new home, set their belongings in the appropriate places and spent the last three weeks just getting through each day. Going to work every morning, coming home in the evenings, cooking tea, watching the TV for a couple of hours and then falling into bed exhausted. The weekends had been taken up with Joe's website building and Tiff's housework regime of running around the whole house with a hoover, just to keep the copious amounts of dust down and perpetually filling the washing machine with its next load. Thank goodness the weather had been on their side and dried their clothes on the wobbly, rotary washing line which was barely standing upright around the side of the house. At least the washing was above par. Although, Tiff did expect to find it all laying in a muddy heap one day, when the ancient rotary line died and crumpled to the ground.

Unable to get the image of the half-naked woman out of her head, Tiff headed down the stairs with a laundry basket full of dirty washing.

"I've finished upstairs. Just need to do down here. I'm not going to spend every weekend cleaning this place from top to bottom though. We'll have to do something about the dust – I don't know where it's all coming from?"

Joe looked up from his laptop. "The carpets. The wallpaper. It's everywhere babe. Once we start decorating it'll settle down."

"When will we ever find time to do that?" Tiff huffed. "We haven't got any time off work for months yet."

"I'm going to make a start – tomorrow. We agreed the first job would be to paint the picket fence white." Joe smiled warmly. "What do you think? Might even meet some of our neighbours."

That was exactly what Joe would want to happen. Meet his neighbours. Make new friends. *Ogle the sexy woman next door...*

"OK. It would look nice. And especially if your parents are coming over in the next few weeks. Suppose we could start from the outside and work our way in."

"Exactly. And certainly while the weather is good at the moment. It'll soon change and then we'll have to wait until there's a hint of summer before we can do any painting outside."

Tiff nodded agreeably. "OK, It'll make a good first impression when everyone comes round, I suppose."

Both sides of Joe and Tiff's families wanted to visit and see the new house. Tiff was an only child but Joe had two brothers and a sister. They had all said that they would visit at some point, apart from Joe's oldest brother who lived in Germany and only returned to the UK now and again. So Tiff's frantic hoovering and cleaning sessions were more to do with the possibility of someone coming to see them and inspect their new home at a moment's notice. At least if the place was clean then the countless other little jobs could be overlooked or noted as 'a work in progress'.

"Oh, and I've been thinking about the small back bedroom," added Tiff. "I might use it as my craft room. Nice view of the fields, out the back."

Joe nodded enthusiastically. "I'll get it decorated for you, babe. That'll be another job done."

"No. I can do it myself. I would err... quite like to do that actually." Tiff stumbled, as images of a giant-sized pair of breasts bouncing around the garden next door, flickered through her mind.

"Choose the colours and we'll *both* do it." Closing the lid of his laptop, Joe continued. "Shall we go into town and get the paint today? I'll need to pick up some white for outside anyway."

Tiff nodded her head and grinned. "OK. Let me put this load on first."

"I'll nip upstairs and gauge how much paint we'll need for that back room," said Joe, pulling himself up from the dining chair and stretching his powerful arms above his head.

"No! I mean – it's OK," she blurted, falteringly. "I mean – I've done it. Measured it. Yes, I've done it already. You've got to be quick to keep up with me. It's err... "

Startled by the urgency in Tiff's voice, Joe frowned questioningly. "What about the skirting boards? Some of those need replacing don't they? I'll check before we leave. No point decorating and leaving rotten skirting boards at the bottom."

"Oh yes. I forgot about them. Wait. Stay there –" she said, dropping the laundry basket on the table with a thud. "I'll go and look – right now." Racing away, Tiff stumbled at the foot of the stairs and screeched, "Ouch!"

"Tiff," called Joe, "what are you doing? What's the mad rush?"

Feigning laughter, Tiff picked herself up from the bottom step. "Nothing darling. Thought I'd help out by doing the measuring for you. Stay there – I'll be down in a minute." Taking the stairs two at a time, she reached the top and halted. Listening out for any movement downstairs, she walked across the narrow landing and entered her newly appointed craft room.

There were two skirting boards that needed replacing. One of them was badly scuffed and chipped and the other one, under the window, was covered in grubby green stuff and brown streaks, both of which Tiff had tried to scrub off in the first week of moving in. Pacing the length of the first wall, she tried to gauge the size of board they would need. *Four and a half metres*, she thought to herself. Reaching the window, she peered out again to see if the woman was still in her garden.

"You're getting a bit possessive about this room, aren't you?"

Startled, Tiff turned around. "Ooh – you made me jump. What are you doing up here?"

Joe laughed. "Tiff – what's got into you? I live here – remember?" he said, leaning on the doorframe. "It's like you're scared that I'm going to take the room away from you. It's yours, babe – chillax. I want to make it look nice for you though."

Tiff stepped back and perched her bottom on the windowsill, obscuring as much of the window as she could.

"You'll need this," said Joe, holding out a tape measure across the small room. "To see how much wood we'll need."

"Did it in my head, but I suppose I can do it accurately." Tiff leant over and stretched her hand out, trying to reach the tape measure without leaving the window. "Throw it," she said as she realised she couldn't reach it.

Joe shot a quizzical look as he threw the tape across the room. "What about the window?"

"What about it?" Tiff snapped.

"I was just going to ask – do you want blinds up there?" Joe edged towards the window.

"No. No blinds," she shrieked, in a panic. "Don't need to measure it. I'll... I'll just paint the frame. It'll be nice to have a bare window – you know, to look out of when I'm crafting."

Joe nodded his head, "OK, your call babe but calm yourself down. It's like you've become crazily obsessed with having this room." Halting in the middle of the room, he peered up at the ceiling. "White for the ceiling?"

"Yes and err... lilac for the walls. I like lilac. It's calming."

"Go on then," said Joe, glancing amusedly at Tiff. "Measure up and we'll go into town."

As Joe disappeared from the room, Tiff turned around and peeped out of the window again. The woman next door had sat up. She was liberally slathering sun lotion over her chest, rubbing it in with circular movements around her breasts. The sun glistened on her skin making her appearance even more alluring. Tiff watched admiringly. If only she had a body like the woman's. It was an attractive sight, if she had to be honest, not that she was that way inclined at all. Nevertheless, she would not want Joe to see the woman. Ever.

Tiff was not worried about Joe's fidelity. Although he was a little flirtatious in his manner, she knew that he loved her dearly and did not have eyes for anyone else. The problem stemmed from Tiff and her own insecurities. Her low self-esteem had improved slightly when she'd met Joe but old habits were hard to shift and gradually, she had slipped back into her old ways. Always wishing she didn't have small breasts and large hips and always wondering whether she was good enough for Joe. Always fretting about her abilities in anything and being far too judgmental on herself. She worried whether she was good enough for anything and that included her job too.

At a mere 25 years old, Tiff had been in her job for the last six years. She loved it. It was varied, interesting and well paid. She could work from home or alternatively, go into the studio, which more often than not, she did. Her working hours were flexible and as long as her production rate met the requirements, she could pick and choose her days off. She liked to work weekdays only, that way she could spend time with Joe at the weekends. Only on a very odd occasion had she done some extra time on a Saturday, during the busy seasons. As a stone-craft artist, her profession was, in itself, an enviable position to have.

The only downfall with her job and her new home was the small green she had to walk around to get to the house. Although picturesque, the position of the house was not best placed for carrying crates of stone-craft backwards and forwards from the car, which was parked in a lay-by on the main, Oakwood Road. Tiff had suggested to Joe that she worked more in the studio and brought less work home to do if they were to buy the house. So the fact that they didn't have their own drive was not going to be an issue for her. She was adamant about that. The house had been too good an opportunity to miss out on, just because it had no road access. Stone-craft or no stone-craft.

Artistic in nature, Tiff had been excited at the thought of having a purpose made craft room once they moved in. She liked to make countless, unique greetings cards to sell at car boot sales, local village fayres, school fayres and anywhere else she could find to sell them. She could put her artistic skills to anything, creating beautiful cushions, jazzy fabric picture frames, plush baby or wedding album covers, jewelry, decorated plastic keyrings and so much more. She was highly talented, yet she was her own worst critic too.

Dropping the sun lotion on the floor beneath her chair, the woman next door stretched back again and basked, semi-naked in the hot sun, in the confines and privacy of her own garden. Her round, oily breasts rose up and down as she breathed in and out.

Tiff shook her head in annoyance. Annoyed more by her own lack of confidence and insecure nature than by the huge pair of tits undulating in the sunshine, next door.

"Right, I've got the measurements – let's go," said Tiff, holding a scrap of note paper in her hand. "Lilac indoors, white for outdoors and six metres of skirting board."

Joe grinned and nodded his head. "You're on the ball today, aren't you?"

"Yes, but how will I fit the skirting board on? Do we have nails?"

Eyes wide in amazement, Joe replied, "Tiff – I'm shocked. Since when did you become a DIY enthusiast? You want to fit the skirting boards yourself? And you *can* stick them on with *Gripfill* but shouldn't we be doing it together?"

"I was thinking that we could do a job each. I want to learn how to do these things now that we have our own house. And... and I want to do the craft room myself – It'll be fun," she lied.

"OK, I get it," said Joe, rubbing his brow in puzzlement. "Well I think I get it. You never cease to amaze me Miss Cuthbert. I take it I'm doing the fence then?"

Tiff smiled warmly. "We're going to make a great team, you and I." Holding up her hand, she beckoned to Joe to high-five her. "Gently," she reminded him as his mighty hand clapped hers.

Chapter 3

The previous day's afternoon outing to the local DIY store had taken far longer than expected and Joe and Tiff had eventually arrived home at 11.15pm. By that time, they were tired and it was too late to carry heavy things across the green so they had left all of the paint, paint brushes, rollers, skirting board, saw, hammer, packs of different sized nails and two tubes of *Gripfill* in the car overnight.

Their shopping trip had turned into coffee and cake in a nearby cafe and a spontaneous visit to the cinema. Joe had then decided that they should try out the newest carvery in town for an evening meal. Tiff had been worried that she was not dressed for the occasion but Joe dragged her along, saying that their money was as good as anyone else's and he didn't want to go all the way back home just to get changed. It was a place to eat, not a fashion show.

Joe liked spontaneity and had been known to drag Tiff along to some of the most bizarre events during their time together. Like the time his rugby club were holding a charity event for the friends and family of the junior teams. Joe had picked Tiff up from work, even though she had her own car in the studios' car park, and whisked her away to an evening of heavily competitive Bucking Broncho – Guys versus Gals. Tiff had no option but to hitch up her flowing, denim skirt and join in the rodeo. Straddling the mechanical horse, with her eyes tightly closed, she squeezed her toes around her flip-flops straps, while her dangly ear-rings flicked painfully across her face. That was one occasion that Joe had completely forgotten to mention to her beforehand.

Another time that Joe had forgotten to mention before, was the hot air balloon ride. They had been in town, in the morning, doing some Christmas shopping for their families. By the afternoon, Tiff had found herself clinging, desperately, to the side of a wicker basket, 3000 feet away from the ground. The ride had been arranged the previous week by a friend of

Joe's at the rugby club. Joe had excused his lack of forethought and pre-warning, by saying that he thought Tiff wouldn't have gone if she'd known about it beforehand. She should be more spontaneous and grab life with both hands. At the end of the ride, Tiff nervously explained that she *had* 'grabbed life with both hands' literally. A lack of blood had left her fingers white, cold and numb as she had gripped the sides of the wicker basket in pure terror.

"It's a bit early to start painting the fence," said Tiff, gazing into her first coffee of the day. "Let's have some breakfast and then I'll help you bring all the stuff in from the car."

"OK. Toast?"

Tiff nodded her head and peered out of the patio doors. "It's going to be another lovely day."

"Perfect for getting the fence painted. Jam?"

"Marmalade – I bought some on Thursday."

"Oh good. Marmalade it is then." It was Joe's favourite. If he had his way, he would eat marmalade with a spoon. Tiff however, would not allow him to indulge often and constantly reminded him about the amount of sugary foods he ate and how bad it was for his teeth, his waistline and his overall health. Since retiring from playing rugby, Joe had had to watch his weight as it could all too easily shoot up, turning his stocky frame slightly plump. But for now, he was in perfect shape.

"Not too thick, Mr Frey," Tiff mocked. "Don't want your trousers getting tight again do we?"

Joe laughed. "I'm a lot more active now – those young lads at the rugby club make sure of that."

"I know they do. Go on then, as it's a beautiful Sunday morning."

"Yes it is, and I've got so much to do around this house and outside that I could probably get away with eating a jar a day. And what's a beautiful Sunday morning got to do with it anyway?"

Shrugging her shoulders, Tiff grinned. "Just thinking about that picket fence outside. It's going to take all day to do both sides of it."

"It'll probably take *you* all day to do your craft room too."

"At least you'll be getting a tan," joked Tiff. "I'll be stuck in a tiny room breathing in paint fumes all day."

"I said I'd help you do it. Let's do both jobs together."

"No," Tiff replied sharply. "No, I'm joking. I can't wait to do my little room."

"Are you sure?"

She peered at him thoughtfully. "I'm sure. Just don't get too burnt out there – wear a hat and make sure you cover your scar too."

"Yes Mother," Joe replied in jest. "I'll get the Factor 50 out."

The old scar around the back of Joe's neck wasn't usually visible and certainly not noticeable when he was dressed but Tiff knew that it would become sore if it got sunburnt, like it had before. The long white mark curved around his neck, from ear to ear. Originally the weal had gone all the way around his neck and it had looked like he had tried to hang himself with a thin rope. Over time, thankfully, the scar had faded at the front, leaving just the back of his neck disfigured.

When Joe first received the wound, years ago, he'd tried to hide it from his parents but his mum, Alex, had known something was wrong when he wouldn't remove his hoodie. He had just returned from a walk with their family dog and was acting peculiar and somewhat cagey. Joe's mum had been horrified when she discovered the deep burn marks on his skin and had rushed to the cupboard to get her first aid box. She always said that the burn cream she applied immediately, had lessened the scarring, particularly around the front of his neck and it had saved him from having to tell his crazy tale to anyone who asked. It had also saved him from looking like a suicidal failure.

"It still makes me laugh you know," said Tiff, eyeing Joe's neck. "Imagine how stupid you would look now if the burn hadn't healed so well around the front. It would have been so noticeable."

"Yes, all right. I'll get the sun cream when I've finished my toast."

The accident had happened whilst out walking his family's dog, Misty. Joe had bumped into an old college friend, on a nearby field. They had decided to sit down on the grass to chat about the old days, like they were two old men reminiscing about the past. They'd only left college the previous year but for the two young men it had felt like a lifetime ago.

Misty was sitting next to them, attached to her retractable lead. During the conversation, Joe had casually draped the lead around his neck and dropped the handle into his lap, while Misty basked lazily, in the afternoon sunshine.

Moments later a huge Labrador had arrived on the field. Bounding around, the sable coloured retriever played fetch with a ball.

Misty's ears pricked up. Energetically, she jumped to her feet and shot off at a 45-degree angle to Joe. The whipping sound of the eight metre cord, reeling out from the handle, was accompanied by a deep guttural squeal. The leash wrapped tightly around Joe's neck and burned deep into his skin as it was pulled away with the dog at considerable speed.

Joe's family had desperately tried not to laugh, once the initial trauma was over. But who wouldn't laugh at such a daft act? Especially when the victim was almost 20 years of age. It wasn't like he was a young, innocent child with no forethought.

The car was empty by the second trip. Tins of paint, skirting board, nails, glue and tools cluttered the hallway. It was ten o'clock and Tiff decided that this was a perfectly acceptable time, on a Sunday morning, to start doing some DIY. Besides, painting was a quiet job. The only noisy part for Joe, would be the banging in of nails to repair a couple of the fence posts.

"Babe, you really shouldn't worry so much about things," said Joe, reaching for an old t-shirt from his drawer. "We haven't made any noise at all since we've been here. A few nails being banged into a fence is hardly going to annoy the neighbours – and so what if it does – this is our house and we're doing it up. It's not like it's seven o'clock in the morning so stop fretting about what other people think."

"OK, OK," replied Tiff. "You're right, I do worry too much. And the little girl next door makes more noise than anyone around here."

"There you go then," said Joe. "Right, I'm going. We'll meet for lunch shall we?" Smiling cheekily, he continued. "Let's say one o'clock, at the dining table, at number 4 Sycamore Close." Winking a long lashed eye, he leant over and kissed her softly on the lips. "Give me a shout if you need help in your little craft room."

Tiff smiled and nodded her head. A warm glow filled her body. He was adorable. Sexy. Strong. He was hers and she loved him immeasurably.

The skirting board, previously cut by Joe at the exact point where Tiff had marked it, fitted perfectly. Now it was time to paint. Tiff had never painted a wall before and although she was very talented when it came to stone craft painting, decorating walls with rollers, was a whole different ball game.

The potent smell of the *Gripfill* wafted up her nose and filled the room. Stepping over to the window, she peered out towards the garden next door before opening the window to let the warm breeze in. The woman was not in her garden today but Tiff guessed that it may be a little too early in the day to be sunbathing – topless.

Opening the tin of lilac paint, she admired the rich colour and smooth texture. She stirred it with a stick, as instructed by Joe earlier, and poured a small amount into the roller tray. *Here goes,* she thought to herself and carefully rolled the roller through the thick liquid.

It was hot work painting four walls as the heat of the sun poured through the open window. Standing back, Tiff lovingly regarded her workmanship. It was a bit patchy though. This afternoon she would have to start all over again and apply a second coat. Peering down at her t-shirt and jeans, she puzzled over how she had managed to get covered in so many lilac dots and smudges.

Taking another glance out of the window before she left the room, she could see that the garden next door was void of people, pets and more importantly, breasts. Not that she was obsessed by the woman next door. She'd only peered out of the window about 28 times during the *whole* morning and that included the time when she was painting the wall surrounding the window. It was more a case of curiosity, rather than an obsession. Tiff wondered whether the elderly couple, who lived next door on the right, could see the woman's garden from their first floor windows too.

Washing her hands in the bathroom, Tiff looked up at the small mirror, precariously hanging from a bent nail (Another little job to do – get a decent mirror and hang it on a proper hook). She was surprised to see the newly acquired lilac streaks in her long, brown hair. She giggled to herself and decided to leave them there. She was bound to get a lot more paint on herself before the day was out. Joe would be amused by it too.

Popping her head around the bedroom door, she glanced at Joe's alarm clock, perched on an upturned cardboard box. She didn't want to be late for her date at one o'clock. Their bedroom was pretty basic at the moment. A king-size bed and two boxes, posing as bedside tables, furnished the back end of the room. There was a rickety set of old wardrobes, two sets of drawers that were barely holding together and an old dressing table that they'd managed to buy for £6 in a second-hand shop, scattered around the rest of the room. Tiff and Joe had discussed the order of rooms to be decorated and furnished and had come to a decision that their bedroom would have to be one of the last rooms to sort out. After all, no one would be going in their bedroom. Apart from their parents maybe, when they came for their initial inspection of the couple's first home.

Noting the time was approaching one o'clock, Tiff was about to go down the stairs when she heard voices coming from the front of the house and one of them was very familiar. Stepping back into the bedroom, she made her way over to the slightly open window and peeped out. She was right. One of the voices belonged to Joe. He was sitting on the pathway which went round the edge of the green, providing easy access to each house. He'd already painted over half of the picket fence on one side. He looked hot and sweaty, his damp hair spiked up untidily. He looked particularly handsome, sitting on the floor, cross-legged, with a paint brush in his hand, smiling up at someone.

Moving closer still, Tiff could see a figure leaning over the unpainted part of the fence separating her house from her neighbours. It was the woman with the tits. Smiling, laughing and flirting. Her arms folded in front to push the swell of her breasts out the top of her low cut t-shirt.

Tiff froze on the spot. She held her breath as she tried to hear what the woman was saying. In her right hand, the women held her dog's lead. The dog was panting as it sat in the hot sun and had obviously been for a walk already, by the way it idly waited by her side.

"So..." said the woman. "... two married?"

Joe shook his head. "No..."

Tiff struggled to hear every word.

"Kids?"

Again, Joe shook his head and smiled up at the woman.

"... handful... off without any." The woman stood upright, dropped the lead on the floor and tied her long blonde hair up in a loose bun. "... dog instead."

Joe laughed and then nonchalantly stroked the paint brush up and down the length of a fence post. "Suppose... answer back, do they?"

This time the woman laughed. "If you annoy... they will." Then she peered up at the blue sky for a moment before turning back to Joe. "Better go... bit of sunbathing... back garden... too hot... love... sun."

Tiff held her breath again. Had the woman just told Joe that she was going to be sunbathing in her garden? Had she told him she would be topless? A lump caught in Tiff's throat. She didn't like this woman. She didn't even know her. Breathe. Breathe. Keep calm. Keep calm.

Watching as Joe rose to his feet, Tiff's heart beat rapidly.

"Time for lunch," said Joe, looking down at his watch. "You'll... come over... meet... girlfriend... get on... together"

The woman nodded. "Thanks... will." Tugging at the dog's lead the woman turned around and disappeared up the path to her house.

Placing the lid on the paint tin, Joe carried it into the front garden and left it by the side of a small bush, in the shade. He put the brush on top, stood back and studied the fence with his hands on his hips. Then he went indoors.

"Tiff," called Joe as the front door closed. "Lunchtime."

Tiptoeing out of the bedroom, Tiff crept back to her craft room and stood in the doorway. "What did you say?" she shouted.

"Are you stopping for something to eat?"

"Oh yes. Coming right now." Slamming the craft room door shut, she sighed heavily and made her way down the stairs.

By the time she reached the kitchen-diner there were already two tall glasses of iced lemon on the table. Joe had removed his t-shirt and was busy making thick-cut ham and salad sandwiches.

"How did you get on?" asked Tiff, grabbing the salad cream from out of the fridge.

"OK – you?"

"Done one coat all the way around already."

"That's good babe." Joe slapped a slice of bread on top of each of the sandwiches, placed one on top of the other and cut through them diagonally. "Oh damn – forgot the salad cream."

Tiff smiled weakly. "Don't worry. I'll squeeze it in."

Fetching two plates from the cupboard, Joe placed the sandwiches on them and carried them over to the table. "Bring it over, I'll squeeze some in mine too."

"Did you get much done then?" quizzed Tiff.

"Not as much as I'd hoped and it's bloody hot out there. Wanna swap?"

"No – but I'll help you if you want. I can do the second coat another day."

Joe paused thoughtfully. "Thought you wanted to get the walls done and finished today."

"I can do them next weekend..."

"No, *we* can do them next weekend if you're going to help me outside."

Tiff gulped down a piece of bread without chewing it properly and froze momentarily as it stuck in her throat. "I..." she coughed. "I'm sure you'll have more jobs by next weekend Joe." The lump slowly slipped down her throat and disappeared. "No, I want to do the craft room myself, you know... just to say that I did it all. But I'll come and help you this afternoon. You never know, we might meet some of our neighbours."

"OK," said Joe, agreeably. "Get your bikini on though – it's hot out there."

Feigning shock, Tiff wondered when or if Joe was going to tell her about the woman he'd been talking to. "I'm not wearing a bikini out there, Joe Frey."

"Ahh, go on. We could have a paint flicking fight. Looks like you've been in one already – and lost." Joe laughed and leant over the table to peck her on the cheek. "It's in your hair too."

"I know. Not quite sure how it got there."

Raising his eyebrows, Joe rolled his eyes and tutted before continuing to eat his sandwich silently.

From the corner of her eye, Tiff watched as he devoured his lunch hungrily. Was he going to mention the woman from next door? When would he tell her about it? Surely he would have said something by now if he was going to say anything. A queasiness crept over Tiff, putting her off her sandwich. Did he fancy the woman? Was he hiding the fact that he had been talking to her? Tiff fought with her envy-monster as she nibbled her way through the sandwich, in silence.

Chapter 4

The afternoon sun beat down on Sycamore Close casting picket fence shadows around the edge of the front garden. It was so picturesque. Almost as soon as the brilliant white paint touched the surface of the wooden panels, it became tacky. Joe and Tiff had spent almost an hour, in silence, painting different sections of the fencing. Only once had Joe gone over to Tiff to top-up his paint tray from the five litre tin. It was a relaxing job, sitting on an old cushion, painting narrow slats while soaking up the heat from the sun. Tiff had had to put her sunglasses on due to the glare of the paint and Joe had removed his t-shirt for the second time today. But still, there had been no mention of the woman next door. Tiff had struggled with her jealous insecurity, through the silence. It was like torture.

"Do you need more cream putting on your back?" asked Tiff, breaking the silence.

"No, I'm good. I'll go and get us some more drinks in a minute."

Tiff nodded and smiled, waveringly.

The front door of number five opened and an elderly man hobbled down to his front gate. Wearing a greying-white, short sleeved shirt, unbuttoned half way down his front and khaki shorts, the extremely hairy, rotund man leant his legs against his gate. "Afternoon," he said in a croaky old voice. "You're doing a fine job there, young man."

Joe stopped painting and looked up. "Cheers. First job of many."

The old man smiled. "Poor old John didn't have it in him anymore – let the place go."

"John? Was he the man who lived here before?"

"Yes. Saw his last days out in that house," said the man, waving a crooked finger towards Joe and Tiff's new home. "Ninety-six I do believe, or was he ninety-five, coming up for ninety-six? Anyway..." said the man, shaking his head puzzled, "he couldn't do much at the end, as I said before.

He outlived most of his family and there wasn't anyone left to do things for him. God rest his soul."

"He lived to a very good age then," said Joe, rising to his feet and towering over the old man. "My name's Joe and she..." Joe pointed through the fence to where Tiff was sitting on a cushion, "is Tiff."

"Hello," said Tiff, smiling sweetly.

The old man offered a handshake to Joe. "Name's Cyril and the dear lady wife – 'er indoors..." Cyril chuckled, "or should I call her the lady of the manor? Is Betty."

"It's very nice to meet you," Joe replied courteously as he shook Cyril's hand.

"She... my Betty, saw you out here this morning. Daft bat – she's made a cake for you. Like's to welcome new neighbours in with a cake."

Joe looked across to Tiff and grinned. "That's very kind of her. We like cake, don't we Tiff?"

Tiff smiled and stood up with the paint brush held in her hand. "Thank you. How sweet of her."

"Date and walnut," said Cyril, proudly. "My Bet makes a good date and walnut cake. Not allergic to nuts are you?"

Simultaneously, Joe and Tiff shook their heads. "No, thankfully," said Joe.

As if on cue, a tiny, frail looking woman appeared at the front door holding a large cake wrapped in greaseproof paper. Her pale pink, flowery apron was covered in flour and smudges of cake mix. Her brilliant white hair was scooped up in a beige hair net and her rose coloured, powdered cheeks dominated her tiny features. She smiled warmly as she stepped out of the door. "Welcome to Sycamore Close," she said in a quiet, gentle voice. "I thought you might like this as a house-warming gift."

"That is so very kind of you," said Tiff, passing by Joe and Cyril and reaching the gate of number five. "It's lovely to meet you too, especially as we live right next door to you. My name is Tiffany – everyone calls me Tiff – and this is my partner Joe."

Betty nodded and passed the cake to Tiff. "I do hope you will like it. It's my speciality."

"Partner? You're married then?" said Cyril, watching his wife pass the heavy cake over the gate.

"No," replied Joe. "If she's lucky, I might just marry her one day." He laughed, embarrassedly.

Cyril darted his eyes across from Joe to Tiff and then cleared his throat uncomfortably. "Ah, sorry. Hope I haven't put my foot in it."

"No, not at all," replied Tiff. "On the contrary – he'll be the lucky one if I decide to accept a marriage proposal." Mouthing a 'thank you' to Betty, Tiff took the cake back to her house and placed it inside, on the bottom step of the stairs before returning outside. "I was joking by the way," she added as she rejoined the small gathering by next door's gate.

"Phew," puffed Joe as he wiped a hand across his brow. "I was worried there for a minute." Placing an arm round Tiff's shoulders, he pulled her in tightly. "We have done things a little unconventionally. Bought the house first. Everything else can come later."

"That's the young folk of today I suppose." Cyril sighed. "We don't have any children of our own but we can see how the youngsters do things a lot differently nowadays."

Joe nodded his head agreeably. "And not always for the better."

"I agree with you." Cyril paused thoughtfully. Leaning over towards Joe's ear, he lowered his voice, "Not like some around here."

Joe frowned and Tiff gave him a quizzical stare as she heard Cyril's last words.

"Her – on your left. Number three."

"Ah, yes," said Joe, waveringly. "I err... met her this morning." Darting his eyes towards Tiff, he grinned. "I meant to tell you babe."

Tiff smiled awkwardly.

"Woman's got no morals," whispered Cyril.

Tiff moved closer and listened to the intriguing conversation.

Little Betty was oblivious to the conversation outside her gate and tended to the well-kept dahlia bushes that lined the pathway up to her front door. She moved along slowly, meticulously picking at the leaves, dead-heading the old flowers and sniffing the new ones. Now and again she looked up and smiled.

"Who is she?" Tiff feigned curiosity.

"Georgie – Georgie Ford." Cyril replied in a hushed breath. "Watch out for her."

Cyril's last statement, or warning, had been solely directed towards Tiff.

Inching even closer, Tiff glanced back over her shoulder, before asking the inevitable. "Why? Why should we watch out for her?"

With his hands buried inside the pockets of his shorts, Joe shuffled uncomfortably from one foot to the other. "Seemed OK when I spoke to her this morning."

Cyril held his chin in contemplation, "Hmm…"

Betty looked up and smiled sweetly before returning to her pruning.

"Kicked her husband out, a good few years back now. She's a devious woman – don't ever trust her." Cyril turned his head, towards number three with a disdainful look in his old eyes. "Betty and I… we keep our distance."

"Oh dear," said Tiff, considerately, "I'm sorry to hear this. It must be very difficult living so close to someone you don't get on with."

Cyril nodded his head and sighed deeply. "We mind our own business. Bet bakes her cakes and nurtures her flowers – I like the cricket on TV and spend a lot of my time doing crosswords. And we've got the birds out the back. We're happy enough. You've probably seen the aviaries from your room upstairs, have you?"

Tiff shook her head. "Oh, I thought they were two large sheds."

"Lovebirds. Like miniature parrots. We have over a hundred of them." Cyril peered down at the ground forlornly. "We had a lot more… before *she* came along." Again, Cyril shot a menacing glance towards number three.

"So," said Joe, "how has she upset you?" He paused momentarily before quickly adding, "If you don't mind me asking."

"I don't mind," Cyril replied. "We lived our dream some six years ago…"

"Anyone like a cup of tea?" Betty moved towards the gate smiling widely. "I have a lemon drizzle cooling in the kitchen if you'd like a slice."

Joe glanced at Tiff and grinned. "That would be most kind of you," he replied, nodding his head eagerly.

"Yes, thank you," added Tiff.

"You're welcome to come in." Cyril beckoned towards his house as Betty trotted off with a handful of dead flower heads. "Come and see the birds."

"Cool," said Joe, gladly. "I'll just get the paint tin covered over." Grabbing the brushes, he quickly gathered the other things from the garden and placed them carefully inside the hallway. He pulled the key out from the inside of the front door lock, closed the door behind him and locked it.

Tiff was already inside Cyril and Betty's house by the time Joe caught up with them.

It was like stepping back in time to a 1950s, retro American diner. Tiff and Joe marvelled at the bubblegum and neon décor. The kitsch was dominated by a huge American jukebox, standing centrally, against one wall. A brilliant red, *Salvador Dali* lips sofa sat under the bay window at the front and black and white, chequerboard vinyl flooring covered the entire, open-plan space. Over in the kitchen area, Tiff could see a huge, pastel pink fridge unit dressed with chrome trim and solid looking, pivoting handles. Matching floor and wall units lined a section of the wall and ended at a pink gas stove. The smaller appliances were all chrome and gleamed brightly in the light coming from the wide kitchen window, which was framed by a pair of sugary-pink and powder-blue, abstract design curtains.

In the dining area stood a Formica topped dining table with four matching chrome and Day-Glo blue chairs. Three flying ducks, increasing in size, adorned the pistachio-green, sprigged floral wallpaper behind the table along with a large, framed photograph of Queen Elizabeth II's coronation.

"Wow," breathed Joe, taking in the colours and intricate detail all around him. "This is truly amazing."

Tiff stood alongside him, speechless.

"Stuck in a time warp," said Cyril, lightheartedly. "My Betty loves it. I, on the other hand, live with it. I've got my birds to keep me happy."

"I'm astounded. It is absolutely incredible." Tiff stared around the expansive space in awe, as the homely smell of baking wafted up her nose.

"Took three years and as many steel beams," said Cyril, proudly. "We have no supporting walls downstairs, as you can see. Just these big, old pillars and the beams across the ceilings." Cyril pointed to three small pillars around the walls and one large solitary one in the middle of the expansive room.

Tiff imagined that the largest pillar was roughly where their own dining room door began.

Joe shook his head in disbelief.

"Old John took one of *your* walls out, at the back, in his younger days."

"Yes," said Joe, still eyeing the bright décor. "We have a kitchen-diner at the back. We've got a lot of work to do in there though." Turning to look at Tiff, he added, "I'd have my work cut out if Tiff ever wanted anything like this."

Tiff giggled, "Not a bad call. I'd love to have a place like this."

Eyeing her quizzically, Joe smiled. "Maybe one day."

"Have a seat," said Cyril, ushering Joe and Tiff towards the 1950s dining table. "My Bet will make a lovely pot of tea."

Betty had already started to prepare a tray on which she had placed a vintage, gilt-edged sugar bowl, milk jug and matching cups and saucers, all decorated with a delicate rose spray. She counted four heaped spoons of tea leaves into the matching teapot and carefully poured in boiling water. Then she popped a sterling silver tea strainer on the top of one of the cups and carried the tray over to the table. Returning to the kitchen area, she cautiously moved the lemon drizzle cake from its cooling rack and placed it on to a cake stand.

"This all looks delightful," said Tiff, eyeing the presentation in front of her. "You are very kind to have gone out of your way to do this for us."

"Ooh, it's no trouble at all dear," replied Betty as she went back to the kitchen to fetch a cake slice.

"She does this every day, my dear old Betty. There's no drinking from mugs in this house." Cyril laughed. "And there is never a day that we don't have cake either."

"It's quite apparent that you like to bake," said Joe. "And you certainly have an amazing kitchen to do it in."

Betty nodded her head and removed her apron before sitting down at the table. Dressed in a pink, floral swing-skirt dress which pinched in at the waistband, revealing her tiny figure, it seemed that Betty's choice in fashion was also stuck in this 1950s time warp. However, it worked. Betty was gracious and pristine in her appearance, and her kitchen was immaculate, bearing in mind she had recently baked two cakes.

Tiff wondered for a moment whether her own kitchen would look so clean and tidy if she had just whipped up a couple of cakes.

"Should I pour the tea?" enquired Joe, politely.

"No, you sit there and have a rest. You've been painting all morning. Lemon drizzle cake?"

Joe nodded. "Yes, thank you."

Tiff watched Joe admiringly. His impeccable manners were second to none. His general thoughtfulness and consideration for others outshone many of his friends and rugby associates. He was a dream-like character in so many ways. So why hadn't he told her about his chat with Georgie Ford this morning?

"So..." said Tiff, tentatively, "you were saying you lived your dream six years ago?"

"Ah yes." Cyril turned to look at Betty.

She nodded her head approvingly and smiled.

"We had wanted to visit the USA for years and years. Tour the states, see the sights and turn it in to a one-month dream holiday." Cyril took a cup of tea from Betty and smiled at her. "But it just wasn't possible..."

"Oh – why?" asked Joe, curiously.

"The birds. We didn't have any family close enough to look after them."

Joe and Tiff nodded their heads appreciatively.

"And at that time we didn't know anyone in the close well enough either."

"The community centre has brought us all together since though. We do love the community centre, don't we Cyril." Betty added.

"Is that the one just along the main road?" asked Tiff.

"Yes, Hillhead Community Centre – very nice place, they have OAP days on Tuesdays and Fridays," said Betty, as she cut large slices of cake and placed them on the small, decorative plates. "Now and again we arrange outings and trips on Saturdays too."

"That's nice," Tiff replied with a warm smile. "Do they do charitable fayres – things like that?"

"Oh yes. You must come along. I'm always there – I like to help out with other events that go on during the week too. They could always do with an extra hand."

"I will pop along and see if there's anything I can do. I'm always interested in helping the local community in any way I can. Thank you." Tiff turned to look at Joe and then Cyril. "Sorry, please do go on."

"John, next door, had been in hospital for some time, after one of his operations. Hip replacement, I do believe it was at the time, so we couldn't have asked him to look after the birds either. God rest his soul." Cyril peered down into his cup.

"So you asked Georgie?" Joe enquired.

"No. Actually we didn't. I was talking to her one day, out on the green. She was giving me this sob story about her terrible husband and how she couldn't take much more of him. He'd already left but..." Cyril took a sip from his tea and then sighed. "Well, she said she needed a holiday and we then got on to the subject of dream holidays."

"She offered – it was her idea," said Betty in a troubled tone.

Nodding his head, Cyril sighed again. "Yes, she did. We were so excited about the possibility of really living our dream. Georgie seemed like a lovely girl. Troubled by marital problems, yes, but she came across as a very kind and caring woman. Her daughter, Sophie, was just two years old so Georgie stayed at home to raise her. We saw quite a lot of her after that day on the green. The more we saw her, the more we liked her." Cyril puffed out his cheeks and let a stream of breath out slowly. "We had no idea of what she was really like."

"Sounds ominous," said Joe, worriedly.

Cyril and Betty simultaneously nodded their heads as sombre expressions crept over their withered faces.

"She insisted that we should have our holiday, especially as we were growing older. She vowed that she would take care of the birds for a whole month." Cyril cleared his gravelly throat and continued. "We offered her £400 to take care of them. She wouldn't take it at first."

Joe and Tiff slowly nibbled their way through the fabulously flavoursome lemon drizzle cake as they listened to the seemingly, incredulous tale.

"So that was that. We were off," said Cyril. "Georgie had clear instructions on how to care for the birds. She knew what to do and when to do it."

"We did get our dream holiday," added Betty, "but at a very high price. I told Cyril not to pay her before, and to wait until we returned." Betty shook her head sadly. "Soppy old Cyril thought she would need the money beforehand and in the weeks leading up to our departure, he'd doubled the amount he'd offered to pay her."

"So you paid her... £800?" asked Joe, reproachfully. "I mean; I don't want to sound rude but I'm guessing that things did not turn out well."

Cyril nodded his head as the corners of his mouth turned down. "No, things did not go well."

Listening in silence, Tiff watched Joe's expression change as the story unfolded.

"My birds are precious to me. I wanted to make sure that they were well cared for so I offered her more money. I thought that £200 a week would help her and also ensure that the birds were very well looked after."

Joe nodded and smiled agreeably. "I take it she didn't look after them?"

"Over half of them were dead when we got home. The cages were in an appalling state. I'm sure she hadn't cleaned them out once – although she said something to the contrary."

"Oh no, I'm so sorry to hear that," said Tiff, softly. "It must have been a terrible shock for you."

"Yes..." mumbled Cyril. "Betty had a nasty shock too – she discovered them first."

"I did." Betty joined in. "There was a nasty smell in my kitchen. I couldn't work out where it was coming from... until I looked in the swing-bin." Shaking her head in disgust, Betty tutted and shuddered. "Yes, there were four dead, rotting birds at the bottom of the bin – buried under sheets of paper towel."

"That woman had not fed them. She hadn't given them water. She hadn't opened the windows every day – especially as it was the summer time – to allow some air to circulate. She hadn't done anything." A look of bitterness crept over Cyril's face.

"What did she say? I'm assuming that you went round to see her?" asked Joe.

"She said she'd fed them and given them water but she didn't think that they looked well. She said that she became ill after the first week and feared that she had caught something from the birds. Apparently, she didn't see the birds for a few days, due to her illness, and when she went back a couple of them had died. She told me that she hadn't known what to do and just kept on feeding them and giving them water." Cyril drew in a deep breath and sighed. "I know she didn't give them water often, as when we returned home, the water trays were bone dry. It was stiflingly hot and acrid in the aviaries too. They hadn't been cleaned out at all – I could tell that, by the amount and consistency of the droppings festering in the heat."

"Anyone like another cup of tea," asked Betty as the atmosphere in the room grew heavy.

"Yes, please," said Joe. "I think we have time for another." Peering across to Tiff, he smiled weakly.

Tiff nodded and smiled back. "That would be lovely. Thank you Betty."

"How many did you lose?" asked Joe, compassionately.

"Including the four in the bin, we counted 53."

"Oh dear, that's a lot. Did she say why she'd put them in the bin?"

"According to her, they were the first ones to die. She didn't know what to do with them and discarded them in the bin. Stupid woman – did she not think that they would begin to fester and rot?"

"We took a mobile phone away with us," said Betty as she poured freshly boiled water into the teapot. "She could have called us. But she didn't."

"What was her excuse for not contacting you?" asked Tiff.

"Lost our number. We don't believe that for a moment – do we Cyril?"

"No." Cyril stretched back in his chair and rubbed at his chest. "I had bred a lot of those birds myself. They were like my babies, you know what I mean, don't you?"

"Yes," replied Joe and Tiff, at the same time.

"Are they worth a lot of money?" asked Joe, before adding, "Not that that is the issue, I'm sure."

"Not really. I suppose I could get £100 for a pair of the more popular ones. But it has never been about the money, for me. They are my hobby – my life. Bet's got her baking, I've got my lovebirds."

"Did you get the money back from Georgie?"

Cyril let out a laugh. "Oh yes, we got £10 back. She said she'd spent it all. Said she'd pay it back in installments. That was six years ago."

"And nothing since?" Tiff was disliking the woman next door more and more.

"Not a penny. Not even a proper apology. Took me weeks to nurse the survivors back to peak health. They were dehydrated, I can tell you."

"That's when she started divorce proceedings on her husband as well," said Betty. "Lovely man – always takes his daughter to her, every other weekend now. Thank God he was awarded custody of the poor girl though. As for Georgie, she's under a psychiatrist, I do believe."

Cyril winced as if in pain, as he rubbed his hand across his chest again. "She's a hussy," he said, forcibly. "Loose morals – and particularly when it comes to young men."

"What do you mean?" asked Tiff, curiously.

"There are always different men going in and out of her house, especially during the week when her daughter isn't there." Pulling himself up further in the chair, Cyril leant over the table, uncomfortably. "So there you are. Watch yourselves. She's a cunning cat."

"Well, thanks for giving us the heads-up, Cyril. I'm sure that we'll be very cautious with her. Won't we Tiff?"

"Oh, most definitely."

Chapter 5

"Come on, let's get the fence finished. We've still got plenty of time." Joe unlocked the front door and reached for the paint tin and brushes.

"Can't believe we've been round there for over an hour," said Tiff as she brushed past Joe and stepped inside. "Beautiful birds – wouldn't mind some of those myself."

Joe looked up and grinned. "Let's get some then – or ask Cyril if we could buy a couple from him."

"Good idea. But let's get the house sorted out first." Tearing up the stairs in front of her, Tiff shouted back, "I'll be back in a minute – had too much tea."

Walking out of the bathroom, she halted at the top of the stairs as curiosity began to build in her mind. She turned and walked into her craft room. The smell of fresh paint gave her the perfect excuse to go and open the window. Was that woman, Geordie Ford, out in her garden, baring her breasts again? It was no good, she had to take a look.

Although it was only late April, the weather had been more tropical than spring of late. And there *she* was. Bathing in the sunshine, wearing nothing more than a thong bikini bottom. At least she wasn't exposing her breasts this time, as she laid on her front, but her bare buttocks would have been just as alluring for any man's eyes. At the top of her right shoulder was a tattoo of some description. She was too far away for the artwork to be seen properly. However, from a distance, it looked like an ice-cream, in a cone. Tiff thought it odd that she would have a tattoo of an ice-cream on the back of her shoulder and dismissed the idea. Opening the top window, as quietly as possible, she peered out at the fields in the distance and the dazzling river beyond. It was a heavenly place. If only the woman next door would keep her clothes on.

Joe had already made a start on the fence when Tiff arrived. "You've been a while," he muttered nonchalantly, engrossed in the sweeping up and down of his paint brush.

"Opened the craft room window – it really stinks of paint in there."

"You know," said Joe, dipping his brush into the paint tin, "you've got the best room in the house there."

"Why do you say that?"

"The view – you've got the amazing view out the back."

"That's why I chose it. I can look out of the window and get those creative juices flowing."

Joe laughed. "Don't think you need any more creative juice do you? You're ultra-creative already – certainly compared to me anyway."

"You can never have enough, Joe."

"If you say so. I might even take my laptop up there – the view could help me to do the weekly round-up report on the website."

Tiff knelt down, grabbed the other brush and dipped it in the paint. "Err... well, I was thinking that it would be just my room. You know how much stuff I've got. I don't want to be worrying about clearing enough space for you to work in there as well."

"I'm joking babe. It's your room." He shot a quizzical glance towards her. "The view's all yours too."

Attempting to back-track, Tiff added, "Well of course the view's not mine. You can go in there just... err... look at the view from the back wall. Once I get my big table in there, it's going under the window. You won't be able to get near the window at all."

"Tiff..."

"Yes?"

"You seem a little edgy. It's like you think I'm going to take your room away from you. It's like you don't want anyone seeing the view."

"No, I don't think that. And yes, of course I want people to see the view. Aren't we being a bit silly now?"

"You just seem a little edgy about the room, that's all."

"I'm not. Really I'm not."

"OK," said Joe, displaying his brilliant white teeth in a smile. "Love you, even if you are a little bit crazy sometimes or should we say most of the time?"

"Love you too and you're not much better than me Mr Frey." Tiff began to paint the fence post next to Joe's. "Why didn't you mention that you'd spoken to that woman next door, this morning?" she whispered.

"Don't know really. Never thought about it." He stopped painting. "She seemed very nice and friendly though."

"First impressions can be deceiving."

"Yes, I know but we haven't heard her side of the story have we?"

"Are you defending her?" snapped Tiff, without meaning to.

"I don't think we should judge her by what someone else has told us."

"So you think we should be nice to her?" Tiff could feel a jealous fear bubbling inside her.

"Well, I think we should be fair. We shouldn't have a preconception of her, just by what our other neighbours say. That would be wrong." Joe had lowered his voice considerably.

"Sounds to me like you're defending her."

"I'm not defending her, babe. I don't even know the woman. She's our neighbour and we have to give her the benefit of the doubt – surely?"

"Well you know her better than I do, after all, you've been chatting to her all morning." Tiff cringed as she realised that she'd let her jealous demon loose. "Sorry – I didn't mean to sound nasty."

"It's OK babe. I can tell that you've taken an instant disliking to her. I'm just saying that we shouldn't be judgemental – particularly as we have to live right next door to her."

"OK... you're right I suppose." Ethically, Joe probably was right. He was a fair man. However much Tiff hated it, she had to agree with him. He was always right.

"Wow," exclaimed Joe. "What a difference it has made."

Standing back on the green, Joe and Tiff admired the front row of picket fencing. Brilliant white and shiny, it stood out amongst the back row of houses.

"Taken longer than I thought it would. Maybe we should finish it off next weekend."

Tiff glanced at her watch. "We've probably got enough time to finish off that side," she said, pointing to the fence adjoining Cyril and Betty's front garden.

"Are you sure? What about the second coat in your room? Thought we might be able to get that finished today. We could both do it..."

"No." Tiff bit down on her bottom lip thoughtfully. "No... err... I'll get it done during the week sometime. I'm way ahead of my work quota. I could probably take a whole day off in the week."

Joe peered at her questioningly. "If we painted it today, you could be moving your stuff in there during the week."

"Hmm..." Tiff feigned contemplation for a moment. "No – I would much rather do the painting myself. You know how much I like doing it. Let's get some more of this finished."

"OK, your call."

As Tiff helped Joe collect the tin of paint and the tray of brushes and carry them into the front garden she noticed a tall, dark-haired man walking straight across the green, towards them. Wearing beige Chinos and a brown checked shirt the middle-aged man held his head high. His black hair swept across the top of his head and down one side of his face, ending in a neatly cropped style around his ears. For a man who appeared to be at least in his early forties, his hair was unnaturally dark. His pointed features and clean shaven, angular jawline made him appear somewhat Dracula like. With one hand in his pocket, he sauntered up to the fence.

"Afternoon," he said forcibly, offering a handshake to Joe over the garden fence. "Alvin. Alvin Snodgrass is the name. Number nine."

Joe reached across and took the man's hand. The grin on his face suggested he was slightly amused, either by the man's name or his demeanor, or both. "Hello, nice to meet you. Joe Frey... and this is Tiffany."

Alvin held his hand out to Tiff and smiled pretentiously. "Good to meet you, madam."

Taking his hand, Tiff winced as he squeezed hers tightly and shook it forcibly. "And you," she spluttered, before snatching her hand away.

"Looking good," said Alvin, eyeing the fence. "Been here long?"

"Three weeks now," replied Joe. "We've got a lot of work to do, to get it how we want it."

"Old John – lived here before you – he let the place go. Died in his sleep apparently. What a way to go."

Joe and Tiff smiled awkwardly.

"We heard he lived to a really good age," said Joe.

"No point living forever if you can't enjoy it." Alvin stroked a hand over his smooth chin and then rubbed a finger across a noticeable nick on the bottom of his jawline. It looked like a deep, old scar.

Tiff tried to hide the look of surprise on her face and Joe smiled stiffly.

"Met any of the Sycamore tribe yet?"

"Sorry?" Joe frowned quizzically.

"Neighbours man, neighbours." Alvin let out a chilling snigger. "4 Sycamore Close, right?"

"Oh, I see what you mean," Joe interjected. "Yes, a couple of them."

Alvin leant closer, over the fence. He glanced down at the wet paint and shuffled his legs backwards a little. "They're all a bunch of nutters," he said in a quiet voice. "Except for Georgie, she lives next to you – there." Discreetly, Alvin signaled with his eyes to the house next door. "She's a good girl. A very good girl."

"Yes... I met her this morning. She seems nice." Joe shot an uncomfortable glance at Tiff. "She had just returned from walking her dog and we had a quick chat."

"Delightful, playful dog," said Alvin, as a cunning grin crept across his thin lips. "I'm talking about the dog – not Georgie." Alvin winked his eye, exaggeratedly and sniggered.

Joe let out a short nervous laugh. "Yes, I knew what you meant. So... err, have you lived here long?"

Tiff could sense the tightness in Joe's voice and could tell that he felt uncomfortable and didn't particularly like the man.

"Depends what you would call long, I suppose, young man." Alvin pulled himself upright and breathed in deeply, puffing his chest out. "Not as long as old John did and I never will do. I'll be long gone before that. Or you'll find me hanging from a tree in the copse, by the river, at the back there." He flicked his gaze over the rooftop of Joe and Tiff's house. "Purple-faced with a limp tongue drooping down my chin." Alvin smirked. "Just hope I don't dribble – don't want to be remembered as the dribbler of Sycamore Close now, do I?"

Dumbfounded by Alvin's words, Joe and Tiff were speechless. They stood motionless with stupefied expressions on their faces.

"Come on my friends – I'm teasing you. The look on your faces." Alvin mocked. "I've been here for twenty years, that I can remember." He sniggered again. "Honestly, the pair of you look like you're just about to be hung yourselves. Lighten up guys."

Simultaneously, Joe and Tiff breathed a sigh of relief and released themselves from their frozen stance.

"You've lived here quite a long time then," remarked Joe, unsure of what else to say.

"Sure have man. I'm not around much though. I work away quite often. In London. I'm taking a short break at the moment."

"What do you do for a living?" asked Tiff, politely.

"Top secret, I'm afraid. Let's just say I work in a particular governmental department. Think – spy. Think – covert operations. Then you'll be on the right track." Alvin eyed Tiff pointedly. His dark and narrow eyes were eerie and intimidating.

"Ah..." said Joe, lightly, "a secret agent of some kind then?"

Alvin nodded his head. "Let's just say I work undercover, now and again."

"Sounds interesting," said Tiff.

"Not for your ears girl," Alvin kinked his upper lip into a half smile.

"Oh," mumbled Tiff, rather shocked by his response. "Is it for men only then?"

"It tends to be a man's world – yes. Have to deal with all sorts in the secret service but I haven't told you that – right?"

"Right." Tiff peered at Joe incredulously, before turning back to Alvin. "Err... so... do you know many of the people around here?" she added, curious to know how he might respond to her next question.

"All of them, I'm sorry to say," he replied, with an egotistical smirk on his face. "You've got the couple at number one – they've got two little brats. Keep themselves to themselves, luckily."

Tiff felt a little braver and challenged the odd looking man. "I take it you don't like kids?"

"Hate the little wretches. Do you have any?"

Both Tiff and Joe shook their heads. "No, not yet anyway," replied Tiff.

Alvin placed his hands back in his trouser pockets and snorted. "Georgie's got a girl. Thankfully, she's not so much of a brat as the rest."

"Yes, we know she has a daughter, we've heard her in the garden." Hesitantly, Joe added, "Sounds a bit of a handful, if you ask me."

"Joe," Tiff retorted. "You shouldn't say that."

"I'm just saying that we've heard her outside and she sounds quite demanding. I'm not being nasty." Joe tried to retract from his words.

Alvin eyed him with contempt. "I think *you* should think twice about having kids yourself, my friend – they're hard work apparently. Unless of course…" He looked down at Tiff disdainfully, "you're going to let your woman do all the nasty work. After all…" He let out a gravelly laugh, "that's what they're for isn't it?"

"Hang on a minute…" said Joe, pulling his wide shoulders back and placing his hands on his waist.

"Err… anyway…" Tiff stepped in sharply, sensing that Joe was beginning to get a little annoyed, "do you know *everyone* here?"

"Not sure you'll want my opinion on the residents of Sycamore Close…"

"I think we'll be best finding out for ourselves," Joe butted in. "It's been nice to meet you though."

"It's not every day that I go around the block introducing myself to people, you know." Alvin grinned through a perfect set of unnaturally white teeth. "I need to keep a low profile most of the time."

"Because of your job?" Joe asked, inquisitively.

"That, and the girls…"

"Girls?" Tiff scrutinised Alvin's well-dressed, well-presented, and slightly false appearance.

Puffing out his cheeks, Alvin let out a slow breath. "Got a lot of young lady admirers you know." He smirked arrogantly. "Can't say more than that."

"Lucky you," blurted Joe, before snapping his mouth shut and giving Tiff a sheepish grin.

"Is Georgie one of your admirers?" asked Tiff, making sure she kept her voice low enough that none of the neighbours could hear.

"Georgie is my number one girl – comes out for a trot with me now and again She likes a good trot."

"A trot?" Tiff was growing more and more curious by the man's utter contempt for women and children.

"A run. You must have heard of the word 'trot' woman?"

"Yes," replied Tiff, stiffly. "I have. I just wondered if that was what you were implying."

"Nothing more, nothing less." Alvin winked an eye at Joe. "We go off through the woods, on the other side of Oakwood. She takes her dog sometimes." Alvin glanced across to the upstairs windows of number three. "Good girl, is our Georgie. A very giving girl." Again, Alvin winked at Joe, a conceited smirk plastered on his face.

"How do you mean?"

"How do I mean what?" Alvin seemed to snarl at Tiff.

"Sorry, I mean – why do you say Georgie is very giving?" Tiff paused thoughtfully. "I don't mean to pry."

"Ah, you ladies are all the same. You do mean to pry. Don't you think so Joe?" Alvin laughed off his comment as being insignificant.

Joe had kept silent for a moment, obviously listening with intrigue, to the strange man standing before him. "Sorry? What was that?"

"These women," Alvin indicated to Tiff with his eyes. "They do like to know what's going on all around them."

"I think most people do, it's not a woman thing," Joe replied, defensively.

"Women do like a good gossip though. Isn't that right girl?"

"I suppose a lot of them do. No harm in that." Tiff retorted.

"Absolutely not. Keeps you going, I'd imagine." Casting an appraising pair of eyes over Tiff, Alvin grinned in a way that made her feel uncomfortable.

"Not me personally. I have far more interesting things to keep me going." With a deadpan expression, Tiff stared into the man's satirical eyes.

"Pleased to hear it, girl. I always say, keep your nose down, mouth closed and eyes all knowing."

"Really?" Placing a tacky paint brush across the top of the tin, Tiff continued, directing her words towards Joe. "Well, I think we need to keep our noses down and get on with this fence."

"Absolutely," agreed Joe. "Time's ticking on."

"I'll be off for an early evening trot later on, if you..." Alvin raised his eyebrows at Joe, "want to join me. Some glorious views out on the hills. Incredible what you can see with a good old pair of binoculars."

"Err... thanks for the offer but..." Joe peered round to Tiff, knowingly, "we have a lot to get done this evening, don't we?"

Tiff nodded her head fervently.

"Your loss. Another time, maybe. Not around for long. Important work to be done in the secret service you know. Until we meet again, I bid you farewell." Turning on his heels, Alvin walked away with an air of opulence about him, his hands still tucked into his pockets.

"Obnoxious prick," muttered Joe, under his breath.

"Lecherous prick, don't you mean?"

"Tiffany Cuthbert – I don't believe I've heard you speak like that before," Joe mocked.

"He brings the worst out in me." She giggled. "What a total wan..." Her words trailed off.

Joe stared, disbelievingly. "You're right – and I'll say it for you. Total wanker."

"And what's his name all about?"

"Total wanker's name I guess," said Joe, nonchalantly.

Giggling heartily, amongst themselves, Joe and Tiff watched, across the green, as Alvin Snodgrass arrived at the last house on the close, opened the gate and strutted up the pathway to his front door. A swift, shifty glance, from left to right, and then he disappeared into his house.

"So," said Tiff, regaining her composure. "What do you think of the neighbours so far?"

"Keep your voice down, babe."

"Sorry," she whispered back. Picking up her brush again, she crouched down and continued to paint an unfinished post. "They're all a bit weird, aren't they?"

"I'd say the only weird one is that idiot at number nine. The others are OK, from what I've seen so far. Why do you think they're all weird?"

"Well, unusual then, not weird. Maybe that's the wrong word to use."

"Why do you think Georgie is unusual, you haven't even met her yet."

A vision of Georgie, sprawled out in her garden, naked, entered Tiff's mind. "Err... don't know really."

"And Cyril and Betty – they're not weird," said Joe quite defensively. "I think they are a really nice couple."

"Oh yes, they are. Most definitely. Just weird in the sense of their house, I suppose."

"No. Brave, committed and unconventional. I like it."

Tiff smiled, warmly. "Yes, so do I to be honest. Anyway, come on, let's get this finished ASAP. We need to get some dinner and try out that date and walnut cake."

"Work it baby, work it."

Chapter 6

The date and walnut cake was just as delicious as the lemon drizzle. Betty obviously enjoyed baking and did it very well. Having finished the painting for the day, eaten a tuna paste bake for their tea, finished off with a hearty slice of cake, Joe and Tiff retired to their minimalistic living room. Minimalistic, not by choice but more by lack of funds, time and inspiration for the time being.

Grabbing one side of the shabby, old curtains, Tiff went to draw it across the large window. She halted and gaped across the green. Under the streetlight at the end of Sycamore Close, right outside number nine, was a tall figure. Wearing a brilliant white vest, bright red, skin-tight *Speedos* with a broad white stripe down the sides, white socks and trainers, Alvin Snodgrass was doing a lunge workout and leaving absolutely nothing to the imagination. Tiff cringed in disgust as the pronounced bulge at the front of his pants appeared to tip slightly from one side to the other, as he dipped into each lunge. Strapped across one shoulder and around his back was a small black binocular case. "Joe – quick – come here – right now."

"Not that old woman again," said Joe, heaving himself out of the armchair. "What's she doing now?"

"No – not her – quick."

Joe arrived at the window with disinterest and glanced out. Then he took a second look. "What on earth..."

"Going for a 'trot', I'd imagine." Tiff continued to stare, incredulously. "What does he think he looks like?"

Switching from the lunges, Alvin moved on to calf stretches and heel digs. He then began to march on the spot, lifting his spindly legs almost as high as his chest. The case hanging around his back bounced up and down as he pulled each leg up high.

"He's wearing bloody *Speedos!*" remarked Joe, peering harder through the window. "They're swimming trunks – they're not for jogging. Bloody hell – the man's a freak."

"It's getting dark. Why is he taking binoculars with him? He won't be able to see anything." Tiff shook her head in revulsion. "I think he's a dirty old pervert."

"I think you're probably right. You know who he looks like?"

"Who?"

Joe let out a short burst of laughter. "He looks like one of those characters from the *118 118* commercial."

Sniggering as she continued to gape out of the window, Tiff replied, "He look worse than that. Those men don't wear *speedos*. It looks like those trunks would cut his legs off at the groin if he bent down too far."

"And he doesn't have a black moustache, I suppose." Joe reached across to the other curtain and began to pull it. "Come on – I've seen enough to put me off food for a week."

"His lunchbox, you mean?"

"What?"

"You've seen enough of his *lycra*-lunchbox to put you off eating for a week."

"Yeah. Can't be doing with a *spandex* scrotum bouncing around Sycamore Close. Shut those curtains."

Tiff giggled. "Perhaps he's going out on a top-secret spy mission."

"Hmm..." Joe mumbled, thoughtfully. "Doubtful."

Together, the couple swished a curtain each across the window and met in the middle. Raising a hand up, Joe offered a high-five.

"I'm going for a bath," said Tiff, pecking him on the cheek.

"Want me to come and scrub your back?"

"If you want to," she answered, with a suggestive expression on her face. "I'll give you a shout when I'm ready."

It ended in a duo-bath. Then a passionate love-making session on top of the bed sheets. Joe was an affectionate man. A seductive lover. Young, strong, healthy and libidinous, his appetite for sex was unwavering.

As Joe climbed wearily into bed and tossed the dishevelled sheets over him, Tiff went back to the bathroom to freshen up.

Alerted by a sudden noise from outside, which filtered through the small gap in the partially open bathroom window, Tiff drew in a breath and held it. Straining her ears for another noise, she could feel her heart beating inside her chest. Exhaling, she remained motionless. Listening. Waiting. She was sure she'd just heard the high pitched gasp of a woman. She was absolutely sure of it. She waited and listened again.

A muffled groan. A hollow clatter. Like something banging against a metal barrel.

Switching off the bathroom light, she tiptoed back to the bedroom to see that Joe had turned over on his side. She crept around to his side of the bed and saw that he was asleep. Creeping back out of the room, Tiff quietly closed the door. Standing on the landing, wearing an oversized, old t-shirt and pyjama bottoms, her heart beat rapidly. She had definitely heard a woman's voice. The noise was coming from Georgie's garden; she was sure of it. Like a top-secret agent, she crept into her empty craft room and approached the window.

It was so dark out the back that it took a moment for her eyes to adjust. All she could see, across the fields, were a couple of twinkling lights in the far distance. Possibly coming from the farm behind the river. Turning her gaze to the left, she stared hard, into Georgie's garden. She certainly wasn't expecting to see the woman lying on her sunbed at this time of the night. As Tiff's vision adjusted further, she could just see the empty sunbed, still situated where it had been before.

Another noise. Again, a woman's voice. Another gasp. A moan. The window above her head was still open and the noises outside could be clearly heard.

Stepping to the far right of the window, Tiff could see movement in the furthest corner of Georgie's garden. A flicker of white. A figure. A man. Long, bare legs. Thrusting his pelvis backwards and forwards, the man was leaning over another figure.

Tiff blinked. The images were getting clearer through the darkness.

Alvin Snodgrass. The white strip, on the side of his trunks, lunged forwards and backwards. Underneath him, and leaning back against what looked like a concrete mixer, dressed in dark clothing, which seemed to be hitched up around her waist, was Georgie. Her long legs were spread apart and she stood on tiptoes, as her dangerously-high heels wobbled on the hard ground.

Alvin's hands were firmly placed on her clothed chest. He rammed his pelvis into her, repeatedly. Forcefully. Now and again a faint gasp or a moan could be heard.

Tiff stood motionless in the darkness. Breathing shallow breaths, she watched disbelievingly. They were having sex. In the garden.

It appeared to be a loveless exchange. Fervent yet crude. Georgie gripped on to the sides of the mixer, her head turned away to one side.

On and on. The tempo quickened. Tossing her head back, Georgie stared up at the night sky. A look of sadistic pleasure, etched on her face. Or was it a look of pain?

A louder gasp. Loud enough to be obviously apparent to anyone who may still be awake and in close proximity to Georgie's house. How could she be doing such a thing? And in her garden?

It was over. Alvin adjusted himself in his trunks and casually walked towards the house and out of sight. He had left Georgie abruptly, without uttering a word to her. There was no gentle aftercare like Tiff would have expected any normal couple to do.

Pulling her dress down to her knees, Georgie appeared to sigh and then she followed Alvin back to the house.

They were gone. The night was still and silent again.

Tiff leant back on the window frame and stared out thoughtfully. Had she really just seen that? Would she think it was a dream by the morning? Should she tell Joe? Would he believe her? She shook her head and slowly crept towards the door. No, she wouldn't tell him. It was bad enough that Georgie was baring all during the day, let alone providing a raw pornographic show in the evenings. As for Alvin, Tiff's thoughts of earlier were justified. He was a lecherous, dirty man.

"Oh," screeched Tiff, smacking a hand upon her chest. "You made me jump. I thought you were asleep."

"What are you doing in there?" Joe's sleepy eyes looked puzzled. "Thought you were coming back to bed. I've been waiting for you."

"Just had a..." Tiff faltered. "I was... checking the paint. Had a quick look out at the view. Was going to shut the window..." She turned her head around. "Oh look, silly me, I forgot to shut it." She rushed across the room and shut the top window quickly. Darting back across the room, she closed the door firmly behind her and grabbed hold of Joe's arm. "Come on, I've done it now. I thought I'd left it open. Wouldn't want to leave the window open all night would we?" she added, as she ushered him back through to the bedroom. "And you had fallen asleep."

"Only for a minute. Why were you looking at the view? It's pitch black out there."

"Yes, I know. You can just see the farm lights though, way off in the distance, but I was admiring my paint work really."

"In the dark?"

"Yes – it looks good in the dark."

Joe nodded, sleepily. "You make me laugh babe – you're mad. Come on. Bed. I need a cuddle." Staring wide-eyed, he blinked his eyes dolefully and then winked and smiled.

A surge of excitement rushed through Tiff. Who could say no to those thick lashed eyes? It had happened several times before. Joe would wake up after just a few minutes of sleep and be feeling amorous again. She felt it too. Even though she had just witnessed a crude, coarse act of fornication in the neighbour's garden, she was ready for another 'cuddle' with Joe. It would be longer, more sustained and emotionally deeper than the last but she hadn't been put off by what she'd seen. If anything, she felt more up for it. More up for a romantic session in bed, with her loved one. By no stretch of the imagination would she ever consider being an exhibitionist, like Georgie, and she hoped that Joe had those same values too. Not that she was going to mention it to him. Ever.

"You never did tell me what you were talking to Georgie about this morning," said Tiff, lying contentedly next to Joe's hot, moist body.

"Nothing really. It was just small talk." Joe's voice was beginning to slur as be started to drift in and out of sleep again.

"What kind of small talk?"

"Hmm?"

"What sort of small talk were you having?"
"Uh…"
"Joe, don't go to sleep yet…"
"Uh-huh."

Peering into the darkness, Tiff realised it was no use. He was falling asleep and once he'd drifted away, a train could come rumbling through the bedroom and he wouldn't hear it.

Monday morning had come round far too quickly for Tiff. Preparing boiled eggs and toast for breakfast, she mused over the previous night's goings-on in the garden of number 3 Sycamore Close. She now felt a little doubtful about the move to their dream home. It was still a dream home and a beautiful place to be – but some of the people who lived there tainted and distorted the overall image and feel. Maybe she was being oversensitive. No. It was totally unacceptable to be shagging in the back garden when some of the neighbours could potentially see them. Surely number two would be able to see them too and possibly even number one. Tiff wondered if Cyril and Betty would be able to see her garden from their top windows as well. She guessed that they would have to poke their heads out of the windows, quite a way, to see that far around.

"Joe – breakfast is ready," Tiff called up the stairs.

Being in the fitness industry, Joe insisted that they always had a good breakfast in the mornings, except at the weekends, when he did like to indulge in thick marmalade on toast. A good breakfast would always see them through the day and, according to Joe, ensure that their weight would remain constant. Tiff struggled with that concept. The more she ate for breakfast, the hungrier she was by lunchtime. It had to catch up with her sooner or later and she had noticed a slight bulge around her waist. But luckily for Tiff, she was still considered, 'petite', by most of her friends and family.

"Coming," Joe replied, and then bounded down the stairs.

On the dining table were two glasses of pure orange juice, a rack filled with four slices of toast, unsalted butter and a glass pepper pot. Tiff carried two plates over to the table, containing two boiled eggs in egg cups.

"I'm taking Wednesday off," she said, placing the plates at opposite sides of the small table. "I'll get the painting done then." She smiled sweetly, pulled out a chair and sat down.

"OK. Good. We'll fix up your table at the weekend then."

"I might even do that as well. I know how to join it all together."

Joe looked across the table. "Are you sure?"

"Yes – once it's in place you could help me get everything else in there."

"OK – sounds like a plan to me."

Wolfing his breakfast down, Joe wiped his mouth with the back of his hand and grabbed the glass of orange juice. He drank the whole glass in one go and set it back down on the table. "Right – got to go. Got a new receptionist starting today. See you tonight." Pecking Tiff on the top of her head, he left the room. He grabbed his coat from the newel post at the bottom of the stairs, checked his pockets and then left the house.

Tiff had another hour before she had to leave. She always got up earlier than she needed to, so that she could get some housework done before she went to work. She much preferred to do her chores in the mornings, rather than come home to them in the evenings. She liked to spend her evenings with Joe, even if it was just sitting in the living room, mindlessly watching the television. It beat washing or ironing any day of the week.

Checking the door was locked securely, Tiff walked down the garden path, admiring the white picket fencing. It would look beautiful once it was finished and once they had tidied up the front garden. As she reached the gate, she noticed Alvin across the green. Wearing a pinstripe grey suit, lilac shirt and deep purple tie, his black brogue shoes finished off his overall appearance of a professional man. His dark hair was neatly swept back across one side and he carried a black laptop case. His look, this morning, was in sheer contrast to the kinky pervert he appeared to be last night.

Tiff cringed as a vision of his antics with Georgie crept into her head. Georgie was an attractive girl and had to be at least ten years younger than him. So why would she be interested in him? Why would she entertain a swift hardcore romp over a rusty old cement mixer?

Alvin raised a hand in acknowledgement as Tiff approached him. "Morning," he chirped, merrily. "Off to work, are you?"

"Yes," she replied as she walked down the path. "I take it you are too?"

Darting his eyes from side to side, Alvin moved closer towards the end of the path. "Big business this morning. Been called up unexpectedly."

"Oh, right." Mimicking Alvin's clandestine approach, Tiff lowered her voice. "Called up? Where are you going?"

Again, Alvin's narrow eyes flicked from side to side. "London. Head office. Can't say any more than that."

Tiff nodded her head. "OK – I understand. Must be difficult having a job like yours."

"It is."

"Well," said Tiff, edging away. "I really must be going. Lots to do today."

"And what is it that you do?" Alvin asked, with what seemed like a genuine tone of interest.

"I'm a stone-craft artist."

"A stone-craft artist? Sounds interesting."

"Not half as interesting as your job, I'm sure." Alvin's behavior was somehow different today. Yesterday, Tiff had not liked him at all. She thought he was belittling of her, yet this morning he seemed to be showing an interest in her.

"No, it's far from interesting – more like stressful. Unpredictable and unnerving at times. Very unsociable hours too."

"Oh dear," Tiff replied, feeling a little sorry for him. "Guess it must be like that. Never thought about it in that way. I'd imagine most people would see you as a *James Bond* type of figure." Tiff let out a short, nervous laugh. "You know, all the glamour and girls that *007* gets."

"Oh yes. That all comes with it too." Alvin paused for a moment, as if he was thinking about something. "But too much of a good thing... well, you know what they say. I'm probably a little complacent with it all."

"Really? Most men would jump at the chance." Tiff smiled uncomfortably. "Right, well, I really must be going. Hope it all goes well for you."

"It will – I haven't failed a mission yet." Alvin winked an eye and placed a hand on Tiff's arm. "Have a productive day, young lady," he said in a low, husky voice, before gently squeezing her arm.

"Err… yes. Thanks. You too." Edging away from Alvin's touch, she shuddered slightly. "Bye."

Walking past him, Tiff headed for her car, parked in the lay-by, on the main road. She didn't turn round once but she could feel his eyes on her. On her bare legs. On her high-heeled shoes. *What a creep.*

Chapter 7

Tiff had almost met her whole week's quota by Wednesday evening. She'd changed her plan earlier in the week and would have today (Thursday) off instead. Knowing that she wouldn't have a huge amount to do on Friday, she hoped that she could get away early tomorrow too. She loved the flexibility of her job and enjoyed doing the work. Her position allowed her to take days off, midweek, providing she could fulfill her order schedule and this arrangement suited her. Also, her craftwork hobby at home had been paying for itself, and more, for some time now, so she had the best of both worlds. Going to work or working from home, either way, she loved what she did and got paid for it.

Luckily, she hadn't seen Alvin again during the week and guessed that he had jetted off somewhere to secretly plan and execute some sort of mysterious undercover mission. Tiff admired him for that. It was just such a shame that he was a total creep in other respects. Also a salacious brute if that night in Georgie's garden was anything to go by.

Peering out of the bedroom window, Tiff watched Joe walk around the green and head off to his car. He worked long hours some days, and today he had a conference to attend near London. He would catch the train though. It beat getting stressed when trying to find parking in the city and his company paid his expenses anyway. So, Tiff had all day to get the painting done and build her new, flat-pack craft table.

A young couple walked out of number seven, both dressed in suits. They marched purposefully down to the main road and got in a small black *Vauxhall Corsa*. Tiff had seen them, briefly, once before and guessed that they didn't have any children as they both looked far too professional, focused and well-polished.

There was a young couple at number eight as well. One morning, as Joe and Tiff had left the house together, they had met the man as he was leaving his house. He'd been polite and wished them a 'good morning'. His partner was standing at the door wearing a rose pink dressing gown and white fluffy slippers. Lovingly, she had waved the man off and at the same time, nodded her head and smiled at Joe and Tiff as they passed by. Joe had thought it was 'kind of cute' that the woman had gone to her front door to say goodbye to the man and wave until he had disappeared out of sight.

Tiff wondered, as she continued to look out of the window, who lived at numbers one and two, to the right of her and also at number six, the last house on the back row, which was shrouded in tall hedges. Number six was the only house that didn't have a picket fence at the front. She hoped that the other residents would be normal, ordinary people, just like herself and Joe and of similar ilk to the residents of numbers five, seven and eight. At least then, numbers three and nine would be far easier to cope with. Tiff liked mainstream. She did not like the goings-on that she had witnessed so far. And Joe hardly knew any of it. But it was probably better that way. Better for Tiff anyway.

The weather wasn't as warm today. Small white clouds puffed up and morphed into bigger ones with a tinge of dark grey, as they floated across the blue sky, changing shape as they went. On several occasions, during the rare moments when the sun did appear from behind the greyish-white billowing masses, and lit up the room, Tiff had peeped out of the craft room window. Just to check. Just to see if Georgie *was* out there. Just curious. But she wasn't there. However, Georgie's rusty old cement mixer, in the corner of her garden, stood as a constant reminder of their weekend's shenanigans.

By lunchtime, Tiff had finished the second coat in the craft room. The lilac walls looked deeper and richer now that the patches had disappeared. She opened the window to air the room and went downstairs. Date and walnut cake and a milky coffee were calling her.

A small envelope lay on the front door mat. It must have been hand delivered as there was no stamp and the address read simply, No. 4. Curiously, she opened the sealed envelope.

Dear No. 4

Welcome to Sycamore Close!

We are having a BBQ this Saturday (weather permitting) and would really like you to join us. We're mainly a close-knit community and it would be wonderful to welcome you to the close, along with some of the other residents.

If you are able to make it, we would love to see you around 7pm. Completely understand if you can't make it at such short notice.

Kindest regards

Hayley and Wayne (No.8)

p.s. Please bring a bottle if you would like to have anything more than the Pimms punch we will be making for everyone. We will be doing the traditional bangers, burgers, chicken and assorted skewers and salad to garnish. You're welcome to bring anything else along with you, particularly if you have any special dietary requirements.

Hope we might see you here.

Look forward to hearing from you.

Tel: 0758982837 (Hayley)

Tiff read the message again and smiled. It had to be the woman she'd seen wearing a pink dressing gown, the other day. How sweet. Tiff was definitely interested in going and she knew, without a doubt, that Joe would be up for it too. He loved a good barbecue and a drink – especially on his own doorstep. At least they wouldn't have far to go home, should the urge arise to down a few drinks. Joe didn't drink often but when he did, he did it big style. Being one of the rugby team, in the past, Joe and his friends were all experts in the art of downing pints at the rugby club. However, Joe also knew when to behave himself. He knew that Tiff would not approve of him getting too drunk when the acceptance of the neighbourhood was at stake. He always knew when he had to rein himself in by the look he got from her. It was enough to stop him in his tracks at any given moment, yet, he never held her accountable for 'The Look'. He just seemed to obey it and all of its connotations.

By five o'clock, Tiff had finally managed to piece together the craft table. It had been far more difficult than she'd first thought. The instructions were sparse and the few diagrams didn't help much at all. But she'd struggled through and completed it. The problem was that the table was upside down on the floor. There was no way she could lift it up and turn it over on her own. She would have to wait until Joe arrived home. She would have to drop her guard about him going anywhere near the window. Tutting to herself, she was well aware that her obsession with 'the view' was becoming absurd. But she needn't be so obsessive about it today anyway, as the weather had been too cloudy for sunbathing. It was also getting late and Alvin had gone off on a cloak-and-dagger operation. So Georgie wouldn't be fornicating in the garden, whilst riding her cement mixer either. Would she?

Joe was later than usual. Peering up at the clock, Tiff noted the time was ten to seven. He should have left London around half past three. Surely he'd be home by now? Just as she was doing her usual worrying about every conceivable calamity she could think of, the front door opened.

Walking into the kitchen, Joe looked weary. He hung his jacket over a chair, loosened his tie and unbuttoned his collar. He smiled and moved across the room, towards Tiff. Kissing her on the lips, he then rested his forehead on hers.

"Good day?" she asked, relieved and excited that he was home.

"Boring." Joe stood upright and stretched his back. "Usual harping on about health and safety issues and new measures. Paving the way forward in management and that kind of stuff. Tedious tripe."

"You sound really fed up."

"Don't know why they have to call us all in for a so-called conference, when they had already sent out the new outlines for progression beforehand."

"I expect it's because, like you, most people don't read any of it."

"Hmm." Joe nodded his head agreeably. "Anyway, how's your day-off been?"

"Very productive." Tiff grinned. "Sit down, I've done some dinner."

Pulling a chair out, Joe sat down.

"Only sausages, mash and peas, I'm afraid. I've had a busy day." Tiff removed the two plates from the oven and placed them on to the table mats, which had been lovingly crafted from a cardboard box. "Careful, the plates are hot. Thought you would have been home earlier, so I've been keeping dinner warm." Returning to the kitchen, she whipped up some gravy in no time and joined Joe back at the table.

"Sorry babe."

Tiff watched as he heartily began to plough through three sausages, a mountain of mashed potato and a splattering of peas. In comparison, her dinner was much smaller.

"Got the room finished," she said, in between mouthfuls of food. "Looks nice."

"Good – you all moved-in there now then?"

"Not yet. I've been waiting for you to come home."

"Huh," Joe huffed. "Sorry, I would have been in a bit earlier but that Alvin bloke stopped me as I got out of the car."

Tiff stopped eating and held her fork midway between the plate and her mouth. "Really? He's obviously back from his latest underground intelligence assignment then."

"His what?"

"All that espionage stuff. He was called up on Monday, apparently. Thought we'd seen the last of him for a while."

"How do you know that?" Joe gave a quizzical look.

"I bumped into him as I was going to work. He told me he was off on a mission."

"Well, he's back then. I had a hard job getting away from him…" Joe paused, bemused. "He was wearing that moronic jogging outfit again."

"Oh no," said Tiff. "And the binoculars?"

"Oh yes. Asked me if I wanted to go with him and did I have my own binoculars as he could highly recommend the ones hanging around his neck, if I didn't."

Tiff shook her head, in disgust. "What on earth is he looking at when he goes out in the dark, how can he see anything?"

"Bird-watching, probably."

"In the dark?"

"Depends what sort of birds he's watching."

"What a creep." Tiff shuddered as she remembered his hand squeezing her arm and the way he looked at her. Sleazy was putting it mildly.

Joe laughed. "He wants me to go over to his for a few drinks on Saturday night –"

"No," Tiff said, emphatically. "You can't. We've been invited out."

"Oh, don't worry babe. I have no intention of going round there."

Pausing thoughtfully, Tiff lowered her fork and placed it on her plate. "If he's invited you to his house on Saturday night, that means..." She smiled with relief. "That means he won't be going where we've been invited."

"You've lost me now."

"We've been invited to a barbecue," she said. "At number eight." Peering around the kitchen, she continued. "There's a note over there somewhere, from... Hayley and Wayne. I think that's their names."

"OK, cool. Take it he, Alvin, hasn't been invited then."

"I guess not, if he wants you to go round to his for a drink. I hope that's not going to be awkward."

"Doubt it," Joe mumbled. "I said I wasn't sure if I could go and would have to speak to you first as you made most of the arrangements. He gave me an odd look as if I was stupid to check with you first."

"He's a freak. Anyway, well done. So you can now tell him that I'd already agreed that we would go to the barbecue – yes?"

"I'll text him." Joe pulled his phone from his pocket and swiped the lock screen.

"Text him?" Tiff was taken aback. "Have you got his number then?"

Peering across the table, Joe smiled. "Well... obviously." He let out a chuckle and then smirked. "Best buddies now – Alvin and me."

"Yuk. Good luck to you."

"He insisted I had his number. Asked me if I had my phone on me and wanted me to put him in my contacts there and then."

"He's creepy. I don't like him at all." Tiff hesitated. "Why... why do you think he wanted you to have his number?"

"Just being friendly, I guess."

"Well don't give him any more details."

"I won't. Stop worrying, babe. He's just the friendless, neighbourhood dork."

Tiff mouthed an, 'OK' and finished her meal with far less vigour than before.

Carrying his plate to the kitchen, Joe picked up the note on the windowsill and read it. "Number eight – that's the couple we bumped into the other day."

"Yes. The furry white slipper woman."

"Waving to her husband or whoever he is. Should be good. Are you up for it?"

"Yes, definitely. They seemed like quite nice people."

Joe nodded his head. "Be good to meet some more of the neighbours too."

"That's what I thought. Now, when you've had your shower, could you give me a hand to turn the craft table over? It's far too heavy for me."

Returning to the table, Joe pecked her on the top of her head. "Your wish is my command, madam. Will we also have to christen the table and the room?"

"Christen?" Tiff shot a quizzical glance at him. "What do you mean?"

"You know… perform some sort of loving ownership ceremony in the room. After all, we've practically christened every other room in this house." Joe squeezed the tops of her shoulders, softly. Then he ran a finger down the middle of her back, causing her to squirm and shudder.

Tiff giggled. "Joe Frey – you're insatiable. And no. My craft room is going to remain virginal. Go and get in the shower."

"OK – how about the shower again, then?"

"No – I've got clearing up to do and you have a table to turn the right way up."

"Garden?" Joe grinned.

"Shower – now. You are sex mad."

Joe slumped off and went upstairs.

Placing her knife and fork on the plate of unfinished food, Tiff stared out of the patio doors as the light began to fade. Why had he said the garden? Was she becoming completely paranoid? She knew that he liked to be spontaneous in their sexual relationship and wouldn't think twice about which room he was in... but he had never, in all the time she'd known him, mentioned the garden. So why now?

"Where do you want this?" shouted Joe from the top of the stairs.

"Coming." Tiff bounded up the stairs, two at a time. "How did you manage to pick it up on your own?" Tiff stood with her hands on her hips, staring, surprised, at the upright, oversized table.

Holding his arms up, Joe struck a strongman pose, clenching his fists to accentuate his muscular arms. "You've either got it babe –or you haven't." He laughed. "So obviously, you haven't."

"I definitely haven't. I thought you were having a shower first."

"No, get the work out of the way first. So, where do you want it?"

Pointing a finger towards the window, Tiff smiled. "There please – right under the window."

Heaving the table across the room, they shifted it into place. Tiff flicked her gaze out of the window, checking for any activity in the neighbour's garden. She was on edge now she knew that Alvin was back home. She did not want Joe seeing anything untoward.

"Are you sure? You'll never be able to get anywhere near the window, babe."

"Yep. I really like it there," she replied, falsely.

Joe frowned and rubbed his chin. "Look, "he said, grabbing hold of one end of the table. "If we turn it around, you could still look out of the window – you'd just have to turn your head. But at least you could get to the window to open it." Joe peered at the window thoughtfully. "What about curtains or blinds – you'd need to be able to get to them to open and close them."

Shaking her head in disagreement, Tiff placed her hand on the table top. "I really want to leave it here. I'll have a lovely view, right in front of me, when I'm working." She searched her brain for other excuses. "And... and I don't need blinds... or curtains. We're hardly overlooked. And I'll get a hop-up stool to open and close the window if I have to."

"It's up to you, babe. It's your room – and your table."

"Then we'll leave it here. Thank you, Mr Muscles, for picking it up." Tiff moved around the table and kissed him on the nose. "Now go and get a shower. I'll put the kettle on and we can have a coffee... and the last bit of Betty's cake."

Chapter 8

To
Hayley and Wayne
We would love to come to your BBQ – thank you very much for inviting us.
From Joe and Tiff at No. 4

Tiff pushed the thank-you card into the envelope and sealed it. Luckily, she always kept some spare hand-made cards in a box, for moments like this. The 'Thanks a Bunch' card was one of her particularly favourite designs. Simplistic yet pleasantly appealing, it was one of her most popular designs for cards such as Mother's day and Easter. It also went down well as a general birthday card for women once the wording on the front was changed. A delicate posy of white and yellow flowers, tied-up in a tiny silk bow, decorated the lower central area of the card and the calligraphy script, in contrasting colours, finished off the top. That was another love of Tiff's – calligraphy. Calligraphy on greetings cards, table place-holders, door plaques, picture frames and more. In fact, anything that she could write on would be subjected to the ancient writing technique.

Pushing the card through the letterbox of number eight, she made her way towards her car. The sun had returned this morning and just for a moment, she wondered if Georgie would be out in her garden this afternoon. Not that it mattered to her as she would be at work most of the day. Climbing into her car, she noticed a piece of paper tucked underneath the windscreen wiper. She pulled herself back out, lifted the wiper, took the piece of paper and opened it. It was a typed note.

> I know you are new to the area and have seen you get in your car most mornings. I hope you will be very happy, here in

Sycamore Close, but please try and keep yourself to yourself. People are not always what they seem around here. Best wishes.

Tiff read the note for a second time – was it meant for her? What did it mean exactly? Who was it from? What was the note trying to say? Who was it aimed at? She had absolutely no idea. Standing by the side of her car, she peered up and down the road and then across the green to the houses in Sycamore Close. The note was obviously from someone there as they had said they hoped she would be happy, 'here' in the close. Unnerved by the fact that someone must be watching her to the extent that they knew which car she owned, Tiff drew in a deep breath. Was this note a warning? Or was it just some idle gossiper, going overboard with the 'neighbourhood watch' ethos? Whatever it was, she did not appreciate having anonymous, printed notes shoved under her wiper blade. Why hadn't they simply posted it through her door?

"I got a very strange note today," said Tiff as she busily prepared a chicken salad, accompanied by large baked potatoes. "Here." Passing the crumpled note to Joe, she frowned.
"Who's it from?" Joe unfolded the note and read it.
"No idea."
"Must have posted it after I went to work. There was nothing on the doormat when I left." Joe read the note again, just as Tiff had done earlier.
"No – it wasn't posted through the door." Tiff picked up two healthy looking, loaded plates and carried them over to the table. "It was under my windscreen wiper. I noticed it before I drove away, this morning."
Following her across the room, Joe took a seat at the table and looked at the note again. "What's it supposed to mean?"
"Not sure." Tiff sat down and proceeded to smother her meal with lashings of low fat salad cream.
"Well, whoever it is better keep their opinions to themselves," said Joe, angrily. "Who do they think they are? Telling us to keep ourselves to ourselves."
Tiff hadn't quite seen it this way before but now that Joe had mentioned it she could see that the note was indeed, a downright cheek. "I get the

feeling that the note is for me though. Rather than, us. Why would it be put under *my* windscreen?"

"So…" mumbled Joe, chewing a mouthful of food, "who do you think it might be then? And who do you think is not what they seem?" He smiled warmly, showing her that he was not quite so het-up about it as he had first appeared.

"I really don't know." Tiff stabbed a chunk of cold chicken with her fork. "We hardly know anyone yet."

"My guess would be that weirdo, Alvin Snotgrass."

"It's Snodgrass," Tiff laughed and the chicken fell off her fork. "Not Snot-grass."

"Whatever. He goes from one extreme to another – bet he's not what he makes out to be."

"Ooh, Joe Frey, now you're not being fair. You're being very judgemental." She gave him a wry smile. "I thought you said that we shouldn't judge people and we should make our own minds up about someone, rather than listen to others."

"I *have* made my own mind up." Joe picked up the glass of water in front of him and took a gulp. "He's a freak and I don't believe for one minute that he's some kind of super-spy. How can he be, when he dresses like a one-hundred-percent-nerd in his spare time? A secret-service agent by day, and a dogtrot-degenerate by night? I don't think so."

Tiff sniggered into her plate. "Maybe we'll find out more on Saturday night. We could do some secret surveillance of our own."

"OK, *Miss Moneypenny*, you do the field work and I'll be your *James Bond*." With a flirtatious wink, he gave an inviting smile before parting his lips and licking them deliberately.

"Finish," Tiff mocked as she pointed to his dinner. "Then I might be your *Moneypenny*."

Another week sailed by at such a pace that Joe and Tiff didn't have time to discuss the note any further, or Alvin, or secret spies or anything else for that matter. The slip of paper had remained in the 'junk-drawer', in the kitchen, since Tiff had received it. Yet, each morning, she had wondered if she was being watched as she walked around the green to her car. She half-expected another note to be poking out from underneath the wiper blade but there was nothing, thankfully. So she really didn't need to feel so spooked every morning.

The weather report for Saturday's barbecue looked favourable. Tiff secretly wondered if Georgie would be invited. She was intrigued by the woman and, as of yet, she hadn't had an opportunity to meet her, face to face. In fact, she had hardly seen anyone in the close, all week. But then again, she was at work most of the time.

Joe arrived home early, as was usually the case on a Friday evening. "Come on babe," he called up the stairs. "Let's get a takeaway tonight. I'm starving."

Bounding down the stairs in her grey tracksuit and pink and grey, cheap trainers, Tiff flung her arms round his neck and kissed him hard on the lips.

"What's that for?" he asked, wiping a hand across his mouth.

Shrugging her shoulders, Tiff smiled. "Don't know. I just felt like it."

Joe laughed and shook his head quizzically. "You're a mad woman."

"I'm looking forward to the weekend – aren't you?"

"I am now…" said Joe, turning to open the front door.

"What do you mean, 'now'?" Tiff followed him out of the door and locked it behind her.

"Had to put Mum and Dad off. They wanted to come and see the house tomorrow."

"Oh – so soon?"

"Well, we have been here practically a month now." Joe placed an arm round Tiff's shoulder as they strolled around the edge of the green towards her car. "But don't worry – I put them off. Told them we were really busy tomorrow and then we have the neighbour's barbecue in the evening."

"Were they OK about it?"

"You know what Mum's like – she wanted to know everything about our neighbours."

"What did you say?"

Joe shrugged his hefty shoulders. "Just said we had the standard quotient of weirdos in the close."

Tiff giggled and peered up at him. "We've only got one haven't we?" she whispered as they passed by number nine.

"Georgie's a bit strange too –"

"What makes you say that?" Tiff snapped. "I mean – why do you think she's strange?"

As they approached the car, Joe walked round to the driver's side. He always drove when they went anywhere together and Tiff was more than happy with that. She wasn't as confident a driver as he was and particularly in unfamiliar areas.

"Chinese?" he asked.

Tiff nodded. "So, why do you think Georgie is strange? I thought you said you liked her."

Joe glanced briefly at her, a puzzled frown across his face. "I hardly know her, babe. Like I said before, she seemed nice enough when she stopped to talk to me that day. I'm purely going by the Cyril and Betty story, if that's what you're asking. Maybe she's not strange – I don't know. And I don't care either. Why do you snap at me whenever her name is mentioned?"

Tiff lowered her eyes and consciously wiped the glare from her face. "Sorry, I didn't mean to snap... Guess I'm just suspicious of everyone around here. You know... the note... and creepy Alvin." She sighed as they pulled out on to Oakwood road and drove away. "I just wondered if you knew something I didn't. That's all."

Shaking his head, Joe kept his eyes on the road. "No. I don't know any more than you do."

Shifting guiltily in her seat, Tiff toyed with the idea of telling him everything she knew. But she couldn't. Not now. He would wonder why she hadn't said anything before. Worst of all, he might want to find out more for himself and become obsessed with the view from the craft room. Just as she was consumed by it. Astonishingly.

The weather was going to be good for the barbecue this evening, going by the glorious sunshine streaming through the slit in the bedroom curtains. The weather reports had remained consistently correct, for a change, although the balmy conditions were more suited for July and August rather than early May.

Tiff dragged herself out of bed, leaving Joe asleep. They had woken an hour earlier but as usual, at the weekends, Joe's daybreak libido was up before him. He was hard to resist in the comfort of a cosy warm bed. His hot naked body was soft and smooth to touch. Sensual and strong, he had taken her in his arms and loved her with tenderness before the birds had even begun to sing.

Quietly closing the bedroom door behind her, Tiff tiptoed into the craft room and leant right over the table. She could just see Georgie's garden if she stretched far enough. Why on earth was she peering into Georgie's garden at 8.30 in the morning? She had no idea. As if the woman was going to be sunbathing at this time of the day. As if Georgie would be fornicating over the cement mixer in broad daylight. Tiff tutted to herself and shook her head in annoyance. She had to stop it. She had to block the bizarre images from her mind.

Across the field, in the distance, she spotted a person walking along the tree-lined path which led all the way down to the river. A dog raced along the pathway, weaving in and out of the trees, stopping to sniff things and then racing ahead of its owner. A woman? Tiff peered with squinted eyes. Was it Georgie? The dog looked like Georgie's, even though it was so far away. She strained her eyes to focus on the figure walking along. It was difficult to see who she was as the trees obscured the view. Tiff knew it was a woman by the way she walked and swung a dog lead in her hand. Frozen to the spot, she watched as the woman got further and further away. Her long blonde hair bobbed up and down as her energetic gait speeded up. It *was* Georgie.

A glint of gold caught the corner of Tiff's eye and she turned to look to the right of the fields. Again, through the trees on the right, chinks of gold flashed as the morning sun reflected on something moving swiftly along the other path.

Tiff held her breath.

She had to get the old set of binoculars from one of the boxes in the cupboard under the stairs. They had belonged to her dad, years ago, when he'd enjoyed a spot of ship-watching from the old harbour walls on the south coast. Tiff had just remembered that she had them. They were buried somewhere in the bottom of a box, along with some sentimental ornaments and childhood memory-boxes.

The gold colour flickered along the path behind the wide trunks of the sycamore trees. Gold Latex. *Speedos*. With spindly legs attached. Pulling his knees high up to his chest as he pranced along, Tiff was pretty sure that it was Alvin, making his way, rapidly, towards Georgie.

Muffling her gasp with a hand cupped to her mouth, Tiff stepped backwards. Were they meeting each other? Why were they both at the back of Sycamore Close? Ordinarily, Alvin and Georgie could have had genuine reasons for their individual romps through the fields, early in the morning, but they weren't ordinary people. And Tiff suspected that they weren't planning to be 'individuals' for too long either, by the speed that Alvin's sleek, gold pants were moving through the trees towards Georgie.

Tiptoeing out of the room, Tiff pulled the door closed and crept down the stairs as her heart thumped with every footstep. She had to find the binoculars. They would come in handy anyway for looking across the fields. For looking at the river and admiring the view. But she would keep them hidden in her craft accessories drawer. There was no way she wanted Joe to use them, 'to look at the view' or to peer into anyone's garden for that matter.

The cupboard under the stairs went as far back as the bottom step. Filled with unpacked boxes, shoes, Joe's old motorbike gear and countless stacks of books, the small box, which Tiff was looking for, had to be somewhere near the back. She scrabbled around in the dark, ducking her head down further and further as the ceiling above her dropped steeply. It had to be in there somewhere. But where?

"Tiff?"

A voice, from outside the cupboard startled her. She froze. Thinking of a plausible reason for being on her hands and knees in the depths of the stair cupboard, she began to shuffle backwards.

"Tiff? What are you doing in there?" asked Joe, amusedly. "What are you looking for?"

Scuffling back through the boxes, books and motorbike paraphernalia, Tiff edged her way out of the cupboard like a breech birth. "Oh... you're awake now." Pulling herself to her feet, she dusted off her pyjama trousers.

"Just looking for any craft bits... you know," she stumbled, "stuff I might have missed..."

Shooting a puzzled stare, Joe frowned. "At this time of the morning?"

"It must be getting on for nine o'clock, mister lazybones." Playfully, she poked him in the tummy, closed the cupboard door behind her and walked away to the kitchen with flushed cheeks. "Cup of tea or do you want coffee?"

Chapter 9

Coffee and the weekend's usual lashings of marmalade on several pieces of toast. Tiff had been on edge throughout breakfast and Joe had noticed her impatience.

"You OK this morning, babe?"

"Yes," she replied, scooping her hair away from her face. "I'm fine. I'm looking forward to getting on with the rest of the fence."

"Cool, we'll get it finished today." Joe paused, thoughtfully. "Is there anything else to do in your room?"

"No." Picking at the piece of toast on her plate, she looked up and smiled weakly. "I... err... I'll sort out everything as I go. No need to worry about that room anymore – it's finished."

"Are you missing some bits though?"

"No, why do you say that?"

"You were looking for something earlier?" Joe propped his chin up with his hand. "I'm sure I put all your craft stuff together."

"Yes – you did. I don't know what I was looking for really. Just wanted to check what was left under the stairs."

"OK," replied Joe. "Come on then. Let's get dressed and get that fence finished."

She'd missed it. Whatever 'it' might have been. Maybe it was nothing. But Tiff had a feeling that it would have been more than nothing. Quite irked by the fact that she hadn't been able to see or watch what Alvin and Georgie were up to, she couldn't help but sulk. What was becoming of her? Was she turning into a freak? Why was she so preoccupied with the neighbours? Tutting to herself, she made a concerted effort to forget about them and enjoy her day, painting with Joe.

"Morning," called Joe.

Tiff turned and looked at him, puzzled. He wasn't talking to her. Peering back over her shoulder, she could see Georgie walking across the green with her tired, heavily panting dog. It was the first time she had seen the woman up close. Surprisingly, she looked a dishevelled mess. Her mud splattered tracksuit bottoms were crumpled and her hair looked fit for a bird to lay its eggs in. She smiled as she approached and mouthed a 'good morning', directing her gaze towards Joe.

Tiff smiled awkwardly. "Hello," she spluttered. "Nice to meet you."

As Georgie drew closer, she lowered her head, coyly. "You too."

Thinking about what she'd seen earlier, Tiff blurted out, "Looks like you've been on a long walk – your dog – he seems to be worn out." Looking down at Georgie's filthy trouser bottoms, she screwed her nose up and added, "Has he been dragging you through mud?"

Peering down at her legs, Georgie replied stiffly. "Yes – near the river. He's hard work. Drags me around all over the place."

"I can see that."

A small, red graze, glistened on Georgie's left cheekbone.

"Looks like you've cut your cheek," Tiff remarked. "Are you OK?"

Placing a grubby hand to her face, Georgie winced as her fingers brushed across the raw wound. "Fell over." She let out an unconvincing chuckle. "Not the first time."

"Georgie was saying the other day that her dog is very strong – needs a lot of walking." Joe smiled warmly. "This is Tiffany – my partner."

"Tiff. I prefer to be called Tiff."

"Hello Tiff," said Georgie. "It's lovely to meet you. You are one lucky lady." Flicking a glance towards Joe, her smirk was flirtatiously unnerving. "Anyhow, I'd better go. I've got a lot to do today." Georgie eyed Joe, who was aimlessly flicking his paintbrush up and down the fence, disregarding the job in hand. "Bye Joe. See you again soon, I hope." With that, she trundled off down her garden path, dragging the weary dog behind her. She disappeared through her front door and slammed it shut.

"Bye Joe – see you again soon, I hope," sneered Tiff, under her breath. "What's all that about? Did you see the way she looked at you?"

Joe tutted and rolled his eyes. "Tiffany – what has got into you?"

"She fancies you – and it's, Tiff, if you don't mind," she whispered.

"Sorry babe. So what if she does?" Placing the paintbrush across the tin of gleaming white paint, Joe stood up and stretched. "Come here, you." Beckoning to Tiff, he reached out a hand and pulled her up, towards him. "She can fancy me all she likes. I don't care. She could never compare to you." Kissing her forehead, he placed his hands on her shoulders and squeezed her. "Now stop being so insecure. I love you Miss Cuthbert and that's that."

And that was exactly what Tiff needed to hear. She knew it anyway. But sometimes she just needed to hear it a little more often. As always, Joe managed to say the right things at the right time.

"I know you do," she sighed, before moving away to the next unpainted section of picket fencing. "I know you do..."

That woman had been out with her dog for a long time though. She looked like she'd been dragged through a prickly bush, backwards – or forwards, it wouldn't have made much difference which way. What had Tiff missed this morning? Had Georgie really fallen over? Or had she met up with Alvin and had rampant sex against a tree trunk, while the dog mooched around the fields? Tiff imagined Alvin's gold pants glistening in the sunshine as he thrusted against Georgie's crotch. Maybe a branch had caught her face as they swung through the trees, playing *Tarzan* and *Jane*? Or had Alvin-aka-*Goldfinger* been rubbing his *Pussy Galore* up the wrong way and they'd got into a bit of a rough and tumble in the bushes? Now Tiff's musing was getting really ridiculous. Wasn't it?

Peering around the green with a hand shielding his eyes from the glaring sunshine, Joe's smug expression said it all.

"It does look good," said Tiff, following his gaze.

"Best one on the close, I'd say."

"Umm..." Tiff lowered her voice. "Shame that house hasn't got a picket fence," she said pointing to number six. "At least they would all be the same then – even though some aren't painted at all."

Joe nodded his head and turned to admire their brilliant white fence again. "Definitely need to have a tidy-up in the garden now."

"We can do it tomorrow. As long as you don't have a hangover."

Grinning sarcastically, Joe walked through the gate and looked around. "Get rid of that thing for a start."

"But it's quite sweet and that little old woman comes in and sits on it."

"Yeah, exactly. Have you found out why yet?"

Tiff shook her head. "No – haven't been able to catch her."

The thing was – Tiff could have caught the old woman on at least two occasions but she just hadn't known what to say to her. *What are you doing in my garden?* That sounded too abrupt. *Why do you think you can come in here and sit down?* Again, that was far too discourteous. Maybe, a softer approach was needed. *Hello there – can I help you at all?* Why hadn't she thought of it before? It was pretty simple really. All she needed to do was strike up a conversation with the woman and find out why she came into their garden to sit on the bench under the window. Tiff subconsciously chastised herself for always creating more of a problem than there needed to be.

"I will catch her next time. Let's keep the bench for now."

"OK, we'll sort the weeds out and cut some of those bushy things back then."

"Think they're fuchsias – not weeds." Tiff giggled. "They'll look nice in the summer." Standing in the middle of the front garden, with her hands on her hips, Tiff surveyed the borders. "We'll keep that," she said, pointing to a small, straggly hydrangea. "I'm sure I could trim it and tidy it up. And that one, we'll keep that... and those."

"OK. So what shall I dig up?"

Tiff shrugged her shoulders, turned her wrist and looked down at her watch. "Suppose we've got another hour." She sighed. "I do need to wash my hair and have a bath before tonight though. Just dig up the weeds in between the bushes."

"No problem. I'll do it and you can supervise. I can't tell the difference between a weed and a bush."

At 6.40pm, Tiff glided down the stairs and wafted into the kitchen. "What do you think?" she asked a gobsmacked Joe before twirling round on her toes.

"You can't go out looking like that."

Tiff frowned and a puzzled look crept across her face.

"I'll be wanting to have mad passionate sex with you all night. You look so sexy."

Although they'd been together for a couple of years, Joe still managed to make her blush. She looked down at her dress coyly. "You like it then?"

"Like it?" Joe advanced towards her with two small glasses of white wine in his hands. "I love it."

Taking a glass, Tiff sipped at the chilled fruit wine. She needed a drink before they went to the barbecue, to calm her nerves. She peered down at her dress and lovingly smoothed it down. "Got it from *ASDA*, would you believe."

"You look lovely babe."

The peach dolly shoes complimented Tiff's new dress perfectly. A strappy little summery number with a pinched-in waist and full, knee-length skirt, the light, cotton fabric felt nice on her skin. The large lemon, peach and rose flower print suited her complexion and hair colour. She'd also applied some make-up, so her small features and large doe-like eyes were appealing. Yet she was very modest about her look and didn't see herself as anything special. Joe always said that she was fairylike in her appearance. Dainty, yet dazzling and certainly a feast for the eye.

Joe hadn't asked how he looked. He always looked great anyway. Wearing blue jeans and a pale-blue checked shirt, his physique made any casual attire look amazing. The aura of confidence and substance which surrounded him, made him entrancing to many an admirer.

Knocking back the wine, Tiff went to the fridge and poured another one from the box dispenser. "Do you want another one before we go?"

Joe shook his head. "No – I'll stick to the beer." Grabbing his pack of twelve cans and the tray of lamb and spicy vegetable kebabs, he went into the lounge and set them by the front door. "You've got five minutes to calm your nerves babe. It's ten to seven now. We shouldn't be late."

"Ready in five." Tiff gulped down the second glass of wine as the effects of the first one began to warm her and ease her nerves. She couldn't get drunk at their first meeting-of-the-neighbours so she'd have to be careful about what else she had for a while. At least for the next hour or so anyway. Two glasses of wine were enough for her. Enough to remove her inhibitions. Enough to make her more sociable and less shy. Any more than that and she would become silly. She did not want to do 'silly' tonight.

Nervously waiting at the front door of number eight, Tiff looked up at Joe and smiled. She'd be OK with him there. He was good at talking to strangers. He had a way with people that she envied slightly. He found it easy to get on with anyone and everyone got on well with him. He made people laugh. He could always break the ice in any strained or unfamiliar atmosphere. People wanted to listen to what he had to say. There was just something about his personality that attracted people to him. Tiff liked it that way. It took the focus away from her and she could comfortably hide behind his loud, gregarious presence.

"Hello!" The front door flew open wide and Hayley stood in the doorway beaming. Wearing a summer print playsuit and purple flip-flops, her casual appearance was friendly and calming. "Come in. It's so lovely to meet you both at last." She tucked a strand of her mid-length brown hair behind her ear and stepped aside. "Joe," she said, holding a hand out. "It's good to meet you." Shaking his hand, she ushered him through the door. "And Tiff, is that short for Tiffany?"

"Yes it is, I much prefer to be called Tiff though."

Hayley smiled warmly. "Lovely name, do come in. So happy you could make it." Placing an arm round Tiff's shoulders, she smiled widely. "Do go on through." She Closed the door behind them and pointed along the corridor. "Through there and straight out to the garden if you like."

The smoky smell of chicken and sausages cooking on an open flame met Joe and Tiff as they reached the dining room. In front of them, patio doors led out to a large decked area, filled with potted plants, chairs, large beanbags and several people. Hayley's husband, Wayne, was standing over on the far left of the garden, by the side of a large metallic barbecue talking to another man.

"Wayne – darling. Joe and Tiff from number four are here."

Wayne looked up and smiled. "Hello," he said, jovially. "Glad you could make it."

Joe left Tiff's side and approached Wayne. "I brought some kebabs along…"

"Great – pop them on the table and we'll get them on in no time."

"Now then, can I get you both a drink?" Hayley's cheery disposition and smiley face were calming and welcoming.

"I'll stick to these, thanks," Joe replied, holding up his cans of beer.

"Tiff? Would you like some *Pimms*?" Hayley pointed inside to a huge glass bowl, in the centre of a long dining table, filled with plates and dishes of salad and various finger foods. A mountain of bread rolls towered precariously at the back of the table and a row of sauces and chutneys lined the front.

"Yes, please. That would be lovely," said Tiff, politely as she followed Hayley back inside. "Looks like you have a few people coming round. The spread looks amazing."

Hayley reached across the table and pulled a plastic tumbler from a stack. "Oh," she said, shaking her head, "not that many really. Wayne always says I do too much and I should remember that I'm not feeding the whole town."

Tiff nodded her head. "I think I'd be the same."

"Good – then I'm not the only one." Hayley dipped a ladle into the punch bowl. "Better to have too much than not enough, I reckon."

"Absolutely."

"Strawberries and cucumber?"

"Oh, yes please. Never thought of putting those in a *Pimms* before." Watching closely as Hayley fished around to catch the strawberries and cucumber slices bobbing around the bowl, Tiff added, "It's very kind of you to invite us here this evening."

"You're very welcome. It's nice to get to know your neighbours, especially on such a small close."

Tiff nodded agreeably before turning her head to see where Joe was.

As usual, Joe had already struck up a conversation with Wayne and the other man stood beside the barbecue. He was doing most of the talking while the other two men smiled and listened.

"I'll introduce you to everyone in a minute," said Hayley, passing over a tall plastic tumbler, filled to the top with strawberries, cucumber slices and *Pimms*. "Be careful with it," she said, winking a pretty mascaraed eye. "I've put as much *Vodka* in it, as *Pimms*.

Tiff giggled softly. "Oh -OK. It's strong then?"

"As always. If you're going to have punch, make sure it gives you a punch, I say."

"I couldn't agree more," said Tiff, really warming to her friendly neighbour.

"Right," said Hayley, taking a sip from her own tumbler and plucking out a piece of cucumber, "let me introduce you to everyone. They're not all here yet but we can do intros as we go. What do you think?"

"Great," replied Tiff, nervously, as she gulped down a mouthful of her drink and ate a piece of fruit. "I'd love to."

Ushering Tiff back out to the garden, Hayley began the introductions. "So..." she said, pointing to the first woman sitting by the patio doors, "this is Karen, my sister-in-law. She's trouble – keep away from her." Hayley giggled before leaning over and hugging the blonde woman's head. "Only joking – I love her really. And that's my brother John – over there." Hayley pointed towards the men at the side of the barbecue. "And the other two are our husbands." She giggled again.

"Ah, that tall one is not my husband – well not yet anyway." Tiff took another gulp of her drink.

"Oh – not yet? So we'll be having a wedding on the close?"

"No, we don't have any plans at the moment." Tiff whispered, as she felt herself cringing. People always thought they were a married couple and she wished they were too.

"We'll work on that one," said Hayley, grinning widely. "Anyway... over here are Tom and Jean. They live at number two, across the green.

The elderly couple smiled and both said 'hello' at the same time.

They had to be at least in their seventies, thought Tiff as she greeted them warmly. They appeared perfectly normal too. The odds were stacking against there being any more weirdos on the close.

"And over here..." said Hayley as she moved towards another elderly, smartly-dressed woman who looked fine and dignified, "is our one and only Lilly. Lilly Watson. She lives at number six, on the corner." Hayley pulled up a chair next to her and sat down.

"Hello – nice to meet you," said Tiff as the effects of her drink warmed her cheeks.

"In fact," added Hayley, "our Lilly is your next-door-but-one neighbour, isn't she?"

Sitting down on a large beanbag, on the other side of Lilly, Tiff nodded her head. "Yes, that's right."

"Hello dearie," said Lilly in a high-pitched squeak. "Do you come here often?" Lilly gave a crinkly smile, displaying her perfectly aligned, unnaturally white teeth.

"No, it's our first time," replied Tiff. "We moved here about a month ago."

"Ah, yes, of course you did," she breathed. "Thought I hadn't seen you before... but I do know who you are. I'm afraid I don't get out much these days, myself," Lilly paused thoughtfully, "and those blasted bushes have grown too high for me to see anything on the close. Are you all settled in now?"

"Lilly we said we'd trim them down for you," Hayley jumped in. "Wayne can get hold of a hedge trimmer, no problem."

"Nope – nope – nope – nope – nope. I tell you dearie." Lilly pulled herself up in her chair. "I'll deal with it myself."

Hayley rolled her eyes and tutted to Tiff. "She's as stubborn as a mule, is our Lilly."

"A very proud lady I'd imagine and yes thank you, we've settled in nicely," said Tiff, unsure of what to say really.

"Good. You say, 'proud lady'? Yes, dearie – I'm proud. As for lady? Not sure I've been one of those since my seventies." Lilly let out a short titter.

Tiff's eyes widened. "Since your seventies?" she remarked.

"Go on," whispered Hayley, into Lilly's ear. "Tell her how old you are."

"Ooh... now then... I think I must be 88 this year," said Lilly in a hushed voice. "Or is it 89?"

"Lilly!" Hayley tutted again. "It's the big one this year – remember?"

Lilly grinned. "So it is dearie. Yes, it's a big one... not as big as being 100 though."

"Wow, that's incredible," breathed Tiff. "So you'll be 90 this year?"

"Yes, that's right dearie. Ninety." Lilly cupped her hands together in her lap. "I don't feel a day over twenty, I don't mind telling you."

"Very sprightly, our Lilly, you know." Hayley placed an arm round Lilly's shoulders. "A bit too sprightly sometimes – aren't you Lilly?"

"You can never be too sprightly dearie. We can't do 'sprightly' in our coffins so we should make the most of it while we're upright."

"True," said Tiff, taking a small sip from her drink as she felt the alcohol warming her entire being. "You are very inspirational. It's been such a pleasure to meet you."

"Are you going somewhere?" squeaked Lilly.

"No." Tiff stumbled.

"Then you should say it 'is' a pleasure to meet me. And not 'it has been' a pleasure to meet me, dearie."

Tiff looked across at Hayley awkwardly. "Yes, of course. My apologies."

"Apology accepted dearie... Now, do you think you could get me a packet of cheese and onion crisps? The hosts are terribly slow."

Hayley stood up and winked at Tiff. "Terribly slow? You're a cheeky one, Lilly Watson. You haven't even asked for a packet of crisps yet. Come on Tiff, I'll show you where they are. Oh... and Lilly?"

Lilly peered up expectantly.

"No popping them – OK?"

"I like to open them myself dearie. You know I do. I won't touch them if they're opened already."

Puzzled by the last part of their conversation, Tiff gave a quizzical stare at Hayley and then followed her back indoors to the kitchen.

"She pops them. Every single time."

"Pops them?" questioned Tiff, amused. "You mean the crisps?"

Hayley shook her head and sniggered. "No, the packet. She's like a little excitable child at a tea party."

"Oh, I see." Tiff smiled and sipped at her drink more cautiously as a slight fuzziness began to enter her head.

"She's a nightmare. Makes everyone jump out of their skins." Hayley reached into a bottom cupboard and pulled out a multi-pack of assorted crisp flavours. "And she won't touch the crisps if she's not the one to open the packet." Hayley found a packet of cheese and onion crisps and returned the rest to the cupboard. "She finds it highly amusing when everyone almost falls off their chairs in fright."

Tiff stifled a giggle. "Oh dear. Perhaps you should warn everyone beforehand."

"Huh," Hayley rolled her eyes, "tried that one. It's like she waits until everyone has forgotten and then she makes an almighty pop with them, showering anyone who might be nearby with sprinkles of disintegrated crisps."

This time Tiff let out a chuckle and placed a hand over her mouth, unsure of the level of annoyance that Lilly might be creating. "Sorry," she said, desperately trying not to laugh again.

"Oh, don't apologise, it used to be funny," Hayley continued "but it's become a little annoying having to pick up all the crisp crumbs around her chair."

"Does she come round here a lot?"

"Oh yes. We can't get rid of her at the weekends sometimes. We don't mind too much, she's a wonderful, dear old lady really."

"She's amazing. Ninety years old..."

"Almost," Hayley pointed out.

"Almost," laughed Tiff. "And she seems to have all her faculties about her."

"Oh, she has. A bit too much really. She can be a danger to herself sometimes." Hayley lowered her voice just as the sound of the front door opening filtered through from the hallway. "She's outlived all three of her children – such a shame for her. She's so tough on the outside but I think, deep down, she's a wonderful woman."

"Oh gosh. That must have been very hard."

Hayley nodded her head agreeably as footsteps could be heard moving along the hallway.

"Hi babe," came a woman's voice, a second before she appeared in the dining room doorway. "Where shall I put these?" Holding up two bottles of *Prosecco*, the scantily clad woman grinned. Her perfect, voluptuous figure was enhanced by a low-cut, lemon mini-dress that barely covered her thighs, patent black shoes with five-inch heels and a small black, silk rose in her long blonde hair. "Hi," Georgie said, grinning at Tiff. "We meet again."

"You've met Tiff before, have you?"

"Yes – just this morning."

"What have you been up to?" asked Hayley, peering at Georgie's cheek.

"Oh – you know." Georgie brushed three fingers across the graze on her face. "Buster the bruiser..."

"He's had you over again?"

Georgie nodded her head and darted her eyes quickly, towards the kitchen window. "Wayne out there is he?"

"Yes – go through. We'll be out in a minute. Just getting Lilly's crisps."

Placing one of the bottles on the table, Georgie picked up a plastic tumbler and carried it out to the garden with the other bottle.

"Right," said Hayley, smiling weakly. "Shall we go back outside?"

"Yes, of course." Tiff couldn't wait to go outside now. She wanted to see where Joe was and also keep an eye on Georgie. The woman's titillating attire suggested that she was all-out for some attention from the opposite sex.

"Sorry it took so long. Couldn't find them." Hayley placed a bag of cheese and onion crisps in Lilly's lap. "And no scaring anyone."

"Oh no dearie. Would I?" She gave a cunning grin.

"Yes – you would," replied Hayley in jest, before gently squeezing Lilly's shoulder and smiling at her warmly.

On the far side of the decking, Joe was still chatting to Wayne and John. Georgie had joined them and was standing directly opposite Joe. She laughed. She drank. She posed. She teased. She flicked her long hair from side to side. Tiff was sure that she eyed Joe with a glint in her eye.

Tiff watched with a distrustful eye and a brewing jealousy.

Chapter 10

A few minutes of torture had trickled by. Tiff couldn't tear her eyes away from Georgie. She had to be discreet in her scrutiny though. She couldn't allow anyone to sense her jealousy. Her innate insecurity.

Seated next to Lilly again, having been ushered to the beanbag by Hayley, Tiff listened politely to the friendly chatter between the elderly couple from number two, Lilly, Hayley and her sister-in-law, Karen. Tiff didn't know what they were talking about really. Or care too much. Now and again she smiled respectfully or nodded at what she thought were appropriate moments. However, her mind and eyes were elsewhere.

"Another *Pimms* Tiff?"

Startled by the direct question, Tiff snapped back from her furtive surveillance. "Oh, yes. Thank you." Passing her empty tumbler to Hayley, she was surprised to see that she had finished her drink entirely. She had unknowingly sipped the punch while being distracted and intrigued by the frivolities going on in the corner of the garden, by the side of the barbecue. The three men were having a jolly good laugh, along with Georgie. They had all weighed the woman up, from top to toe. Tiff knew it. She'd watched each and every one of them. Including Joe.

"Are you OK?"

Again, the direct question shook Tiff. Looking up she smiled falteringly. "Yes, I'm fine thanks. Would you... err... like me to help you with those?"

Hayley nodded her head and passed two tumblers to Tiff. "Let's get these filled up and then we can come back out here."

"OK," Tiff replied, resignedly.

As they entered the dining room, the peal of the doorbell surprised Tiff.

"Come in," shouted Hayley, "the door's open."

Tiff immediately recognised the young couple as they walked through the door, laden with cans of beer and cider. Dressed far more casually than their usual attire of smart suits and briefcases, the couple smiled weakly.

"This is Alfie and Kelly, from next door," said Hayley. "Hi you two – finished work for the day?"

The couple nodded in unison and stood in the middle of the dining room looking awkwardly shy.

"Let me get you both a drink," said Hayley. "Try some Punch first, before you start on yours." Hayley began to dart around the room collecting clean glasses and more plastic tumblers. "Have you met Tiff? She's just moved in to number four."

"Hello," said Kelly, quietly. "Nice to meet you."

Alfie nodded an acknowledgement and peered out of the patio doors, into the garden.

"Hello," said Tiff, trying desperately not to slur her words, "I've seen you a couple of times – going off to work in the mornings."

"Oh yes – that's all we do. Six days a week, most of the time."

"What do you do?" asked Tiff, genuinely curious.

"We run an estate agent – in the town."

"Oh, I see. So do you work together?"

Kelly nodded her head and smiled. "Yes, all the time. Live, work, sleep, eat and breathe together."

Detecting a hint of sarcasm in Kelly's voice, Tiff smiled awkwardly. "Must be very difficult. I mean, it must be hard work running an estate agent."

"You get used to it." Kelly shrugged her shoulders.

Alfie had already taken his cans of beer and exited the dining room. He was heading for the corner of the garden where most of the noise was coming from.

"Thanks," said Kelly, taking a tumbler of punch from Hayley. "Is Lilly here?"

"Yes, she's in the garden – go through." Hayley grinned, "Watch out – she's got her crisps."

Kelly let out a short burst of laughter and left the room.

"They seem like a nice couple," said Tiff. "Anyone else coming from the close?"

"No – think that's it. I did ask Gary and Sarah, at number one, but they're busy tonight. Their eldest will be six, tomorrow. Think they're having a sleepover for him tonight and then off out for the day tomorrow." Hayley scooped more punch into a fresh tumbler and passed it to Tiff. "Take it slow," she giggled, "you'll be on the floor at this rate."

Embarrassed, Tiff took the drink, peered into the tumbler and pulled out a slice of cucumber. "I'll suck on this for the rest of the night then."

Giggling to herself, Hayley continued to fill another four tumblers. "You're funny – I can see we're going to get along really well."

Tiff nodded her fuzzy head. "Yes – so can I. Let me take those out for you."

Doing her very best to walk normally, Tiff carried two drinks out and passed them to the elderly couple, Tom and Jean. She glanced across at the small crowd, gathered by the barbecue. Joe was oblivious to her whereabouts and totally engrossed in a conversation with Georgie. Tiff had to join them. Show her face. See what they were talking about. Reluctantly returning indoors, she picked up two more tumblers and took them back outside to Lilly and Karen. Then, hearing her name being called from the kitchen, she went back inside.

"Sorry Tiff... would you mind just giving me a quick hand with this?" The mountain of baps and finger rolls had been moved from the table and were piled up on the kitchen worktop. "While I'm slicing through this lot, would you stir the onions for me?"

"Yes, of course." Actually this was the perfect place to stand. While stirring the fried onions, Tiff could see Joe through the kitchen window. She could watch the interactions between him and Georgie. His face was lit up with smiles and laughter and he looked like he was having a fun time. Georgie had her back turned slightly, yet Tiff could tell that she was laughing too. By the way she flicked her long hair back and tilted her hips, Tiff knew she was flirting as well.

"Are you sure you don't mind doing that?"

Hayley's voice had interrupted Tiff's deepest thoughts once again. "No, no. Not at all. Sorry – I was daydreaming."

"Joe seems to be getting on well with everyone."

"Yes – he always does. He's a very sociable person."

"And so are you."

Tiff was really beginning to like this woman. She was her kind of person. "I'm quite shy really."

"Me too. I was so nervous about you two coming." Hayley giggled as she sliced through the bread rolls. "I'm OK once I've met someone for the first time though."

"Yes, I'm the same." Tiff turned the onions over as they began to brown. The smell was making her feel quite hungry. "I've met almost everyone on the close now."

"Oh, have you?"

"Yes – Cyril and Betty, next door to us. Are they coming?"

"No, I... I didn't invite them."

"Oh, OK." Tiff sensed an awkwardness in Hayley's voice.

"Your other neighbour? Alvin?"

"Absolutely not. No, he's not coming either."

It was now obvious, that there was a contemptuous tone to Hayley's voice.

"I'm guessing that you don't like him."

"I don't care either way to be honest. I have nothing to do with him. And I don't have much to do with Cyril and Betty either. I'll say hello if I see them but that's it."

"We liked Cyril and Betty when we met them. They invited us into their house for tea and cake. Amazing house they've got, you know."

"I bet they have. Cyril's very hardworking and Betty just looks the type to be a perfect housewife."

"She is." Tiff smiled warmly at the thought of Betty's endearing cake-making skills and hospitality.

"It's awkward for me," Hayley said, resignedly. "I have to think of Georgie."

"Oh, OK." Tiff deliberately sounded nonchalant. She had to pretend she knew nothing of the goings-on in Sycamore Close.

"They don't get on. Georgie had a falling-out with them a couple of years ago. It's awkward for us but we do like Georgie."

"Yes, she seems like a very nice lady," Tiff lied.

"She's got her faults..." Hayley peered out of the window to the barbecue crowd.

"I suppose we all have." Tiff was curious as to why Hayley liked Georgie so much. "So... what about Alvin, next door? What is it that you don't like about him?"

Hayley shrugged her shoulders and rolled her bottom lip down. "Again, it's more to do with Georgie. I wouldn't say that I don't like him. I don't really know him to be honest."

"Oh – has something happened between Georgie and him then?"

"Not sure what's going on really. One thing I do know for sure though is, she absolutely hates him."

"Hates him?" Quickly, Tiff snapped her mouth shut. "Oh dear... why does she hate him?" Visions of the garden shenanigans flashed through her mind. How could Georgie hate him? Tiff could not reveal what she'd seen. It could not get back to Joe that she had been watching Georgie. Spying on the neighbours from her craft room. No, that sounded awful. She'd only been living there a month and already she'd probably seen far more than anyone could imagine. What would the neighbours think if they knew what was really going on and that Tiff had actually witnessed some very bizarre behavior and kept it all to herself? What would anyone think if they knew how obsessed Tiff had become with the view from her craft room. What would Joe think?

"He's so nasty to her, apparently. I only know by the things she tells me."

"Why is he nasty to her?"

"He asked her for a date, after her husband left her but she turned him down. Since then, he's been sending her nasty messages now and again and generally being an arsehole."

"I see," Tiff replied, vacantly. Actually, she didn't 'see' at all.

Suddenly, Tiff pulled herself upright and focused her gaze on the sizzling onions. Stirring them frantically, she had an awakening. A horrifying realisation. A sickening understanding. Had she actually witnessed a rape that night in Georgie's garden? She felt queasy and more uneasy than before. What should she do now?

The food was ready. Wayne had brought trays, full of cooked meats, into the dining room while Joe and the others continued to chat. The rolls were cut and the onions were fried. Just like Tiff's brain.

Everyone began to filter into the dining room, grabbing a paper plate as they passed by Hayley. Tiff stood by the pan of onions, serving spoon in hand, attempting to look busy, sober and casual as Joe eventually walked through the doorway.

"There you are," Joe said a little guiltily. "Where've you been? I thought you were with me when I went outside."

Tiff grinned falteringly. "I've been busy, helping Hayley get things ready."

"You're getting on well with her then?" Joe whispered.

Tiff nodded. "She's really nice."

"Are you in charge of onions?" He smirked and winked an eye, before leaning over and softly kissing her cheek.

"Looks like it. So what have you been doing in the garden? Have you had a chance to talk to anyone much?"

Joe looked into her eyes, a puzzled expression on his face. He peered round at the guests milling around the dining table and then turned back to Tiff. "Yes, of course I've had chance to chat to people – haven't you?"

"Yes... so... what have you been talking about with...?" Tiff shot a reproachful look at Joe.

"You mean with her?" Joe flicked his eyes sideways, indicating to Georgie, who was standing at the far end of the dining room with an empty plate in her hands.

"No, I mean with anyone." Tiff darted her eyes around the room to make sure that no one was listening to their conversation. "I just wondered if you were having a nice time here, that's all?"

Reaching down for Tiff's hand, Joe took it and stroked it lovingly. "I am... and you should be too."

Pulling her hand away, Tiff smiled falsely. "Yes, I am – everyone's lovely." Lowering her voice, she whispered, "I do like Hayley – she's really nice."

"They're all a good bunch," Joe replied in a hushed voice, "Wayne's as funny as you like."

Tiff nodded her head and grinned. "Onions?"

"Let me get my burger first." Winking an eye, he turned away and headed back over to the dining table.

"Come on Tiff," shouted Hayley. "You don't have to serve them as well – let everyone get their own."

Placing the spoon back into the pan of onions, Tiff walked over and took a plate from Hayley. "Thanks. I'm hungrier than I thought actually – I'll just grab a burger."

"You'll have to eat more than that. This lot has got to be cleared before anyone can go home tonight."

"Yes – that's true," called Karen from the other end of the table as she picked up a roasted vegetable skewer. "She won't let you leave until, either the table is clear or you're prepared to take a doggie-bag home with you."

Several of the guests laughed and nodded their heads agreeably.

"How's your face?" Tiff peered at her drink on the table. She felt better, having eaten a cheese-burger, hot dog, plate of salad, coleslaw and homemade potato salad. She was practically sober again and slightly bolder than her norm.

Joe had gone back out to the garden with everyone else. When Tiff had returned from the downstairs toilet she was surprised to see Georgie standing alone in the far corner of the dining room nibbling away on a cheese straw.

Georgie placed a hand on her cheek as if she was remembering how she got the graze below her eye. "Oh... it's fine. Tough as nails, me."

"Did you say you were walking your dog through the woods?"

"No – I didn't," Georgie snapped.

"Oh, I'm sorry. I got the impression you went for a walk across the fields, out the back." Tiff began to retract from her words. "It's a lovely area. I bet there are lots of nice places to walk a dog around here."

"Suppose." Georgie's unfriendly gaze was unnerving. "If you like walking dogs."

"I've never had one myself. Think I'd prefer cats – they can do their own walking." Tiff let out a small, chancy giggle.

"Hate cats."

Georgie's blunt tone was enough for Tiff to realise that her neighbour did not care to talk. "Oh, well, OK, think everyone has gone outside now... err... I think I'll join them... speak to you again soon." Tiff gathered up her drink and a cheese straw of her own and walked out to the garden.

There was still a cold chill in the evenings, so early in May, but the two patio heaters, one at each end of the paved area, did a grand job of warming the air underneath the gazebos. Tiff's mind wandered again as she thought about Georgie, in her garden. It must have been cold for her, sprawled out against a cement mixer with her skirt hitched up to her waist. Tiff shook her head to disperse the haunting images.

Again, the men were clustered together under the gazebo furthest away and the women under the other. Kelly stood just behind Alfie, trying to join in the conversation with the men but she didn't appear to be having much success. Once again, the main focus of the male group was Joe. They all listened and laughed with him.

Tiff lowered herself down on to the huge, paisley design beanbag. There were several of them scattered around the garden and Tiff had been surprised how comfortable they were. She had half expected to sit on it and end up sinking down to the floor with her legs up in the air, in a very undignified fashion. But, thankfully, they weren't those kind of beanbags. She looked up and smiled at Lilly who was sat next to her. Lilly hadn't moved from her chair. "Hello again," she said, feeling much more relaxed, knowing that Georgie wasn't anywhere near her beloved Joe.

"Hello again dearie." Lilly smiled and sipped at her drink. The packet of cheese and onion crisps lay unopened on her lap.

"Not eaten them yet?"

"In my own time... in my own time."

"Yes, of course."

A moment later, Georgie came sauntering out from the dining room with a tumbler of punch in her hand. She glanced across at Tiff and then casually strolled over to the group of men. She walked straight past Kelly and joined the group around the other side, right next to Joe. A surge of disdain filled Tiff's head. She had to go over there and stand with Joe. She'd hardly spoken to Wayne anyway, so that would be a good enough excuse to join them...

BANG!

Tiff's whole body jolted at the sound. Her drink shot up in the air but luckily most of it fell back into the tumbler. Just a few drops landed on her new dress and she quickly brushed them away with her hand. She turned at the same time as everyone else to peer at Lilly incredulously.

"Bloody hell, Lilly, you've done it again," scoffed Hayley across the garden. "You're going to give yourself and everyone else a heart attack one of these days."

Lilly sat motionless in her chair, a conceited grin on her face and a pile of cheese and onion crisps in her lap.

Everyone turned back to the conversations they were having before the explosion went off, as if they'd all seen and heard it many times before.

Tiff smiled awkwardly and looked up at Lilly's white curls. "You've... err..." Pointing with a finger, she indicated to the top of Lilly's head. "Crisps – you've got crisps in your hair."

Lilly giggled and bent her head over her lap. She brushed the crisps from her hair and then began to nibble from the pile in her lap.

"Are you OK there?" Tiff indicated to the pile of crisps.

"Couldn't be better dearie." Lilly scooted the crisps around in her lap and picked out the smallest bits.

"Right, well – I'd better go and have a chat with Wayne. Haven't been over to meet him properly yet." Tiff pulled herself up from the beanbag. She brushed several crisp crumbs from her dress, daintily waved three fingers at Lilly and grinned. "Speak to you again soon."

Edging as close as possible to Joe, Tiff tried to push her way into the circle. No one was moving. She could feel Georgie's eyes following her every move.

"Oh, hi babe – didn't see you there," Joe placed an arm round her shoulders and pulled her in.

Looking sideways to Georgie, standing on the other side of Joe, Tiff smirked.

Georgie giggled at the sight of her and shook her head. Then she carried on listening to the men talking about rugby and football.

With his arm still round Tiff's shoulders, Joe carried on the conversation with the other men, oblivious to the fact that he was sandwiched between two women who apparently had such a dislike for each other.

Georgie had now turned her focus towards Kelly, who was standing opposite her, and for just one moment, Tiff could have sworn that she was mouthing something to Kelly about her. Georgie's shifty eyes and cunning grin suggested that she was finding something quite funny and secretively sharing it with Kelly. Kelly's eyes slyly darted from one side of Joe to the other. From Georgie to Tiff and back again. Only once did she meet Tiff's eye and she very quickly averted her gaze. Yet, all the time, a grin stretched across her face.

A few more minutes passed and Georgie now had the giggles. She grabbed hold of Joe's arm as she leant over and chuckled. Tiff felt uneasy again but her apprehension was masked by a raging jealousy and rapidly growing hatred for this woman.

"Oh God," breathed Georgie as she pulled herself upright and sighed.

Joe and the other men stopped talking and stared at Georgie with puzzled looks on their faces. Kelly scooted away in a fit of laughter, clutching her tummy, coughing and spluttering as she went.

"Oh... Joe..." Georgie gasped as she continued to grip his arm. "You're going to have to..."

Joe turned to Georgie and frowned.

"Tell her..."

Tiff glowered. Tell her what? She gulped hard. *What* should Joe tell her?

"Ha, ha," Georgie snorted before grabbing Joe's arm with both hands and resting her forehead on the top of his arm.

The other men stood motionless, perplexed by Georgie's display of hilarity.

"What?" asked Joe, a tense tone in his voice.

Georgie laughed louder, still clinging on to his arm. The other men twitched from one foot to the other. Tiff glared as her heartbeat strengthened and grew in rapidity.

Kelly was over the other side of the garden laughing loudly while Hayley and the others watched her in amusement.

"Tell her... go on..." Georgie giggled.

"Tell her what?" Joe flicked his eyes from Tiff to Georgie and then around each of the men standing in the circle. "What?" His voice was uptight.

Pulling her head away from Joe's arm, Georgie sighed deeply and glanced around at the puzzled faces staring back at her. "Well... look," she spluttered, as she pointed directly to Tiff, before bursting into laughter again.

Joe was the first to turn and look at Tiff. Followed by everyone else.

"Your hair... babe."

"What?" Tiff peered into Joe's eyes, searching for a clue. "Hair?"

"Crisps babe..." Joe withdrew his arm from Tiff's shoulders. "You've got crisps in your hair. I'm sorry... I didn't notice." Shaking Georgie off his other arm, Joe proceeded to pick the small fragments of crisps from the top of Tiff's head.

Georgie chuckled. "Oh, I'm sorry... you did look funny when you came over here. I couldn't... I couldn't tell you, I wanted to laugh so much."

The other men smiled or diverted their gaze elsewhere.

Brushing Joe's hand away, Tiff snorted, "Leave it, I'll do it myself." She stepped back and scuttled away from the circle, heading straight indoors to the downstairs toilet.

Once safe in the confines of the small, nicely decorated room, Tiff looked into the round mirror hanging above the washbasin. There were still bits of crisps speckled on top of her hair. She flicked her head upside down and teased the fragments out. Then she scooped the bits from the floor and dropped them down the toilet. Her eyes burned. She could not cry. Not here. And if she spent too much time in the toilet, Georgie would be sucking-up to her boyfriend. She had to get back.

As she reached the dining room, Hayley walked in from the garden with two tumblers in her hands. "You OK?" she asked, genuinely. "Lilly got you with the crisps, didn't she?"

Tiff nodded her head and pulled a sad face. "Yes, I didn't realise I had them in my hair."

"She's a little devil you know. Sits there for hours, squeezing the bag, trying to crunch the crisps up, before she makes the bag explode." Hayley smiled warmly and held a tumbler up. "Want another one?"

"Err... I've got one still. I left it out there, next to Lilly, I think."

"OK," Hayley replied, brightly. "Come and sit with me and Karen. We can get drunk and have a giggle. Lilly's quite happy sitting on her own in the corner, now she has her crisps."

"Are you sure?"

"Yes, absolutely. She will be perfectly fine on her own. She loves to sit and watch other people, you know. And I'm sure she is planning her next crisp-victim when she does sit there all quiet and observant."

"OK, thanks. I'll get my drink and come over."

Returning outside, along with Hayley and two refilled tumblers, Tiff went over to Lilly's table and picked up her drink. "I'm going to have a chat with Hayley and Karen. Will you be alright sitting here on your own?"

"Oh, don't mind me dearie." Lilly beckoned with her hand. "Here, my dear. Just a moment."

"Yes?" Tiff leant over to listen.

"Your husband," she whispered, with a slight whistle in her voice. "Look after him. He looks like a very nice man."

Tiff nodded her head and grinned. "He is."

"Watch out dearie. Others might think that too." Ushering Tiff away with her delicate hand, Lilly attempted a wink but both of her crinkly eyes closed tightly at the same time. "Sorry that I crisped you. Make sure you enjoy the evening."

"Thank you, I will try to."

Chapter 11

Tiff wasn't sure if she had enjoyed the evening or not. As she stumbled home with Joe at 1.25am, her fuzzy head and blurred vision marred any real issues that may have arisen during the evening.

Joe was just as drunk as she was. Hayley and Wayne's generous hospitality and their cocktail-making skills had wrecked them both. As Joe pulled Tiff along the pathway to their house, the silence around the close was comforting. It was bedtime and she would very soon be in hers. Snuggled under the warm quilt. Sleep, and not having to think too much, were a welcoming combination.

A murky, grey sky greeted Tiff as she slowly opened her eyes and looked across at the window. Alone in the bed, she contemplated dragging herself up while her skull squeezed at her brain and her eyes squinted from the pain. Turning slowly, she peeped at the alarm clock resting on top of the cardboard box. Blinking away blurry spots, she focused on the red numerals, glowing so brightly that they burned into her eyes. Twelve fourteen – quarter past twelve – afternoon. Had she really slept that long? Lying still for a moment, she listened to the sound of the wind whistling through the unkempt windows. She assumed that Joe was downstairs already and probably feeling much the same as she did. She pictured him sitting at the dining table, chin propped up with his hand and a strong cup of steaming hot coffee in his other hand. Coffee. That was what she needed. Yet, just the thought of moving was painful.

A gentle nudge of her shoulder alerted her. Tiff opened her eyes to see raindrops leisurely trickling down the glass of the bedroom window.

"I've made you a coffee," a voice spoke gently from behind her. "Are you getting up?"

Turning over, Tiff looked up to see Joe crouching by the side of the bed.

"It's nearly two o'clock – lazy bones."

Rubbing her forehead, she opened her eyes wider. "Really?"

"Yes, really. Come on, or it'll soon be time to go back to bed."

Smiling through the pain of her pounding head, Tiff pulled herself up to a sitting position.

"Here," said Joe, passing a mug of coffee over. "I'll do you some toast – that'll make you feel better." As he went to leave the room, he turned. "Do you want it up here or are you coming down?"

"I'll be down in a minute."

Sipping the sweet coffee, Tiff watched the raindrops hit the window. Dark grey clouds sped past as the wind continued to find tiny gaps in the window's seals to whistle through. It was a miserable day. Or what was left of it. Annoyed with herself for wasting over half a day in bed, she sighed. And then she began to think about the previous evening. Laughter. Hayley – and how well she had got on with her. Draining the punch bowl down until just a few pieces of soggy cucumber were left in the bottom. Cocktails. Wayne's expertise in making a whole caboodle of colourful concoctions. Lilly's humorous departure because she needed to go home for 'a little poo' as she discreetly put it. Lilly had never pooed in public or at anyone else's house for that matter and she never would, as long as she had the mind and legs to carry her home. Alfie and Kelly's drunken exit, which must have been before midnight. Karen and John's farewell. Surprisingly, after several little waltzes under the gazebo and an endearing peck on the cheek from time to time, Tom and Jean had also left the party with a wobble and a giggle. Hand in hand they had tottered out of the garden, graciously thanking everyone for a wonderful evening. Then there was Georgie. Georgie Ford. Georgie the sly, flirtatious bitch. And Joe. The man who was dutifully buttering some hot toast downstairs. *Her* man.

"How do you feel?"

Tiff tied the belt of her dressing gown tighter and padded through the dining room and sat down on a chair. In front of her, two slices of toast lay on a plate. "Terrible."

"Want some painkillers?"

"Please. What the hell were we drinking by the end of the night?"

"Everything, I think. I have no doubt that we had tried every single type of cocktail that was going by the end of the night." Joe placed a big hand on Tiff's back and rubbed her gently. "I've been up a few hours – only just starting to feel better now."

Shrugging his hand away, Tiff smiled stiffly. "Please don't rub my back, my brain is shaking around inside as it is."

Joe snatched his hand away, looking like a scorned child. "Sorry babe, I'll get you some tablets." Hurriedly, he went over to the kitchen junk-drawer and scrabbled around for a box of painkillers. "Have you seen the fence?" he asked upon his return, as he popped two tablets from the foil sleeve.

"The fence?" Tiff frowned as she took a tiny bite from her toast.

"In the garden. It looks like someone has kicked it in, if you ask me."

Turning her head around to the patio doors, Tiff peered out through the sheet of rain lashing down from above. One fence panel at the end of the garden had been demolished at the bottom. Strangely enough the top of the panel was still intact and wedged between the posts. A gaping hole, about a metre square, was missing. Debris lay on the grass suggesting that the fence had been damaged from the other side, as it had caved into the garden. "How did that happen?"

"I don't know. Saw it when I got up this morning."

"Great, now we'll have to get it fixed quickly. Could get foxes and things coming in."

"I'm sure they could jump the fence anyway, but that's beside the point. I'll get a new panel for next weekend. I'm not doing anything out there in this weather."

"No, of course not." Picking up the two painkillers from the table, Tiff took a gulp of coffee, pushed them in her mouth and swallowed them awkwardly. "So, did you enjoy it?"

"The party?"

"Yes."

"Sure I did. Didn't you?"

"Yes, it was OK." Tiff finished her coffee and began to eat the toast with more vigour. She had to start making herself feel better. Currently, she felt utter crap and thick-headed and there were a few things she wanted to get off her alcohol addled mind so she needed to be clear-headed first.

"Wayne's a good man – I really like him."

"Thought you did. You were by his side most of the evening."

"We had so much in common, yet completely different interests." Joe paused, thoughtfully. "He asked me to play a round of golf with him, next Friday."

"You'll be at work," Tiff reminded him.

"Well... I was thinking of asking Lee to swap a shift. Would you be happy for me to work on the Saturday?"

"Sure – do what you want to do." Tiff rubbed at her tight forehead. "You've never played golf before though."

"Always a first time."

Joe's cheery voice annoyed Tiff slightly. There she was feeling completely hungover and miffed by the antics of the bionic-boob woman last night. There she was irked by Joe's apparent lack of sensitivity and reflective consideration and there he was – happy as a lark and carefree, like an amnesic blossoming golf pro.

"Why Friday? What does Wayne do for a living? I've forgotten... or maybe he never told me."

"Buys houses. He does them up and sells them on."

"Oh yes, I remember now. Didn't really talk to him much last night."

"Too busy laughing your head off with Hayley."

Tiff smiled as she thought of the ridiculous conversations they were having about all sorts of funny things. "Yes, I like her. We got on really well." Finishing her coffee, Tiff added, "She was telling us about some of the things she sees and has to deal with in her job."

"Ah yes – a nurse."

"Hmm," mumbled Tiff, before finishing off the first slice of toast.

"Another one?" Joe had picked up Tiff's mug and pulled himself out of his chair.

Nodding her head, she looked up and smiled. "Thanks." As Joe walked over to the kitchen, Tiff felt a little pang of guilt. Perhaps she was being too harsh thinking the worst of him. Maybe he really was oblivious to Georgie's persistent pestering and coquettish conduct. But then, Tiff supposed it *was* conceivable that she'd imagined it all and was simply fixated by Georgie and her demonstrative ways. Even so, it still bothered her. Perhaps she shouldn't mention it though.

"Georgie was all over you last night." Too late, she'd blurted it out.

Joe turned and shook his head worriedly. "That was embarrassing. She wouldn't leave me alone."

"The more you talked to her, the worse she got."

"I know. Look, if you're worried that I have any sort of attraction to her, you'd be completely wrong." Joe looked uncomfortable.

"No... I don't," Tiff lied. "But don't you think you might have made her worse?"

"I felt uncomfortable babe. I didn't know what to do. I knew you wouldn't like it. I was talking to her about us – you and me – in the hope that she would get the message, loud and clear."

"Bloody cheek. Trying it on with you, right in front of me."

"I don't think she was really trying it on babe. I think she's just a bit over-friendly."

Tiff sighed. "Oh dear, you don't see it do you. She fancies you and she had the nerve to flirt with you, right in front of me."

"Well, you might have seen it differently from your angle. I showed no interest in her little remarks or sexual innuendos."

"There you are," scoffed Tiff. "You've just said it. She *was* flirting with you. Sexual innuendos? It wasn't my imagination then."

"Oh – I don't know," he huffed. "The point is – I am not interested in her and I made it abundantly clear. I know I did."

"Let's hope so."

Joe poured the boiling water into two prepared mugs. Stirring the coffee mindlessly, his expression was one of frustration. Peering up he turned to look at Tiff. "Look – I don't want to get into any arguments about that woman next door."

"Neither do I. It's just that..." Tiff thought hard for a moment. There was so much that she knew about the woman already, yet she couldn't bring herself to reveal anything. It was awkward and she wouldn't have known where to start. After all, Joe already thought that she had an obsession with her craft room and the view. If only he knew. "Well... it's just that I really don't think she likes me at all. I get the feeling that she is trying to upset me somehow."

"Why do you say that?" Joe carried the two mugs over to the table and sat down, an inquisitive expression replacing the look of frustration.

"She hardly said two words to me all night. And when she did she grunted at me, rather than talk to me. And why did she have to make such a show of hanging on to your arm every five minutes? She deliberately tried to embarrass me about the crisps in my hair as well."

"She was drunk – really drunk," Joe replied, awkwardly.

"Sounds like you're trying to defend her."

"Don't be silly. She was pissed by the end of the evening – you must have seen the way she staggered out of the house."

"Oh yes. Kissing everyone goodbye on the way."

Joe sighed heavily. "Well then, there you are. She could hardly stand upright – probably why she kept hanging on to me."

"Didn't need to kiss you though." Tiff knew that she now sounded like a jealous partner but she couldn't help it. She had to vent her feelings. Clear the air.

"Tiff," Joe stared pleadingly, into her eyes. "She kissed everyone – she was hardly going to leave me out, was she?"

"Didn't kiss me – in fact, she deliberately bypassed me and went straight to Hayley."

"Well, I don't know about any of that and... and I can't believe we're getting into an argument about her this morning."

"We're not arguing. I'm just stating a few facts but you're trying to turn a blind eye to it all. And it's not morning – it's the middle of the afternoon."

Joe tutted. "Afternoon then. And what am I turning a blind eye to?" The tone in his voice had risen.

"Georgie's infatuation with you."

"Good luck to her – I couldn't really give a shit what she thinks. On the other hand, I do give a damn about what you think. It's all becoming a bit tiresome though babe." He stood up, grabbed his coffee and marched through to the living room. Flicking the TV on, he sat down and stared at it, expressionless.

Tiff hated herself. Why had she made such a fuss? Now she'd caused an atmosphere between them. She knew that he only had eyes for her. Once again, her lack of confidence and self-worth had reigned over their relationship. If she carried on like this she would be guaranteed to lose the love of her life, one day. Following him through to the living room, she sat next to him and rubbed her hand up and down his back. "I'm sorry. I felt a bit left out, that's all. I know you wouldn't encourage her. I do love you."

"Love you too," said Joe, turning to kiss her softly on the lips. "More than you know. You have no idea."

Chapter 12

The week was whizzing by. Joe had managed to convince Lee to swap a shift so that he could play golf on Friday – weather permitting. It hadn't been a good week for weather at all. Constant downpours, dreary grey days and a chill in the air had turned the early part of May into, what felt like, the return of winter. One thing was for sure though – at least Tiff didn't have to obsess over the *view* from her craft room.

Morning sweetie, hope you have a nice day at work. I was wondering if you fancied having a girlie shopping day with me on Saturday – I've got the whole day off! What do you think? While the cats are away (working, hee hee) the mice can play (ha ha). Hays xx

Tiff had never had many friends and certainly not a close friend, since leaving school. The other women at the studio, where she worked, were just colleagues and any school friends she'd had in the past, had drifted away, as they usually do. She had always struggled to bond with people and make lasting friendships. It wasn't that she was aloof or ignorant – far from it – it was more a case of keeping herself to herself, politely declining invitations and smiling her way out of most things. Yet since exchanging mobile numbers with Hayley, last Saturday evening, she was beginning to feel different about friendships. She was starting to welcome Hayley's efforts to kindle a relationship. She believed in this incipient companionship. Hayley had texted several times over the week. Firstly, asking Tiff if she had a hangover like *she* did. Then she had texted about the miserable weather and how lucky they'd been to have their first barbecue of the year, last week, when it felt like summer had arrived and yesterday, she had texted about Alvin Snodgrass. She had remarked on his jogging attire *(OMG! Have you seen Alvin when he goes out running?)* and how he went out, whatever the weather, wearing the same skimpy pants and vests. The only difference being that he had his binoculars draped round his neck, in a *Sainsbury's* plastic carrier bag when it was raining.

I would really like that. Thank you for asking me. See you Saturday, Tiff. Tiff paused before sending the text. Then she added two kisses, just like Hayley had done. *xx*

So that would be the weekend gone. The broken fence would have to wait until the following weekend. On Sunday, Joe's parents were coming to see the house. Tiff felt a little nervous about them coming. She couldn't help but be shy when she saw them. She never knew what to say, what to do, how to talk to them or whether she was being polite enough. She'd met Joe's parents on several occasions, the last time being the funeral. Joe's grandad had sadly passed away over the last Christmas period and Tiff and Joe had gone to stay at his parent's house overnight. It had been as stressful a time for Tiff as it had been for Joe. Tiff had to meet his grandma, aunt, cousin and his not so nice wife, his younger sister (who had seemed a little self-conscious and preoccupied about her teeth) and two older brothers, one of whom had flown home from Germany. Tiff had tried to keep a low profile during the whole affair, opting to be the taxi-service, gate-keeper (ensuring Joe's grandma's house was locked when everyone left for the funeral) and tea-maker during the wake. Yet, no matter how daunting the whole episode had been for Tiff, she had liked Joe's family and particularly his sister, Emma. Emma seemed to be somewhat similar to herself, in that she was self-effacing, lacking in confidence and a little shy.

In contrast to Joe, Tiff was an only child. Her parents were very old fashioned and she had had a strict, but harmonious upbringing. Her father was a mathematician at a top university and looked like one too. His tufty moustache, unruly beard and straggly, mid-length, greying hair coupled with an array of tank tops and checked shirts ensured that he upheld his *Albert Einstein* image. Tiff's mum, in comparison, was more conventional. As a one-hour-a-day dinner lady, in her local junior school, her career was starkly dissimilar to her husbands. Both Tiff's mum and dad were surprisingly introverted people, considering their jobs were so vastly public orientated. Keeping themselves to themselves, just as Tiff had always done, they spent all of their free time nurturing and tending to their expansive, well-loved, immaculately landscaped garden. Tiff loved her parents dearly and valued time spent with them, each time she returned for a visit – even if she did have to get her old muddy wellies on and join them in the garden.

Friday's were Tiff's favourite day of the week. The weekend was imminent and the upbeat atmosphere at the studio was always fun to be a part of. Friday's always went quicker than any other day.

Looking out of the bedroom window, Tiff marvelled at the early morning sun lighting up Sycamore Close in a vibrant orange glow. Having dressed in a pair of blue skinny jeans and a lilac viola print blouse, she pulled her denim plimsolls on and then trotted down the stairs. "Looks like you'll have the perfect day for golf," she said as she entered the dining room.

Joe was sitting at the table, dressed in black chinos, a collared pink t-shirt and an old pair of black trainers. "Luckily, yes. Tiff..." he hesitated, "do you think I look all right for golf, wearing these?" He lifted a foot out from underneath the table.

Nodding her head, she grinned. "They look OK. You can't be expected to have all the correct gear for golf when you've never played before. Wayne said you could wear trainers didn't he?"

"Yeah, but I should have at least got some new ones."

"They're fine. If you really like it, you could always buy some proper golf shoes later."

"Sure, yes, OK – I'm going to get off now, we start at eight." Joe stood up and straightened his trousers. "And if I really like it, you could get me my own set of golf clubs for Christmas." Joe grinned, cheesily. "They'll only cost you about three hundred."

"Three hundred pounds? You might get them for the next three Christmases then." Kissing him on the lips, Tiff continued. "Have a lovely day and I hope that you really enjoy it. Think of me sitting in the studio, peering out of the windows at the glorious sunshine."

"I will. Have a good day yourself. Love you quite a bloody lot Miss Cuthbert – bye."

Pulling into the lay-by, Tiff peered across the green as she pulled the handbrake up and turned the engine off. She didn't know if Joe was home yet as he'd gone off in Wayne's car early this morning. She thought he might be, as the time was fast approaching four thirty. After all, how long did it take to play 18 holes of golf? Actually, she had no idea.

As she strolled around the green she admired their white picket fencing from afar. It was the start to the overall new appearance of the front of their house. Once they had new windows installed and a coat of paint applied to the brick frontage, it would look delightful. Tiff had wanted yellow for the front, as it was her favourite colour but Joe's horrified expression had put a halt to that idea. OK, maybe she would be happy with white to match the fence.

Pushing her key into the front door, she stepped into the house and paused. Holding her breath, she listened. The sound of a woman's voice, giggling, had stopped her in her tracks. It was a strangely familiar noise. She'd heard it before and the vexatious laughter that was growing in intensity held Tiff rooted to the spot in fear. Her heartbeat quickened. Her cheeks flushed and a sickly saliva filled her mouth. Freeing her anchored legs, she walked hesitantly, through the lounge towards the dining room. A babble of words. More laughter. This time it was a duo of mirth. The bass tones of Joe's laughter. The nauseous high pitch of Georgie's.

Entering the room, Tiff froze as her eyes darted across to the kitchen where Joe and Georgie stood. Each one leaning against a kitchen unit facing each other. Tiff couldn't stop the incensed curl of her top lip rising, as she glared at Georgie with a deep antipathy. Wearing frayed denim shorts, which exposed the lower half of her bottom cheeks, a baggy vest-style see-through top over an underwired, bright yellow bikini top and purple trainers, Georgie stared back, wide-eyed. The laughter had stopped.

Opposite Georgie, stood Joe. Practically naked. With a bath towel wrapped round his waist, his wet, spiky hair and gorgeous, muscular frame made him look appealing and Georgie looked delighted to be his audience. Tiff was only thankful that Georgie was not wet too.

"Babe... H... Hi... We... err... I..." Joe stuttered, as a look of fear and regret washed over his face. "The... err... the dog... the fence."

Dropping her mouth open to speak, Tiff tried to say 'what' but nothing would come out. Her voice had left her. Her legs had solidified on the spot again. Her arms hung down by her sides, unable to move, not knowing what to do. Should she fold her arms? Should she wave them around in the air and scream? Should she just gather her whole body together, turn around and run? Or should she lunge at Georgie and claw her beautiful mascaraed eyes out?

"Babe, look... sorry. I know this must... err... well, it probably looks a bit... err." It was clear that Joe was desperately fighting to find the right words.

"Looks?" Tiff managed to drag the word from her throat.

"Anyway," interrupted Georgie, brightly. "I'd better go –"

"Yes. Time for you to go." The words were beginning to flow from Tiff's mouth more freely now.

"I... I need to get my dog," said Georgie, pointing to the patio doors. "Can I?"

Joe remained glued to the kitchen unit. Staring down at his bare toes, he wiggled the ones on his right foot.

"Get it." Flicking her glare from Joe to Georgie and then back again, Tiff walked over to the door and opened it. The big, black brute bounded towards the door and stopped. Tiff's heart beat rapidly. The dog looked much bigger than she had remembered. "What's it doing in here anyway?"

"Buster... come here, naughty boy." Georgie leant over and grabbed the dog by its collar. Her pert bottom cheeks were exposed more as she pulled the dog towards her, clipped the lead on to its studded collar and pointed a finger in its face. "You are a naughty boy." Pulling herself upright, she adjusted the cups of her bikini top with her free hand and then pulled the dog into the house. "Sorry about that. I'm sure Joe will explain. Thanks again – I'll be off now. Nice talking to you Joe. Sorry and goodbye Tiffany."

Following Georgie and her dog to the front door, Tiff grabbed hold of the door handle as they passed through. "And it's, Tiff – not Tiffany."

Georgie shot back a scornful look as she went outside. She turned and sneered before walking off down the pathway, her partly exposed buttocks tightening and stretching as she went.

Tiff slammed the door shut and leaned against the hall wall. Tears filled her eyes. Her heart hurt. She had to go back through to the kitchen. She couldn't cry. Not yet.

"Tiff." Joe had appeared at the living room door. "Babe – that must have looked really bad." Edging closer, he raised his arms to cuddle her. "Come here."

"No," said Tiff and brushed past him. "You can talk to me in the kitchen – I need a coffee."

"Let me make it for you." Joe followed her back into the kitchen.

"Get dressed Joe. You must be feeling a bit cold in that damp towel." Tiff scoffed, as she flicked the kettle on.

"OK – I'll be back in a minute babe. I need to talk to you about this."

"Do you?"

By the time Tiff had made a coffee, just for herself, which she knew was a bit childish, Joe arrived in the dining room, fully dressed. Sitting down next to her, he awkwardly fumbled with the buttons of his shirt. "Babe... I know you're pissed off... but I can explain exactly what happened."

Looking up, Tiff eyed him incredulously. "Don't tell me – she dropped by whilst out walking her dog, wearing half a bikini and barely a pair of shorts and you invited her in for a coffee and a friendly chat."

"No, it wasn't like that at all. Will you just hear me out babe?"

Tiff raised a sneering smile at him. "Or were you having a competition to see who could look the most naked – without being naked?"

"Tiffany." Joe peered at her, despairingly. "Please – listen."

"It's Tiff – not Tiffany. You can tell me later. I'm not interested now – I'm too tired. I need a lie-down." She stood up, grabbed her coffee from the table, walked out of the room and headed for their bedroom. She really did need a lie-down. To cry. She needed a chance to think things through. Find a way that the situation she'd encountered would be perfectly plausible.

Waking from what felt like only a brief moment of sleep, Tiff opened her eyes. Peering at the clock she guessed she'd only been asleep for about half an hour at the most. She'd laid on the bed earlier, trying to make excuses for the situation between Joe and Georgie. Then she'd embellished her hopeless ideas, turning them into seedy little clandestine meetings or even a sordid act of wanton fornication, having been spurred on by frustration and their sexual attraction to each other. But her creativity had then worsened with thoughts that they were simply having a full-on affair behind her back.

Joe hadn't been to the bedroom once. She had been there for over an hour now. Why hadn't he come up to see what she was doing or how she was?

Guilt.

Obviously.

Dragging herself off the bed, she left the bedroom and tentatively went down the stairs. A clattering of pots and pans and the homely smell of cooking wafted out of the kitchen.

"I've made your favourite," said Joe, smiling apprehensively. "Spaghetti Bolognese – I was going to wake you in a minute." Stirring the meat sauce, he seemed edgy as he moved the wooden spoon around the pan. "There's wine in the fridge. Thought we could have a couple of drinks tonight."

Tiff sat down at the table without saying a word. She had mocked any attempts that Joe had made earlier to rectify the situation. She had to give him a chance to speak now, to explain, or to wheedle his way out of it.

"Wine?" asked Joe, taking two glasses from a cupboard.

Tiff nodded her head and watched as he took a bottle of fruity white wine from the fridge and poured two large glasses. Taking a large gulp from his glass, he carried the other one over and passed it to her. Bending over, he kissed her delicately on the forehead. "I'm sorry I've upset you, babe. I can explain everything. I know how it must have looked."

"OK," whispered Tiff and took a long sip of her drink.

"Let me get this dished up and then I'll tell you."

Tiff was hungrier than she'd realised. With her favourite meal set down in front of her, alongside her preferred choice of wine, she couldn't resist.

The atmosphere was tense as Joe joined her at the table. He gulped half of his glass of wine down, then picked up his knife and fork. "Do you want me to tell you now or shall we eat this first?"

"Eat this first," Tiff echoed, before swilling her whole glass of wine down.

Joe looked at her astonished. "Thirsty?"

"A bit," she replied.

"I'll bring the bottle over." Jumping up, he hurried over to the fridge and grabbed the bottle. Then he returned and refilled Tiff's glass straight away.

"Thanks." Almost instantly, the wine went to her head. She'd eaten hardly anything all day and she realised that the sooner she ate her dinner, the quicker it would lessen the effects of the wine. But the slightly numbing, tingly sensations in her head felt good. It was where she wanted to be right now.

Placing his knife and fork on his empty plate, Joe picked up his wine and drained the glass. He poured another glass and set the bottle back in the centre of the table. "Right," he said with strength in his voice. "Let me tell you what happened."

Tiff looked fixedly at him.

"I'd only just got out of the shower when she knocked on the door." He paused thoughtfully. "I ran downstairs in a towel, thinking it was Wayne at the door. He'd said he would give me his mobile number but we'd forgotten to exchange them."

Tiff nodded her head, while propping up her chin.

Joe glanced nervously at her and then continued. "So, anyway. It was Georgie, not Wayne – obviously. She was in a bit of a flap. Her dog had gone under our broken fence and wouldn't get out of our garden."

"You're telling me that she was walking her dog around the back fields wearing just a bikini top?"

"And shorts... and that top she had on."

"Well, yes – of course. Could hardly have called them shorts though. More like a wide G-string. And there was absolutely no point in wearing that top."

"Whatever. I don't know what you women wear," he replied, defensively. "And I don't care. Anyway, she asked if she could get her dog from the garden – Tiff I knew you would be home from work soon so I said that I would get it."

"So why didn't you?" Tiff jumped in.

"She said that she would have to get him as he might attack me. What was I supposed to do? I told her to come on through." Joe heaved a sigh. "I even apologised to her about having just got out of the shower."

"Oh, I bet she loved it."

"I don't know or care about that."

"She'd hardly complain about getting a little eye-candy, would she?" Tiff's top lip curled disdainfully for the second time today.

"Like I said, I don't know babe – and I don't care."

"When I arrived home, it didn't look to me like she was trying to get her dog out of the garden." Tiff took another gulp of wine. "How long had she been here?"

Joe raised his eyes to the ceiling as if he was calculating the length of time.

"Why do you need to think about it? How long was she here? It's a simple question."

"It must have only been about... twenty minutes?"

"Twenty flaming minutes?" Tiff shrieked. "Twenty long minutes? What were you doing for twenty minutes Joe?"

"Talking."

"Talking while you're semi-naked and undoubtedly dripping wet?"

Joe nodded his head hesitantly. "Yes, I'm sorry babe. I know how it looks."

"Well I'm relieved that you know how it looks. I'm sure you have no idea how it feels though."

"Yes, I do."

"What the hell were you talking about for twenty minutes?"

Shifting in his seat uncomfortably, Joe combed a hand through his hair. "I don't know really – she was doing most of the talking."

"About what?"

"You know, it was so trivial, I can't even remember." He averted his eyes and gazed down at the floor.

"It wasn't that long ago Joe – you must remember what she was talking about." Tiff could feel the anger rising up through her body again. "Sounded like you were both having a right good laugh when I walked in." Grabbing her glass from the table, she gulped the wine down quickly, hoping to ease some of the tension in her neck and shoulders. "So what was so bloody funny then?"

Joe flicked his eyes up to the ceiling and rubbed three fingers across his lips as if in deep thought. "I think... err... I think it was about... err... oh yes, I know. She was telling me how she'd gone for a sunbathe over the back, by the river and err... I think she said she'd left her proper t-shirt there... or something like that. She was worried that I'd think she was a weird one, walking around in a see-through vest and a bikini top."

"And you said – of course not, I think it's lovely."

"No, I didn't. I felt a bit embarrassed actually. Laughed it off I guess."

Somehow, Tiff sensed that her beloved boyfriend wasn't telling her the complete truth. His averted gaze, his lack of composure and the awkwardness in his speech were all tell-tale signs that he was finding the situation unusually difficult or he was hiding something.

"I know what you're thinking babe and you couldn't be further from the truth. I do not fancy the women one little bit. Please believe me. I love you and only you."

"Sure you do," Tiff replied sarcastically. "Not sure I'm getting the t-shirt thing though Joe. Why would she have two t-shirts with her? Think about it."

Joe shrugged his wide shoulders and peered down at the floor. "Don't know babe. I don't get it either." He lifted his head and met her eye. "But I really don't give a damn about her or her t-shirts. Can we drop this? I've told you the truth, I love you and that's all that counts."

Chapter 13

Today was shopping day. Today would also be snoop day. Tiff had to find out more about the woman next door – she couldn't even bring herself to mention the woman's name without a bitterness welling up in her mouth, waiting to be spat out.

Having finished two bottles of wine by the end of the previous evening, Joe and Tiff had gone to bed together. They'd come to a bittersweet ending on the escapades of the 'woman next door' as Tiff had started to refer to her. And Tiff had still managed to keep quiet about the things she knew of the woman, even though she wanted to scream about it and tell Joe everything at times.

Their lovemaking had been emotionally charged, uninhibited and frantic. Tiff had wanted to resist his drunken charms but her own inebriated state let him in. Although she was still angry with him, with *her* – that woman, it was the best sex they'd ever had.

Shuffling around the bedroom with a pounding head, Tiff gathered up fresh underwear, a pair of clean jeans and a pretty floral top. Most of her tops had floral patterns on them, she hated plain fabrics. Carrying her clothes to the bathroom, she went in and locked the door behind her. The bath was almost full with warm bubbly water and the moist air was filled with the calming scent of lavender. Time to relax and unwind from the anger that she felt was still buried deep inside her. Time to let go. She had to, otherwise Joe would get fed-up with her insecure ways. She might even lose him and that was inconceivable.

"Morning." Hayley stood at the front door looking radiant in a black and yellow checked, cotton coat, skinny black jeans and knee-high, flat, black boots. "Are you ready?"

"Yes, definitely. Been looking forward to it. I haven't been into town for ages." Grabbing her handbag from the bottom stair, Tiff stepped out of the door and locked it behind her. An image of Joe flashed through her mind, sitting behind the reception desk at the leisure centre, looking bored and nursing a hangover. "I'd like to get some nice table mats today. We've got Joe's parents coming for the day tomorrow, from Portsmouth. We've been using bits of cardboard as table mats but I'm sure we could go all-out for our guests."

Hayley giggled. "It's hard when you're just starting out. I can remember when we first moved into our house. We had cardboard boxes as tables."

"Really?" Tiff laughed. "So have we. Bedside tables to be precise."

"There you go. It happens to us all. Come on – lets hit the town. I'm sure we'll find some amazing table mats for you." Placing an arm over Tiff's shoulder, Hayley ushered her down to the lay-by where her shiny deep-red supermini was parked.

"I wondered who this belonged to. It's gorgeous."

Hayley grinned. "It's my little burgundy-baby. Jump in."

"Ever had any strange little notes placed under your wipers?"

"Sorry?" Hayley frowned as she started the car.

"I had a note pushed under my wipers a while back."

"What did it say?"

Tiff peered across the green. "It was from someone on the close – don't know who. Said I should keep myself to myself – not get involved in anything."

"Really?" Hayley peered at her incredulously. "Wonder who would have done that?"

Tiff shrugged her shoulders. "No idea." She let out a giggle. "Take it, it wasn't you then."

"Definitely not." Hayley began to pull out of the lay-by. "Probably that weirdo next door to me."

"Hmm... I did wonder if it might be him. I'll ask him next time I see him."

"You do that." Hayley nodded her head as she drove along Oakwood Road. "Bloody cheek, whoever it was."

The town was heaving with shoppers of every size, shape, religion and age. Once again, the weather was glorious and half way through the morning, both Tiff and Hayley had had to remove their coats. Darting in, out and around every shop along the precinct was hot work. Hayley had bought several clothing items from various places and dragged Tiff to all the upstairs household floors to look for a nice set of table mats but to no avail.

"We'll find the right ones. We'll keep looking – but first, let me buy you lunch."

"No, I can't let you do that," said Tiff, surprised by Hayley's generosity.

"Yes you can. Come on, let's go in here." Grabbing hold of Tiff's arm, Hayley pulled her into a quaint, little tearoom-style café.

"This looks really nice. Haven't been to one of these afternoon-tea places before," whispered Tiff.

"I love it here. Me and Georgie came here once, a couple of years ago. She wasn't quite so keen, bless her, more like she hated it – said it reminded her of her tormented childhood, but I love it here." Hayley's tone of voice had a hint of sarcasm in it.

"Sounds ominous – tormented childhood?"

A young girl with two perfect French plaits through her brown hair ushered Hayley and Tiff to a small table-for-two, next to the window.

"Thank you," said Hayley, politely, as she pulled a chair out and sat down.

The girl smiled sweetly, placed a dainty, stainless-steel table-number card holder on the table, along with a fresh posy of cut daffodils and brilliant red tulips and then walked away.

"Ooh, tulips – my favourites," said Tiff, stroking the vibrant petals.

"Nice aren't they. Prefer the daffs myself. I do like yellow."

"So do I," Tiff exclaimed. "That's my favourite colour."

"One of mine too," Hayley raised her eyebrows and grinned. "We're starting to sound like twins."

"As long as we don't turn into terrible twins." Tiff giggled and gazed at the vase of flowers, contentedly. Hayley was her new friend and she liked it.

Hayley picked up two menus and passed one over to Tiff. "Here – if you fancy it, we could go for a deluxe afternoon tea. I highly recommend it."

"Thanks," Tiff replied as she began to scan through the menu. "Yes, that sounds lovely." She peered over the top of her menu card. "Could I pay half?"

"No, absolutely not – my treat." Hayley looked up and grinned. "There is a method to my madness however."

"Sorry?"

"Why I'm offering to pay."

"Oh," Tiff replied, a little unsure of what to say.

"It's so that you will owe *me* an afternoon tea and then we'll have to come out and do it again sometime."

"Aah, I see," said Tiff. "Yes of course, I'd love to. The food looks really nice – from what I can see over there." She flicked her gaze across the room to two older women who were tucking into generous sized fresh cream and jam scones. "So..." she clasped her hands together and propped them under her chin, "you were saying... about Georgie. A terrible... or was it tormented childhood."

"Oh yes, she's had a tough time, that girl. Poor thing."

"Oh dear – really?"

Hayley was nodding her head as the young girl returned with a notebook in her hand. "Are you ready to order?" she asked with a wide smile.

Hayley looked across at Tiff. "Yes please. We'd like two deluxe teas. Tiff, which sandwich and cake would you like?"

As Hayley reeled off her choice of sandwich and cake, Tiff looked through the menu again.

"Oh, I'd like a tuna-mayo and cucumber sandwich please, and... lemon drizzle cake."

The young girl scribbled quickly on her notepad. "Would you like ready salted or cheese and onion crisps?"

Tiff glanced down at the menu again. "Oh gosh, we get crisps as well – I'll have ready salted then please."

"Ready salted for me too," echoed Hayley. "Thanks."

"It's very kind of you to treat me like this. I really appreciate it. Thank you so much."

"Don't mention it. Like I said – you'll have to owe me one."

Tiff nodded her head and smiled. "So, I know I keep going back to Georgie but I'm just interested. She is my neighbour after all. You said she err... had a tough time... when she was a kid."

"Yes – so she told me anyway."

"You don't believe her?"

"It's not that I don't believe her." Hayley let out a sigh. "I do. It's just that she tends to wallow in her own misery at times."

"Oh, I see."

"She was physically and mentally abused by her father from the age of seven. She claims that her mum knew about it and allowed it to happen. Georgie has memories of her mum being there several times, as an onlooker, when she was severely beaten by her father or mentally stripped of her self-esteem and confidence"

"God, that's awful." Tiff shuffled in her seat, uncomfortably. Perhaps she had been too harsh on the poor woman.

Hayley shook her head disgustedly. "The thing that I can't get my head around is – Georgie has forgiven them both."

Tiff stared at her new friend with a shocked expression on her face. "Did anyone else know about it? Did her parents get away with it?"

"No, and yes, they did. This is where I struggle with it all a bit. For her to forgive her parents for what they did is completely beyond me. It would take me all day to tell you how bad it was. Georgie missed so much school when she was young, purely because she had to be hidden away until the cuts and bruises had vanished."

Tiff was stunned momentarily. "I… I don't know what to say."

"I know, it's terrible isn't it?"

Tiff shook her head disbelievingly. "Does she still see her parents?"

"Yes – apparently so. I've never seen them myself – don't think I want to."

"How could she forgive them?"

Hayley let out a long sigh. "I don't know but I feel so sorry for her. It's almost pathetic."

"Pathetic?" Tiff stared questioningly.

"She said that her parents were all she had when her husband and daughter left. She told me that she needed them – no matter what they'd done in the past."

"But what about her daughter? Surely she's putting her own child at risk. Her parents are nothing more than child-beating monsters – both of them – if this is true. Sorry to sound so opinionated about it but I find that kind of thing absolutely terrible."

"I know. I do too. She doesn't let her daughter see..." Hayley stopped abruptly as the young girl appeared, carrying a tray loaded with two pots of tea, two tiny milk jugs, two vintage-floral, porcelain teacups with matching saucers and a bowl of white and brown sugar lumps. "Thank you," said Hayley, leaning back as the waitress placed the items on the table.

"Ooh, this looks lovely." Tiff smiled and politely moved her elbows from the table. "Thank you so much."

A moment later, the young girl returned with two three-tiered stands, decorated in the same vintage-floral pattern as the cups, loaded with sandwiches, crisps, cakes and scones. She placed two small matching plates on the table and said, 'enjoy' before she left.

"Wow," uttered Tiff. "This looks amazing."

"It is – trust me. Just wait until you start eating it." Hayley took two quarters of her triangular-cut sandwich and placed them on her plate, followed by a handful of crinkle-cut crisps.

Tiff followed Hayley's lead and did the same with her tuna sandwich. She'd never been to such a quaint little tearoom like this before. Her mum's birthday sprang to mind – her mum would really like something like this. "My mum would love this place – she likes things like this. I'm just thinking about taking her to one of these places for her birthday."

Hayley let out a giggle. "I did that for my mum's birthday a couple of years ago. Actually, to tell you the truth, I bought a voucher for afternoon tea for two and she invited me to share it with her."

"Oh, they do vouchers do they?"

"Yes, just ask at the counter when I pay for this. You can get a voucher for any value you like and you can use it in any of their cafés around the south coast. The one I got, covered the cost of two deluxe cream teas – like we're having now."

"OK, that's great – thanks. I think I have seen one of these cafés in the town where my mum lives. She'd enjoy this. Thank you again – it's truly delicious."

"Stop thanking me and just eat." Hayley grinned before biting into her first quarter of egg and cress sandwich.

Two hours later, Tiff had found the perfect place mats, a black leather-bound set of four table mats and four matching coasters. In addition to these, she hadn't been able to resist a brilliant white tablecloth too. "Later on, when we can afford it, I would really like a black and white kitchen."

"That's the trouble when you buy your own home. There are so many things you need to buy or do that the big things, like a new kitchen, have to wait a while."

"Well, I suppose we've got all the time in the world."

"Exactly," replied Hayley. "It's taken us four years to get to where we are now. Ours was very run-down when we bought it."

"Joe says we should take one step at a time and not worry too much. He says that the house will evolve before our eyes and we should take photos as we go."

Hayley giggled. "Same as we've been doing then. We have a lot in common don't we?"

"Yes, we do."

"Would you and Joe like to come along to a quiz night at the community centre, next week? We have such a giggle there."

"That sounds like fun and I've been meaning to check it out. Betty, next door to me, was telling me about the fayres they have there."

"Oh yes, they do those quite often – helps raise money for the elderly people who run clubs there. Why? Are you thinking of selling things there or just buying?" Hayley appeared genuinely interested.

"I make a lot of greetings cards and crafty things, usually try to sell them at car boot sales, places like that," said Tiff, proudly.

"Sounds like fun. You'll have to show me sometime."

"I will." Tiff grinned widely. "Right, I'd better go and pay for these place mats – then I'm done."

"OK," said Hayley. "I'm done too. We can head off home if you like."

"Yes, that's fine by me, and Hayley?"

"Yes?"

"Can I just say thank you again for a lovely day and for the scrummy food."

"No you can't." Hayley laughed. "You can just say – when am I coming out to lunch with you?"

Nodding her head, Tiff giggled. "I will, I promise. I'll check arrangements with Joe and ask you very soon."

"Quick – hide!" Suddenly, Hayley grabbed Tiff by the arm and pulled her around the end of an aisle, while trying desperately to stifle a giggle.

"What?" whispered Tiff, as she crouched alongside Hayley, unaware of who she was hiding from.

Hayley peeped around the end of the aisle and pulled back sharply. "Quick – this way," she whispered through her tittering. "Follow me."

Edging along the aisle, Tiff followed to the end. They moved around the corner and stopped. "Who are we...?" she began to question.

"Snodgrass – look," Hayley whispered, pointing her finger towards the checkouts. "Don't want to bump into that creepy bloke – we'd never get away."

"Oh – him. What's he buying? Looks like a..."

"A bright red dog lead? What's he buying a dog lead for – he hasn't got a dog," Hayley remarked.

"And a big studded collar," muttered Tiff, amusedly.

"Really?"

"Unless he has got a dog..."

Hayley and Tiff watched as Alvin Snodgrass stood waiting in the small queue. His shifty stare around the shop and his arrogant stance made him look like a suspicious character.

"Couldn't have a dog, could he? He's away a lot. On his secret missions."

"Maybe he's bought it for Georgie's dog," said Tiff, without thinking.

"Why would he be buying a lead and collar for Georgie's dog? She hates him. Her dog probably does too."

Tiff giggled and cupped a hand across her mouth. "Oh yes, of course, I forgot she hated him." She tried to backtrack on her words. "Perhaps he's got a mission coming up that requires a dog then."

"Hmm... whatever it is, he's a bit of a weirdo."

"I agree with you. We'll have to watch *his* space – in Sycamore Close – see if a dog appears on the green."

"As long as it doesn't wear gold *speedos*, eh?" Hayley let a burst of laughter out before she too, smacked a hand over her mouth.

As Alvin waited impatiently in the queue, swinging the dog lead and collar backwards and forwards, he was completely unaware of the two women sniggering uncontrollably behind the nearest aisle.

Chapter 14

She was at the front door. In broad daylight. How could she be? Why?

Feigning ignorance, Tiff climbed out of Hayley's car and grabbed her bags. "Thank you. I've had a great day."

"Yes, me too." Hayley locked her car and joined Tiff on the pavement. "Looks like you have a visitor," she said, looking across the green.

"Oh, yes. It's... err... it's Georgie isn't it. Wonder what she wants." Tiff replied, waveringly.

"Probably being a pain. Has she asked to borrow any sugar yet?" Hayley winked an eye. "Oh, and please don't mention that I told you about her parents – I think she'd kill me."

"Absolutely not. I wouldn't dream of saying anything. I promise you." Tiff forced a grin at her new friend. Her mind was now frantically worrying about something else. "So, I'll see you next Friday night – all being well with Joe."

"OK, let me know. Text me," called Hayley as she walked down the path, towards her house.

"I will. Bye."

Joe was leaning against the front door frame and thankfully, fully dressed. "Hi babe, had a good day?" he called out.

His wide-eyed expression suggested he was worried. Worried that he'd been caught out again? "Great, yes thanks." Tiff approached the garden gate apprehensively. She had to be polite. She had to play things cool. She wanted to scream – what the hell are you doing here again? "Hello Georgie, everything OK?" Peering at Joe, Tiff opened her mouth again and couldn't stop the words coming out. "You've got some clothes on today."

Wearing a pair of tatty jeans, muddy trainers and a sloppy t-shirt, Georgie still looked gorgeous even when she looked a mess. She was one of those types of women who Tiff envied. She could be wearing a black, plastic bin liner and still look appealing.

Georgie turned and sneered. "I do wear clothes…" Glancing up at Joe, she giggled, "sometimes."

Joe's cheeks began to colour. "Err… Georgie, here… she, err… wanted to know if we wanted a fence panel. She's got a spare one in her garden."

Tiff could hear the fear in Joe's voice. She sensed he was on edge again. Nervous. Caught out. Guilty?

"Might be something to think about." Tiff couldn't help her deadpan expression and the wooden tone in her voice. "Thanks," she mumbled.

"Well, you've got my number if you do want it, give me a call – or just pop round, any time," said Georgie, directing her flirtatious gaze at Joe.

Joe smiled awkwardly and nodded his head as he scrunched the tiny piece of paper in his hand and shoved it in his trouser pocket.

"See you again soon Tiffany." Georgie turned away from Joe and smirked as she passed by Tiff and trotted out of the gate.

"It's Tiff – I prefer to be called Tiff. Remember?"

"Of course." Georgie turned her head to one side as she entered her front garden. "Sorry Tiff, I forgot you prefer Tiff, rather than Tiff-an-y. I prefer Tiffany myself." Georgie opened her front door, waved to Joe and went indoors.

Fumblingly, Joe went to raise a hand to wave goodbye but was both too hesitant and also too late. He grinned sheepishly and stepped aside to let Tiff through the front door.

"You don't need to hide her phone number in your pocket." Tiff eyed him sharply before walking through to the kitchen.

"I was not hiding it." Joe followed her into the kitchen. He pulled the piece of paper from his pocket and threw it on to the worktop. "Here, I was going to show you. I thought maybe you would prefer to have her number. There's no need to be so nasty to her."

"What do I want her number for? And I haven't been nasty to her." Tiff couldn't help the rising anger in her voice.

"You could text her if you want the fence panel. And you weren't very polite – commenting on her clothes." Joe reached for the kettle and began to fill it.

"Firstly, I'm not doing your dirty work for you – she hardly talks to me – she gave the number to you. And secondly, I merely stated the fact that she had proper clothes on today."

"What do you mean by 'dirty work'?"

"Oh for heaven's sake Joe." Tiff slumped down in a chair and rested an elbow on the dining table. "Can't you see what she's doing?"

"No I can't." Joe's face had changed from the fearful, caught-out look he had a few moments ago to one of disappointment. "So what's she doing then?"

"Well..." Tiff stumbled. "Actually... I wouldn't be surprised if she had a glass tumbler stuck on the wall outside or... or a telescope out on the fields." Tiff paused to take a breath. "To watch us arguing over her."

"I'm not arguing. You're the one getting irate about things."

"I'm not getting irate! All you seem to do is protect her – stick-up for her if I say something bad about her."

"OK," muttered Joe. "I'm going to make you a coffee, then we'll talk about this in a cool, calm way."

"Don't patronize me."

"Tiff," Joe turned around from the kettle. "I am not patronizing you. This is getting a little bit silly, don't you think?"

"Silly – silly is it? Then why does she always come round to see you when I'm not here?"

Shaking his head despairingly, Joe heaved a deep sigh. "Oh babe, she's been round here twice. She must have seen me come home. I had only just taken my jacket off at the door, when she came round."

"Obviously been looking out for you then. Why did she give you her number? She could have said, just knock on the door if you want the fence panel?" Tiff's face was burning. She knew she was being a little unreasonable. But Joe didn't know what the woman was really like – or did he and he was actually more than happy to have a romp in her garden?

"Err... I don't know," Joe replied falteringly. "She just gave it to me. I didn't ask for it." His eyes averted before he turned round to finish making the coffees.

"Joe?"

"Yes?"

"Are you telling me the truth?"

Turning around with a coffee in his hand, he snatched a glance at the piece of paper on the other worktop. "Yes, I am. Can we leave this now?"

"Why are you home early anyway?" Tiff peered up at the wall clock in the kitchen. "Thought you didn't finish till five."

Joe shrugged. "I got fed up. I had enough staff in from three o'clock so I came home."

"You *have* been to work haven't you?"

"Yes Tiff – I have been to work. Where the hell do you think I've been?"

Forcing an exaggerated shrug, Tiff turned down her mouth. "I don't know. You're the boss – you can go anywhere you like."

"Here," said Joe, fumbling in his pocket for his mobile phone. "Do you want to phone work and check?"

"Now who's getting silly?" Storming into the kitchen, Tiff took the coffee from him. "This is getting us nowhere. I'm going to have a bath and tidy up – we've got your parents over tomorrow."

"Fair enough. And I'll help you clean up. We've got to stop this babe."

As Tiff left the kitchen/diner her eyes began to sting. Two arguments in less than three days. That was not good. Especially when the heated exchanges were over a woman. The deliberately sly, surreptitious woman next door who obviously fancied Joe and would do anything to upset Tiff's relationship with him. Carrying her coffee and a carrier bag up the stairs, Tiff threw the bag on the bed, placed her coffee on the windowsill and went through to the bathroom to run a bath. The housework could wait. She needed a good long soak and a think. Maybe even another cry.

Sinking into the bubbles, she lay still as the hot water surrounded her and soothed away her pent up anger. Joe had to be telling the truth. There couldn't be anything cagey going on. He wouldn't do that to her. But that wasn't to say that Georgie wouldn't stop trying to get her long, manicured nails into him. Desperate bitch.

The sound of the hoover ripped Tiff away from her tormented muse. Obviously, Joe was trying to creep around her by doing the cleaning downstairs. 'Guilty' was becoming the word of the week. Tiff couldn't help the negative thoughts that were stomping through her mind with steel-cap military boots on. Or was 'paranoid' actually the real word of the week?

"Did you give her your number?" Tiff was standing in the doorway of the living room, dressed in her pyjamas and a pink toweling dressing gown.

Joe turned round from the television unit, a duster in one hand and a can of polish in the other. "No...I... err." He stalled for a moment. "Err... no, I didn't. Can we forget about it now?" Turning back to the television, he wiped the cloth along the top, then walked through to the dining room. "Do you want another coffee?" he called back.

"I'll make it." Tiff joined him in the kitchen. Scanning the worktops, she added, "where's that bit of paper gone?"

"Paper?"

Tiff rolled her eyes and tutted. "Yes – the one with Georgie's number on."

"I threw it in the drawer. If you want the fence panel you can contact her. I'm fed up with all the drama to be honest, babe."

"Do we want it?"

"Well she doesn't want anything for it."

Joe still sounded a bit edgy, but then Tiff wasn't really surprised after her outburst earlier. "Look, I'm sorry Joe. I didn't mean the things I said. I find it hard to like that woman when she is so stand-offish with me all the time and so obviously accommodating to you."

"I'm sure you're imagining it babe. She likes you... well, I'm sure she does."

"That sounded like you know she likes me. Like she's spoken about me."

"No, err... she hasn't. I'm sure she must like you though. Why would she want to be helpful by offering us a fence panel for nothing?"

"Because she fancies *you* – you just can't see it can you?"

"I really don't care," said Joe, moving towards Tiff. "You're the one *I'm* interested in." Sweeping his arms round her waist, he pulled her into him. "You're the one I want, even when you are being completely paranoid." Bending his head down, he kissed her softly on the lips. Then again, harder. "You must know it. I want you... I need you, babe... I love you more than you could know."

Joe kissed her repeatedly, slowing the pace as she responded. She was reluctant at first, but then she submitted and succumbed to the passionate temptation. It didn't matter that they were standing in the kitchen. The desire was too great. She allowed him to untie her dressing gown. She assisted him in removing her cropped pyjama bottoms. He pulled at his own trousers, loosening the belt and unzipping them. Lifting her up, he pushed her against the edge of the worktop. Resting her hands back on the kitchen surface, she let him in. A crescendo of intense devotion brought their frenzied intimacy to an end within minutes.

"I love you too," she whispered, as a tear welled in her eye. "I'm sorry to keep going on about things. You must hate me sometimes."

"Never."

Downstairs done. Upstairs done. Bed changed – tick. Ironing finished – tick. Washing on – tick. *Domino's* pizza, garlic bread and potato wedges ordered – tick, tick, tick.

Tiff and Joe slumped down on the sofa with hot cardboard boxes on their laps. They'd worked so hard, cleaning the house from top to bottom in preparation for Joe's parents coming for the day tomorrow. The fresh smells of the polish and other cleaning fluids were slowly diminishing as the potent aroma of warm garlic bread filled the air. Two large glasses of white *Blossom Hill* stood on the coffee table in front of them and the TV was tuned into the movie channel. This was Tiff's favourite kind of evening – eating pizza and drinking wine before she snuggled up with her dream man and watched a romantic comedy. Heaven.

"Do *you* want to let Georgie know that we'll have the fence panel?" Tiff spoke softly.

"I don't mind babe. You can do it if you want to, or I'll do it if you want me to. Whatever *you* want babe."

"You can tell her and offer her something for it. Some money, I mean." Tiff shot a wry grin at Joe.

"OK, only if you're sure." Joe pulled her closer to him and rested an arm round her shoulders. "Love you Miss Cuthbert."

"Love you too, Mr Frey. I'm sorry for being such a paranoid freak. And yes, I'm sure."

"You are an attractive paranoid freak though." Joe laughed and kissed the top of her head before finishing the drink that was in his hand.

Chapter 15

They were arriving at ten and although both Tiff and Joe had cleaned the house last night, from top to bottom, back to front and inside and out, Tiff was still running around looking for something that they may have missed. She didn't know why she was always so anxious as Joe's parents, Alex and Grant, were lovely people. They were kind, helpful and generous too. They had been so eager to help financially when it came to buying the house in Sycamore Close. Joe had refused to accept any money from them and said that they should keep their money for themselves. 'Take a well-deserved holiday Mum', Tiff had heard him saying one day. 'We will manage – and if we can't – then maybe I'll come calling.' Joe wanted to prove that he could do this on his own, with Tiff's help, of course. He was incredibly independent, if not a little stubborn too. 'Save it for the grandkids, Mum.' His last statement had sent a little flutter through Tiff's stomach – kids – there weren't any grandkids on this side of the channel, as of yet, so maybe Joe hoped that he would have his own children one day. Tiff hoped even more, that this was true.

"Babe – the house is spotless. Will you stop stressing and calm down? They're not coming to do a dust inspection."

"I know," she replied, resignedly. "I just want it to look as nice as it can for them."

"It does – they'll love it. They won't be expecting a pristine mansion."

"OK, I'll try to relax."

Joe's mobile phone pinged, indicating a text message. Pulling it from his pocket, he peered at the screen.

"Is that them?"

"Err... no," said Joe, shoving the phone back in his pocket quickly. "It was... Wayne... yeah, Wayne. Wants to play golf again... next week."

"Oh, OK. Aren't you going to reply?"

"No, I'll... err, do it later. Come on, let's check the garden is tidy."

"Thought you said you didn't have his number."

"No, I didn't. Got it the other day… bumped into him."

"OK," Tiff replied, just a little skeptically.

Why had she got herself so het up about Alex and Grant coming? They loved the house.

"It's bigger than it looked in the pictures," said Alex, taking a seat at the dining table. "And I love your little craft room – you've done it out beautifully. And the view is amazing. Are you happy with it all so far?"

"Oh yes," Tiff replied, joining Alex at the table, "and we have so many plans to change the place to how we want it." Peering out of the patio doors, Tiff could see Joe with his dad, at the bottom of the garden. They were looking across the fields whilst chatting and pointing to different things in the distance. An image of Alvin Snodgrass, in his gold *speedos*, flashed through Tiff's mind.

"What about the neighbours? Have you met any of them yet? Joe said they're weird – but then Joe would say that."

"Yes, err… we've met most of them actually. We went to a barbecue at number eight a couple of weeks ago. There are some very nice people on the close. They're not all weird." Tiff smiled awkwardly.

"Ah, that's good," said Alex. "So who have you got on either side?" She waved a pointed finger from left to right.

"We've got a woman of about 30 on that side," said Tiff, pointing a thumb behind her. "She's got a little girl… well sometimes. It's a long story, and Cyril and Betty live that way." Tiff nodded her head towards the dining room wall in front of her. "They are an elderly couple – very nice people – they made us a cake after we moved in."

"That's nice."

"Yes – and you should see their house inside – it's like stepping back in time to 1950's America."

"Really?" Alex looked genuinely interested. "So I'm guessing it's very retro, pastel pinks and blues?"

"Oh yes, and dear old Betty even dresses like she's just stepped out of the fifties."

"That's so cute."

Tiff nodded agreeably. "Yes, we were stunned when we saw inside the house. Her husband is not so keen on it all but then he keeps himself busy in the garden with his lovebirds."

"Lovebirds?"

"I think that's what they are, yes. Like little parrot type birds – apparently."

"Ooh, it does sound like you have some interesting neighbours."

Tiff giggled slightly. "Oh yes, and some are much more interesting than others."

"Oh?" Alex's eyes widened. "Tell me more – I do like to be nosey. Why does the woman that way..." Alex indicated to the left side, "have a daughter sometimes?"

"Don't think she has custody of her daughter – only visiting rights."

"Oh, I see. That's difficult."

"Hmm... anyway, we also have a secret agent living at number nine – last house on the right, as you stand facing the close."

"A secret agent? How do you know that?" Alex sat up straight and leant forward eagerly.

"Well, he's some kind of secret agent type person. Not sure exactly. But apparently he does all kinds of top secret stuff. He told us."

"Well..." said Alex, "that is super cool. So you have your own *James Bond* living on the close?"

"He's no *James Bond,* I can assure you of that." Tiff shuddered and then smirked. "He gives me the creeps actually. He's a bit of a weirdo."

"Oh, why?"

"When he's home, which isn't very often as he gets sent out on all these special missions, so he tells us. Anyway, when he's home, he goes out jogging a lot."

"And? I feel there's more to this." Alex let out a short burst of laughter. "Jogging's not weird."

Tiff giggled into her cup of coffee. She was actually enjoying telling Alex all about the neighbours. She was relaxed and may as well have been sat with a friend, drinking coffee and giggling about things. "No, it's not – on its own." She giggled again. "It's just that he wears these awful gold coloured *speedo* shorts when he's doing it."

"Really? Is he a bit of a hunk?" Alex grinned cheekily.

"No way. Far from it. He looks like *Dracula*. He's tall and skinny, with a ghostly white face, a scar on his chin, a pointed nose and jet-black hair swept across the top of his head. He's so false."

Alex screwed her nose up. "Doesn't sound great."

"No – exactly. And he always has a pair of binoculars with him when he goes out jogging."

"OK," said Alex, stifling a giggle. "I shouldn't be judgemental but why would you take binoculars out with you when going for a run? I can see why you think he's weird."

"Who's weird?" Joe and his dad had just walked back into the dining room.

Tiff looked up and smiled. "Just telling your mum about Alvin."

Joe rolled his eyes and tutted. "Our freak in red *speedos?*"

"Gold," shot Alex.

"Forgot to tell you Joe," Tiff added, "I saw him in gold pants a couple of weeks ago – out the back – looked worse than the red ones."

Joe turned to his dad. "Haven't told you Dad – we've got our own top secret spy lives down the end of the close."

Grant looked puzzled. "A spy?"

"Yeah." Joe glanced at Tiff and grinned. "Her Majesty's secret service – he works on some sort of governmental assignments. It's all very hush hush."

"Thought that kind of stuff was only in the films. And you're telling me he wears gold *speedos*? I think you're having me on."

"Not to go to work in, Grant." Alex tutted and shook her head. "When he's out jogging."

"So he works for the secret service as a jogger – in gold pants?"

A resounding 'No' shot around the room and everyone, except Grant, laughed heartily.

"OK – take it I've missed something here," said Grant, peering around the room puzzled.

"Don't you always," spluttered Alex, "I'm sure Joe will fill you in."

132

Tea was a joint effort between Tiff, Joe and Alex. Grant had ended his tour of the house in front of the television and had told Joe that he needed to rest his eyes before tea as he had to drive all the way home again later on. Joe had joked that they lived barely twenty miles away and it was hardly an epic journey home but Grant insisted on some 'shut-eye' before the meal.

"That was delicious," said Alex, placing her knife and fork, neatly on the plate. "Thank you."

"You're very welcome." Tiff smiled confidently. Somehow, today had been different. Her usual jangling nerves and awkwardness had been replaced by a warm, friendly and relaxed feeling. She assumed it may have had something to do with the fact that Joe's parents were now on her own territory, therefore the roles had reversed and changed. It felt good whatever it was.

"I'll help you, wash-up," said Alex, getting up from her seat and gathering the plates together.

"There's no need – I can do it later."

"No, I'll do it now. That way, you and Joe can have a sit down this evening when we're gone. Last thing you want to be doing on a Sunday evening is all the washing-up after the in-laws."

"That's very kind of you. Thank you." Tiff smiled with embarrassment as the word in-laws went through her mind several times.

Joe and his dad remained at the table talking about future plans for the house and garden. Then they moved on to rugby, football and just about every other sport currently televised.

Tiff and Alex washed and dried all of the saucepans, plates and cutlery, in relative silence. Just now and again they commented on something that either Joe or Grant were talking about.

A harmonious blend of chatter and laughter filled Tiff's kitchen/diner. She had enjoyed the day with Joe's parents and had realised that she could be a good hostess, she could communicate well with them and she *was* good enough. If it turned out that Alex and Grant did become her in-laws in the future, that would be the royal icing on the top of a giant fruit cake.

Joe and Tiff stood with an arm round each other as they waved goodbye to his parents. They had walked across the green and down to the lay-by together to say their farewells. It had been perfect timing. At the exact moment that they all left the house, Alvin Snodgrass had come out of his. Joe and Tiff had whispered, mumbled and signaled to the end of the close as Alvin arrived at his front gate. Barely dressed in his red *speedos*, a white vest and his binoculars, Alvin acknowledged the group and then began his stretching exercises out on the pathway. His overly exaggerated lunges were alarmingly unabashed and his skimpy red pants only just managed to contain their load. Yet he had no inhibitions to continue in front of Joe's parents.

Slowing their pace, Tiff and Joe could see that Alex and Grant were trying to hide the stunned looks on their faces. Politely, they all passed by Alvin, not daring to look too much as he began to stretch his hamstrings with one foot on the ground and the other placed on top of the garden fence. His shorts stretched at the seams and bulged dangerously around his crotch. It was an astonishingly hideous sight and not one to be reckoned with.

"Has he gone?" whispered Tiff as Alex and Grant's car disappeared down the road.

Turning his head slightly to the left, Joe replied in a hushed voice, "No, still there."

"OK, let's just wave at him politely and walk up the other side of the green. I can't be bothered to talk to him. Can you?"

"Oh – God!" cried Tiff. "You... you made me jump."

"Evening." Alvin was practically on top of them, he was standing so close. "Joe, dear chap, do you fancy a trot out this evening?"

"Err... thanks – but no thanks." Joe looked as shocked as Tiff felt. Alvin had been by his gate a millisecond ago. He must have leapt over the end of the green in one gigantic stride, the moment Joe had turned back around to Tiff.

"Ah now, that is a shame. It's a beautiful evening for filling your lungs with good fresh air and energizing yourself – ready for the week ahead."

Joe stared in silence.

"Come on young man – you would enjoy it. Leave the lady to get on with her chores." Alvin's small beady eyes bore into Tiff's. "Does he hinder the housework my sweet?"

"No. Actually, he helps." Tiff glared up at Alvin's cadaverous face. "But we've done everything already."

"Good woman." Alvin smirked conceitedly. "A good housekeeper has forethought and well planned out days."

"Pardon?"

"Allowing room for your man to have his 'man-time'." Alvin continued to stare fixedly at Tiff.

Joe let out an awkward laugh. "I'll be having my man-time when I watch the rugby. Thanks all the same Alvin."

"Another time young Joe. Another time, for sure."

Joe nodded his head. "Yes, maybe another time Alvin. Thanks."

"And get this poor young girl some rubber gloves." Eyeing Tiff's hands, which were clenched together tightly, Alvin continued, "Dry, dishwashing hands are not appealing on a woman of any age."

Alvin turned on his heels and trotted off along the main road, leaving Joe and Tiff standing by the lay-by, utterly speechless.

"What a completely chauvinistic freak he is," said Tiff, managing to gather her words together as she walked back to the house with Joe.

Joe tittered. "I'll get you some hand cream tomorrow."

"Don't you dare." She slapped him on the back as they entered the house. "How dare he make judgements like that. A housekeeper? Dishwashing hands? How dare he?"

"Alright, babe, calm down."

"Well – I can't believe his nerve. He makes me feel sick."

"Aren't you taking all this to heart a bit too much? Ignore him – he's just a sad and lonely middle-aged man who can't get his kicks any other way."

"Huh," huffed Tiff. "That's a joke, he..." Snapping her mouth closed, she collected her thoughts and realised that she had nearly told Joe about what she'd seen over the last couple of weeks. "He... he's supposed to be this big secret agent isn't he? Surely he gets plenty of 'kicks' from that?"

"I can imagine that it's a pretty miserable and lonely existence."

"Well, I don't care what it is. He's not going to keep on talking to me in that condescending way – I won't have it."

Joe turned his mouth down. "Come on babe, forget about him and don't worry, I have no plans to watch any rugby tonight, let's watch a film instead."

Tiff nodded and smiled. "OK – oh, and while we're talking of plans – did you text Wayne back?"

"Wayne?"

"Yes, Wayne. Did you text him back?"

"What for?" Joe looked puzzled.

"Golf? He texted you this morning. Remember?"

Joe's eyes widened. "Err... oh yes... thanks... for reminding me."

"Which day does he want to play?" Tiff picked up the television remote control and flicked through to the film channel.

"Err... can't remember. I'll sort it out... tomorrow. Come on – let's snuggle up and watch a good film."

Chapter 16

Hmm... As Tiff reflected on the weekend and Joe's parents visiting, she mindlessly applied a layer of brown scumble to an ornamental rabbit. Sitting in the warmth of the studio, scumbling, brushing and then buffing one tray of rabbits after another, she had subconsciously left the vast work space and the gossipy chatter around her and drifted off into her own world. *Hmm...* There was something that bothered her about the weekend, something she couldn't quite get a grasp of, something to do with Joe. Replaying the events of yesterday in her head, she watched carefully as her mind's eye traced through the day, with Alex and Grant, the farewells and the unexpected meeting with Alvin. And then their return home to snuggle up on the sofa and watch an old film... and bedtime... and the amazing sex.

So what was it that was eating at her? What had bothered her – if only for a fleeting moment that it hadn't managed to embed in her mind?

"Hey – Tiffy."

A woman's voice smashed through Tiff's deepest, most intimate thoughts as she was reliving the sex she had enjoyed last night.

"Tiffy – come back to planet earth."

Looking up from the *Wordsworth* rabbit, she held in her hand, Tiff grinned. "Sorry Pat, I was miles away."

"Sharon's getting coffees – do you want one?"

"Yes please." Tiff nodded her head and dipped the rabbit into the pot of scumble. Then she placed the dripping stoneware onto a drip-tray, along with thirteen others which had been dripping for a minute or so.

"You're quiet today." Pat moved closer to Tiff's table. "Everything dandy with the new house? Is Joe OK?"

"Yes, yes thanks. Everything's going well – we had Joe's parents over for the day yesterday – I'm just a bit tired today."

"Ooh – I bet that stressed you out, Tiffy."

Tiff shrugged off a laugh. "No, it was OK. They are very nice. We had a lovely day."

"Jolly beans," said Pat before wandering off to do her usual inspection around the tables, checking for any paint misses, sloppy jobs or untidy work areas.

As the supervisor of the scumble and shading department, Pat liked nothing more than to listen to other people's gossip and offer her worthless opinions about any subject matter going. She'd been with the company for over forty years and everyone had tried to guess her age on several occasions but dear old Pat wouldn't give in to the guesses and questions. She was well past retirement age, that was for sure. Every day she wore the same grey overall, smeared with ancient scumble from days gone by, the same brown trousers and the same white shirt. She had assured everyone that she had several sets of the same clothing and didn't believe in wearing anything else just to go to work. She often boasted about the number of children, grandchildren and great-grandchildren she had and for those who had never met her before, the figures were quite astounding.

Pat had seven children, fifteen grandchildren and six great-grandchildren and didn't mind telling anyone about them. All of them. Far and wide, her family had spread out across the whole world. She had family in America, Japan and Canada, to mention just a few, and one of her grandchildren had spent several years in Antarctica, studying penguins. On the whole, she was a kind, fair and supportive supervisor even if the stone craft artists had to endure a weekly run-down of who was doing what and who was travelling where, in the world of Pat's descendants.

Golf... That was the issue. It had eluded her all day but suddenly, on the way home, it had come to her. When she'd asked Joe about the text message from Wayne, he had seemed a little edgy and forgetful. Had he really received a message from Wayne? How would she know? Who else could the message be from that might send him into a jittery mess when asked about it? Tiff swallowed hard as a queasy lump filled her throat. It was Georgie. It had to be. But how could she find out for sure? She could hardly ask to see the message. Their relationship had already been strained over the last week or so and it had all been Tiff's fault. She feared that the subject of 'Georgie' had to be left well alone, for some time. Let things die down. Cool off. Maybe she could sneak a look at his phone when he was in the bath or sleeping. She shuddered as she pulled into the lay-by. It was wrong to distrust him. It was not right to go snooping around. Yet she had no choice – she had to know the truth. One way or another.

"Hi babe." Joe's face beamed. "You're late tonight."

Throwing her handbag on the sofa, Tiff removed her jacket. "Could do with a day off to be honest. Thought I'd get as much done today as possible."

"You deserve a day off – I'll make you a coffee." Joe stood up, kissed her on the top of her head and went through to the kitchen. "Made a lasagna for tea."

"Oh great, I fancy that. Have you had a good day?"

"Usual kind of day – nothing much happens in the leisure industry on a Monday."

"Have you had a chance to... to reply to Wayne?"

"Err..." Joe had his back turned and was busying himself making two coffees. "Damn – I knew there was something. I'll... Do you know what? I think I'll nip over to his house – that way I can reply to his face."

"OK, do you want me to come with you?"

Joe turned sharply. "No babe, you relax. I'll run a bath for you after tea. I'll... err... I'll be back before you know it." Joe smiled and winked an eye. "Back in time to wash your back."

"OK." Tiff forced a smile back but the doubting-queasiness had resurfaced. There was definitely something funny going on. Joe was still on edge at the slightest mention of the text message he received yesterday. It had to be Georgie and Tiff was going to find out for sure, at the first opportunity she could get to investigate his mobile phone.

"Your bath is done," Joe called down the stairs. "I haven't put any bubble bath in it, in case you want to put one of your fizz-ball things in."

Tiff reached the top of the stairs. "They're called bath bombs."

"OK, but they're like fizzy balls aren't they?"

"Yes, I suppose they are. Anyway, you'd better get over to Wayne's if you're still going."

"I am. I'm going over there now. Are you getting in the bath yet? Do you want a hand removing your clothing?" Joe gave a suggestive smirk.

"No I don't," she replied, slapping his behind. "Off you go."

"I'll only be ten minutes max." Joe began to descend the stairs. "Keep the water for me – but not too much of that fizzy stuff."

"OK, see you soon."

Standing just inside the bathroom door, Tiff listened for the front door closing. Then she sneaked across the landing to their bedroom, and hurried over to the window. Joe was just crossing the green, wearing just his work shirt and trousers. He walked through the gate of number eight, pressed the doorbell and stood waiting for an answer. Tiff hadn't expected him to actually go over to Wayne's house so maybe he was telling the truth and he had received a message from him about golf. Was it her who made him edgy with her questions all the time? Was Joe feeling suffocated and unable to be himself in case she accused him of anything? There was one way to find out. Joe wasn't wearing his jacket and the likelihood of his phone still being in his jacket pocket was high.

Racing down the stairs, she found his jacket hanging by the front door. She rifled through his pockets, inside and out. His phone wasn't there. Hurrying through to the kitchen, she scanned the table, the kitchen worktops, any obvious places that he would leave his phone. It was nowhere to be seen. He had to have it on him still. Maybe in his trouser pocket. Or was it in the bedroom and she hadn't noticed it when she was spying from the window. Racing back upstairs, she searched the bedroom. Nothing. Where could it be? Joe did not normally carry his phone in his trouser pockets and especially once he was at home. He usually had so much change jingling around in them that he had scratched the screens of his phones in the past. He couldn't stand screen protectors as the tiny bubbles and imperfections annoyed him Again, things were looking suspicious as far as Tiff was concerned. Why would he be hiding his phone – even if he was now in Wayne's house, supposedly arranging another game of golf? Actually – why didn't he just text Wayne back? Then he wouldn't have needed to go over to his house at all.

Tiff grabbed a bath bomb from her small collection, unwrapped it and dropped it into the hot water. Instantly, the bomb began to fizz and she watched as pink froth exploded out from the violent blast of tiny bubbles. Rings of pink, red and white froth drifted outwards, across the water. The aroma of raspberries filled the room as she knelt down by the side of the bath, mesmerised by the constantly changing coloured circles of bubbles. Transfixed, she continued to watch. The bath bomb's magical creations were relaxing to observe. They helped take her mind off other things. Bad things. Worrying things that just couldn't be real. Could they?

As the last specs of the bath bomb fizzed away to nothingness, Tiff pulled herself up from the floor, closed the bathroom door and locked it. She tied her hair up, got undressed and stepped into the softened water. Sliding down into the frothy bubbles, she closed her eyes and breathed in the fruity aroma. Ten minutes had passed since Joe had left the house. He was sure to be back any minute. She lay still as the frothy warm water surrounded her body. Still and quiet. Listening and waiting for the front door to open. Wondering if Joe had his phone with him, buried in his trouser pocket along with lots of loose change. It would be unusual if it were in there.

Startled, Tiff opened her eyes wide. Joe was on the other side of the door, knocking and calling her.

"Tiff – have you fallen asleep in there? Tiff."

"Oh yes, I must have. I'm getting out now."

"Sorry I'm so late back. Couldn't get away from Wayne. Think he was a bit lonely, to be fair. Hayley's on a long night shift. I expect that water is cold now."

Tiff hadn't moved. The water had chilled somewhat and the thought of moving a muscle sent shivers through her. "Yes – it's cold."

"Don't worry, I'll get a shower. I'll make us a coffee. You coming down?"

"Five minutes," called Tiff, wondering how long she could stay there before she really grew cold. If she kept still, it was OK. But sooner or later she would get too cold. Dragging herself up, she quickly jumped out, grabbed the bath towel which had been draped over the radiator, and wrapped it round her. She began to tremble as she pulled the plug from the bath. Too cold. She had to dry herself and get dressed in her pyjamas and dressing gown as fast as she could.

Joe had already prepared the drinks when Tiff reached the living room. "Did you sort the golf out?" She eyed his trouser pockets discreetly, looking for the bulge of his phone. She couldn't see one.

"Yeah – he wants to play on Saturday. Are you OK with that? I said I'd get back to him, you know, once I'd spoken to you."

"I don't own you. You can do what you want."

Joe looked a little disappointed. "I wanted to check that we didn't have any plans, that's all."

"Oh we do. I'd forgotten. Well, not until the evening though, so you should be OK during the day. Surprised Wayne didn't mention it."

Joe frowned and shook his head.

Tiff let out a giggle. "Unless *he* doesn't even know about it yet, either."

"I'm guessing he doesn't then – never said a word to me."

"Hayley has invited us to a quiz night on Saturday – at the community centre down on Woodford Road." Tiff sat down next to Joe and snuggled into him, wrapping her arm round his waist. Maybe she could delicately feel her way around his trousers without him noticing.

"OK – sounds interesting."

"Hayley said it's a good laugh. We can take some drink with us and they provide hot dogs and chips for a small fee."

"Cool, so that's Saturday night sorted out. We were going to play early – about seven."

"In the morning?"

"Yes, obviously. Wayne said it's the best time to play. That way we can get home and have an afternoon nap. Well, that's what Wayne does anyway."

"Oh, I see." Tiff poked his side. "So that's you pretty much, wrapped up for the whole day then."

"Looks like it." Joe peered down and grinned. "Don't mind do you?"

"No, it's fine. I'm pleased that you like playing golf. At least it's something you can do. I know you miss your rugby games.

"Yeah, not quite the same as getting into a rugby tackle though. Unless I come across a hefty squirrel, refusing to give me my ball back – that's the only likely tackle I'd get into on the golf course."

Tiff laughed and rubbed a hand up and down his trouser leg. "I can just imagine that. You and a giant squirrel wrestling on the green."

Joe squeezed her closer to him and kissed the top of her head, as he always did. "I'd prefer to wrestle you on the green, on the bed, or anywhere you'd like."

"Joe Frey – go and get yourself showered and changed. You're a sex maniac."

The sound of the water running from the shower and frequent splashing noises, indicated that it was safe for Tiff to search the bedroom once more. Joe's clothing lay on the floor in a heap. She picked up his trousers and went through the pockets. Nothing. Apart from his wallet which had been secured in his back pocket by a small button and some loose change in the front. Stuffing the wallet back, she searched through the rest of his clothes – even feeling his socks for any lumps and peering into his shoes. Where was his phone? He always had it with him, in case there was a problem at the leisure centre. He didn't want his staff to have his home number as he didn't believe that they should be contacting him or Tiff for that matter, on their private number.

Returning to the living room, she took her own phone from her bag and began to type a message to him. *Fancy that wrestling match? Meet me in my bedroom at 10.30pm xx*

By nine o'clock, Joe and Tiff had settled down to watch a documentary on the TV about Antarctic penguins, which reminded Tiff of her boss, Pat and her large family. The washing and drying-up had been done, tomorrow's lunch sorted for Tiff and she had also managed to reduce the ironing pile by several items although she didn't normally like to have to do that in the evenings.

"Did you get my text message?" Tiff gave a sultry stare.

"No – what message?"

"I sent you a message earlier, have you read it?" She raised her eyebrows provocatively and smiled.

"No, what did it say?"

"You'll have to read it…" Seductively, she placed a finger in her mouth, sucked it and then pulled it out slowly. "And soon…"

Joe looked at her puzzled and then laughed. "Just tell me. What are you up to?"

"You'll find out if you read your message." She raised her eyebrows again and gently rubbed her wet finger around her partially opened mouth.

"I think I've left it in the car babe. Tell me."

"Uh-uh, you'll have to go and get it…" She smiled suggestively. "Go on…"

"What – like this? I'm not dressed. I'm not going across the green in just a pair of shorts – Alvin might think I want to go running with him."

"Put your dressing gown on and run down to your car."

Joe sighed heavily. "Oh babe – can't you just tell me."

The game was wearing thin and Tiff was starting to feel a little annoyed, if not a bit silly. "Oh, it doesn't matter. Why's your phone in the car – you never leave it in the car?"

"Don't know – I just forgot it."

"What if someone has tried to ring you from work?"

Joe perked up and pulled himself out of the chair. "That's a good point. I'll go and get it."

Joe entered the living room, puffing and panting. He'd ran down to his car and back. Wearing a pair of baggy tracksuit bottoms, a plain white t-shirt and his brown moccasin slippers, he stood there breathing rapidly. "Don't know where it is… must have left it at work."

"That's not like you, Joe Frey."

"I know… I… err… well, I can only think that I *must* have left it there."

"Here," said Tiff, holding her own mobile out to him. "Phone work – see if someone's seen it."

"Nah, it's a bit late now. They'll be shut in half an hour."

"You've still got time – call them. At least, that way, you won't be worrying all night."

"I'm sure I would have just left it on my desk. I don't really want to go bothering them about it now. They'll be starting to clear up."

"Do you want me to give them a quick call for you?"

Joe shook his head and screwed up his nose. "Nah, don't bother babe. I'll find it in the morning." Dropping into the seat next to Tiff, he leant over and whispered in her ear. "You'll have to tell me what that message was about now, won't you?"

"Oh, it doesn't matter anymore. The moments gone to be honest with you."

Chapter 17

Huh. Well that hadn't gone down very well. Joe had gone to bed early, with a face like a rebuked child and Tiff was still no further in her quest to get a sneaky look through his phone. The following morning wasn't any better either. But this time it was Tiff who moped around the house, getting ready to go to work with an air of disdain about her.

Ha ha. I got your message. Sorry for being a miserable sod. Found my phone on my desk, as suspected. Love you xxxx
Love you too xxxx and sorry for being a miserable moo this morning.

She'd met her quota during the week and managed to secure the day off today. Friday was her favourite day and to have it off was a bonus, as it meant she had a long weekend to look forward to. Tiff had plans today. Plans to get up in her craft room and get her materials and tools sorted into drawers, stacked on to shelves, and the regularly used things, neatly positioned on the sizable table top. Afterwards, she was going shopping to the garden centre. She wanted a few 'flowery' plants for some empty patches in the front garden. If the weather was nice tomorrow, she would plant them in the morning while Joe was out playing golf. Then they were going out tomorrow night with Hayley and Wayne – weekend sorted. Sunday would be a housework catch-up day and a be-extra-nice-to-Joe day so that he would go round to Georgie's and collect the much needed fence panel. Of course, Tiff would make a 'Thank-you' card for the woman, with restrained contempt.

The sun was shining in a cloudless, blue sky so Tiff would have a picturesque view to look out upon while she organized and sorted through her stuff. Momentarily, she wondered whether she would see Georgie across the fields, walking her dog. She also speculated on the possibility of seeing Alvin cantering through the trees like a stallion dressed in a golden saddle. Whatever he or they might get up to along the tree-lined paths, she didn't care much today. She was on a mission and Alvin and/or Georgie could keep their own missions to themselves.

Yet, when it came to it, Tiff did care. Her curiosity was far too great to be ignored. It was like she could go to her own private viewing in her craft room, any time she liked, and there would always be something to see.

Wearing a peach coloured, ankle-length summer dress and white pumps, Georgie had walked along the pathway on the far left, with her dog, about half an hour ago. She had looked pretty, from a distance, and her long blonde hair had splayed out behind her as the wind blew gently through it.

The craft table was piled high with boxes and crates, carrier bags and an ancient, red hand-luggage case, filled with patterned papers and coloured card. However, Tiff still managed to keep an eye on the window by peeping in between the boxes and crates. Keeping watch. Waiting for a glimpse of Georgie's return or a sighting of the repulsive gold *speedos* flashing through the trees.

It wasn't long before Tiff's curiosity awarded her. Sure enough, as if it was a regular TV soap, Alvin appeared from the right. Jogging along the pathway, his gold shorts flickered through the trees. Yet, he looked slightly different today. He didn't have his binoculars hanging from his neck. He had a small rucksack on his back, which bounced up and down freely, as he gained momentum. He ran past the back gardens of Sycamore Close and disappeared up the pathway to the left. Now and again, Tiff could just see his gold shorts glisten in the sunshine.

Binoculars. She had to find them. Purely to find out why the odd couple should meet, way across the fields, deep in the woodland.

Racing down the stairs, she reached the cupboard under the staircase and wrenched the door open. Her heart pounded as she climbed into the cupboard and began frantically searching through the numerous boxes of items still waiting to be unpacked. She had an idea where the binoculars were and typically, they were right at the back, at the lowest point of the cupboard.

The loud peal of the doorbell startled her and she froze momentarily. Who could it be? Georgie? Alvin? Georgie and Alvin? Had she been caught out?

She had just spotted the binoculars, at long last, at the bottom of her 'Memorabilia' box. But they could stay there for the moment. Hidden away. Just in case.

Dragging herself back out of the cupboard, she stood up and brushed the dust and dirt from her legs. She could see a figure, clothed in a fluorescent orange sleeveless waistcoat, waiting at the door. The bell pealed out again. Rushing to the front door, she yanked it open.

PARCEL*FORCE. A tall, bearded man with an impatient expression leant on the doorframe. "Can you take this for number six?

Tiff stared mindlessly. "Sorry?"

"Number six, love. Can you take it in?"

Tiff peered at the huge parcel standing next to the man.

"What? That?"

"I can lift it in for you."

"Yes, of course." Tiff had come to her senses. "Err... sorry – busy working – not thinking straight. Please, just put it there."

The man lifted the enormous, tall box into the hallway and shuffled it to one side, resting it against the wall. "What's your name?"

"Err... Tiff... sorry no, it's Cuthbert."

The man nonchalantly typed the name into his electronic signature gadget and passed it over, with an attached stylus. "Sign there," he said, pointing to a box on the screen.

Returning the gadget and stylus, Tiff smiled at him. "There you go."

"Cheers," said the man and left without a reciprocating smile.

The box was almost as tall as Tiff. She stared at it puzzled. Number six – that was Lilly, on the corner. She wondered for a moment what could be in such a big parcel. There was no way she would be able to carry it along to Lilly's house. It would have to wait until Joe came home.

Back to the binoculars.

Tiff crawled back into the cupboard and retrieved the dusty binoculars from her memory box. Dusting them off, she placed them outside the cupboard and carefully moved everything else back into place. The contents of the cupboard appeared untouched. Grabbing the binoculars, she raced back up the stairs to her craft room. She sat at the table, wiped the lenses on her t-shirt and then positioned herself between the boxes on the table. Twisting the focus wheel, she held the binoculars in a fixed position, pointing towards the trees in the far distance, near the river.

She gasped. She held her breath.

Snatching the binoculars away from her face, her heart pounded in her chest. She'd had such a clear view, way over the fields, towards the river, in amongst the copse. So unobstructed that she momentarily felt like she was actually there. Peering back through the eyepiece, she held her breath again. This intrusive act felt wrong. Could they see her as well as she could see them? Of course they couldn't.

Alvin was carrying the small rucksack by his side. He nonchalantly swung the bag as he walked away from the clump of trees. Georgie's dog was further away, by the riverside. Sniffing along the bank of the river, the dog looked disinterested in his owner – Georgie, there she was. Propped up against a tree, she was pulling white underwear up her slim legs. She had one shoe on and the other one lay on the ground beside her.

Oh my God, Tiff breathed out.

A thick red collar was wrapped around her neck. Tiff turned the focus wheel again. A dog's collar. The dog collar that Alvin had bought in town, last week. Georgie was wearing it.

Patting her dress down, Georgie clutched at the collar, trying to undo it in a violent, angry way. She managed to pull it free and tossed it to the ground. Then she turned her head towards Alvin who was now further away from her. She glared at him disdainfully.

Tiff let out a puff of air and realised she'd been holding her breath again.

Georgie continued to scowl in Alvin's direction. She hated him. Tiff could see it etched, painfully on her face. So why was she allowing him to do these things to her? What hold did he have over her? Suddenly, an overwhelming feeling of compassion for Georgie, engulfed her. She knew what had just happened, even though she hadn't actually witnessed the event. She was relieved that she hadn't seen it. As Georgie moved around the tree and called out to her dog, Tiff slowly removed the binoculars from her eyes and placed them on the table.

Emptiness filled Tiff's whole being. What was really going on with those two? Had she completely misjudged Georgie? Or was Georgie simply an unrestricted temptress? Tiff had to find out. She was possibly the only person who knew what was going on. How could she share this with anyone? But, then again, what if Georgie wasn't a slut? What if she had witnessed a rape, that night in the garden and just missed another one now. It couldn't be rape – Georgie was allowing him to do it. Tiff gulped back the queasy feeling rising from her stomach. She had to talk to Georgie, somehow, without appearing to be some voyeuristic crazy woman herself.

Placing the binoculars at the very back of a drawer, Tiff covered them over with a piece of fabric from her spare materials box and closed the drawer quickly. Why did she have to be so curious? If she hadn't seen Georgie in her garden sunbathing, weeks ago, she wouldn't have become overly obsessed with the view from her window. She wouldn't know about any of the goings-on out in the fields or indeed, in Georgie's back garden. She wouldn't have known anything. She wished she knew nothing.

The plans to sort out the craft room boxes had faded away and completely disappeared into a bout of anxiety. Tiff had to get out of the house. Get away from Sycamore Close. Or was it Sick-amour Close? The garden centre was where she wanted to be right now. Strolling around the outdoor aisles, in the sunshine, without a care or thought of anything else but pretty, colourful flowers.

Ten plants later, Tiff had consciously removed herself from the images of earlier and had a spring in her step as she carried the tray of bedding plants across the green. She'd been away from home longer than expected but the quaint little café, located inside the garden centre, had 'called' her on two occasions while she shopped in the warm sun. There had been so much to see around the garden centre and it had been very thirsty work. She liked looking at the ponds and the wide variety of fish for sale. Koi, goldfish, tropical fish and marine. It was time-consuming to see them all but it had to be done and it had been the best medicine to rid her of her anxiety and the horrible images tainting her mind.

Joe was home already. Tiff had noticed his car in the lay-by when she'd arrived back. Luckily, he wasn't propped up against the front door, nonchalantly chatting to Georgie. Tiff placed the tray of plants to one side, underneath the bench on the left and then pulled at the front door handle. Unlocked – he was in – and not round at Georgie's doing, God only knows what. No sign of Georgie in her house either. That could only be a good thing.

"Joe," Tiff called up the stairs. "I'm home."

Silence.

An image ran through Tiff's mind. Joe. Georgie. Upstairs. In bed. She shook her head and tutted to herself. It had to stop. Her imagination would be the destructive source in their relationship if she continued. "Joe – I'm home."

Still and quiet.

Placing a foot on the first step, she tentatively lifted herself up. "Joe?" Another step up. "Joe – are you in?"

Nothing.

Steadily rising up the staircase, she listened for any movement, the slightest of noises. Alert senses pricked through her body. Was he in her craft room, ogling the 'view'? Unusually, their bedroom door was closed. Why? Reaching the top, she halted. What would she see behind the bedroom door? Two figures, under the duvet, frozen with fear? Caught out?

Bang!

The sound of the front door closing made her jump in fright.

"What are you doing standing up there?"

Tiff turned to see Joe at the bottom of the stairs, beaming up at her.

"Oh God – you made me jump. I thought you were upstairs." She turned around and went back down.

Joe laughed. "Did you think I was hiding upstairs?"

"Something like that. Where were you?"

"Just taken that bloody great big box to Lilly's."

"Oh..." Tiff reached the bottom of the stairs and kissed his cheek. "I didn't even notice it had gone." She giggled nervously.

"Yeah – she was so excited." Joe shook his head despairingly. "She said she's been in all day. Must have not heard her door. Do you know what's in the box?"

"No."

"It's a whacking great big petrol hedge trimmer. Reckons she's going to trim her hedges tomorrow. It's got to be two and a half metres long when fully extended."

"Oh gosh – she can't do that on her own. Did you offer to do it for her?"

Joe shook his head. "No – well I'm out tomorrow, aren't I? Golf in the morning. Surely she won't really do it herself. I thought Wayne was going to do it anyway."

"Well, let's hope so. She's a stubborn woman though. I dread to think what might happen if she tries to use it herself."

"Yeah – me too. She probably hasn't got any petrol for it anyway."

"Petrol? I do hope not. Let Wayne know in the morning."

"I will babe – or I suppose I'll have to do it myself tomorrow afternoon."

"That would be nice... and while you're at it... I was thinking..."

"Yeah?" Joe ambled out to the kitchen, turning his head once or twice to make sure that she was following him.

"About that fence panel."

Reaching the kitchen, Joe turned around. A worried expression had crept over his face. "What about it?"

"Well... I was thinking that I could make a thank-you card for Georgie, if you wanted to pick it up over the weekend." Tiff smiled weakly. "You said she didn't want any money for it so.... I thought maybe I could make a card and get her some flowers or chocolates... or something. We don't want her dog getting in again, do we?"

"Sure," Joe replied, indifferently. "If that's what you want."

"Well we do need it don't we?" Tiff sensed the awkwardness in Joe's voice since the subject of Georgie had come up.

"Yes, we do. I could get it sorted on Sunday, if the weather's OK."

"Do it then," said Tiff, forcefully. "Text her or pop round there and ask if we could have it on Sunday."

Joe nodded his head like an obedient schoolchild before turning around to flick the kettle on.

"So, which will you do?" Tiff stood behind him, tapping her fingers on the worktop impatiently.

"What do you mean?"

"Are you going to text her or go round there?"

"You could do it if you want to babe."

"No – I don't want to. She hates me."

Joe sighed as he pulled two mugs from the cupboard above his head. "She doesn't hate you, babe. It's all in your imagination."

"There you go again, talking like you know her so well."

"Oh please... babe... let's not get into this again."

"We're not – I'm not. I just think it will be better if you go or text her. I haven't got her number anyway. And she did offer the fence to you."

"OK, I'll go round tomorrow afternoon."

"You could just text her if you want to – you've got her number haven't you?"

"Err... no... I haven't. Didn't we throw it away?"

"No, you put it in the drawer over there." Tiff pointed to a top drawer on the other side of the kitchen.

"Oh OK, I'll..." Joe fumbled with a spoon, attempting to scoop up the last granules of coffee from the jar. "I'll... err... knock her door tomorrow."

"OK – fair enough." Tiff tried to sound upbeat. "How about I pick up some flowers *and* chocolates and make that card, ready for Sunday."

"Yeah, good."

Chapter 18

Tiff was still in bed when Joe left, early the next morning. She had pretended to still be asleep as she listened to him tip-toeing around the room, finding clothes to wear. Again there had been an air of discomfort last night and it was plainly obvious how both herself and Joe had tried to keep the atmosphere harmonious and the subjects of conversation as far away as possible from the topic of neighbours. They had gone to bed together but both had excused themselves from any amorous activities by mentioning how tired they were, or in Tiff's case, the addition of a thumping headache.

She waited to hear the front door close then she leapt out of bed and peeped through the curtains to see Joe walking down to Wayne's house.

Pulling her dressing gown around her, Tiff wandered through to her craft room and peered between the boxes still piled up on the table, out to the view beyond. A mist lingered along the length of the river in the distance and rose up to the treetops, creating a pretty, early morning picture of calmness and mystery. Curiously, she opened the drawer next to her and reached in for the binoculars. *No,* she muttered to herself, *you have to stop this Tiffany Cuthbert.* Closing the drawer again, she left the room and shut the door behind her. Today was not going to be all about Georgie and her antics, or Alvin, for that matter. Today was going to be her day for planting her new plants in the front garden and then taking a long, relaxing soak, ready for their evening out with Hayley and Wayne.

Two plants in the ground and the day was already warming up considerably. Tiff hadn't seen anyone on the close, although it was approaching eleven o'clock. She hadn't seen Georgie go out for her morning jolly around the back fields with her dog and she hadn't caught a glimpse of Alvin's pants prancing about either. All was quiet in Sick-amour Close. Tiff giggled under her breath as she thought about her new name for the close. If only she could share it with Joe. It would be so funny. But she couldn't. He would want to know why she had renamed it and that was one question she would not be able to answer. Or even want to. She was in too deep now. She'd seen far too much. She didn't want to tell a soul.

The bedding plants were adding some much needed colour to the front garden and Tiff was thoroughly entertained by digging out little holes to place the plants in and then marking out where the next one should go...

A loud grating, whirring sound interrupted Tiff's meandering thoughts. Looking up from the soil, she could tell where the irritating noise was coming from. It stopped. It started again. She stood up, brushed her knees off and walked down to her gate. Lilly Watson. Peering across to Lilly's front garden, she could just see the tip of a huge hedge trimmer waving around carelessly. *Oh my God,* she mumbled under her breath as she opened the gate and briskly walked towards Lilly's house.

"Lilly." Tiff halted at her gate. "Lilly – stop!" she shouted over the rasping reverberations of the gigantic double-edged blade, swinging about in the air recklessly.

Lilly was desperately gripping the powerful machine as it pulled her along the length of the hedge. Upon hearing Tiff's scream, she turned awkwardly and stumbled, before swinging the extended end of the blade across the garden towards Tiff and almost falling over.

"Lilly – please – stop! Turn it off!" Tiff jumped backwards, away from the gate, fearing that her head might be removed in one swoop of the blade. "Turn if off!"

The frightening sound stopped suddenly. Lilly lowered the machine to the ground and heaved a sigh. "It's too heavy dearie," she panted. "Can you help me?"

"Lilly... step away from it, please." Tiff tentatively opened the gate and walked in. "I couldn't do that," she said, pointing to the long trimmer, lying on the grass. "I thought you were going to wait for Wayne or Joe to do it. That is so dangerous Lilly. You can't do it yourself and I'd be terrified of using a thing of that size – it's much bigger than either of us."

Lilly peered down at the machine and tapped it with her foot. "Thought I'd give it a little go."

"No, please. It's far too dangerous."

"Where are the men then? There's no bugger around when you need them."

"Wayne and Joe are out playing golf. They'll be back this afternoon. Maybe one of them could do it for you then."

Lilly huffed and bent down to pick the trimmer up again.

"What are you doing?" Tiff's heart shot up to her throat. "Lilly – please don't turn it back on."

"I'm not dearie. Like I said, it's too heavy and far too powerful for me." She dragged the machine across the grass and pushed it under the hedge. "At least I gave it a go though. Do you think one of the boys would do it?"

"Yes, I'm sure they will." Tiff thought for a moment. "But if they are too tired this afternoon, after their golf day, I know that Joe will come over and do it for you tomorrow, for certain. How does that sound?"

"Oh, I suppose another day can't hurt, can it dearie?"

Tiff shook her head, relieved. "Now, you promise that you won't try to start it up again?"

"Hmm..."

"Lilly, I can't leave until I know that you will be safe. Please just leave it there and I'll get Joe to pop round later today. That way he can let you know when he can do it. How does that sound?"

Lilly nodded her head, resignedly. "I suppose so."

"OK. Anyway, it's nice to see you again." Tiff smiled warmly. "I'm just putting some plants in my front garden. Good job I was too." She giggled. "Otherwise we could have had you being dragged around the entire close by a giant hedge trimmer. I dread to think about it."

"Decapitating everyone –"

"Yes, most definitely. Actually..." Tiff shook her head, alarmed by the thought, "I can't bear to think what might have happened."

Shrugging her tiny shoulders, Lilly glanced over at the trimmer. "All right dearie. I'll be getting indoors for a brew now then – out of this sun. No good for the skin you know. It'll give you cancer if you stay out in it too long."

"I know. Luckily, I've got sun cream on so I'll be OK to finish my planting – without having to worry about what you're doing. Please don't frighten me or anyone else like that again. Using that thing is murderous," Tiff pointed to the trimmer with a wobbly finger, "could have turned out far worse than getting skin cancer."

Lilly waved the back of her hand as she tottered off, up the path to her house. "Cheerio dearie. Nothing like keeping the neighbours on their toes though."

"Goodbye Lilly – you certainly did that. I'll send Joe round later."

"Thank you, dearie."

Tiff drew in a deep breath and then exhaled slowly as she watched Lilly's tiny frame disappear inside her house. She wasn't quite sure what Joe would say about her offering his services to Lilly but she dreaded the thought of Lilly getting impatient and attempting to start the motor up again to have another go.

Wandering off, back down the path towards her own front garden, Tiff played the scenario through her head. Joe would come home from golf, feeling exhausted. She would tell him he'd have to trim Lilly's bushes today or tomorrow. He would sigh exaggeratedly and possibly grumble and moan about having to do the fence as well. She would plead that it was literally a matter of life or death. He would agree to do it, resignedly. Sorted. No decapitations on Sycamore Close. Although there was just one – or maybe even two heads – that sprung to mind as possibilities. If only she could get away with it.

"Good morning."

Tiff turned around quickly, startled by the gentle voice behind her. "Oh – hello Betty. I didn't see you there."

Seated on a low gardener's stool, Betty was looking over the fence with a wide smile on her powdered face. "Hope I didn't make you jump."

"Well – yes – but not as much as someone else did, a minute ago. Sorry, I was deep in thought."

Hauling herself up from the stool, Betty pulled a pair of pink gardening gloves from her dainty little hands and tucked them into her apron. "What on earth was going on over there?" she whispered, gesturing with a hand towards the tall hedge on the other side of her garden.

"Oh my goodness," Tiff whispered back. "Lilly – she was trying to use a huge, petrol, hedge trimmer. It's twice the size of her."

"Thought so. I was on my way out here when you were shouting at her."

"I didn't mean to shout at her so loud but she couldn't hear me over the trimmer. It was so scary."

Betty shook her head. "Oh dear," she mumbled. "The dear old lady is mad."

"Very impatient, that's for sure. Nearly took my head off as she swung it round." Tiff let out a little giggle. "You wouldn't have recognised me on the way back."

Betty gave a puzzled look. "Why do you say that?"

"If she'd taken my head off? You wouldn't have…"

"Oh, I see now. Yes." Betty laughed into her hands. "I would have sent Cyril out to help…" Betty paused and looked down at her hands, "but he hasn't been so well lately. I tell him to go to the doctors – but he won't go."

"Oh, I'm sorry to hear that. What's wrong with him?"

Betty shook her head and frowned. "I don't really know but there's something not right about him. He sleeps a lot and he's got no energy."

"That doesn't sound too good. Could you ask the doctor to come out to him?"

Betty shook her head. "Cyril would hide away with his birds, if he thought a doctor was coming round."

"It must be difficult for you."

"It can be sometimes. No point in dwelling on it though." Betty peered over the side of Tiff's garden fence. "I see that you've been busy this morning. It will look very pretty when you've finished."

"Yes – I thought it would look nice with a few more flowers." Tiff giggled. "I just hope I don't manage to kill them off. I'm useless with houseplants."

"Oh, they will be fine in the ground. Give them a little water once you've finished and then water them regularly until they are established and especially during the dry periods."

"Thank you, Betty, I will. You never know – I might even turn into a full-grown gardener."

Betty giggled into her hands again. "You might like to come and see my fairy garden out the back."

"Fairy garden? What's a fairy garden?"

"Would you like to come and see? We could have a cup of tea and a slice of fruit cake? I made it this morning. It's still warm." Betty giggled again. "Fruit cake always tastes best when it's still warm."

Tiff's tummy gurgled hungrily. "Are you sure? What about Cyril? I don't want to be a nuisance."

"Not at all. Cyril's pottering around with his birds at the moment anyway."

"Well, if you're absolutely sure, that would be lovely. Thank you." Tiff smiled warmly, she really liked Betty. "I'll just go and lock my front door."

"All right. I will pop the kettle on. Please, just walk in the door – no need to knock."

"Thank you, I will."

Once again, Tiff stepped back in time as she walked through Betty's house towards the kitchen. "Only me," she called out, politely. A rich, homely smell of freshly baked cake drifted up her nose, making her tummy rumble loudly.

Betty was already preparing two teacups and saucers on to a tray, along with two small plates. "Have a seat," she said, gesturing to the classic 50's dining chairs.

Tiff pulled out a chair and sat down. "The cake smells lovely."

"I'm sure it will taste very nice too. We'll have this..." she said, gently pushing a cake slice through the fruit cake, "and then I'll show you the fairy garden."

"Is Cyril not joining us?" Tiff had noticed that there were only two cups on the tray.

"No, I made a flask of tea for him earlier and he has a big slice of cake, wrapped up in a serviette – just how he likes it. He'll be out with the birds most of the day. He cleans them out thoroughly at the weekends."

"Oh, OK."

Carrying the tray across the room, Betty placed it on the table. "Would you like me to pour yours?" she asked, staring down at the teapot.

"Thank you. That's very kind of you."

"Help yourself to some cake." Betty grinned and picked up the teapot.

Tiff's hunger had been satisfied after she'd hesitantly agreed to have another, larger, piece of cake. She stretched back in the chair and patted her tummy. "Thank you Betty, that was so nice."

"You are very welcome." Patting her mouth with a serviette, Betty smiled. "Now, would you like to come and see the garden?"

"Ooh – yes please."

Betty's fairy garden was behind the aviaries. "That's odd," said Betty as they passed by the second birdhouse, "I thought Cyril was down here cleaning out the birds." She peered through a small window, in the wooden shed-like building. "Cyril? Are you in there?" she called, rapping her knuckles on the glass.

Nothing.

"I'll just check he's all right," said Betty, a worried expression on her face. She walked back round to the door and opened it hesitantly. She looked back at Tiff. "Don't want to let any birds out if the cages are open."

Tiff nodded her head and mouthed an 'OK'.

"Not in there." Betty closed the door and frowned. "I'll check the other one."

Waiting patiently, Tiff could see that Betty was a little concerned about Cyril.

"Not in that one either. He's a little devil, he must have sneaked back upstairs when I was out the front." She sighed. "I wouldn't mind betting that he's gone for a lie down, half way through the job. He does that quite a lot lately."

"I can imagine it's tiring work, cleaning out those sheds every week."

Betty sighed again. "Yes, it is. I have said to him that there will come a day..." she paused thoughtfully, "when he won't be able to care for the birds anymore."

Tiff stared down at her shoes, awkwardly, before looking back up. "I suppose we all have to retire at some point, even from the things we love doing." She smiled stiffly. "I can't imagine I'd be able to do such intricate craft work when I'm older."

Betty drew in a deep breath and exhaled slowly, through her nose. "I can't imagine not baking cakes ever." She let out a tiny giggle. "I'll still be whisking up cake-mix on my death bed, I'm sure."

"Don't tell me – then you'll ask someone to put it in the oven for you?"

"Yes." Betty beamed. "That's right – but the oven will be right next door to my bed, so I can watch the cake rise and cook. I do like watching them bake." She gently took Tiff's arm and pulled at it. "Come and have a look at the fairy garden."

Going behind the aviaries was like walking into yet another world. A magical miniature world filled with the most endearing, woodland landscapes carved out in perfect proportion to the little fairy houses, their adjoining dinky gardens and the well-hidden fairies.

"Oh – wow – this is just amazing." Tiff scanned the area, searching for the tiny fairies, dotted around under bushes, tucked away in the gardens and partially hidden under tree bark. "Oh, Betty – I love this." Crouching down, Tiff peered at each garden's furniture, the minute garden tools, stoneware pots, some filled with microscopic plants and the tiny benches. "Are they real?" she asked, pointing to the potted plants.

"Yes, they are just single stems of a variety of alpine plants." Betty giggled. "They don't last very long – the pots just aren't big enough, but I do enjoy helping the fairies to do their gardening."

"Oh, this is just incredible. I absolutely love it."

Moving around the side of the miniature garden, Betty picked up an oval dish and passed it to Tiff. "Do you like this?"

Taking the dish, Tiff stared down at the mini world in her hands. Several, tiny, flowering plants lined the outer edge of the dish. In the middle was a miniature swing, made from sticks and string. Underneath it, a pathway of small pebbles weaved across the soil to one of the plants and then disappeared under a little bush. Five brightly coloured toadstools were scattered around the soil and as Tiff took in the magical scene, she spotted the smallest set of gardening tools and the tiniest pair of wellington boots that she had ever seen. "Betty – "she exclaimed, "this is so beautiful."

"Would you like it?"

Tiff turned and stared Betty in the eyes. "No, I couldn't. You must have put so much work into this."

Betty smiled graciously. "I make the swings myself." Tapping the teeny twig-seat, she beamed as it swayed backwards and forwards for a moment before stopping.

"You are so talented. I love this."

"Then you can have it."

"No, I really couldn't..."

"Yes you can – take it."

"Let me give you something for it then." Tiff wrapped an arm round the dish so she could free up her other hand. She gently tapped the swing's seat and watched it move. "I'll only have it if you will take some money for it. This must be worth at least twenty, twenty-five pounds."

"I sell those ones for eight pounds," said Betty. "However, that one isn't for sale because it's yours and I don't want anything for it. Please, do me the honour of taking it."

"Oh, Betty, this is so very kind of you." Tiff grinned and felt a tiny tear prick in her eye. She really liked Betty a lot. It wasn't because of her generosity. It wasn't because she had fed Tiff on two occasions now. It was because she was such a beautiful, kind and gentle person. She was caring and serene. There was a fairy-like quality to her. Tiff wondered, just for a moment, whether she was actually a real fairy. Then she smiled to herself. Of course she wasn't a real fairy – fairies aren't real. Are they?

Placing the dish carefully on the ground, Tiff crouched down again and gazed in wonderment at the teeny tiny gardens. It didn't matter how long she stared at it, she still managed to find something new, hidden away somewhere, between the cute little bushes, under pieces of bark and behind rocks. "I wish I were a fairy," she whispered, "this place makes it look like the little fairies have so much fun in their gardens."

"Oh, they do," Betty whispered back, before letting out a tiny giggle. "They have lots of fun."

The bright sunshine warmed Tiff's back as she continued to survey the gardens with admiration.

"Would you like another cup of tea?" Betty had been tidying the plants by pulling little, unruly shoots from them and popping them into a small, galvanized bucket, by her side. "I'm sure you could squeeze another slice of cake in."

"I'd love another tea – thank you. And then I'll have to get home. Joe will be back soon." Tiff laughed. "But I really don't think I could squeeze another slice of cake anywhere."

"Then I'll cut up a couple of slices to take with you. I'm sure Joe would like some when he gets home."

"I'm quite sure he would. Thank you Betty, you are too kind."

"I don't think you can ever be *too* kind."

"That's true." Tiff smiled and pulled herself up from her bended knees. She leant over to pick up the dish and peered, lovingly, at the swing. "Are you sure?"

"I'm quite sure. Come on – let's have another cup of tea and I can see where that young Cyril has got to."

Tiff grinned and proudly followed behind Betty, carrying her new prized possession.

Chapter 19

"Where shall I put this?"

"Ah, just pop it on the table, there, on top of that newspaper." Betty pointed to a paper with yesterday's date on it. "Cyril collects them – for the birds. They make a good base for underneath the gravel paper."

Tiff carefully placed her fairy garden on top of the paper and took a seat.

Once again, Betty filled her tray with clean teacups and saucers. She cut two thick wedges of fruit cake and wrapped them in white serviettes. Then she popped them into a food bag. "That should be all right," she said, passing the bags to Tiff.

"I feel like you're really spoiling me – what with all this cake and the little garden."

"I don't have anyone else to spoil, so why not my nice new neighbours."

"Thank you again Betty."

"No need to keep thanking me. I should thank you for coming in to have a cup of tea with me. I do get a bit lone..."

"Not feeling good..."

"Cyril?"

Clutching his chest, Cyril stood behind the central pillar looking as grey as pewter. Wearing only a brown, towelling dressing gown, he held on to the pillar in an awkward stance as beads of perspiration dripped down his face.

"Cyril?" Betty peered at him with a fearful gaze. "Where've you been? I didn't hear you come downstairs."

"Leaning... here... behind the pillar... I... can't move..."

Tiff stood up and looked from Betty to Cyril and back again to Betty. "Is there anything I can do?" she asked, feebly. "Should you sit down? Would you like me to lea..."

Cyril made a horrible rasping sound, screwed his face up and slid down the pillar.

"Oh my goodness – Cyril?" Betty dropped the sugar bowl on to the tray and scuttled across the room. "Cyril?"

"Shall I call an ambulance?"

Reaching Cyril's side, Betty took hold of his face and directed his wide-eyed stare towards her. "Cyril?"

Groaning and grimacing, he continued to hold on to his chest as he slowly slumped further down.

"Where's your phone?" Tiff called out, patting at her pockets to double check that she didn't have her mobile with her.

"Cyril – dear. Cyril?" Betty wasn't responding to anything else other than her distressed husband.

"Betty! Please – where is your phone?"

Cyril was now lying flat out on the floor. He writhed around, moaning and gasping. "Am...bulance. Bet –"

Betty shot a sideways glance. "Over there – by the sofa. Please – hurry." Clinging on to Cyril's hands, she turned back and leant over him. "We're getting an ambulance, Cyril. You stay still now."

Tiff stepped over Cyril and reached the phone, expecting to be able to grab it from the side table, call the emergency number and take it over to Betty. However, as was the case with everything in Betty's house, the phone was as ancient as they were. It was a typical retro 1950's, pastel pink, rotary phone. Picking up the receiver, Tiff placed a finger in the number nine of the rotary dial and pushed it all the way round. She assumed she was doing it correctly as she had seen them being used in the old, classic films that her mum and dad used to like to watch. The dial returned to its starting position and Tiff quickly repeated the process another two times. Too scared to turn round and look at Cyril or Betty, she peered out of the window as the ringing tone started.

"Nine, nine, nine, which service do you require?" asked a woman's voice, systematically.

"Ambulance, please."

A brief click could be heard down the phone line.

"Ambulance service. Is the patient conscious and breathing?"

"Err…" Tiff turned her head and looked over at Cyril's body lying on the floor. "Is he breathing?" she shouted out.

"Are you still breathing Cyril?" Betty shook his shoulder and Cyril moaned.

"Yes – I'm sure he's still breathing. Please hurry."

"What's the address madam?"

"Err…" Tiff had to think quickly where she was. "Number five, Sycamore Close."

"Thank you. What's the patients name?"

"Cyril… err…" Tiff looked over to Betty again. "Betty – what's your last name?"

Cyril continued to writhe around on the floor. The twisted grimace on his face was alarming.

"Hanley," replied Betty, "H-A-N-L-E-Y."

"Got that," said the woman on the other end of the phone. "And how old is Cyril?"

"How old is he, Betty?"

"He's 69."

"Sixty-nine."

"Thank you," said the woman. "A paramedic is on his way. Could you open the front door please?"

"Yes, of course… should I… err… hang up now?"

"If Cyril is breathing and conscious you may hang up. The paramedic is almost with you."

"Oh – OK – gosh, that's quick. Thank you." Tiff placed the receiver down and went to the front door. She peered out across the green but couldn't see anyone. She left the door ajar and returned to the pillar. As she got closer she halted abruptly as her eyes peered down at Cyril's torso. His constant writhing around on the floor had made his dressing gown twist and turn around, revealing his loose black underpants. Tiff gasped as she stared fixedly, at a tiny, shrivelled grey-haired penis, resting on the side of Cyril's leg. Her mouth dropped open but her eyes continued to stare rigidly at the ugly sight before her.

The strange sound of a car's engine filtered through the house. Tiff thought it odd as there were no roads close by. She looked across to the front door as a uniformed man appeared, carrying bags and equipment. He walked right in and moved swiftly across the room to where Cyril lie on the floor.

Tiff looked again, she didn't mean to but it was almost as if she had to be sure she'd seen what she'd seen the first time round. She was right. For sure. Cyril's crinkly, old penis was poking out of his underpants proudly.

"Hello," said the paramedic, directing his words towards Betty. "Can I get down there?"

Without hesitation, Betty pulled herself up and out of the way as the paramedic moved in closer and opened his bag. Quickly, he sprayed something into Cyril's mouth, under his tongue. He opened Cyril's dressing gown and began to stick little circular pads on to his chest, which he then connected to a machine. "Cyril – you are having a heart attack. I need to help you sit up."

Cyril was semi-conscious but managed to heed the man's words and co-operate with him to pull himself up to a half-seated position. Perspiration dripped from his nose and his grey complexion had worsened.

"Oh, my goodness." Betty squealed, having just seen Cyril's groin area. "Oh dear me."

The paramedic was crouching down alongside Cyril, continuing to administer treatment.

Betty's face flushed and her panic-stricken expression made her look quite different to the gentle, timid old lady that Tiff had come to know. She straddled the paramedic's back and leant forward, over his shoulders, trying to reach Cyril's private parts.

"Ugh..." grunted the paramedic as he almost fell into Cyril's lap, right on top of his protrusion.

"I just need..." mumbled Betty, trying not to lose her balance as she continued to lean on the paramedics back, "to tuck him... back... in." Grappling around with Cyril's underpants, she tried to flick his penis back under the baggy material. She failed.

The paramedic shrugged her off and peered round at her incredulously. "Please. Stop. I am trying to treat this man."

"But..." Betty pulled herself up once again and looked awkwardly at Tiff. "I need to wrap his dressing gown over," she muttered, embarrassedly. "He's indecent."

"Betty," said Tiff, calmly, "it doesn't matter. The important thing is that Cyril gets treatment." Putting an arm over her shoulder, Tiff gave her a reassuring squeeze. "Let the paramedic do what he needs to do."

"But..." cried Betty, pointing at Cyril's pants.

"No – leave it. It's not important." Tiff tried to comfort her by keeping an arm round her.

An ambulance arrived on the green. Tiff watched through the window as it quickly drove across the grass, coming to a halt next to the paramedic's car. A young man and a beefy looking woman jumped out, both carrying bags. They entered the house, calling out as they did so, and went straight over to the paramedic. The young man and the paramedic started up a conversation straight away and Tiff could just about get the gist of what they were saying. They were taking Cyril to hospital. He was having a massive heart attack. Tiff gulped as fear began to rise in her. Was Cyril going to make it? How would Betty deal with it if he didn't make it? She had no one else.

The woman paramedic went back out of the front door and walked to the back of the ambulance as the two men continued to work on Cyril. She returned moments later with a wheelchair. Between the three of them, the paramedics hauled Cyril up and into the wheelchair and the woman covered him over with a blanket, hiding his little, shrivelled pecker from prying eyes.

"Mrs Hanley?"

Betty turned and peered, dazedly, at the young man from the ambulance. "Yes?"

"We are taking Cyril to the General. Do you want to travel in the ambulance with him?"

Betty turned and looked at Tiff, worriedly.

"Yes – go on. You need to go with them." Tiff rubbed her arm affectionately. "I'll come and pick you up later if you want me to."

Betty nodded her head.

"Are you a family member?" asked the paramedic.

"No, I... I live next door."

"Perhaps you could assist Mrs Hanley in ensuring the house is locked safely."

"Yes – yes, of course. Betty, have you got a piece of paper and a pen? I'll give you my phone number," said Tiff as her mind spun round in circles.

Betty nodded again and tiptoed past the paramedics who were just about ready to leave. She fetched a piece of paper and a biro and handed them over to Tiff.

"We'll be in the ambulance, Mrs Hanley. Please come in when you've locked your house up."

Betty responded obediently with a nod of her head. Her dazed expression and nervous rubbing together of her hands made her look vulnerable.

"Betty, get a coat and your handbag, if you use one. It might be cold later," said Tiff, feeling quite nervous herself. "This is my number. Give me a call when you need to come back home or call me if you just want me to sit at the hospital with you."

Betty took the slip of paper from Tiff and went to get her coat and bag.

Tiff watched as the paramedic car and the ambulance drove across the green, slowly bumped down the pavement and sped off down the road. Once out of sight, she could hear the peal of the siren starting. She desperately hoped that Cyril would be all right as the ambulance's warning sound sent shivers through her.

Both Tom and Jean, from number two, were walking along the path towards Tiff. They'd been in their front garden, watching the goings-on at number five. No one else from the close was out, which surprised Tiff. She'd imagined that everyone would have been wondering what was going on and come out of their houses to see. Maybe it was because the ambulance hadn't had its sirens going when it arrived or indeed, when it left, not until it was out on the main road anyway.

"Was that old Cyril?" asked Tom, as they arrived at Tiff's front gate.

"Yes, it was. He's... had a heart attack."

"Oh dear me," said Jean. "Will he be OK?"

"I don't know to be honest with you. Betty went with him." Tiff slumped against her gate as the adrenalin began to wear off. "I do hope he will be OK. I'm going to pick Betty up from the hospital later."

"Please, tell her... if there's anything we can do, she should let us know," said Jean.

"It's a good job they've got a friendly neighbour like you," said Tom. "You're nothing like that little madam next door to you." Tom shot a cursory glance towards Georgie's house. "She's a good for nothing..."

"Tom!" Jean poked him in the side with her elbow. "That's enough. Come on, let's go. We have some gardening to do." Glancing at Tiff, Jean frowned. "Sorry about that. I can't take him anywhere."

"It's fine, honestly."

Jean shoved her arm through Tom's arm and pulled him away. "Please could you let us know how he is?"

"Yes, of course I can." Tiff smiled waveringly as the realisation of what had just happened, began to sink in.

Slumping on to the sofa, Tiff closed her eyes for a moment and relived the last couple of hours. She'd almost had her head hacked off earlier by a six and a half foot jagged-toothed-blade. Lilly's hedge trimming capabilities were well below par. The dear old woman was a danger to herself – a menacing old maid. Then there was Betty and poor old Cyril with his withered penis. Tiff cringed as she tried to stop the images from entering her mind. But she couldn't. They came and they were vivid. Right down to the tiniest of hairs. How could she ever look at him the same way, again? Poor Betty – she must be so worried and alone at the hospital.

"Caught you."

Tiff opened her eyes wide and looked up, startled by the voice. She'd been asleep. She rubbed her face and peered at the clock on the wall. The time was 1.30pm. Unsure of how long she'd been asleep, she pulled herself up. "Oh, I must have nodded off when I got in."

"Got in? Where've you been then?" Joe kicked off his shoes and walked through to the kitchen.

"Huh," huffed Tiff. "Where do I start?"

Joe frowned and then flicked the kettle on. His face was bright red, it looked burnt by the morning's sun.

"You've burnt your face."

"I know – it's probably wind-burn more than sunburn." He touched his forehead and screwed his face up tightly. "It's bloody sore."

"I'll get some cream for you in a minute. There's some in the bathroom," mumbled Tiff, sleepily.

"So, where have *you* been?"

"Next door, mostly. Cyril's had a heart attack – he's been rushed into hospital."

"Oh no – is he OK?"

"I don't know. Betty's got my number. She said she'd call me if... or when she needs a lift home."

"Doesn't she drive?"

"Yes," said Tiff, hoping she hadn't already missed a call, "but she went with Cyril in the ambulance."

Joe nodded appreciatively. "OK, I'm with you now."

"I'd better check my phone," said Tiff, trying to think where she'd left it. Peering around the kitchen and dining area, she couldn't see it anywhere. *Bag*, she thought to herself. She probably hadn't even taken it out of her handbag since her shopping trip yesterday. That wasn't unusual for her, she didn't use it much and didn't get many text messages or phone calls from anyone apart from her mum anyway and maybe sometimes, Joe, but that was very rarely. "It's probably in my bag," she said, thoughtfully, "I'll get you some cream while I'm upstairs too." She giggled and gently kissed Joe on the cheek. "That's really going to burn up by tonight – you'll look like an embarrassed radish by the time we go out."

"Thanks for that," Joe replied and tapped her bottom with his foot as she left the kitchen. "I'll make a drink and you can tell me what's happened with Cyril. Poor old sod."

No messages or missed calls. Tiff couldn't even contact Betty as she didn't have her number. Maybe it was too soon. Maybe they were still treating Cyril or maybe... No, Tiff couldn't let the other thought enter her mind. He couldn't die. Could he? Grabbing the after-sun cream from the makeshift bathroom cabinet, she returned downstairs to Joe, who was resting his weary feet on the sofa, a mug of coffee in his hands. His eyelids looked heavy and Tiff knew it wouldn't be long before he was asleep. And probably for the whole of the afternoon.

"Left yours in the kitchen babe, sorry."

Tiff smiled and threw the tube of cream into his lap as she walked past and headed to the kitchen. "Anyway," she continued, "that was just one thing that happened this morning. I tell you..." She returned with her cup of coffee and sat down on the sofa opposite. "Sycamore Close has all sorts of things going on when you're not around."

"Like what?"

"Like, I nearly had my head chopped off this morning, before I went to Betty's."

"Your head chopped off? How the hell...?"

"Lilly..."

Joe laughed. "Don't tell me... She didn't use that great big trimmer did she?"

"Uh-hu." Tiff nodded her head slowly and deliberately.

"Bloody hell – how did she manage that?"

"Well, she didn't – that's the whole point."

Joe eyed her, puzzled.

"She didn't *manage* it at all. The monstrously big thing nearly took her flying across her garden. And she almost decapitated me in the process."

Joe shook his head despairingly. "Blimey. Are you OK? Why couldn't she just wait?"

"Well, I've told her that she has to now. She soon realised that she couldn't handle it. And I wouldn't have been able to either. It's very powerful."

"It would be. It's probably more powerful than an electric one. She's bloody mad."

"Anyway..." said Tiff warily, "I've, err... told her that you'd do it." She screwed her face up and waited for the aftermath. "Either today or tomorrow?"

"Great." Joe tutted. "It'll have to be tomorrow then – I really can't be bothered this afternoon, I'm knackered."

"That's fine. I did say it might be tomorrow. Thanks Joe."

"Huh – I can hardly say no, can I?"

Shrugging her shoulders, Tiff turned down the corners of her mouth and gave him a sad look. "Sorry babe. It's for the best. If she started that machine up again and tried to do it herself, she'd end up killing someone, if not herself, believe me."

"Yeah, suppose." Joe's eyelids were getting heavier and heavier. "What about Cyril? Will he be OK?"

"I really don't know. He didn't look good..." Tiff broke off. "Joe?"

"Hmm?"

"I can't believe you're falling asleep while I'm talking to you."

"Hmm... sorry babe..."

"Don't worry, I'll tell you later. Finish your coffee, put some cream on your face and have a nap. I'll go and finish planting the new plants." Suddenly Tiff remembered that she had left her fairy garden and the slices of cake at Betty's house. She shrugged to herself and wandered outside as Joe's breathing became deeper and turned into just a faint little snore. There were more important things to think about than the miniature garden and cake. She desperately hoped that it would turn out all right at number five.

Chapter 20

Finally, Tiff pulled herself up from the mud, took an admiring glance around the front garden and dusted off her jeans. She picked up her phone from the empty plant tray and peered at it. Still nothing from Betty. It was almost five o'clock. Had Cyril died and she was still at the hospital, sitting in a corner somewhere, crying her eyes out, alone? Tiff shook her head. No, please.

Sycamore Close had been quiet all afternoon and she hadn't seen a single person. Not even Alvin. She'd half-expected to see him limbering up, outside his house in his ridiculous gold pants, before prancing, ostentatiously, away with his binoculars or even another rucksack.

Clearing away the garden hand-tools she'd been using, Tiff stretched her back and walked down to the front gate. She had to pop into Lilly's and tell her that Joe would do the hedges tomorrow. She hadn't dared to ask him to go and tell Lilly himself, as he looked a little rough when he came home and he was also burnt to a crisp.

Lilly eventually opened her front door and thanked Tiff for letting her know about tomorrow. She seemed oblivious to the goings-on next door to her, earlier that morning and Tiff had decided not to enlighten her. It wasn't really her place to go around telling all the neighbours about poor Cyril's misfortune. She still hadn't had any further information as to his condition so she didn't know whether she might be speaking of the dead if she said anything. She was sure that Lilly would find out for herself sooner or later.

Returning home, Tiff scooped up the tray and hand-tools and carried them indoors. Surprisingly, Joe hadn't moved from his spot on the sofa all afternoon. She walked straight through to the back garden and dumped the tools underneath a tough plastic sheet (their makeshift shed). Then she returned indoors and put the kettle on.

"Oh – you're awake now," she said, startled by Joe, standing behind her looking crinkly faced and glowing from ear to ear. "That looks really bad."

Joe opened his mouth to stretch out his face and winced. "It is. That cream hasn't done a lot of good."

"There is a limit Joe. It's not going to cure third degree burns."

He smirked and went to sit down at the dining table. "I'm sure it's not as bad as that. What are we having for tea anyway?"

"I haven't thought about it to be honest. I've been busy all afternoon and I've just come back from Lilly's."

"Oh dear lord, has she been – ?"

"No, before you ask, she hasn't. Thankfully."

Joe sighed. "Good."

"Oh wait," said Tiff. "I just thought – we're going to that quiz night, aren't we? I'm sure Hayley said there'd be food there."

"Oh, yeah. Think there is. Well that's that sorted then. We can get something there. I need a bath before we go anyway so we can scrap the idea of cooking."

"That's a relief. I'm a bit worried that I still haven't heard from Betty yet. I'm supposed to be picking her up at some point."

"Call her and find out what's going on." Joe pulled himself up from the chair as if every muscle in his body ached. "I've got to go and have a bath babe."

"But I don't have her number."

"Phone the hospital then. Find out what's going on."

"Could do I suppose."

"You'll have to, surely. You can't exactly go out for the evening and leave her there."

"I know," said Tiff, resignedly.

"Right, I'm going for a bath. Do you think I should put more of that cream on after?"

"Yes, definitely." Tiff grinned as he hobbled past her. "Why are you walking like that?"

"Ache everywhere. Don't know what's worse, rugby or a round of golf?"

"Surely golf is nowhere near as energetic as rugby."

"You'd be surprised," he replied as he reached the bottom of the stairs. "All that walking up and down hills, grappling around in the bushes and swinging the clubs many more times than most people because I couldn't hit the bloody balls – it's hard work when the sun's beating down on you."

"Fair enough," said Tiff, rolling her eyes. "Go and soak those weary old bones of yours in the bath then."

Tidy up the kitchen first. Avoid making a phone call to the hospital. What was she supposed to say anyway? She didn't have a clue where Cyril or Betty might be. Sort clothes out to wear tonight. Still avoiding making that phone call. Iron said clothes. She wouldn't know which department to ask for or anything. Avoiding a phone call further. Text Hayley to check what time they were going tonight. Avoiding the inevitable. And what if Cyril was dead – she did not want to hear that over the phone. Avoiding the inevitable further.

Tiff heard Joe's footsteps upstairs. He was obviously out of the bath. She couldn't avoid it any more. She had to call the hospital. Time was ticking by and she'd heard nothing from Betty – which wasn't really a good sign. The inevitable had caught up with her.

She opened Joe's laptop and searched *Google* for the number of the General hospital. She typed it into her dial pad. The doorbell rang. Excuse to avoid the inevitable again. Placing her phone on the arm of the sofa, she went to the door.

"Oh," she said, surprised by the visitor. "What are you doing here? I... I was... just going to call you. I mean call the hospital. Betty, please come in."

Betty was standing at the door holding the fairy-garden dish with the cute swing. Also, hanging from one of her hands, was the food bag containing the fruit cake wedges she'd lovingly sliced earlier. She smiled sweetly and stepped into the house. "Thank you," she said. 'I caught the bus home. I thought it was a little too late to be dragging you out from your home. I hope you don't mind me popping these things round to you. I think they were overlooked – what with all the hullabaloo earlier today. My sincerest apologies."

"Oh, Betty, please don't apologise. I was just about to call the hospital to see what was happening." She *was* just about to do it. She really was. "I was all prepared for coming to get you and it would not have been any trouble at all. Anyway, you're here now but more importantly, how's Cyril?"

"He's all right. They fitted two stumps into his veins. He had a very large blood clot."

"Oh dear. But I'm so pleased to hear that he will be OK. By the way, I think they're called 'stents'."

"Yes, that's right. Stumps, stunts, stents – it means nothing to me."

"They open up the veins, I do believe, to allow the blood to flow easier."

"Yes, that's right – I do remember the doctor saying something like that."

"Let me take that from you," said Tiff, graciously accepting the dish from Betty's hands and carrying it through to the dining table. "Would you like a cup of tea? Then you can tell me all about Cyril."

"That would be very nice, thank you. Are you sure I'm not stopping you from doing anything?"

"No, it's fine, honestly. We're going out later, with Hayley and Wayne from number seven so Joe's having a bath at the moment. But we have at least an hour. Only problem having a cup of tea is... I don't have posh teacups like you do."

Betty giggled sweetly. "A mug, or any sort of cup, will do just fine. I've brought yours and Joe's cake round too," she said, holding the food bag up.

"You are so thoughtful Betty, even when everything is stacked against you. You still manage to think of others first." Tiff gladly took the bag from her.

"I may as well spoil others while I can," she replied, "Cyril won't be able to eat cake like he used to."

"Oh?"

"I do believe they will be advising him to go on a strict diet. It's his waistline, you know – he's far too round."

"Did they think it was to do with his weight then? Is that why he had a heart attack?"

Betty nodded her head, sadly.

Tiff took three clean mugs from the cupboard. "Are you sure a mug will be OK?"

"Of course – I do like tea in a mug from time to time."

"Hello," said Joe, padding into the dining room in his dressing gown and slippers. "How's Cyril? Tiff told me the news."

"He will be all right," said Betty. "They said he could be home by Monday."

"That's good to hear," Joe replied. "Once he's home, he'll be able to relax better."

"Oh yes," Betty said sternly. "And relaxing will be all he'll be able to do. There won't be any birdcage cleaning for him. I think I might have to start doing that myself." Betty peered down at her feet. "It's not something I'm looking forward to doing either."

"Then we will help you." Tiff shot a swift glance at Joe. "Won't we Joe?"

"Err...yes, sure we will."

"I couldn't ask you two to do something like that?"

"You're not asking – we're offering."

Tiff met Joe's eyes and he gave her a polite smile.

"That's most kind of you both – thank you. And I am sure that I am speaking on behalf of Cyril too. The doctor said he will have to take things easy for some time when he comes home."

"Understandably," said Joe.

"We will help you for as long as you need us to."

"You can even feed us in cake," laughed Joe. "We'll eat Cyril's share. I heard what you were just saying about his diet."

Betty giggled. "Now that is one thing that I'll have to discuss in length with dear old Cyril. He will miss his cake."

"I'm sure he will. I'm relieved to hear that he is OK though." Joe smiled and picked up his mug of tea from the worktop. "Now, if you'll excuse me, I need to get dressed and tend to this scorched face of mine."

Betty peered at his face, thoughtfully. "I thought you looked rather... burgundy, in colour."

Tiff nodded. "It's even worse now he's had a bath."

"I take it you got burnt this morning?"

"Yes – far more than I realised."

"So..." mumbled Joe, "that's now the hedge trimming at Lilly's house, cleaning bird cage's next door, collecting a fence panel from next door the other way, and fitting said fence panel in our garden – I've got a busy Sunday haven't I?"

"Well, obviously, I will help you to do the birds and I can go to Lilly's with you – I'll help pick up all the trimmings as long as you don't slice my head off in the process. And if I really have to, I'll go next door and get the fence panel, that's if I'll be able to lift it," replied Tiff, defensively.

"Between you and Georgie, you'd be able to carry it round."

Tiff nodded her head, reluctantly. "So it's not as bad as you first thought."

"No, I suppose not. I was looking forward to a day of rest though, to be honest with you."

"I know you were but we should help our neighbours out, don't you think?"

"I've already agreed, haven't I?" Joe opened his mouth and began to contort his face this way and that. "This is getting worse," he mumbled, grumpily.

"Put some more cream on then – we've got to go in a minute. Your face is probably soaking the cream up straight away, it's so burnt. I don't know why you didn't..."

"What?"

"Oh, it doesn't matter. Just make sure you take sun cream with you next time."

As Joe and Tiff left their house to walk down to Hayley and Wayne's, there was an air of indignation seeping from every singed pore in Joe's face. Partly because he had so much to do tomorrow, on his day off, but mostly to do with the fact that his face was on fire and it was all his own fault.

"Come on Mr Beetroot," Tiff whispered, linking arms with him, "we'll get through tomorrow together. Even *with* that face of yours."

The small community centre was just a ten-minute walk away from Sycamore Close. A new build, the centre was fresh-looking and very white. Everything was white. Both the inside and the outside were so white that

Tiff wished she had brought her sunglasses along. Of course, the glare inside the community centre only accentuated the glowing faces of both Joe and Wayne. Tiff and Hayley had spent the whole of the ten-minute walk, strolling behind the men and giggling discreetly, so as not to upset them any more than they were already. Both of their faces looked like the inflamed back-end of a baboon.

An extremely elderly man, wearing black trousers, a white shirt and a silver waistcoat ushered the small crowd into a large room on the right side of the building. He appeared to be enjoying his all-important job and Tiff wondered, for a moment, if this was the highlight of his week. It was quite endearing.

The room was filled with round, white tables, each with four white chairs which were tidily tucked underneath. There was a small, curtained stage on the right side of the room, with two white chairs and a smaller, white table on it. Over on the left was a wide serving hatch with a closed shutter. Rows of plastic beakers lined the hatch and a small, 'Help yourself to beakers' sign hung from the shutters. A smell of fried onions wafted around the room making Tiff's mouth salivate and her tummy rumble. She was starving and wished she'd had at least a tiny bite of the delicious fruit cake, still in its food bag, on the kitchen side.

Hayley grabbed Tiff by her arm and pulled her along to the back of the room. She placed her handbag and a carrier bag, laden with alcohol, on a table. "Shall we sit here? Don't know about you but I hate being at the front."

"Sure – I wouldn't like the front either." Tiff did the same with her bags and pulled out a chair."

"There's some hard-core quizzers here. They take it very seriously. That's why I don't like sitting at the front." Hayley giggled. "We get most of the questions wrong."

"Oh dear – I doubt that me or Joe will be of any help to you then."

"I came for the giggle, so don't worry. Wayne takes it far more seriously than I do – don't you Wayne?"

Wayne and Joe had just strolled over to the table.

"Sorry? What was that?" Wayne was still looking as miserable and scorched as Joe was.

"I was just saying to Tiff that you take these quiz nights more seriously than I do."

"Oh, yes. No point coming otherwise." He turned around to Joe and they started to talk in low, inaudible voices as they slowly wandered off to the hatch to collect some beakers.

"I'm surprised by the number of people coming in."

"Oh yes, it's quite popular around here."

"Anyone else from our close come to these quiz nights?" Tiff asked, scanning the sea of faces walking into the room.

"Haven't ever seen anyone – except for Georgie, of course."

"Georgie? Wouldn't have thought that this was her kind of thing." Tiff tried not to show her disappointment.

"I thought I told you – she helps out here sometimes. She quite often does the cooking for the quiz nights. She's probably behind those shutters right now, covered in grease and up to her elbows in onions."

"Ah, right. You probably did. Sorry." *Great!* Tiff thought quietly, whilst conveying a polite, contented smile.

There must have been at least 80 people in the room. Taking their seats, talking in groups or milling around the entrance, the crowd were mainly middle aged to elderly. Only a few were of a younger age group, similar to Tiff, Joe, Hayley and Wayne. Tiff hadn't expected it to be quite such a big affair and she was starting to feel a little nervous about her utter lack of general knowledge.

"Ladies and Gentleman…" A rotund, middle-aged man, wearing black trousers, a white shirt, a black bow tie and holding a microphone, called out from the stage. "Please be seated."

Joe and Wayne joined their table and sat down. The rest of the crowd scrabbled through the maze of tables and chairs, trying to reach their seats as quickly as possible. Every now and again, someone would take a double-take at Joe or Wayne's face and shake their heads, either amusedly or sympathetically.

"This all looks so serious," Tiff whispered as Joe sat down next to her.

"Thank you," said the man on the stage. "What a turn-out we have here. Welcome to Quiz-night number thirteen. Unlucky, some would say."

The audience laughed and many people mumbled to their friends.

"As always," the smartly dressed, authoritative man continued, "we have the delightful and sophisticated, Peggy Swanson, joining us. Our very own illustrious adjudicator and administrator – and the only woman who is able to keep me in-check."

Again the audience laughed, followed by a babble of excited voices.

"A round of applause please, for... Peggy."

Tiff clapped her hands together heartily and watched as a figure appeared on stage, from behind the curtains. She squinted and frowned as the white-haired woman came into full view. Nudging Joe, Tiff leant over and whispered in his ear. "I know that woman."

"Who?" shouted Joe, over the continuing applause and cheering.

The woman stepped out to the front of the stage, wearing a very similar attire to the man next to her and bowed several times. Then she waved her hand around the room, like she was royalty, and smiled widely.

"That woman – up on the stage."

"Do you?" Joe's burnt face appeared a little worried.

"Yes, I'm sure that's the woman who... I'm sure it is her..."

"Who?"

"Well, I haven't seen her for quite a while now but I'm sure it's her."

"Tiff," said Joe, impatiently, "who do you think she is?"

"The woman who keeps coming in our garden and sitting on the little bench – remember?"

"Oh, really?" Joe peered up at the stage. "Are you sure?"

"Yes, I'm pretty positive." Tiff looked at the woman again as she continued to point at groups of people at the tables and wave to them, as she mouthed, 'hello'.

"Thank you Peggy. I'm sure you've had quite enough accolade for now," said the man on the stage.

A roar of cheering and laughter filled the room again and one man called out from the tables over on the far left. "You're only jealous Charlie. Our Peggy's more popular than you."

"You're probably right. Now, please, calm yourselves down and we shall begin the quiz evening."

"You're not going to say anything to her, are you?" said Joe, eyeing Tiff in a way that she thought was just a tad suspicious.

"Why do you say that? I thought you wanted me to ask her why she was in our garden."

"No – just forget about it now."

"But?"

"Forget it Tiff. You can't say anything to her tonight – that wouldn't be right. Just leave it now."

"I don't see why it wouldn't be right." Tiff frowned at him. "It was you who said I should go out and talk to her – that day when I pointed her out to you."

"Yes but… that was then. It's different now. You can't say anything – that would be embarrassing." Joe paused, thoughtfully. "Like you said – you haven't seen her in our garden just lately anyway. Let it go babe."

"OK," said Tiff, resignedly, as a little niggling doubt began to grow in her mind again. A doubt about what? She really wasn't sure. But Joe just didn't seem to be the same as he used to be. OK, there were no problems whatsoever in the bedroom, but there was something that wasn't right. She just couldn't work out what it was though. He was snappier than usual and on edge sometimes. As for his elusive mobile phone? Well, that remained elusive despite Tiff's constant searching to try and track it down when he wasn't looking or when he was in the bath. He'd apparently left it in his car or at work on at least two more occasions since the first time. Tiff had casually commented on his apathy one day, but only the once, as she hadn't wanted to sound overly concerned. His reply had been brusque, 'I must be getting forgetful in my old age – it's just a phone, Tiff'.

Placing an arm round her shoulders, Joe pulled her closer to him and pecked her on the forehead as the hubbub around the room died down. "Don't say anything to her please – just forget it."

"OK, if you say so." She eyed him skeptically as he watched the couple on the stage. A slight grin etched on to his crispy face.

The tables were equipped with answer sheets and pencils. Wayne picked up a sheet and looked around at everyone on their table. "What shall we call our team then?"

Hayley turned to Tiff and Joe. "I think you two should name our team. What do you say?"

Tiff held her tongue momentarily, as her automatic response was to shout out, 'Sick-amour-four'. "Ooh, I don't know. What do you think Joe?" she said instead.

"Err... no idea. Guess it could be something like... The Sycamore-close-gang?"

"What about..." Tiff grinned. "The Sycamore Four?"

"I love it," squeaked Hayley. "Sycamore-four. Wayne – write it down."

Wayne scribbled on the top of the sheet and then looked up as the man on the stage spoke.

"Here we go then... question number one. Good luck everyone. In which television series might you hear *Victor Meldrew* say, 'unbelievable'?

"*One Foot in the Grave*," whispered Tiff, instantaneously.

Joe peered at her, astonished.

"I thought you said you wouldn't be any good at quizzes," remarked Hayley. "Well done you."

Tiff grinned and her cheeks flushed pink. "I only know that one because my mum and dad used to watch it all of the time."

"That should have been an easy one for the more mature of you. OK. Number two..." said the man. "What is the square root of 729?"

The crowd groaned and mumbled.

Hayley leant back in her chair and locked her fingers together on the top of her head. "Not a clue," she mumbled before rolling her eyes.

Wayne shook his head and looked directly at Joe.

Joe shrugged his shoulders. "Don't know mate – useless at maths. Tiff might..."

Leaning right into the table, Tiff whispered, "Twenty-seven."

Wayne peered at her incredulously. "Are you sure?"

"Yes, write it down."

"Apologies ladies and gents – this is a tough one. I can promise you that neither Peggy or myself know anything about these questions before they arrive."

Peggy was seated behind a table on the stage and nodded her head agreeably.

"Moving on to question three then... In which films does *John Hurt* play the following roles? And you'll get one point for each correct answer. The roles are, A – *Kane*. B – *John Merrick*. C – *Winston Smith*. D – *The Marquis of Montrose*. E – *Quentin Crisp* and finally, F – *Mr Ollivander*."

A sea of whisperings washed around the room as people locked their heads together, across the tables, and began filling in their answer sheets passionately.

"Can you repeat the roles, Charlie?" One man shouted across the room.

"A – *Kane*. B – *John Merrick*. C – *Winston Smith*. D – *The Marquis of Montrose*. E – *Quentin Crisp* and finally, F – *Mr Ollivander*."

"That one is *1984*," said Tiff pointing to the space for C. "From the book by, *George Orwell*."

"Clever girl, Tiff," said Hayley, grinning. "Never heard of it but I'll take your word for it."

"I've read all of *George Orwell*'s books. Again, my dad loves them. I read them when I was a teenager."

"Knows more than she lets on," said Joe, winking an eye at Tiff.

"We're three questions in and Tiff has answered all of them." Wayne laughed and shook his head, amusedly.

Tiff smiled and poured some wine into one of the beakers. "Looks like it's going to be a good night," she replied, unconvincingly.

Tiff's luck had run out after question three. But the silly answers the group were prepared to settle for, and bravely write down on their sheet, certainly gave them all a good giggle as the wine and beer gave way to addled, un-quiz-worthy minds.

"Thank you ladies and gentleman," said the man who Tiff now knew as, Charlie. "We will stop for refreshments and a recharge of that grey-matter. Part two will commence in 45 minutes." Charlie placed the microphone on the table and exited the stage, along with Peggy, via the back curtains.

The whirring sound of the shutters opening made Tiff look over at the hatch. And there she was, looking radiantly beautiful (even if she was a little greasy) in a black and white, stripy blouse as she stood behind the counter. Georgie – the hot dog lady.

"Ah, food," said Wayne, patting Joe on the back as he passed him.

Joe looked across to the serving hatch and then back to Tiff. "Are you coming over to get some food babe? I'm starving."

"In a minute. You go over with Wayne. I'll wait for Hayley."

Hayley had darted off to the toilets as soon as the last question was read out. She had drunk far more wine than Tiff had and already, she sounded tipsy and giggly.

The queue at the serving hatch was lengthening at quite a pace when Hayley returned from the toilets with an alcohol-induced flush on her cheeks.

"They're over there already," said Tiff, pointing to the hatch.

"Blimey, look at the queue." Hayley pulled her chair out and sat down. "Shall we wait until it goes down a bit?"

"Yes, I don't mind."

"Well, knowing my Wayne, he definitely won't think to get anything for me and I don't want to stand in the queue for the next 20 minutes."

"They're all the same," Tiff giggled. "Think of themselves and their bellies first."

"Oh, yes."

"Is this Georgie's job then?" Tiff averted her eyes towards the hatch momentarily before fixing her gaze on Hayley.

"She helps out a lot here. Voluntarily. She claims benefits, so she can't work properly."

"Why can't she get a paid job? I mean, anywhere, not just here."

"She's on the sick – but please don't say that I told you." Hayley glanced across at the hatch.

"Oh, really?"

Hayley lowered her voice although the din in the room was rowdy. "Depression."

"What did you say?"

"I said, she's suffering from depression."

"Oh, I didn't know that." Tiff feigned compassion. "There's a lot more to Georgie than meets the eye."

"No, I think what you see is what you get actually."

"Oh, OK." Tiff paused and sipped at her drink. "I haven't seen or heard her daughter lately."

"Staying with her dad a lot more."

"What do you mean?" Tiff asked, curiously.

"Georgie doesn't have custody of Sophie, does she. Don't think things have gone too well on the visits just lately." Hayley peered over at the hatch as if she was worried she might be overheard.

"Ah, OK. Awkward. Sorry, I shouldn't be so nosey."

"It's OK," said Hayley, "just don't repeat anything."

"I won't. I promise."

"Wayne doesn't even know everything about her. He's far too judgemental and especially when it comes to kids."

"Would I be classed as super-nosey if asked why Georgie doesn't see her daughter so much now?"

Hayley laughed and drained another beaker of wine. "Yes you would... so as long as you're prepared to have the title of 'super-nosey-Tiff' I don't mind telling you."

Tiff giggled and took a long sip of her wine, trying to finish the beaker full and catch up to Hayley. She didn't know why but she wanted to be drunk tonight. It seemed that everything would feel easier that way.

Hayley leant across the table and mouthed, "She can't cope. She's been depressed from the start or should I say end, of her marriage. She's got much worse just lately."

"So the visits, have they stopped? I've seen her with Sophie on some Friday nights. Collecting her from school?"

"Yes, they did have pre-arranged sleep-overs now and again. Usually at the weekends as Georgie's ex-husband works a lot over the weekends. He's in the hotel industry. But there's been a break just lately. I think Georgie is seriously going downhill again."

"Oh dear," said Tiff, "that explains why I haven't seen or heard her daughter much lately. Downhill again?"

Hayley nodded her head. "I thought I'd told you about her set-up before?"

"You probably did but I'm half-piddled now." Tiff giggled, hoping that she might be able to find out a little more about her strange neighbour. She didn't want to sound like she was too interested in Georgie's life story but she was sure she hadn't heard of the woman's downhill depression before.

Hayley joined her and laughed. "Just keep it to yourself – please."

"Yes, of course I will," Tiff replied expectantly.

"Come on, let's get some food, I don't want to spend the evening talking about depressing things."

"Oh, OK," said Tiff, resignedly. That was it, it seemed. Hayley was hungry so there'd be no more poking and prying into Georgie's life. She was off the agenda, unfortunately for Tiff.

Joe and Wayne had reached the front of the queue. Leaning over the counter, the two men appeared to be chatting and laughing with Georgie and another woman, who was helping to serve. As Tiff and Hayley left their table to join the end of the queue, Tiff watched as Georgie clearly placed a hand on top of Joe's and then laughed. He stood up quickly and turned his head towards the group's table which was now empty. Then he turned back to Georgie and appeared to be talking to her again. At the back of the queue, Tiff's view was obscured by the two-deep row of chattering quiz contenders in front of her. How long would it take for Joe to return to their table? How long was he going to talk to *her*? Tiff's eyes darted from the hatch to the table and back again. It was happening again. A queasiness rose slowly from her stomach and stuck in her throat. Jealousy. Undeniable insecurity. Every second counted and the sooner that he returned to the table with Wayne, the better it had to be.

Shuffling along the line, Hayley chatted to the people standing in front of them and now, behind them as well. Tiff grinned, politely, at any pauses in Hayley's incessant chatter and tried to make it look like she was joining in. However, that couldn't have been any further from the truth. She was frantically awaiting the appearance of Joe or Wayne at their table. But Wayne on his own would have been even more worrying. Suddenly, she realised that they were shuffling along the line. How could that be, if Wayne and Joe were still being served at the counter? Because they definitely weren't back at their table. Where could the queue be moving to then? Tiff tapped Hayley on the shoulder and whispered in her ear. "I'm going to the loo – back in a minute."

Hayley nodded and smiled.

Still there. Still talking and undoubtedly flirting, in between eating. Joe and Wayne were now standing by the side of the hatch chatting to Georgie and the other woman while they continued to serve the slowly decreasing queue. That was why the queue was moving. The men had stepped out of the way to let others be served but they remained in full-on conversation and hilarity with *her* and the other woman.

Tiff marched to the ladies' room with a mixture of fury and sickening worry filling her whole being. What the hell did Joe think he was doing? It was starting to look more than plainly obvious that he was drawn to her, every time he saw her. Tiff had to stop this somehow. There was no way she was going to give up her man easily. Especially now that they had bought their first home together. Her head was in a turmoil of disturbing thoughts as she sat on the toilet seat, fully clothed. *Joe Frey is mine... you'll have to kill me first, Georgie-effing-ford, before you'll ever get your grubby little claws into him. Dirty little bitch.*

Chapter 21

"Where have you been?" Hayley pulled Tiff back into the line and put an arm round her shoulders.

"Sorry, there was a long queue in the toilets."

"We all thought you'd gone home." Hayley giggled. "Only joking – but I think Joe was getting a bit worried, bless him."

Tiff peered around to see Joe and Wayne sitting at their table, stuffing their faces with hot dogs and burgers. She watched as Joe took a bite from his hot dog, scanned the room briefly, like he was searching for something, or someone and then washed his mouthful down with a long, drawn-out swig from his beaker of beer. He looked decidedly drunk by the way he was making heavy-handed gestures.

"Tiff?"

Startled, Tiff turned back to see that they had reached the front of the queue.

Georgie grinned. "Hi Tiff, what would you like? Burger, cheeseburger or a hot dog?"

"Err..." Tiff pretended to be thinking when actually, she was a little flummoxed by Georgie's apparent politeness. "I'll have a hot dog please."

"Onions?"

"Yes, please."

Georgie's long, blonde hair had been tied up at the back in a messy bun. Ringlets hung down both sides of her pretty face. Her eyes were round and dark with mascara and eyeliner which had been perfectly applied. *Bitch!*

Tiff peered closer, just inside the collar of her blouse. "Oh – are you OK, Georgie?" Leaning into the hatch, she beckoned to Georgie to move closer.

"Pardon?"

"Looks like you've got a rash on your neck. Are you feeling OK?"

Georgie pulled back, wiped her hands on a paper towel and placed one hand inside the collar of her blouse. Then she tugged at the collar, in an attempt to pull it further around her neck "Yes – I'm fine. I... I don't know what that is...it... well, I don't know. It keeps popping up."

"I'd get it looked at, if I were you. See your doctor."

Without moving her head, Tiff swivelled her eyes sideways to check that Hayley wasn't listening. She wasn't. Hayley was talking incessantly with the other woman, like they'd known each other for years. A young man behind her, had also joined in their jesting banter.

"Yes, maybe I will. Anyway... here's your hot dog. The sauces are over there, on the table." Georgie pointed a finger behind Tiff. "Enjoy the evening" She shot a cursory grin at Tiff and then turned to the next person in the queue. "Yes – what would you like, Joyce?"

"Where've you been my b-a-a-a-by?" Joe's voice slurred.

Tiff pulled a chair out and sat down. "Toilet – why?" she replied, sharply.

Joe brushed a tendril of hair from the side of her face and stroked her neck. "I missed you."

"Did you?" she sneered in a hushed voice. "Thought you were too busy chatting at the counter."

Joe pulled his head back and frowned. "Babe, I was being polite. I could hardly leave Wayne at the counter and completely ignore Georgie," he whispered.

Wayne looked up and smiled, his cheeks stuffed with food.

Tiff reciprocated with a cringe-worthy grin, desperately hoping that he hadn't heard any of their conversation over the hubbub of laughter and talking all around.

Wayne turned away, unaware, and watched as Hayley came wobbling over to the table with a plate filled with two hot dogs and two burgers.

"Got some extras, in case you boys are still hungry."

Both Joe and Wayne stared at the plate with wide eyes. "You first," said Wayne, holding a hand out and gesturing to the plate.

Joe grabbed another hot dog and dropped it on to his plate. "Thanks," he said, eyeing Hayley and then Wayne. "I'm bloody starving."

Peering down at her own hot dog, Tiff pushed it around the plate, picked a piece of bread from the roll and popped it in her mouth. She didn't want it, although she was quite hungry. Georgie had put it together and piled onions on the top. She despised Georgie. She despised Georgie's hot dog. Of course, it might have been poisoned anyway because, didn't Georgie despise her too? "Do you want mine?" Tiff asked, looking at Joe disdainfully. "I'm not really hungry."

"Babe, you've had nothing to eat," Joe mumbled, between chewing his mouthful.

Tiff shrugged nonchalantly. "Not hungry anymore."

Pouring another beaker of wine, full to the very top, Tiff sipped at her drink while she watched the others heartily munch their way through the food.

"Ten minutes, ladies and gents," came Charlie's voice, through the microphone. "Feed that grey-matter but prepare to be discombobulated."

The sounds from the crowd rose.

"A little teaser while you finish eating, ladies and gentlemen. What does it mean? Discombobulated."

"Sounds to me a bit like someone called Bob has been decapitated," said Hayley, indifferently.

Wayne peered at his wife and smirked.

"Think it means, confused, or something like that." Tiff smiled weakly. *A bit like I feel now*, she thought to herself.

Joe was so wrapped up in his hot dogs that he remained silent and didn't even offer any appreciation of Tiff's knowledgeable contribution.

He tried once. Then twice. Then again, he reached out for her hand. Tiff snatched it away as they staggered along the road, behind Hayley and Wayne. Their team had come twelfth out of twenty-two. Hayley and Wayne had been delighted and exclaimed that they had, never before, achieved such a high score. They had all, including Joe, put their success down to Tiff's efforts. Tiff, on the other hand, couldn't have cared less as she blundered through the rest of the evening in a bleary-eyed state. Drunk. As pissed as she could possibly get on one and a half bottles of wine. Deliberately drunk. Unlike Joe, who had been sloshed earlier, but was now sobering up.

Joe peered down at her and screwed his face into a questioning frown. "Babe, hold my hand."

"No," she grumped. "I just want to get home."

"I'll pull you along – come on." Once more, he extended a hand towards hers.

She shunned his offer and continued to sway from one side to the other as she navigated her way along the footpath. "I'll be just fine, walking on my own, thank you."

"Thanks for coming, we'll have to do that again sometime," Hayley chirped in a high-pitched, giggly tone. "Tiff – you're the best. Next time we'll smash it."

Tiff smiled and rolled her eyes. "I was just lucky. I'm really not that intelligent. But thank you, both of you."

Joe sneaked up behind her and wrapped his arms round her waist. "Yes you are intelligent and beautiful to go with it," he breathed into her ear, before kissing it.

Shrugging him off, Tiff gave Hayley a sheepish grin. "Thanks for inviting us. I'm sure we'll do it again."

Hayley nodded her head, "See you again soon then."

"Golf next Saturday. Cheers mate," said Wayne, taking hold of Joe's hand and shaking it.

Joe nodded and patted his new-found friend on the back. "Thanks mate. Good night."

"Bye," Hayley called from her front door. "See you soon."

"Bye," said Tiff as they wandered away down the path around Sycamore Close.

"What's wrong with you?" Joe enquired as they both undressed in the bedroom.

"Nothing."

"Yes there is babe. You've been off with me all night."

Tiff stopped, mid-way through removing her jeans. "I saw her... holding your bloody hand."

"What?"

"When you were talking to her."

"Are you referring to Georgie when you say, 'her'?"

"Georgie. Georgie-pie – kissed the boys and made them high. Yes – who else do you think I'm freaking well talking about?" Tiff held her breath momentarily, this was not going to go well, she could sense it.

"Oh, for Christ's sake Tiff. I thought we'd moved on from that."

"Hoping, more like. Hoping I'd forget about it." Tiff pulled the legs of her jeans off, violently.

"Come on babe..." Joe started to crawl over the bed towards her. "You know how much I love you."

"Huh – how would you like it if I held someone's hand?"

"I did not hold anyone's bloody hand. And certainly not Georgie's."

"I saw you."

"You must be seeing things then. I'm going to sleep – before this gets any worse." Joe slid under the quilt and turned on his side.

"Yeah – that's right. Hide away. Guiltily." She turned the light out and remained seated on the edge of the bed, still partially clothed. "I'm going to visit my mum and dad tomorrow. You can do what you want. I'm sure you'll enjoy a day without me around to disturb you."

"Oh babe, this has got to stop. I did not hold Georgie's hand."

"I saw you. I need to get away from this place. I'm going, tomorrow."

"Do you want me to come?"

"No. You've got things to do, haven't you?" Tiff paused for a moment, in the gloom. "And it's you I need to get away from."

"Babe?"

"I'm serious. Goodnight Joe."

Had she really said all of that last night? Why didn't she just sort things out with him? Probably because he was snoring within 30 seconds of his head hitting the pillow. But maybe he wouldn't remember the conversation this morning anyway. Yes, he would because he'd asked if he should go with her. *Damn.* Now she would have to travel to her parent's house, some 50 miles away and hope that her visit was 'convenient'. At least it might get a point across to Joe that she would not tolerate him holding other women's hands. Or anything else for that matter.

Hi Dad, how's it going? I was wondering if you and Mum would like a visit today. Only me – Joe is busy with things in the house. I can't wait for you both to come down and see it. Love Tiffany xxxx

Her dad was her everything. Her mum was not quite her everything. Her mum was not as nurturing as her dad was. She used to be… but not now.

Morning sweet-cheeks! You want to travel all the way home – for a day? I'm not at home this weekend. Conference in Birmingham. Why don't you come for the weekend, next week? We can put both of you up. Love Dad xx And we will get down to yours as soon as possible. But you know what your mum's like!

Good idea, thanks Dad. I might even come on my own. Joe is up to his neck in jobs – not only our jobs but half the neighbours too, ha ha xxxx explain when I see you. Love ya! x

Tiff put her phone on the dining table and stared out of the patio doors. Yes, she did know exactly what her mum was like. It was quite inhibiting for her dad, yet he always managed to grin his way through it and shrug it off. Her mum had a fear of travelling, whether it be by car, boat, train or plane. Even a bicycle ride had put the fear of God into her once. The only type of travel she could tolerate, and it was a very short journey of no more than two stops, was her bus journey to work and back each day. Tiff had always known that her moving so far away would cause problems for her mum. Their relationship had been a little strained ever since the day that Tiff told her parents she was leaving. That wouldn't have been so bad on its own but to tell her mum she would be leaving *and* moving 50 miles away was the bit that upset her mum so much.

Joe appeared in the dining room, wearing a pair of grey shorts and a white t-shirt, looking like a sun-kissed Chinese man. The skin around his eyes was puffy, making them appear like two slits on his two-tone face. Luckily, he was one of those people who could get burnt by the sun one day and have a glorious tan by the next. Except there was still a trace of the redness along the length of his nose this morning.

"Babe…" he said in a huskier than normal voice, "can we talk? Please don't go to your mum and dad's."

"I'm not," she snapped back.

"Good." Joe stared at her longingly. "We can sort this out."

"I'm going next weekend instead."

"Fair enough." Joe flicked the kettle on and turned back to peer at her. "I've been thinking... about what you said last night."

"Bet you have."

"No, Tiff, you've got it all wrong. I remember now."

"Go on then."

"It was when I said to her that I would go round today – to pick up the fence." Joe threw a tea bag into a mug. "Do you want one?"

"Got one," she replied, stiffly.

"OK, well... anyway, that was when she put her hand on mine. She said something like 'of course you can'. That was all it was babe."

"Why did she have to hold your hand?"

"She didn't hold it – she patted it."

"Didn't look like a pat to me. Why touch you at all?"

"I really don't know babe. Maybe she's just a tactile person. One thing I do know – I wish to God she hadn't." His face was one of pitiful sadness.

Tiff resisted a powerful urge to get up from her chair and leap into his arms and embrace him. "So do I."

"I even considered selling up and moving, last night."

"Well that's just bloody stupid."

"I don't know how else to prove to you, prove how much I love you and that I do not fancy her."

Tiff peered out to the garden, without replying. What was she doing? Why was this happening? Was it because she'd seen so much and knew so much about Georgie that she couldn't get her out of her head and could only see a bad side to the woman?

"I don't want to get the fence today babe – that's how much you mean to me – I'd rather go and buy a new one."

Maybe she did need the break. Maybe going to her parent's house next weekend would be a good thing for both of them. "Just get it. I'm sure I'll get over her."

"Why do you hate her so much? You should try to make friends with her. She's not that bad."

"There you go, defending her again."

"I'm not defending her, babe. I'm defending you."

"How the freaking hell are you defending me?"

Joe filled his mug with boiling water and turned to look her straight in the eyes. "From yourself," he muttered, waveringly. "From your own self-destruction."

"Oh, here we go again." Tiff shoved her chair out from under her and stormed out of the dining room as tears welled in her eyes and her stomach churned. "You turn it all around, on to me, don't you?" she shouted out. She shot up the stairs, two at a time, and into the bedroom, before slamming the door shut. Her heart raced as adrenaline surged through her body. Why? Why was she treating him like this? Why couldn't she believe him? She could lose him if she carried on being so jealous. Yet, there was something not right about any of it. She definitely needed that break away and maybe the time apart would clarify things. Or at its worst, give Joe and Georgie the opportunity to really get it together. That would clarify everything and simply be the end.

The bedroom door opened and Joe peeped his head around the door. "I'm going to Lilly's now."

Tiff nodded her head. "OK."

"Then I'll go to Betty's – get the birds sorted out. I don't mind doing it. Stay here babe and have a chilled-out day."

Again, Tiff nodded as little tears began to develop. "OK, and... I'm sorry."

Joe opened the door fully and stepped in. "You don't have to be sorry babe. I know how it must have seemed." He reached the side of the bed and sat down next to her. "I don't know how many times or how else I can show you that I love you. I want to spend the rest of my life with you." Putting an arm round her back, he pulled her closer and kissed the top of her head. "Speak to Georgie, babe. That might make you feel better."

Tears dropped on to Tiff's cheeks and she wiped them away instantly. "If I..." she stuttered, "If I carry on... like this... you won't want to spend the rest of your life with me."

"You won't carry on like this," breathed Joe and hugged her tightly. "Because one day, I will prove it to you."

"Prove?"

"Prove how much I love you."

Tiff sighed heavily, "I know you will. I'm so sorry. I really don't know what's got into me lately."

"Don't be sorry. Let's try and forget it and move on."

"Do you want me to come and help you at Betty's."

"You don't have to babe – if you don't feel up to it."

"No, I will. I'm sorry. I'll come over to Lilly's with you too."

"Are you sure?"

"I'm sure, just give me ten minutes to sort myself out."

Joe pulled himself up from the bed. "OK, I'll make a quick drink for us. We can have one before we go." He smiled, lovingly, and left the room.

Tiff shivered as tears flowed freely from her eyes. When she was with him, she believed in him. The rest of the time she doubted him.

"Hello Lilly. I thought you weren't in for a minute there." Tiff grinned. "Joe's here, to do your hedge for you."

"He's a good man. Joe, please come through and collect it. I've pulled my back out. I suppose that it serves me right. I shouldn't have pulled the damn thing indoors last night. I should have left it under the hedge. It would have been safe there."

"Oh no, can you manage – indoors, I mean. Do you need me to help you with anything?"

"Oh no, dearie. Stubborn as the mule – that's what they call me. I can manage. But thank you."

Joe stepped into the dark, antiquated hallway.

"Just along there, dearie. See?"

Joe nodded his head and shuffled along the narrow corridor. "Good grief – this really is a bit of a monster, Lilly. How on earth did you…"

"I didn't dearie. That's why you are here and my backbone is not."

Joe shook his head and picked up the trimmer. "I can't believe you even attempted it. I'd think twice about using something like this."

"Oh, I can assure you, I did think twice…" Lilly gave a little giggle. "Upon thrice, I decided to give it a bash."

Tiff smiled and shook her head from side to side, amusedly. "You are dangerously amazing."

"Why do you think that dearie?"

"Well, just because you are prepared to give things a go, no matter how difficult they might be and at such an age."

"Age has nothing to do with it dearie. My head thinks it's still 18. It's only the body that says differently."

Joe stepped out of the house backwards, carrying the lump of machinery, and kept reversing until the end of the blade was outside of the front door. He peered down at Lilly and raised his eyebrows. "I still can't believe you even considered attempting this on your own."

"Do it, not think about doing it. That's always been my ethos. And 'considering' comes under the category of thinking." Lilly gave Joe a stern look. "Life is far too short to be thinking, rather than doing, dearie."

"You're probably right there. But sometimes it's probably safer to think and *not*, do."

Tiff pulled a dustbin liner from the carrier bag she was holding. "I've bought some bags along to put the trimmings in. Would you like us to take it all to the tip for you?"

"Oh, no dearie. Keep your bags – please put them away. I have some in the kitchen, if you'll just give me a minute to fetch them."

"But we can..."

"No. I won't have you using up your bags. You will need those yourself."

"But..." Tiff started to say.

"No buts. I will get some. Bear with me dearie. But that would be very helpful if you could take them to the tip for me." Lilly turned and began to make her way, awkwardly, down the hallway. With a hand placed on her back, just above her hip, she waddled off into the darkness.

"She doesn't look very good with her back, does she?" Tiff said in a hushed voice.

Joe shook his head and crouched down to examine the petrol motor of the trimmer. "Well... here goes," he said as he started up the motor and picked it up determinedly.

Lilly had been quite adamant that the hedges should be chopped down at least by several feet. The amount of trimmings was astronomical and Tiff had given up after five bin liners full. "What are we going to do with all this?" she asked Joe as he put the trimmer down on to the grass and stretched his back out.

"We'll have to burn it – there's just too much of it. We'd be running down the tip all week with this lot."

"Burn it? Where?"

Joe peered down at Lilly's front lawn and frowned. "Can't do it here really. She'll end up with a big scorch mark in the middle of her lawn."

"Where then?"

Joe thought for a moment. "We could take it to ours?"

"But..."

"We haven't done our garden yet – we could burn it at the back." Joe grinned and added, "Get some marshmallows and we can toast them on the fire."

"Oh, very funny." He was doing his best to be funny. To make Tiff laugh. And most of the time he was succeeding.

Joe started the motor up again and moved outside to the pathway and began to trim the hedge from the other side.

"Lilly," Tiff called through the dim hallway. "Lilly."

A moment later the hallway lit up as Lilly opened a door at the far end. Tiff could now see that the shabby, brown wallpaper curled away from the walls at the top revealing mottled black damp patches in places.

"Yes dearie?"

"There's so much rubbish to get rid of here – I'm on my fifth bag already. We've decided to take it all over to ours and burn it in the garden."

"Your garden? Why would you want to take all of that to your garden dearie?" Lilly reached the front door and peered out at the hedge cuttings laying in big piles around the lawn.

Tiff looked at the piles and then the five bags, already filled and overflowing. "We haven't done anything to our garden yet – it wouldn't be a problem to take it all round there and burn it."

"Bring it through here then dearie. You can go out through my back gate, if you'd like. It will be easier to take that way. You do have a back gate don't you?"

"Err... no we don't but we could throw it over the fence. We have a low fence at the back."

Lilly stroked her chin, thoughtfully. "Hmm… you might want to get some higher fences dearie. And a gate. With a nice big padlock. Strange things happen around here."

"Why do you say that?" Tiff shot a cursory glance across the garden to where Joe was, on the other side of the hedge. The sound of the motor ensured that he couldn't hear the conversation at the front door.

"There are some strange goings-on out the back dearie."

"Strange? What do you mean, strange?"

Lilly shrugged her shoulders. "Just strange."

Tiff frowned. "You've got me worried now, are we safe?"

"Oh, I am sure you are quite safe dearie."

"So what do you mean by strange?" Tiff leant closer to Lilly. "I'm very curious."

"Let's just say that there is far more to the wildlife, across those fields and up to the river, than what first meets the eye."

Tiff eyed Lilly with a puzzled expression on her face. "You've got me completely flummoxed," she lied. "Please tell me what you mean?"

"That's all I'm saying dearie – now, would you like to start bringing those bags through?"

"Yes, sure," Tiff replied, reluctantly.

In stark contrast, the dark, dingy hallway was not anything to go by, compared to the rest of the ground floor of Lilly's house. Bright and breezy, the living room and kitchen/diner were extremely old-fashioned yet neat, tidy and clean. As Tiff carried two bags through the house, she marvelled at the vast collection of highly polished horse brasses, pinned to leather straps and hanging in rows above a cast iron fireplace, surrounded by a beige marble mantelpiece. Bunches of satin flowers sat in vases, baskets and ornamental watering cans, around the hearth. The décor throughout was certainly an odd mix of bits and pieces of bygone ages but all were perfectly placed, dust-free and intact.

Finally, Tiff reached the garden, having slowly walked behind a hobbling Lilly, and stepped out, through the back door. Waterfalls, fountains and just about every conceivable type of garden water feature that Tiff had ever seen, filled the entire garden. Some were small while others were taller than Joe. Gravel paths weaved in, out and around statues and other stone sculptures, like a maze. "Wow, Lilly, this is amazing."

"Why thank you, dearie. Follow me. This way. I'm quite sure you'll be able to carry those bags through here." Lilly limped off along a path on the left, which looked like it would end at the fence which adjoined Betty and Cyril's garden. Turning sharply to the right, she guided Tiff down another pathway. Then another sharp turn to the left. Right, left, right.

"It's like a maze. I can't believe it." Tiff wondered if she might be walking round in circles.

"It is a maze. Nearly there, dearie."

Tiff passed by terracotta urns and stone pitchers, fountains with frogs and giant granite balls, columns and pillars, barrels with pumps and granite cascading bowls, all of which were flowing with water. "Sounds like I'm at Niagara Falls."

Lilly turned and gave a fleeting grin, before continuing to navigate her way through the winding paths to the back gate.

"Here we are dearie," she said as she pulled a key from her skirt pocket. "Do you think you can find your way back through, in a minute?"

"I think so," Tiff replied, doubtfully. "Well, I do hope so."

"I can wait here for you, if you'd like me to."

"I'm sure I'll be fine. I'll call for help if I get stuck." Tiff let out a short laugh and went through the gate as Lilly held it open.

Apart from a couple of horses lazing in the sun, in the distance, the fields were empty. Along the pathways, the trees stood motionless and not a hint or a flicker of gold pants could be seen anywhere. In the distance the river sparkled under the blazing sun and just for a moment, Tiff thought about how lucky she was to have such a beautiful scene, right at the back of her house. There were just a certain couple of *things* that spoiled it.

She carried the bags to the back of her own fence and emptied them over the side. She had never been on this side of the fence before and it seemed quite odd to be looking at her house from the other side.

Navigating her way back through the maze of pathways and bubbling, fizzing, cascading water, Tiff politely tapped on the back door before entering Lilly's house.

Lilly was sitting in her antiquated dining room, sipping at a cup of tea. "Found your way back, dearie?"

"Yes, just about." Tiff glanced at the drink in Lilly's hands and then quickly stole her eyes away from it. "I'll go and get some more bags. Are you sure you don't mind me going through your back garden?"

"Not at all, dearie. I don't mind at all. You carry on."

Tiff smiled weakly and walked through to the front garden.

Joe was still busy trimming as she stepped outside. She grabbed two more bags and turned on her heels, entering the gloom of the hallway again.

It was thirsty work, trimming hedges and karting the cuttings backwards and forwards through Lilly's house and exceptionally beautiful back garden, yet Tiff had noticed how both her and Joe hadn't been offered a drink of any description, not even a glass of water.

Joe placed the trimmer on the lawn and moped his brow. "Think that's it," he said, wiping his brow again as beads of sweat continued to trickle down his forehead.

"Good." Tiff rolled her eyes upwards. "That's nine bags now." She turned her head to make sure that Lilly wasn't lingering in her hallway. "And not a hint of a cup of tea, or a cold drink. Not even a drop of water."

Joe shrugged. "Not to worry – we can nip home for one, before we go to Betty's."

Tiff nodded and turned the corners of her mouth down. "Yes OK, but first, I've saved a couple of bags for you to take through and I'll take the last two." Tiff began to pick up the last cuttings from the pavement.

"Why?" Joe's reddening face frowned.

"You have got to see her garden."

"OK," he said, indifferently. "Let's go."

"Thank you very much," said Lilly, holding on to the front door frame. "It looks absolutely wonderful. I can see the close again." She smiled warmly and watched as Tiff and Joe strolled away with aching backs, burning skin and parched throats.

"Hang on a sec," said Tiff, as they reached Betty's house. "I'll quickly tell Betty that we'll be round as soon as we've had a bit of lunch and a drink."

"OK, I'll go and put the kettle on." Joe grinned and pinched her bottom as she opened Betty's gate.

"Oi." She giggled. "Behave." As she trotted up the path to Betty's door, she smirked at Joe who was now walking up their pathway.

"See you in a minute," he mouthed, across the gardens.

"Hello Betty." Tiff grinned at the friendly little face peeping around the door. "We – as in me and Joe, will be round to clean the birds in about half an hour. Would that be OK?"

"Oh, thank you Tiff. That is so very kind of you."

"Don't mention it. How's Cyril? Have you heard any more?"

Betty opened the door further and smiled. "I called the hospital this morning – he's doing very well." She paused in thought for a moment. "I was going to visit him this afternoon. You don't suppose I could give you a key, do you?"

"Err… yes, if that's OK with you, but will you be around long enough to show us what we need to do?"

"Oh yes, I was going to go over there about three o'clock. That should be plenty of time."

"OK, thanks. We're just having a bit of lunch and a much needed drink, then we'll be round."

Betty nodded her head and grinned. "I heard you over there this morning." She turned her head and peered at the bushes. "It looks much better now. Is Lilly pleased with it?"

"Seems to be."

"Good. You and Joe are such good, helpful people."

Tiff shrugged her shoulders. "Thank you, right, I'd better get going. We'll be round in the next half an hour."

"Thank you Tiff."

"You're more than welcome." And Tiff really meant it as far as Betty was concerned.

Chapter 22

"Told Betty we'd be there in half an hour."

"Cool," said Joe, placing a cold drink in front of her.

"Can't believe that Lilly didn't even offer us a drink." Tiff gulped down the fresh orange juice quickly. "She had one herself, while we were there – I saw her drinking tea."

"Maybe she didn't think to offer us one."

"She could see how hot *you* were. At the very least she could have offered you one. Or some water at least."

"Well it's done now. It doesn't matter."

Joe strolled back to the table carrying two plates loaded with sandwiches and crisps. "Bet you're glad you didn't go to your mum and dad's today," he said sarcastically.

"Huh – would have been offered a drink."

"Well I'm glad that you didn't and even if we are doing jobs for other people, I'm having a good time because you're here."

Tiff feigned a gagging reflex. "You are such a smoothie, Joe Frey."

He picked up his cheese and ham sandwich and shoved almost half of it into his mouth as his phone tinkled in the pocket of his shorts. He stopped chewing momentarily and gulped. Rolling his eyes, he shook his head and then continued to chew the rest of the sandwich, filling his cheeks.

"Are you going to see who it is?"

"Wayne," Joe mumbled through a full mouth. "Golf probably."

"How do you know that?" Tiff eyed him suspiciously. "Didn't you sort that out last night?"

"Thought we did." Joe gulped again and quickly drew his phone from his pocket. He peered down at it, moved his thumb around the screen and popped it back into his pocket. "Wayne, asking if I have a hangover." Joe grinned sheepishly and stuffed another large piece of sandwich in his mouth, followed quickly by several crisps.

Tiff looked down at her plate and picked up a single crisp. She popped into her mouth and sucked at the salty flavour. "Aren't you going to reply then?"

"Tiff – what is this? Every time my phone goes off, I get the third degree." Joe gulped hard again. "I'll reply to him later. I'm enjoying eating my sandwich at the moment. Come on, eat yours. We've got to start again in 20 minutes."

Tiff sighed and picked up her sandwich. She had suddenly gone right off her food again.

"Come through," said Betty, leading the way out to the back garden. She turned and smiled as they reached the first aviary. "Could I just tell you what needs to be done – rather than actually help. I've just changed, ready to go to the hospital."

"Yes, of course. We didn't expect you to do any of it anyway." Joe smiled back.

"You look lovely Betty," said Tiff, admiringly.

Betty brushed-up pretty well for a woman of her age. Dressed in a *Vivien of Holloway* navy and white polka-dot circle skirt, a three-inch-wide, white, elastic belt and a white raglan blouse, she looked like a 1950s model, albeit an ageing model. Her tiny heeled, white ballet pumps completed her look.

"Oh," she said in a high pitched voice, "thank you, this is my best outfit. I thought I'd wear it to the hospital today." Betty lovingly brushed the skirt down and twisted the belt around her waist.

"Cyril will be delighted to see you. You look radiant."

Betty's cheeks coloured, through her already powdered pink face. "Why thank you, Tiff, you are such a sweet girl. Do come in," she said, opening the aviary door.

Tiff and Joe followed Betty into the foul-smelling aviary.

"Now, it is a bit whiffy in here, I'm afraid. The poor birds are long overdue a clean." She bent over and picked up two scoops. "Cyril didn't get anything done really, the other day, before... his heart went." She smiled falteringly. "Anyway, these are for collecting the mess on the floor of the cages and these..." she grabbed a packet of gravel sheets, "are clean sheets. That's all there is to it really."

"What about food and water?" Joe asked as he took the scoops and sheets.

"I came in early this morning. I can do their food and water each day. It's just all the scooping out and reaching inside the cages that I struggle with. I am so grateful to you both for doing that."

"Not a problem," said Joe, "and you only need this doing once a week?"

"We can certainly get away with once a week," Betty paused and stared out of one of the square windows, "Cyril's always out here, pottering about. He cleans them when they need doing. Sometimes two or three times a week, but that's just because he gets bored, I'm sure."

"I don't mind coming over twice a week if you want me to," said Joe.

"Wouldn't dream of it. You have your own home to look after – on top of going to work." She handed a tiny set of keys to Joe. "These are for the little padlocks here – see?" Betty picked up a lock, hanging from one of the cages. "You'll need to keep the main door firmly closed when you open the cages. They do like to have a little flutter about."

"OK." Joe peered at Tiff and opened his eyes wide, conveying worry. "What if... what if they won't go back in the cages?"

"Oh they will. I was just going to say that you can also hang some small bags of dried fruit inside, once you've cleaned them. The birds love it and it brings them back into the cages in no time." Betty smiled and patted Joe gently on the back. "Just here, in this box. One bag for each cage."

"OK."

"Now," said Betty, turning to a shelf behind her, "you'll need some gloves and I have an antiseptic hand wash here for when you've finished."

Joe and Tiff nodded their heads simultaneously.

"Looks like we have everything we might need," said Tiff, grinning at Joe.

"Now, before you start, I'm sure you might be able to manage a cup of tea and some fruit cake." Betty moved towards the door. "And if you really don't mind, I'll give you the keys so you can lock the doors behind you when you leave. Would you be so kind as to post them back through the letterbox?"

"Yes, of course," Tiff replied. "And we would love a quick cup of tea before you leave, wouldn't we Joe? Thank you."

"Yes – thanks." Joe put the tiny keys in his pocket and followed Betty and Tiff through the door.

While they were eating cake and drinking their tea, Joe's phone tinkled again. Tiff peered across the table at him but said nothing. He pulled the phone from his pocket and appeared to turn it off completely. He looked across at Tiff and smiled uncomfortably.

"The cake was lovely. Thank you."

Betty rolled a blue plastic mac into a neat roll and stuffed it in her handbag. "It might be chilly by the time I leave the hospital this evening."

"Please, wish Cyril well for us." Tiff smiled waveringly as she cursed at herself, for not making a 'Get Well Soon' card for him. It wouldn't have taken her long to do this morning. *Joe's fault really*, she thought as the crushing suspicions engulfed her again. His phone never went off on a Sunday. Was it really Wayne?

"I most definitely will and thank you again for helping me. Goodbye." Betty grinned so much that her little face scrunched up. She picked up her bag and left with a little spring in her step.

It had certainly been an experience cleaning the bird cages. On many occasions Tiff had yelped as a lovebird landed on the top of her head. Joe found the whole encounter highly amusing, and more so because the birds seemed to be attracted to Tiff more than they were to him. He hadn't had one bird land on him.

Tiff locked the front door of Betty's house and posted the keys back through the letterbox, as instructed, while Joe gazed at the hedge next door.

"Wayne's down there," said Tiff pointing to a figure, seated on the ground, painting the fence of number eight. "Afternoon, Wayne!" she shouted.

"Tiff." Joe tugged her by the arm. "Leave it – I'm knackered. I need a kip. Let's just go indoors," he whispered.

Wayne looked up and waved his paintbrush in the air. Then he heaved himself up from the floor and strolled up the path. "Thought I'd better get our fence painted – you've set the benchmark around here."

Joe smirked and peered down at his feet.

"So, did *you* have a hangover, Wayne? Joe looked really rough this morning." Tiff giggled. "Did he reply to you?"

"Reply?"

"Yes – didn't you message him this morning – asking if he had a hangover?"

"Err..." Wayne shifted his gaze quickly away from Tiff to Joe and back again to Tiff, without actually meeting her eyes. Then he peered down at the ground and shifted his feet from side to side. "Err... yes... well, I think so anyway." He turned and desperately searched Joe's face again. "I was still drunk this morning – must have texted you without realising." Wayne let out a nervous laugh.

"Yeah, probably mate," Joe mumbled. "Well, we'd better get off now – we're going to put our feet up for an hour. Come on Tiff."

"Yes, OK. See you later mate." Wayne shot a swift, shifty glance at Tiff. "See you again soon Tiff." He then turned and hurried off, back to his fence.

Tiff said nothing and walked to their front door and opened it. Once inside, she turned to face Joe who was just closing the door behind him. "So it wasn't Wayne who texted you this morning."

Joe frowned. "Yes it was. He just said so. He forgot."

"How can he forget that he's texted someone, just a few hours ago?"

"I don't know." Joe stepped past and headed for the kitchen. "Do you want a cold drink?"

"Yes please, I don't believe you though Joe. I could tell Wayne didn't know what I was talking about."

"He's probably still pissed now."

"Oh, don't be stupid." She sat down at the table and rubbed her hands around her face. "Joe, I don't believe you. Who texted you?"

"I told you, Wayne."

"Let me see then?" The usual queasy feeling, that appeared every time the conversation with Joe became heated, was beginning to resurface and she had to swallow hard. "Let me see your phone."

"Tiff." Joe's voice had risen in tone. "Why don't you believe me?"

"Just let me see, then I will believe you and I won't bother you again."

Joe snatched two tall glasses from the cupboard, placed them on the kitchen top with a thud and grabbed the orange juice from the fridge. "I've deleted it."

"Oh, I see." Tiff snorted an artificial laugh. "Why would you go to the trouble of deleting a message when you've been so busy this morning?"

"I don't know – just did. Automatic I suppose."

"No it's not just automatic. You deleted it because you didn't want me to see it." Tiff held fast as her eyes prickled. "By the sound of it…" She gulped back the rising fear and sickness. "Wayne's covering up for you."

"Tiff – stop, please. You're doing it ag…"

She cut him short. "Doing what?"

"Letting insecurity get the better of you."

"Are you so surprised that I'm insecure? Wayne's in this with you. I just can't believe it."

"In what, babe?"

"Covering something up for you, he knows." Tiff couldn't stop the tears from escaping over the rim of her eyes. "What about Hayley? Is she covering up for you as well?"

"Babe," Joe looked as though he was about to cry too. "Please Babe, there is nothing going on."

"I don't believe you. Who was the second text from then? Don't tell me – that was from Wayne as well. Yes, of course it was Wayne because he'd forgotten he'd texted you the first time. And then, miraculously, he'd forgotten that he'd sent either text. Silly me, why didn't I think of it before. I suppose you've deleted that one as well, have you?"

Joe nodded his head, a deep frown marred his handsome, tanned face.

"You make yourself look suspicious Joe. Why delete messages so quickly, like you're hiding something?"

He shrugged and shook his head. "I don't know babe."

"Don't 'babe' me." She stood up and stared him in the eye. "I'm going to my mum's – I don't care if Dad's not there. I need a break – from you!" She turned away and left the room.

"Tiff," Joe called after her. "Please don't go. I need you here, with me. I promise babe. There is nothing funny going on."

Tiff ignored his plea and darted up the stairs in tears. She opened drawers, grabbed clothing and underwear and stuffed them all into a holdall. She opened the wardrobe and tore clothes from the hangers. In a rage, she stuffed a pair of shoes into the bag. Storming through to the bathroom she snatched up her toothbrush and a flannel and threw them into the bag too.

Joe appeared at the top of the stairs. "Please don't go babe. I love you. You must know that I do."

"I'm going – for a few days, at least," she muttered as she searched the bathroom for anything else she might need. "That'll give you enough time to sort your mess out and maybe you could even give Wayne a lesson on lying – he's totally useless at it!"

"But... what about your work?"

"I'm phoning in sick. Goodbye."

"Babe... please..."

Tiff tore down the stairs, grabbed her phone, the charger and her car keys. Yanking her coat from the hook she drew in a deep breath as she stopped by the front door. Wayne would be outside. She'd have to walk past him. He'd ask her where she was going. He'd see that she'd been crying. Turning back, she went to the front window and peered out across the green. He wasn't there. He must have finished or gone indoors for something. She went to the front door again. She'd have to make a run for it.

Joe had reached the bottom of the stairs and was hanging on to the newel post with a sullen expression across his face. "Tiff – please don't go. I love you more than anything."

"Need a bit of space. Hopefully, I'll be back – one day."

"You must come back – I love you."

As a lump filled Tiff's throat, she opened the door, checked the green for any neighbours and walked out. With her head held high, and trying to appear normal, she took a shortcut straight across the grass to the lay-by. When she reached her car, she glanced through her fringe, across the green to see Joe slumped against the door frame. She threw the holdall on to the passenger seat and climbed into her car. She drove away. Regretfully.

For the first 20 miles, Tiff drove on automatic pilot. The next five were spent wondering where the nearest petrol station was. Her mobile phone had beeped twice, indicating text messages, and had rung once.

She pulled into a garage and filled her car up. Then she drove into a small carpark, behind the garage and turned off the engine. This was the half-way mark. Did she carry on or turn back? She grabbed her phone from the bag. As expected, the missed call was from Joe and he'd left two messages.

Babe, please come back soon. I miss you already. Love Joe xxxx

I know things might have looked odd over the last few days but I can assure you, there is nothing odd going on in the slightest. It's all coincidence or misunderstandings. Please babe, come back soon. I love you xxxx

Tiff read the messages and the queasiness returned. She wanted to go back right away. Back to her home. Back to her job, tomorrow. Back to Joe. Be in his arms. But pride and a stubborn streak would not let her return. She had to make a stand. She had to show him that she was no push-over. She also had to give herself time to sort things out in her head. She knew her mind could play cruel tricks with her. She knew her head was capable of making up all sorts of bad things. This was her problem more than it was Joe's. She had to do something about it. She also had to get over the guilt of not going to work tomorrow as well.

I need a break away. To sort stuff out, in my head. I hope I will be back next weekend. I pray we can move on from this. You need to stop with all this secrecy and deleting messages. Your phone does have a memory you know. You can store messages in it! Thought you knew that already.

We will move on babe. I can't live without you. You are my whole world. Love you xxxx p.s. yes I know about the message storage, Tiff, I deleted them automatically. Don't know why xxxx

"Hello Mum – it's me," Tiff called out from the front door as she stepped inside.

"Tiffany? What?" Tiff's mum stood in the hallway wearing her old, tatty tracksuit and her 'gardening' trainers. Her round, rosy face looked completely surprised.

"I know I said to Dad that I'd come next weekend but..."

Her mum leapt towards her and flung her arms round her. "Oh, Tiffany, it's so lovely to see you darling."

Tiff eyed her mum in shock. She didn't usually get this type of response from her. Her dad, yes, but not her mum. Not since she'd left home anyway.

"I... err... can I stay for a few days or... maybe until Dad gets home?"

Her mum stared at her curiously. "Well, of course you can darling. But don't you have work? What about Joe? Where is he?"

"I've... got a week off. Joe couldn't get any time off at the moment as he's got a few training days away. We've... err... been doing lots of jobs in the house. I wanted to get away for a little while." Tiff cringed as the lies continued to pour out of her mouth. "It was Joe who said I should get away for a break while he's stuck on this training course, in... err... London."

"Come on," her mum said, reaching out for her hand and pulling her into the living room. "I'll make you a drink."

"Thank you." Tiff met her mum's eyes. "Are you alright Mum – it's just that you seem to be very pleased to see me."

"Oh, Tiffany," she sighed. "I've come to realise how much I've missed you. I know I was a little cranky when you left." She peered down at her trainers, thoughtfully. "But I was so sad and then, when you said that you were moving so far away I... I didn't know how to deal with it."

"Oh, Mum, come here." Tiff reached her arms out and hugged her mum tightly. "I'm not that far away. I can always come to see you, if you can't travel to mine."

"I'm working on that," said her mum, seriously. "I went to the doctors last week. I can get some therapy for it. And I *will* go on the short course that was offered to me." She looked up and smiled. "Apparently, they find out where your fear stems from and work from there."

"That's great news. Gosh Mum, your world will change so much if you can get over it."

Her mum nodded her head enthusiastically. "Yes, it will. It's costing your dad quite a bit though. They're private sessions."

"I bet he thinks it's worth it though."

"Yes, he does." Mum agreed. "Now let's make you a nice cup of tea and then if you'd like to, I could show you the new trees in the garden." She reached for Tiff's hand and led her through to the kitchen.

"I'd love to see the new trees, Mum but it's dark outside."

"Oh, don't worry yourself about that, we have outside lighting now." Mum beamed and squeezed Tiff's hand, excitedly. "They're changeable – you can have whatever colour you'd like when we go and have a look at them. Green looks the best."

"Cool, OK. That'll be great."

"And after that, we'll get you settled into your old room."

"Thanks Mum, it's so lovely to be back home for a few days."

Guess you're there by now. Hope your mum's OK – send her my love. Love you loads, Joe xxxx

Yes, here. Mum's fine.

However much she tried, Tiff couldn't bring herself to send a nice, lovey-dovey message, with kisses on. She wanted to, deep down. Yet, she couldn't do it.

Tiff's bedroom had been at the front of the house when she was a child, and it still was, but now it had been redecorated and turned into a guest room. Not that her parents ever had any guests staying. A small double bed had taken the place of Tiff's old, high-bed which had had a matching desk and shelving underneath. And her pink, flowery wallpaper had been replaced with a beige and brown striped paper which, along with the matching bedding, made the room look and feel like a hotel room. A cheap one at that. Yet, it was a place to stay. A place to get away from the torment, jealousy and anger she couldn't help but feel for Joe. And for Georgie too.

Opening her holdall, she pulled the shoes from it. Odd shoes. In her moment of rage and tears, she'd managed to pick up two different shoes. She tutted to herself and looked down at the tatty old trainers she was wearing, still covered in green stains from the hedge trimmings, earlier in the day. Adding to the overall grubby appearance was a slight yellowy-brown tinge across the tops, from a misplaced scoop of slushy bird droppings which she managed to drop on to her trainers, completely missing the rubbish bag earlier. At the time, Joe had bitten his lip in an attempt not to laugh as she tried to scrub the mess away, creating colourful smears across the once-white canvas of her trainers.

I'm going to bed now babe, got a headache. Hope you will have a nice break with your mum and dad. Tell them I said 'hello'. Miss you madly. I'll call you tomorrow. Love you more than you could ever imagine. Joe xxxx

Goodnight Joe.

And don't forget to phone work and call in sick – or do you want me to do it? xxxx

I'll do it myself thanks, goodnight.

Chapter 23

"I'm off to work now," Tiff's mum whispered through the partially opened door. "Help yourself to breakfast. I've got some muffins in the cupboard – you always liked muffins"

"Thanks Mum." Tiff peeped over the top of the quilt and smiled. "What time are you home?"

"Around two, depending on the bus. They've changed the routes of some of the buses now and completely removed other services altogether."

"Oh, OK."

Mum sighed. "If I want to get a bus into town, from here, I have to walk down to the bus stop on Hillhead Road now – it's ridiculous."

Tiff pulled the quilt down and sat up. "Mum, I need to go into town today. I brought the wrong shoes with me. Do you fancy coming with me, after work?"

"Oh... I..."

"How about I pick you up from school? It's five minutes in the car from your school."

"Well... I..."

"I will drive extremely slowly. It's not as if I could go fast anyway, what with the new one-way system."

Mum nodded her head unconvincingly. "Yes, OK, I suppose I've got to start somewhere. Pick me up at 1.15pm then. If you're staying this week, I could also do with popping into *Sainsbury's*. Just to pick up a few extra bits. Would that be all right?"

"Yes, of course it would. See you at quarter past one."

"Hello."

"Hello babe, how are you? Did you sleep well?"

"Not bad, I guess. Did you?" Tiff gulped hard. The queasiness was creeping into her throat again but with a sad, loneliness about it this time.

"Didn't sleep hardly at all." There was a melancholic tone to Joe's voice. "The bed's too big without you in it."

"Oh..."

"What are you doing?"

"Nothing." The stilted conversation was heartrending. "Aren't you supposed to be at work?"

"I am at work babe. I... I had to call you... to speak to you. To hear your voice. I miss you Tiff."

"Oh, OK."

"I bumped into Wayne this morning. He said to say sorry that he'd been a bit hungover yesterday and a bit disconcerting."

"Did he." Tiff sighed heavily, down the phone.

"Are you all right?"

"Yes."

"When will you be coming home babe?"

"I'll stay until Dad gets home. He's back on Friday night."

"So... will you come home on Saturday?"

"Hope so." Tiff hated herself for giving such short answers but she couldn't bring herself to say anything else.

"Thank God for that."

"Why do you say that?"

"I just can't wait for you to come home babe – where you belong."

"OK."

"Did you call work?"

"Yes."

"What did you say?"

"Said I had suspected tonsillitis and I would let them know for sure, once I'd been to the doctors."

"And they were fine about it?"

"Yes, I've never had a day off sick, remember?" Tiff sighed down the phone.

"No, you haven't. They won't mind, I mean, I'm sure they'll believe you."

"Hope so." Tiff cringed at the thought. She hated lying to her boss and up until now, she'd had a 100% attendance every year. She'd been proud of it and it had earned her a yearly bonus of one extra day's holiday.

"It'll be all right babe." Joe sighed heavily.

"Yeah, well I'd better go now – picking Mum up from work."

"OK…" Joe's breath sounded loud and drawn out. "Shall I call you tonight?"

"If you want to," Tiff replied, stiffly.

"I do want to."

"Then do it," she said, fearing the end of the conversation coming because, she too, missed him terribly. "Talk later."

"Bye babe, have a good rest of the day."

"I will – bye."

"And I love you."

"OK, bye." Tiff pressed the 'end call' button and clutched the phone to her chest as tears welled in her eyes. Why was she being so stand-offish with him when it was clear how he felt about her? Why did everything seem so absurd now that she was away from Sycamore Close? Yet, when she was there, it all seemed so wrong.

"Hi Mum." Tiff beamed a huge smile as her mum opened the door and got in the car. "Had a good lunchtime?"

"Yes. Quiet today – our year fives are out on a school trip. It makes a lot of difference to lunchtimes when just one of the year groups is missing."

"Right," said Tiff, putting the car into gear, "I thought we'd park in *Sainsbury's* carpark. That way we could get your shopping after I've picked up some shoes and we won't have far to carry it."

"But isn't that car park dangerous? What with all those spiral ramps and pillars to get around?"

"No Mum, it'll be quite safe. If you want me to drop you off at the bottom, I can go up on my own." Tiff resisted the urge to tut and roll her eyes.

"Let's see how busy it is first."

"Mum, try to brave it out. I bet when you go on that course, you will have to leave your comfort zone at some point. They'll probably give you some kind of tasks to do."

"Yes, I know." Mum fixed her seatbelt firmly into place and heaved a sigh. "I'm sure that being aware of the problem is half-way there. I'm determined. I've got to do this before…" Mum broke off sharply.

"Before?"

"I mean… so that we can come and visit you… before the summer is over."

"There's no rush."

"No, I know. But I'd like to visit as soon as possible."

"That would be nice. Anyway, let me know if you want to go up the multi-storey or not. I don't want to push you."

Mum smiled and clutched on to the passenger door handle as if she was about to drop from the highest point of a roller coaster.

Tiff pulled away slowly and carefully. It was difficult to be ultra-cautious when driving with a petrified passenger.

They'd made it. Tiff's mum had even overcome her deep-rooted fear of multi-storey car parks. She'd perspired, she'd held her breath and muttered many interjections like, Ooh, ah, eek and oops but the most bizarre one was, brrr, which she spluttered on several occasions.

"Sounds like you're cold Mum." Tiff giggled as they pulled into a parking space.

"Sorry?" Mum was mopping her brow with a tissue.

"When you go, brrr – it sounds like you're cold."

"I read somewhere that making noises can make you deal with difficult situations better. And the noise can be anything that your mind decides to make. I do, brrr, a lot. I really don't know why."

"Never heard of that before, except maybe in childbirth or if you're terrified and screaming."

"Same thing. Noises for different things."

Tiff's mind wandered back to Sycamore Close and the noises that were made in her bedroom sometimes. Not frantic, screeching noises or groans or even howling but subtler sounds like gasping, gentle moaning and affectionate, tender whispers of adoration and all-encompassing love. She pictured Joe, naked and damp. His muscular fawn coloured, smooth skin. His big brown eyes, staring deeply into hers.

"Tiffany."

"Yes?"

"Are we getting out – you looked like you were miles away there?"

"Yes – sorry Mum. I was."

"Anywhere nice?" Mum grinned before heaving herself out of the car.

"No – not really. Just thinking about the house and all the work we have to do," Tiff lied as she too, climbed out of the car and locked it behind her.

"Oh my goodness, I hadn't really noticed them before." Mum peered down at Tiff's trainers in disgust. "What on earth…"

"Betty, next door. I told you about her husband and the birds."

"Ah yes."

"We cleaned the bird's cages yesterday."

"And that's the mess your shoes got in to?" Mum screwed her nose up.

"I dropped a scoop of droppings on them."

"Oh dear. And what's wrong with the other shoes you brought with you?"

"They're odd ones."

Mum giggled into her hand. "Did you pack your bag in the dark?"

"No, I… I was in a bit of a rush yesterday. After all the work we'd done for the neighbours, it was getting late in the day and I wanted to get here before it got too dark."

Mum nodded her head. "Come on then, what type do you want?" she asked as she pointed to the rows of trainers, neatly set out on the stands.

"These will do," said Tiff, grabbing a pair of pink and white canvas pumps. "I'll try them on. And I'm going to wear them just as soon as I've paid for them."

Sainsbury's was reasonably quiet. The clientele consisted mainly of elderly couples doing their weekly shop and young Mum's, pushing prams and dragging toddlers behind them.

Tiff's mum grabbed a basket. "I haven't got too much to get – this should be OK," she said, hanging the basket on her arm. "Anything you need?"

Tiff shook her head and peered around the shop. "No, don't think so. These shoes are hurting a bit though."

"Wait here, by the magazines. I'll be no longer than ten minutes."

"Are you sure you don't mind?"

"Of course I don't mind. Won't be long." Mum hurried off down the first aisle, swivelling her head from left to right as she glanced at the shelves.

Tiff pulled her phone from her pocket and looked at it. No messages. She pushed it back into her jeans and glanced around the front of the shop. To her right, a small tobacco kiosk busily served a string of customers. To her left, alongside the magazine shelving, further along, was the customer service desk. A tall man and a short, dumpy woman were sorting through paperwork and talking. Tiff turned away and watched the checkout girls, ardently scanning goods through their tills. Then she averted her eyes back to the customer service desk and noted the striking difference in the man and the woman's uniforms. Hers was very short and wide... while his was...

She looked harder. His was long... and thin. He was tall. She strained her eyes to pick up the features of his face... his dark hair... his beaky nose... his angular jaw...

The distinctly repelling, Dracula-like facial characteristics had to belong to...

Tiff edged closer to the customer service desk. The man's voice was exactly the same. Yet different in its tone. Gentler, kinder and far less patronising.

Closer still, she could now see his staff name badge – Jeremy. Her heart raced.

The man had to be...

She was sure he was...

Alvin Snodgrass.

The likeness was faultless. His mannerisms were foolproof. He *was* Alvin.

Tiff approached the desk just as Alvin/Jeremy turned away.

"Can I help you?" The short, tubby woman asked.

Tiff peered at her name badge – Tina. "Err... I..." she stumbled. "I..." She pointed to the man behind Tina. "I know him. I was... err... just going to say hello."

"Oh." Tina beamed. "Jeremy – there's someone here to see you."

Jeremy turned around, with a handful of receipts in his hands. His eyes met Tiff's. He dropped several of the receipts on the floor and instantly bent over to pick them up.

"Here," said Tina, gathering up the last receipts and taking the rest from Jeremy. "Let me sort those out – you have a quick chat with this lady here."

Tiff gulped as Jeremy/Alvin walked over to her side of the counter.

"Yes, madam – can I help you?"

"Alvin... is that you?" she whispered.

"Sorry, Miss?"

"Alvin Snodgrass," Tiff repeated. "What are you doing here?" There was no mistaking it. This man was not just a 'double', it really was Alvin. Tiff peered at his super-white teeth and the tiny nick in his chin, which she'd noticed the first time she ever spoke to him. "Are you undercover?" she whispered.

"I'm sorry, Miss – I don't know what you are talking about."

"Alvin, it's me. Tiff – from number four, Sycamore Close. Tiff and Joe? We moved in a few months ago?"

Alvin/Jeremy shook his head and rolled his bottom lip. "I'm sorry – I don't think I do know you." He frowned and turned his head from side to side again. "No, I haven't heard of a Sycamore Road either."

"Close – it's a close – not a road," replied Tiff, impatiently.

"Close," repeated the man. "Nope, still can't say I've heard of it."

"Alvin – I know it's you," Tiff whispered as frustration began to rage through her. "Why are you working here?" She indicated to his badge, "And what's that? Your name's not Jeremy."

"Madam," he said, quite sternly. "I have no idea what you are talking about or who you are talking about. Now, can I help you with anything else today?"

Tina turned to stare at Tiff incredulously.

Tiff peered at Alvin/Jeremy, resignedly. "No... I... err... Thank you and goodbye." Heat tingled in her cheeks as she turned and walked away from the desk. He *was* Alvin Snodgrass; she was absolutely sure of it. But why was he working in *Sainsbury's*? Why did he have a different name? Something very strange was going on and she had to find out what it was.

But how? She walked back past the magazine rack and snuck behind it, so that she was out of view. She was slightly embarrassed and must have looked like an absolute nutcase to the other woman, Tina. She had to think clearly and get her head around this, then she could work out some sort of plan to find out what was really going on with him. Surely, if Alvin *was* on a secret mission, he could have whispered so, or even indicated that he was with his eyes. The man she had just spoken to was very convincing when he said he had no idea who she was. Tiff was more than intrigued. From behind the magazine rack, she watched him going about his chores. He moved like Alvin. He smiled at the customers, like Alvin. There was no mistaking it, he most definitely was Alvin Snodgrass – secret service agent extraordinaire.

"All done. Sorry it took longer than expected, I bumped into Joan, from school. She talks non-stop."

Tiff took two of the bags from her mum. "That's OK, I was miles away. Didn't actually realise you were that long." She smiled as they started heading towards the multi-storey car park. "There was a man in there – behind the customer service desk. I know him… well, I'm sure I do."

"From school?"

"No, from home. He's one of our neighbours."

Mum peered at Tiff with a puzzled expression on her face. "I doubt he could be one of your neighbours, Tiffany."

"I know it sounds bizarre but I'm absolutely convinced it's him."

"Who?"

"The one I was telling you about last night, Alvin Snodgrass, the one who works for the government, as a spy. He's a secret service agent."

"Oh, that one." Mum eyed Tiff in disbelief. "Are you sure?"

"Yes – definitely."

"Do you think he's on a mission in *Sainsbury's* then?"

Tiff sighed loudly. "I don't know. His name tag said Jeremy and he was acting like he didn't have a clue who I was."

"Are you completely sure it was him then?"

"Yes Mum, I'd put my life on it."

"Then maybe he is doing something secret." Mum giggled. "I wonder what's going on in *Sainsbury's* that they would need to have a government spy working for them."

"I really have no idea. It all seems a bit odd to me."

"This is exciting stuff."

"No it's not Mum – I think there is something fishy going on."

"Oh?" Mum looked disappointed. "Like what?"

"I don't know but I'm going to try and find out."

Hi Joe, hope you're having a good day at work. Could you do me a favour on your way home? I need to find out if Alvin is at home. I'll explain later, when you phone. Tiff x

There – she'd done it. She'd put a little kiss on the end of her message.

Curious! How am I supposed to find out if he's home? P.s. you sound a lot happier now.

I'm OK and knock on his door?

And if he answers? What do I say? Oh, hi – just checking whether you're at home or not? Lol xxx

I'm expecting him to not be at home. Because I think he's here but I'll explain that later. Too longwinded on a text message. Unless you can call me now.

Can't call now. I'll ring you when I get home, but what do I say if he does answer?

Say that you've been thinking of going jogging and you were wondering which trainers were the best ones to buy.

OK – not sure I like this though xxx

Please x

OK. Call you later. Love you xxx

Love you too, and sorry xx

No need to be sorry, I understand how things must look sometimes xxx

Thanks xx

"Mum, I'm going back into town tonight – do you know what time *Sainsbury's* is open till?"

"I think it's eleven o'clock tonight. Can I ask why?"

"I want to see if 'Alvin aka Jeremy' is still there and if he isn't, then I'm going to see if I can talk to someone about him."

"Surely you can't do that!" Mum stared worriedly. "What if... if you are meddling in something much bigger than yourself? I don't want you getting in any kind of trouble. Especially if you're sticking your nose into government business."

"I won't get into trouble Mum. I'll play it very cool. I'm not sure that I believe any of this secret service stuff anyway. Please don't worry. I've texted Joe to ask him to find out if Alvin is at home. If he is, then I am hugely mistaken and I won't go. In fact, I'll never be able to step foot in your *Sainsbury's* ever again. But if he's not at home, then I will go to the shop and do some secret investigations of my own."

"Why are you so obsessed about him?"

"I'm not obsessed about him. It's just that..." Tiff paused thoughtfully. "It's just that he's a very strange character."

"There are lots of strange people about," said Mum, wisely. "I'm not too sure that you should be sneaking about, poking your nose into other people's business and especially not someone like this man, Alvin Snod-whatever."

"Snodgrass."

"Snodgrass," repeated Mum. "It's rather an odd name isn't it?"

Tiff jumped up from the sofa. "That's what I'll do! Why didn't I think of it before?"

"What?"

"Can I borrow your computer?"

"Why?" Mum eyed Tiff suspiciously.

"I could check his name. I might be able to find out... well, something. Anything."

"Your dad took it up to Birmingham with him."

Tiff sighed and slumped back on to the sofa. Her phone wasn't much use anymore. She used to be able to surf the internet on it but since the last update, only a couple of days ago, her mobile had repeatedly warned her that the memory was full and now half of the apps didn't work properly. "I'll ask Joe, when he phones. He might be able to find something."

Mum shrugged her shoulders. "I think you're getting too involved in this. You don't want to go upsetting your neighbours do you? Think carefully about what you are doing. Now, what would you like for your tea?"

"So, that's where we're at, at the moment."

Joe sighed down the phone. "Just because he wasn't in, doesn't mean to say that he's not home at all, babe. He might well be out jogging. How can you be completely sure that this, Jeremy, is him?"

"Do you remember that little nick in his chin – at the bottom?"

"No."

"Well, I noticed it the first time we spoke to him and this Jeremy fella has exactly the same mark."

"OK, blimey, you're observant."

"Maybe a bit too much sometimes." There was silence down the phone. "Anyway, I'm now going back to the shop – to see if I can talk to someone about him. I'm hoping he won't still be there."

"Tiff, babe, are sure that's a wise thing to do?"

"Oh don't Joe – you're starting to sound like my mother."

"It's just… if you've made a mistake… well, you're going to feel a bit silly, aren't you?"

"I'd rather feel silly than have one of our neighbours make me look really stupid by denying all knowledge of knowing me or having heard of Sycamore Close."

Joe huffed down the phone. "Babe, you are not getting it, are you?"

"What?"

"If it really is Alvin then he must be on an undercover mission or something like that."

"There's more to him than meets the eye, Joe."

"Yes, I know that. He's a complete weirdo."

"Exactly…" Tiff bit her lip. "More than you… or should I say, *we*, might know."

"OK, have it your way. Just… just be careful babe."

"I will. Shall I call you tomorrow?"

"Yes, I'll be home by six. But babe…"

"Yes?"
"Text me tonight if you do find anything out."
Tiff smiled to herself. "But what if you're asleep."
"Then at least I'll know tomorrow morning." Joe yawned loudly.
"OK, goodnight."
"Nite babe. Love you."
"You too."

Forgot to ask you if you could do a quick search on the internet for me – Dad's taken his computer away with him. Look up Alvin Snodgrass and check his address. Maybe the electoral role? Text me if you find anything odd. Love Tiff xx

I'll have a quick look then I'm going for an early night – so tired babe xx

Chapter 24

"Mum, I'm going now. I won't be long."

"I'm still not sure you should be doing this." Mum stared at her incredulously. "You should leave things well alone."

"I've got to find out. Please don't worry, I'll be back soon enough."

Mum sighed. "I'll wait up for you then."

As Tiff pulled into the smaller car park, at the side of *Sainsbury's,* her phone beeped.

Cannot find the name Alvin Snodgrass anywhere and can only view electoral register at the main library – unless I open an account on line! According to 192.com, there is no one by that name living in a Sycamore Close anywhere. It's hard to look any further as I would need to create an account for that one too. And it costs money. Sorry I haven't been much help. Goodnight babe, miss you loads xxx

Thanks Joe, I'll text if I find anything out – at the shop again now xx

Please, be careful xxx

The store was practically empty of customers. Any noise or movement was coming from the staff members who were dragging large cages, filled with stock, around the aisles. Tiff turned her head as she walked further into the shop and discreetly peered at the customer service desk. Empty.

A middle-aged woman, with dark roots peeping through her highlighted hair, stood at the end of the fruit aisle, piling packs of strawberries on to a sloped display shelf. Tiff watched the woman for a moment and wondered what she could say to her. She hadn't planned her investigation at all.

The woman turned and smiled. Her name badge glinted under the bright lights above their heads – Joanne-Assistant Manager. Their eyes met briefly. "Can I help you at all?" she asked, a jovial tone in her voice.

"Err... yes. I..." Tiff turned away embarrassed and pointed to the customer service desk. "Is... Is anyone working at the customer service desk?"

"Not at this time of night – can I help you with anything?"

Tiff lowered her finger and placed it on her top lip thoughtfully. "I'm not sure if you can..."

Joanne smiled cheerily, placed another pack of strawberries on to the shelf and dusted her hands off. "Oh, I'm sure I can. I haven't worked here for 23 years for nothing, you know." She shuffled past Tiff and beckoned for her to follow. "Follow me, we'll have you sorted out in no time."

Tiff trailed behind obediently until they reached the customer service desk. Her mind raced with questions, scenarios, statements, make-believe stories and tell-tale lies, all of which sounded completely ridiculous in her head. What should she say?

Joanne whipped around, the moment she was behind the counter and peered at Tiff, questioningly. "Now then," she said, "what can I do to help you?"

Tiff averted her eyes for a moment and glanced around the shop. "Well... this is a bit of an odd request..." she said as she turned back and eyed the woman ruefully.

"Oh?" Joanne's eyes lit up. "Go ahead then."

"It's... Jeremy. The one who..."

"Our Jeremy? Who works here?" The woman nodded her head. "Yes, I know Jeremy. What about him?"

"Well... this is a bit awkward... I mean..." Tiff wracked her brain trying to come up with an excuse. She scanned the aisles and peeped back over her shoulder before continuing. "I... err... well, I've been on a few dates with him recently."

"Oh my goodness – have you?"

"Yes, about six actually. I... I thought we were meeting here tonight but I've been waiting outside for the last two hours."

Joanne peered at Tiff doubtfully. "Well, I have no idea where he might be now. He was working here earlier today."

"Yes, he said he would be." Tiff could feel her cheeks beginning to glow. "It's just that..." She peered down at her shoes sorrowfully. "It's just that

I'm..." she shook her head quickly, "Oh, I just don't know what to do, you see... I'm pregnant."

"Oh my goodness." Joanne stared disbelievingly. "I'm so sor..." she slapped a hand to her mouth and held it there as her eyes widened. "I meant to say... are you happy or sad about it? The look on your face tells me you're extremely worried, if you don't mind me saying so." She eyed Tiff compassionately.

Tiff looked down again, unsure of where this was going and why she had chosen the jilted-pregnant-woman scenario. "I don't know. I'm... confused. To make things even worse... I... I have that condition that you sometimes get in pregnancy and... I have memory loss." Tiff blinked her eyes exaggeratedly, forcing tears to well. They were almost real tears as she worried how on earth she was going to get herself out of this pitiful little pack of lies.

Joanne shook her head and peered at her delicately. "I've never heard of that before. I'm very sorry to hear it. What's the condition called? Purely out of interest."

"It's... err... would you believe it, I can't even remember that now. Oh dear... I think... I think I'm falling apart. Please help me."

"What can *I* do to help you?"

Tiff swung her head from side to side, willing the tears to fall. "I know that I can't ask you for his number. I know that would be against company policy."

"Well, yes. I'm..."

"It's just that..."

"Yes?"

"I can't even remember..." Tiff sniffed and rubbed at her nose. "I can't even remember his last name. If I knew it, I could look up his number."

"Oh dear." Joanne held her hands together in front of her and looked decidedly uncomfortable. She glanced around the front of the shop and then turned her attention back to Tiff. "Don't you have his number saved in your phone?"

Tiff shook her head. "I've lost my phone."

Joanne tutted. "Oh dear me." She paused thoughtfully. "OK, it's Greene – with an 'e' on the end," she whispered. "But please don't mention that I have told you."

"Oh my God – yes – I remember it now. Yes, of course it's Greene. Thank you so much. I should have remembered that. My old Greeny, yes, that's what I call him. I do remember – how silly of me. Thank you so much... Joanne. Is it OK if I call you Joanne?" Tiff flung a hand across the counter, offering a handshake.

Joanne stood back and grinned sheepishly. "Yes, you can, it's my name after all."

"When will he be back here?"

"To work, you mean?"

"Yes – I must see him but I just don't remember his address either."

Again, Joanne scanned the shop floor like she was on a surveillance assignment of her own. "He lives with his mum. Does that help you to remember?"

Tiff shook her head distressfully. "No... I don't think so... could you tell me when he'll be back here again?"

"I can't I'm afraid – it's not because I don't want to – on the contrary. He's on a gradual-return-to-work scheme at the moment, since both he and his mum have been so very poorly for the past few years. So he's not here a lot of the time."

"But he's worked here for a long time?" Tiff knew she was clutching at straws. "I'm sure he said that..."

"Yes – that's right. Almost as long as I have."

"Ah, I remember that now as well. So... over 20 years? Now that is a long, long time."

Joanne nodded her head and shot an uncertain grin.

"He does live with his mum. I can recall that too..." Tiff peered downwards again. "But... I still can't remember *where* he lives."

"I'm not sure that I can help you any further, sorry, what did you say your name was?"

"It's Ti... Ti-ti-anna. Yes," Tiff giggled into her hand, "thank goodness I can remember my *own* name."

"OK, Titianna, look, I have an idea. As I can't give you either of his addresses..."

"Either? Have I... Have I forgotten that as well?"

Joanne stared at her woefully. "His other house, on the outskirts of Hampshire, somewhere?"

Tiff placed three fingers to her lips and feigned deep thought. "Oh, hmm... that's not..." She screwed her face into a focused frown, "Sycamore Road, is it?" She thumped the palm of her hand against her head. "No – Close – Sycamore Close. Is that the one?"

"I have no idea, to be honest with you. Not unless I look at his file." Joanne appeared a little disconcerted. "And I really couldn't do that."

"No, no, of course not. But I think you have jogged my memory. I'm sure I've been there." Tiff gave a fake grin. "Thank you so much Joanne, you have been very helpful."

Joanne smiled back. "Phew! That's a relief. However, I was going to suggest that you give me your number and I'll get him to give you a call. Does he know?"

"Know what?"

"That you're pregnant and you have this memory-loss condition?"

"Oh my goodness, no he doesn't. I... I'm not sure that I want him to know either." Tiff sighed exaggeratedly. "I was going..."

"But I thought you were meeting him tonight," said Joanne, shuffling from one foot to the other and looking uncomfortable.

"Err...yes, I was. But... it was to end the relationship actually."

"Oh, I see. Oh dear, I'm sorry to hear that," she said, regretfully.

"No, please don't be sorry... it's just that... well, my mum said it would be best for everyone. And Joanne?"

"Yes?"

"Would you please not tell him that I've been here tonight?"

Joanne nodded her head affirmatively. "Yes, if that's what you want. But..."

"In hindsight... I think he may have jilted me first and that's why he hasn't turned up."

"Oh, I see..."

"Thank you for your help tonight, Joanne. You have helped me far more than you could ever imagine."

"Good. I'm pleased that I have been able to assist you in some way, Titianna. Please take care of yourself." Joanne leant over the counter and lowered her voice, "And to be honest with you... I think you would be much better off without him as well."

"Why do you say that?" Tiff whispered across the Formica counter.

Stretching back to an upright position, Joanne glanced around the shop floor again. "He's a very odd one, our Jeremy. Very odd. I don't trust him myself."

Tiff nodded her head. "Thank you, Joanne, I did think so myself and I've never trusted him either. I really must go now. Please don't mention this to him."

"I won't, I can promise you that. Goodbye."

"Bye and thank you again."

OMG Joe! You won't believe it! I now know that Alvin Snodgrass – or Jeremy Greene – is leading a double life. Look up Jeremy Greene (make sure you put an 'e' on the end) to see if there is someone of that name in Sycamore Close. And he has worked for Sainsbury's for more than 20 years! What the hell is he playing at? Hope I haven't woken you. Speak tomorrow. Tiff xx

"Well? Did you find out anything?"

"Yes. Just about everything I needed to know. We have a very strange neighbour in Sycamore Close and I think I might have figured him out now."

"I don't see why it should be of such great concern." Mum yawned and uncurled herself from the sofa. "Anyway, I'm going to bed now that you're back, safe and sound."

"I'll be up in a minute Mum... and I've locked the front door. Goodnight."

Saw Alvin this morning. In those gold Speedos you were talking about! What an utter dork! He must have travelled back late last night – if that was really him, you saw. Wouldn't he have to lead a double life if he's a spy? Will check that name out when I get home tonight. And Cyril's home, saw him being wheeled around the green by poor old Betty, this morning. He looks a bit rough though. Love you, Joe xxx

"Do you want a lift to work Mum?"

"No thank you. I'll get the bus as I always do."

"But you could stay at home for another hour, if I gave you a lift."

"Yes, that's quite true but I would much rather go on the bus. I have my pass to use up by the end of the month anyway." Mum pulled a small plastic wallet from her pocket and waved it in the air.

"Then I will cook tea for us tonight. What do you fancy? I could prepare something."

It was only Tuesday and Tiff was already bored. She desperately wanted to get home. To find out what was going on in and around Sycamore Close. She was missing Joe and now felt that her leaving him so easily and hastily had been a little senseless. But then again, it was like it was meant to be. After all, she would never have found out about Alvin's true identity if it hadn't been for her little outburst and departure from home.

"I have everything prepared. There's nothing for you to do." Mum peered at her puzzled. "Why did you come for the whole week? I knew you would soon get bored."

Tiff shrugged her shoulders. "I just fancied coming to spend some time with you. I'm not bored," she lied.

"I'll be home in a few hours. Why don't you sit in the garden, have some lunch and read a book?"

"Good idea. Except I didn't bring any books with me."

"I have the whole collection of *Agatha Christie's* novels now. Would you like to read one of those?"

Tiff smiled and nodded her head enthusiastically. "Yes please – I quite fancy a bit of crime."

"In my room – help yourself. Oh... and Tiffany..."

"Yes?"

"Please don't turn the corners of the..."

"Yes, I know Mum. Don't dog-ear them, right?"

"Right. See you this afternoon."

Chapter 25

Two *Agatha Christie* books – read. A catch-up with her dad – done. Several lovingly long phone calls to Joe – sorted and back to normal. Daily check-ins as to Alvin's whereabouts – one successful (he was out jogging again), three unsuccessful (Joe hadn't seen him and was not going to knock his door again). A stay with the parents – done. Bonding time with Mum – done.

Tiff packed her few belongings into the holdall and merrily trotted down the stairs with it. "Right, I'm all done, time to set off home."

Her dad and mum stood by the front door beaming. "We will be down to see you very soon Tiffany," said Dad. "Sooner than you think."

Mum smiled, smugly. "Yes, you just wait and see. I'll soon be flying around all over the place."

"That's so good to hear, Mum. I cannot wait for you both to see the house." Tiff flung her arms round her dad's neck and squeezed him tightly. "Sorry I haven't seen you for very long, Dad, but I really need to get home early this weekend."

Dad patted her gently on the back. "Not to worry. We will see you again and like your mother says, it will be soon."

Tiff pecked her dad's cheek and then moved over to her mum. "Bye – and thank you Mum. Those books were really good reads and thank you for having me."

"And thank you for believing in me and for our little chats." Mum smirked.

"Oh?" said Dad, eyeing Tiff and Mum suspiciously.

"We've had some chats about the counselling Mum's going to be getting," said Tiff. "And I know that she will be able to do it."

Mum held her head high and nodded proudly.

Tiff kissed her mum's cheek and hugged her. "Thank you again – both of you. I'll see you soon." She turned towards the door and picked up her holdall.

"Let us know when you get home," said Mum.

"Yes, of course I will. Bye – love you both loads."

Sycamore Close was just as quiet as it usually was when Tiff pulled into the lay-by. A fluttery sensation bubbled and fizzed in her stomach as she stepped out of the car. She had missed Joe a lot more than she thought she would. As she walked around the left side of the green, she peered across at Alvin's house. Was he home? What would she say to him when she saw him next? Did he find out about her visit to *Sainsbury's* that evening? She hoped he hadn't.

She opened the front door and walked into the cool interior. It smelt like home. An aroma of sweet and musky aftershave wafted around as she went through to the dining room. She peered out of the patio doors and there he was. Gorgeously tanned, wearing a pair of blue shorts and a white vest-style t-shirt, Joe was at the end of the garden, leaning over a repaired fence, his hair spiky and damp.

Tiff placed her holdall on the table, took a deep breath in and exhaled slowly. She opened the patio door and stopped as Joe turned around.

"Babe." His whole expression lifted. He quickly walked across the patchy, muddy grass and held his arms out as he approached her.

Tiff couldn't help but beam as he came closer. A surge of excitement rushed through her.

He whipped her up into his arms and held the back of her head in one hand as he kissed her lips feverishly. "God, I've missed you, babe," he said, brushing his lips over hers.

"Missed you too." She pulled away from his mouth and hugged his head tightly.

Lowering her to the ground, Joe kept her in an embrace and rocked her from side to side. "No, you really don't know how much I've missed you." He stopped still and peered down at her. "I'm taking you out tonight. Just the two of us – for a romantic meal."

"Sounds nice."

"But for now, I bet you need a cuppa."

"I do. Traffic was terrible past Reading." Tiff stepped back indoors to let Joe through. "I see you've done the fence. The hedge trimmings have gone as well."

Joe met her eyes. "Yes, I did the fence just this morning. Wanted to get it done before you came home."

Tiff nodded her head. "Is it... the one from Georgie?"

Joe walked over to the kettle and flicked it on. "Yes, she's been pestering me all week about it, so I thought I'd better get it done. I also had a bonfire last night." He laughed. "You missed the toasted marshmallows – they were delicious."

Tiff said nothing but nodded her head and forced a smile.

"So..." Joe sounded edgy, "how are your mum and dad?"

"They're OK." She grinned falsely. Just the mention of Georgie's name had flared up her hatred for the woman. She couldn't allow it to have a noticeable effect. Not again. "I bet Georgie was pleased to see the fence go, wasn't she?"

"Yes, well I had said I'd get it last Sunday, but..." Joe broke off.

"How's she been pestering you?" Tiff did her utmost to sound nonchalant. "Coming round? Or calling you?"

Joe grabbed two mugs from the cupboard and turned away to prepare the drinks. "Err... she just asked each time I saw her."

It still hurt. It still grated on her. Tiff couldn't stop the hateful, jealous feelings. She had to hide it though. She could not risk getting into another argument with Joe. Yet he appeared to be just as nervous about any conversation which involved Georgie, as he was before she left. Maybe it was Tiff who was making him nervous and not just because it was Georgie they were talking about.

"Did you see her quite a bit then," Tiff feigned laughter. "I mean, more than that elusive Alvin-Jeremy freak."

Joe turned and smiled. "No, I only saw her... in passing really."

"So she didn't share marshmallows with you last night?" Tiff laughed her comment off as if she was jesting.

"No, she didn't. I was completely on my own. Thinking about you." Joe gave a wavering smile. "And I didn't really have marshmallows anyway."

Tiff nodded. "I'm joking with you. So, you've hardly seen Alvin – or should I say, Jeremy."

"No, so what the bloody hell is going on there?" he replied in a more relaxed tone.

"I really don't know. I'm wondering what he might say to me if I see him."

Joe laughed. "I couldn't believe the story you came out with, babe. Pregnant?"

"I just hope he hasn't found out about it." Tiff paused thoughtfully. "Is my craft room OK?"

Joe gave a quizzical stare. "I fed and watered it, if that's what you mean?"

Tiff giggled. "So you've been in there?"

"No, I haven't. Not at all. Why?"

"Just wondered. You know what I'm like. Guess I just missed it while I was away."

"Well it's still there if that's what you're worried about."

"Good. I was having visions that you might have turned it into a golf trophy room or something like that."

"No, nothing like that."

Tiff forced a smile to hide the relief she was feeling. "I was going to ask you what you think I should say to Alvin when I see him. Should I come straight out with it and call him Jeremy?"

Joe's face turned serious. "No, I don't think so, that could get a little awkward. I'd say that you should ignore him. Let him come to you if he wants to talk." He carried two mugs of tea over to the table and sat down. "Anyway, enough of him, let's talk about us... and our home... and how much I've missed you."

"OK," Tiff smiled. "Go ahead."

Joe really was a smooth talker and even before they'd finished their tea, he'd whisked her up the stairs to the bedroom. Passionate and lingering, their togetherness was mind-blowingly clear. There was no mistaking his deeply-affectionate love for Tiff. Why had she ever doubted it?

Tiptoeing out of the room, she closed the bedroom door behind her, leaving Joe to have an afternoon nap. He always fell asleep straight after their lovemaking, whereas, she was all-fired-up and ready to go and clean the whole house or dig the garden up. If it had been night time, she would have quietly read pages and pages of her latest romantic-comedy novel while he slept beside her, a faint humming of a snore resonating across the quilt from him.

She opened the craft room door and stepped inside. It still smelt of fresh paint and there were still boxes and odd bits of crafting materials strewn across the desk, by the window. It didn't look like Joe had been in the room at all. So it seemed that he'd been telling the truth on that count. Certainly nothing seemed to have been touched or moved since the last time she was there. She'd missed the room and she'd been curious all week long as to what might be going on in the deceptively picturesque view. Moving across to the window, she peered out to the sunlit fields and the gently moving trees. There were no gold flashes, flickering past the trunks of the trees. No copulation in the copse. No sparsely clad women walking their dogs.

Instinctively, she reached into the drawer and took the binoculars from the back. She put them up to her eyes and scanned the landscape. She had to be sure. Just to check. A couple of horses grazed leisurely in a field on the right, and to the left, she could just see the area where she had last spotted Georgie. There was something red on the ground, several metres away. Long and red. Tiff twisted the focus wheel, trying to zoom in on the red... dog lead. Uncannily like the lead that Alvin bought a couple of weeks ago. Tiff froze as it dawned on her. She'd seen Georgie with a collar around her neck and now the discarded lead. What the hell were they playing at?

Moving along the tree-lined paths, she turned the focus wheel as she scanned the area, closer to the backs of the gardens. Turning to the left, she could see the back of Georgie's fence. She carried on further, into Georgie's garden. There was the cement mixer. Georgie's recliner and the small table... and...

Tiff froze in horror and gasped. Peering straight up at her, Georgie was standing at the back of her garden, hands on her hips and her head tilted upwards. She was frowning. Their eyes met for a brief second, although it was through the binoculars. Tiff snatched herself away from the window and held her breath. Georgie had seen her with the binoculars, scouring the fields and paths... and her garden.

Guiltily, Tiff threw the binoculars into the very back of the drawer and slammed it shut. Edging backwards, she moved towards the door. Cringing and cussing to herself, she vacated the room and closed the door firmly behind her. She'd been caught spying.

Housework was the only *normal* thing that Tiff could think about doing. What could she say, if questioned by Georgie? She was admiring the beautiful view? Checking out the wildlife? Watching the horses? Studying the mating ritual of the common, immorally debauched jogger? But why was she looking into Georgie's garden? Trying to focus the binoculars? She had tripped up and the binoculars had accidentally veered to the left? She was checking out the sexy cement mixer? It was no use. Tiff could not think of a plausible reason for spying into Georgie's garden. She would simply have to avoid the woman. Forever.

One long, blonde hair may have been purely coincidental. But two? Three?

Joe had been asleep for over an hour, so Tiff had avoided the hoovering, not wanting to wake him. She had decided to sweep the kitchen floor and collect the dirt up with the dustpan and brush. It was like the first strand of pure blonde hair had jumped out on her, saying, 'here I am – look at me!'. The second strand had been far more elusive and was discreetly curled into a corner of the kitchen floor. The third was lounging on the floor on the opposite side of the kitchen. Three long, blonde hairs. Obviously Georgie's. They had to be. Yet Tiff knew that she had hoovered thoroughly last week. So where had they come from? The same old sick feeling crept back into her throat. Why was it that every time she was home, something would happen or appear, to make her feel suspicious of Joe's actions? She emptied the contents of the dustpan into the bin, with a feeling of disgust.

It was sitting on the dining table – just waiting to be read. It was like it had been left there purposely. One way or another, the contents would reveal the truth – surely.

Tiff snatched Joe's phone up from the table and unlocked it. The inbox had only two message threads in it. Her own and Wayne's. Working nimbly, she tapped on the message thread from Wayne. Strangely, there was only one message received from him, which had been sent weeks ago. In fact, it was when Joe first played golf with him. It read: *Hello mate, booked 18-hole for 8-15am. Be at mine for quarter to. Wayne.* So Joe did have Wayne's number before their first game of golf?

Tiff stared at the date and time of the message. Where were the other ones from Wayne? Where were the ones that Wayne had supposedly sent when he was hungover last Sunday? Why would Joe delete all messages apart from one old one? Surely it was easier to delete a whole thread, rather than individual ones?

It was happening all over again. The pain of mistrust was starting to nibble away at her. Deeper and sharper. She couldn't run away again. But they'd had such an exceptionally, emotionally charged closeness earlier. Did she need help? Was it all in her head? Was her mind playing tricks with her? Or was it really Joe that was the problem? The blonde hairs were a fact – they definitely weren't in her mind.

Leaving the housework, midway, Tiff slumped on to the sofa, feeling weary and drained. The journey this morning, and the torrid patch-up with Joe had taken it out of her. She closed her eyes and drifted off, into a troubled, uneasy sleep.

Chapter 26

Joe staggered down the stairs, looking half asleep. He squinted his eyes as the late afternoon sun poured through the window, behind Tiff.

Tiff had just woken too but she was instantly wide-eyed and alert. The uncertainty of earlier slowly crept back into her mind as she pulled herself up from the sofa.

"You been asleep too?" Joe muttered before heading out to the kitchen.

"Yes, I came over all tired." She followed him through and sat down on a chair. "I was trying to tidy up but I gave up half way through."

"Don't worry about it babe – we'll do it all together, tomorrow." Joe turned and offered a cheeky grin. "In the meantime, we'll have this," he said, holding up an empty mug, "and then get showered. Don't forget I'm taking you out tonight."

Tiff nodded. "Oh yes, I'd forgotten about that. Where are we going?" *Blonde hair, blonde hair.*

"I know a really nice country pub and restaurant. It's way out in the sticks – you'll love it."

"OK." Tiff furrowed her brows in puzzlement. "Have you always known about this place then or is it a new discovery?"

"It's... err... well, I've always known about it. I'd just forgotten about it," Joe replied, falteringly.

Blonde hair, blonde hair. "OK, good." Tiff peered out of the patio doors. "Fence looks better now."

"Yeah, fitted perfectly." Joe continued to prepare two mugs of tea without turning around. "New one slid straight in."

"Did Georgie bring it round then?"

Joe stopped, midway through spooning sugar into the mugs and turned around. "No, I went to get it." His eyes had opened wide now, compared to their half-closed, sleepy state a few minutes ago.

"Oh, OK... I just wondered if she'd been round here at all."

"No, not at all. I've been at work all week and... and I went to bed early most nights, except when I was talking to you on the phone."

"Hmm..." Tiff turned the corners of her mouth down, thoughtfully. "I just thought that maybe she'd been here. You know, to bring the fence round. Or to pop in and ask you when you were going to collect it."

"No," Joe said, adamantly, "she hasn't been round here. I bumped into her and she asked about it."

"Hmm... O...K..."

Joe peered at her worriedly. "Why do you say that?"

"What?"

"Like you said it. Hmm... O...K..."

"I was just saying OK." Tiff eyed him with skepticism.

"It's the way you said it, babe. I feel like we're back to the, not believing what I say."

"Not sure what you expect me to believe when I find hundreds of blonde hairs all over the filthy kitchen floor." Tiff cringed, she'd blurted it out without thinking it through. She'd embellished on the state of the floor and exaggerated the number of hairs. And it sounded terrible.

Joe stood in silence and met her eyes. He searched her face, desperately trying to find answers. "Where?"

"I've got rid of them all now. In the bin." She averted her gaze away from Joe's. She was starting it all again. She knew it. She just couldn't stop it. "I wouldn't have found them all if I'd hoovered. But I was being thoughtful by not hoovering. I didn't want to wake you so...."

"So?"

"So I got down on my hands and knees, being the considerate person I am, and swept the floor with the dustpan and brush."

"But..." Joe's face turned pale.

"So where did they all come from?"

"Babe – I really don't know." Joe thought for a moment. "I've had the doors open. It was hot on a couple of evenings, when I was cooking my dinner." He shrugged his broad shoulders and peered at Tiff, pleadingly. "Maybe they blew in here from next door... or something?"

"Oh dear." Tiff shook her head and buried her face in her hands.

"Now, hang on a minute, Tiff." Joe's tone of voice had changed. "I do not know why you would find blonde hair everywhere. Isn't this all getting a bit out of hand now?" he blasted, tiresomely.

"You're the one getting out of hand, Joe. You're obviously stressed out by it. I can hear it in your voice."

Joe rolled his eyes and tutted. "I am getting stressed out with you, babe. Don't you see it? It's starting all over again. Didn't that mean anything to you, earlier?" He pointed to the ceiling, indicating upstairs.

Tiff stared at him, speechless.

"It meant something to me. I thought it showed how much I love you. I thought you would have felt that too."

Tiff continued to look fixedly at her beloved Joe, fighting back the emerging tears. Then she darted her eyes away from his and blinked rapidly as she stared out of the patio doors.

"Tiff – please. Let's not go back to that."

"That?"

"To how things were getting before you went away." Joe tentatively carried two hot drinks to the table. "I thought we'd..."

She continued to look out of the doors. "What?"

"Ended all of that." His voice had returned to a low, husky whisper.

"So did I."

"So, let's leave it – please babe."

"Like that wouldn't you – make it easier wouldn't it?"

"What are you talking about?" He pushed her mug across the table, under her nose.

"If I wasn't so intuitive – would that make things easier for you?"

Joe brushed his thickset hands through his ruffled hair. "No, babe. Would it make it easier for you if we put this bloody house up for sale and moved somewhere else?"

"Oh don't be ridiculous." Tiff grabbed her drink, took a couple of slurps and then clutched it to her chest.

"I'm being serious."

"Well, what am I supposed to think? I come home after a week away to find long blonde hairs all over the place."

"I don't know where they came from. I wish to God I did."

"So, you think they just blew in here, from next door?" Tiff's voice was filled with sarcasm. "Is that what I'm supposed to believe?"

"Believe what you like, babe. All I know is that I love you, I'd sell this house and move for you, I'd cut my right arm off if I could prove to you that there is nothing funny going on and I'd take any lie-detector test that you wanted me to."

Tiff was still glaring, pointedly at the doors. She returned her mug to the table and rubbed her hands around her face. *Text messages.*

"Babe – I want to take you out for a nice meal and a few drinks tonight. Just you and me. I want to prove to you how much I care about you. It's a beautiful, romantic place." He reached across the table and beckoned for her to hold his hand. "Please."

Text messages... can't mention text messages... I'm such a snoop. He doesn't deserve this – maybe I'm wrong. Save the messages for later, perhaps. "I'll..." Tiff ignored his hand lying on the table outstretched, palm facing upwards, with beckoning fingers. "I'll go and have a soak in the bath. Sorry."

"Don't be sorry babe. Be happy and believe in me. I don't have a clue how the floor got covered in blonde hair."

She had to make the effort, although it really was burdensome to search through her wardrobe, trying to find the right clothes to wear, style her hair and apply lashings of make-up. But it would be worth it. She would have Joe salivating over her. She would have him right where she wanted him and then, maybe, she could even bring up the subject of deleted text messages while he gazed lovingly into her eyes across a candlelit table for two. But hadn't Joe had enough of all the suspicious remarks and the sarcastic comments? Yes, probably, he had. But she couldn't carry on a true and loving relationship with him unless she found out all the answers to her questions. She was so terribly confused.

She stood up and glanced at herself in the long mirror. Wearing a navy-blue shift dress, red shoes and accessories to match, her hair was swept up into a messy bun on the top of her head, while several strands framed her tiny face, creating an overall glamorous look. A rush of anger filled her. Georgie often had her hair up in messy buns. Should she have hers down?

No, that was being simply ridiculous. And anyway, her messy bun looked much better than Georgie's ever could.

Joe entered the bedroom with a towel around his waist. "You look stunning babe. I can't believe I'm lucky enough to have you. You are so beautiful." He moved around the bed and placed both hands on her tiny waist. "I love you, Tiffany Cuthbert – and don't you ever forget it."

Tiff smiled waveringly and looked down. "I'll try not to. Come on, get dressed. I'll wait downstairs."

Joe was right. The old, converted cottage, deep in the centre of the New Forest, was indeed, quaint and romantic, just as he had said. He had been a true gentleman all evening. He'd opened doors for her, assisted her across the pebbled car park, situated on the right of the thatched cottage and treated her like a true lady. How could she not fall in love with him all over again. He smelt gorgeous. He was clean shaven and wore a pair of black chinos and a plain purple, short-sleeved shirt. His glorious tan accentuated the whites of his eyes and his perfectly aligned teeth. His voice had been low and husky all evening and he had done nothing but compliment her, express his feelings for her and talk about how lucky he was. He had also spent some time reminiscing about their lives together, so far.

"Do you remember when I took you up in that balloon?"

Tiff nodded her head and smiled, before she took a sip from her third glass of wine. Joe had insisted that she have a few relaxing drinks during the evening and that he would drive. She hadn't argued, on the contrary she agreed that she needed to relax a bit more.

The food was amazing and it had been noticed that the restaurant was the proud owner of a cordon bleu chef.

Tiff placed her spoon into the tall glass and sat back in her chair. "I'm absolutely full."

"Aren't you going to finish that?" Joe pointed to the small amount of strawberry ice-cream left in the bottom of her tall glass.

"No, I can't. Think I might pop."

Joe flicked his eyes around the restaurant and then beckoned for her glass. He pushed his own towards her and swapped them over.

"I don't know where you put it all," she said, giggling as the effects of the wine began to take a hold on her, despite all the food she'd eaten. *Text messages – not going to spoil a lovely evening. Forget about them Tiffany Cuthbert... at least for now.*

Tiff propped her chin up and watched him devour the last few mouthfuls of the fancy Knickerbocker Glory. She loved him dearly. She fancied him madly. She feared losing him dreadfully.

The last glass of wine had done it. Tiff had to cling on to Joe with an iron-like grip as they traversed the pebbled car park. The journey home was a blur and she could do no more than to put her hands in her lap, lower her head and stare downwards as her alcohol addled mind drifted around aimlessly.

Once they were home, she kicked off her shoes in the living room and took the shortest route straight to Joe's trouser belt. Fervently, she undid it and pulled it free from the loops.

Joe looked down at her, surprised. "Are you OK babe?"

She ignored his question and continued to undo his trousers.

He laughed and reached behind her back to unzip her dress. Their garments fell to the floor at the same time. He undid his shirt buttons, feverishly, and whipped the shirt from his back while she watched and swayed a little.

Then he pounced. A frantic attack ensued. Across the sofa, against the walls and finally ending on the floor in a crescendo of heat, moisture and moans of pleasure.

"Tiffany Cuthbert," Joe slurred, sedated by the surge of hormones filling his head, "you are a sex maniac..." He drifted off to sleep, lying naked on the sofa.

"Joe." She shook his shoulder and then pulled her dress over her head. "Wake up – you can't sleep there." A grunt and a snuffled snore signaled that he had already slipped into sleep. "Joe – wake up." She pulled his arm out from under him. "Joe, come on, let's go to bed."

He stirred and looked up hazily.

"Bed," demanded Tiff. "Come on." Again she pulled at his arm.

Heaving himself up from the sofa, he grabbed his clothes, staggered to the staircase and pulled himself up each step, laboriously.

Following closely behind, Tiff admired his buttocks as he climbed the stairs. That was just the most rampant sex they'd had to date and she'd initiated it. There was no way anyone was going to be better than her, when it came to having sex with Joe Frey. She'd practically knocked him out and blown him away with her amorous advances and active participation throughout. And that was how it was going to stay. How could he be interested in anyone else when the dynamics between them were so electrifying?

Chapter 27

Opening her eyes to the glare of the sunshine pouring through the window, Tiff squinted and turned her head to look at the time – 9.35am. She was surprised she'd slept so long. The other side of the bed lay empty and she assumed Joe would be downstairs making some breakfast.

The house was strangely quiet as she went down the stairs, wearing just her pyjamas and a pair of slippers. As she reached the dining room, she realised that Joe was not there or even in the garden. "Joe?" she called, backtracking to the stairs. "Joe..." She swallowed back the bitter taste of mistrust, rising from her stomach – the only place she hadn't looked was her craft room. Was he in there? If he was, what was he doing in there? She tiptoed back up the stairs. If she was going to find him in there, she wanted to catch him out – whatever he might be up to.

He wasn't there.

Tiff sighed heavily, was she becoming completely neurotic? She returned to the dining room and walked over to the kitchen. Immediately, she caught sight of a piece of paper lying on the worktop, next to the kettle.

Morning babe,

I'm next door, didn't want to wake you this morning and thought you'd need the lie-in after attacking me so spiritedly last night. Won't be long, then we can crack-on with the house. Love you xx

Tiff read the note again, looking for surreptitious clues between the lines. Next door? Why had he gone next door? How could he be so brazen about going next door? After everything they'd been through...

Perhaps he had meant Betty and Cyril's house. Why would he go there? Tiff took a mug of coffee upstairs and started to get washed and dressed as a cloud of undesirable mistrust hovered above her head. If he was at Betty and Cyril's house, why didn't he just say that in the note? Was he deliberately trying to stir things up between them? Sitting down heavily on the bed, she rubbed her forehead wearily. She wasn't in need of more sleep, just a break from the rage and self-destructive envy that she couldn't shift. However ridiculous it might all seem in the heat of their intimate moments.

It was just too tempting to leave the binoculars safely stashed away at the back of the drawer. Just one little look. Just to check. Then she would try to get on with her day. Just one quick peep...

She would risk the possibility of Georgie seeing her again. What were the odds of that happening twice? Just one quick peep...

Nothing.

Not even a randy wild rabbit, skittering through the fields. Tiff was standing well back in the room, out of view from the gardens below. She hated herself for doing this. For prying into other people's affairs but it was like it had become an unhealthy obsession. She was beginning to question her own sanity.

A clicking sound came from the front door. She froze and strained her ears to listen. The door opened. She pulled the binoculars away from her face and tiptoed towards the drawer. Thudding footsteps pounded the stairs. Joe arrived at the top of the stairs just as she threw the binoculars in the drawer and closed it behind her. Their eyes met and puzzled frowns furrowed their brows. "What..." began Tiff.

"Are you..." Joe said at the same time.

Their mutual gaze continued momentarily, before he staggered to the bathroom and closed the door behind him. "Won't be a minute – busting for a pee," he said from behind the door.

Tiff inched out of the craft room and quietly closed the door behind her. Moments later, the toilet flushed and Joe appeared from behind the bathroom door. "Are you OK?" he asked, a worried expression on his face.

She nodded.

"What were you going to say as I came tearing up the stairs?"

Tiff smiled sheepishly, "I wondered why the heck you were charging up the stairs – you made me jump." She let out a sigh of relief. "I can see why now. What were *you* going to say?"

Joe reached out for her hand and guided her down the stairs. "You looked like you'd seen a ghost babe – I wondered if you were OK."

"Oh – yeah, fine."

"What were you throwing in the drawer?" he asked, impassively, as he pulled her through to the kitchen.

"Oh... just some old craft stuff. Trying to sort that room out still."

"OK." Joe turned and beamed. "Sorry if I made you jump." He pulled her close and kissed her gently on the lips. "I should have used the loo round Betty's but I just wanted to get the job done and get back here, to you." He kissed her again, softly and purposefully. "She kept making me one tea after another."

It was dawning on her. How could she have been so narrow minded, so skeptical and suspicious? It was plainly obvious, yet she had forgotten about the birds, about Cyril's incapacity, about their promise to clean the aviaries for as long as it took. How could she doubt Joe? Was she going mad? Anyway, she needed to take a look at her own actions, her own sly behaviour, long before she accused Joe of anything underhand.

Housework had never been so much fun. Between kissing and hoovering, petting and polishing and full-blown sex while attempting to clean the bathroom, Joe and Tiff had completely rekindled their love affair in the privacy and comfort of their beautiful new home. Beautiful in the sense that it was theirs and not in the overall appearance – there were still so many odd-jobs to do.

"Why didn't you wake me up this morning? I would have helped you with the birds." Tiff stroked a hand across Joe's bare chest. She looked up to see his eyes closed and smiled to herself. Wrapped snugly in his arms, an overwhelming contentment filled her. She would stay here, in their bed, and drift off to sleep for a while, just like he was doing. There was no rush to jump out of bed and carry on with the housework. It could wait. Moments like this were too precious to leave. The doubting issues were contrived by her own folly. She had to realise that now.

"Meant to tell you," muttered Joe as he ploughed through his perfectly made Sunday roast. "Aaron said hello. He called me this morning while I was up to my elbows in bird shit."

"Aaron?"

"My brother, Aaron?" Joe raised his eyebrows, amusedly. "He wants to visit us soon – he's got a girlfriend he wants to introduce to us."

"Really? Aaron's finally got a girlfriend who's worth introducing to the family?"

Joe sniggered. "Yeah – he must consider her to be something special. He's never wanted anyone in the family to meet his previous girlfriends."

Tiff rested her knife and fork on the sides of her plate. "What's her name – do you know?"

Joe frowned, thoughtfully, while he chewed the piece of chicken in his mouth. "Think it's... err... Jenny," he said, gulping down the last piece in his mouth. "Yes – Jenny. She's got a shop, like Mum's."

"When are they coming?"

Joe eyed the food on his plate and tossed a few peas around. "Err... couple of weeks, maybe."

"OK," said Tiff, nodding her head amicably, "that'll be nice." She picked her knife and fork up again and proceeded to finish her meal. "You've done a great job with the dinner – might have to let you cook all the time."

Joe grinned, proudly. "And another thing..." He broke off and stuffed half a roast potato in his mouth, chewing it at speed.

"Yes?"

"We've been invited out next Saturday."

"By who?"

"Wayne and Hayley." He shoved another fork-full into his mouth, as if he were nervously racing to finish his meal. "They..." he mumbled, "It's a big night out. At the err... community centre again."

"Oh, another quiz night?"

"No, not a quiz night, it's a charity disco... or something like that. You know, new dress and all that."

"New dress? Really? For the community centre?"

Joe set his knife and fork neatly across his empty plate. "Yes, why what's up with that?"

"Nothing. I just wondered. What's it for then?"

"I don't know really. Wayne just said we should go as their charity nights are really good."

"OK."

"There'll be food there, I think." Joe shifted his gaze away from Tiff's and stared pensively through the patio doors. "Thought we could go and have some fun – what do you think?"

"Yes, OK. Do I really need to get a new dress though?"

"Yes, Hayley is. I'm sure that's what Wayne said anyway. It's about time you treated yourself to a nice new dress. We might go off somewhere else after the disco, like a casino or something."

Tiff eyed him doubtfully. "So when did you plan all of this?"

Joe peered down at his plate and straightened his perfectly straight knife and fork. "Err... this morning. He texted me so I called him while I was doing the birds."

"Blimey," Tiff could hear the sarcasm building in her voice, "you were busy this morning. How did you find time to clean the bird cages?"

Joe shrugged his shoulders and said nothing.

"Who else called or texted you this morning?"

"No one else. Just them two." Rising from his seat, he picked both plates up and carried them across to the kitchen sink. Then he turned to the kettle and flicked it on. "Tea or coffee?"

"Tea please and that meal was lovely. Thank you."

Joe winked a long-lashed eye at her before pulling two mugs out from the cupboard. "I'm going to... well, Wayne said I should wear a suit. Especially if we do go to a casino after. I'll get a new one in the week. I could do with a new one."

"Blimey – we're going all-out then?"

"Why not, babe. It's about time we had a bloody good night out."

"We had one last night."

"That was special – just you and me. But we've made some good friends in Wayne and Hayley, so we should go out a lot more with them. Don't you think so?"

"Yes." Tiff nodded and smiled. "Yes, I suppose we should."

"Good," Joe replied, like he was thankful. "It's not all about the house – we will enjoy our hard-earned money in other ways too. So, it's a date, yes?"

"Yes, yes, yes." Tiff giggled and suddenly felt the most at ease with him, that she had felt in quite a while.

Joe beamed and raised his eyebrows at the same time. "New dress – get one by Friday or... I'll go out and buy one for you myself."

"I will, without fail – there's no way you are buying me a dress. No way, Mr Frey."

It had been a little awkward to go back to work on Monday and dish out a bank of lies, to anyone who cared to listen to Tiff's tales, about her terribly sore throat, which had then led to Tonsillitis. She hated lying to people and was sure that her ruddy complexion should have given it all away. Yet, they believed her. She'd had such a good attendance record in the past that it was only natural that they would soak-up every deceitful word she said. She even surprised herself with how easy it was to lie to people and get away with it.

Thursday came around very quickly and Tiff's hard work, all week, had paid off. Guiltily, she was taking the afternoon off to go shopping for a new dress. She wasn't going to at first, but having mentioned the fact that she was going out on Saturday night, to her boss and her other colleagues, they had practically insisted that she take time off to go shopping – even if she had had the previous week off.

The girls in the studio had spent the week discussing the best colours for Tiff's complexion and hair colour, they'd deliberated over dress styles, shoes, accessories and even underwear. Tiff was perplexed by their attention to detail and unexpected interest in her weekend wear, yet she took all the advice on board and now had an image in her mind of exactly what she wanted.

Laden with paper bags, from boutiques she would have never normally considered shopping in, Tiff left the lay-by and started to walk up the path, around the green. It had been another glorious week of sunshine and according to the weather experts, it was set to stay for another week or so. Tiff's week had been full of sunshine, inside and out. The envy monster, within her, had retreated thankfully, and her week with Joe had been calm, trusting and loving. She had decided not to mention the text messages; it was better left that way. For now, at least. It had all become a little too confusing now and Tiff had decided that those questionable things were best left well alone.

Dazedly, she halted and looked up at the figure standing directly in front of her, on the path. "Alvin?" she muttered, instinctively.

Glaring down at her, his beady, dark eyes, burned into her own.

"Or should I say Jeremy?" she whispered, her heart beating rapidly in her throat.

Alvin's tight features turned into a scowl as his brow furrowed. He swivelled his eyes from one side to the other and spoke in a hushed voice, "You... You, stupid woman."

Tiff gasped at his words. "I beg your pardon."

Alvin shifted his gaze from one side to the other like he was checking for anyone within listening distance. He leant over and glared deep into Tiff's eyes. "It's not, Jeremy," he spat. "Do you have any idea?"

"Sorry?" Tiff's heart raced in her chest. "I know..."

"Know what?" Alvin chimed in. "What do you *think* you know?" His pointed nose screwed up disdainfully and his eyes narrowed. "You know nothing."

Taking a step back, Tiff puffed out her chest and stood tall, while clutching hold of her bags with a vice-like grip. She was surprised by her own resolve, "I... I know all about you."

"Have you any idea –" Alvin broke off sharply, straightened his back and cleared his throat. Again his shifty eyes twitched as he viewed the green. "You nearly blew my cover," he said in a quiet voice.

Tiff stared at him incredulously. "But you're not Alvin, you're Jeremy, I check..."

"Don't you get it?" Alvin cut in, "That's my cover." He rubbed a hand across his brow and sighed. "You nearly blew the whole thing apart. This can't go any further."

"Well, I'm sorry but... I don't believe you." Tiff drew in a deep breath and held it.

"Quite frankly, I don't care what you believe," he whispered, "it's got nothing to do with you and you should not get involved in things much bigger than yourself."

"But you're..." Tiff broke off thoughtfully. "I know who you are Jeremy. Jeremy Greene."

Alvin met Tiff's eyes with a hateful glare. He gulped and his prominent Adam's apple rose and fell sharply.

"Yes," Tiff continued, "I know exactly who you are. I know exactly what you do and... and I know you live with your mum."

Alvin took a step back, shook his head and stared at her suspiciously. He opened his mouth but no words came out.

"You've been working at that shop for over 20 years. Isn't that right Jeremy Greene?" Tiff swallowed hard as her nerves jangled and her heartbeat felt like it was thumping in her throat. Pure fear fueled her onwards. "Well? I am right, aren't I?"

"I don't know what you're talking about. I am a secret agent," he muttered. "You blew it and you should keep your nose out of my affairs. I'm the spy – not you. Don't forget it. I'm Alvin Snodgrass, working for the secret service, a spy-extraordinaire, the very best and you'd better... you'd better watch your back."

"Oh, you're threatening me now, are you?" Tiff stepped back terrified but continued to feign a strong front.

"Not threatening you," Alvin rubbed his nose nervously as his eyes continued to dart around Sycamore Close. "Warning you, that's all. Don't interfere in things you know nothing about." Alvin's persona had become edgy as he shifted from one foot to the other, looking uncomfortable.

"But I do know." Tiff looked past him and pointed to his house. "That house, your house... it's in the name of Jeremy... Jeremy Greene. That's you!"

Alvin appeared to freeze momentarily, his eyes fixed on hers, as if he was contemplating his next point of attack. "Just keep well away from me – you don't know what you're talking about," he snarled, before pushing past her and scurrying off towards the lay-by on the main road.

Tiff took a deep breath and pulled back her shoulders. She turned and watched Alvin/Jeremy climb into his car and shoot off down the road. She stared, incredulously, as the car weaved across the lanes, as the engine revved noisily, going faster and faster. He was guilty of a pack of lies. She knew it. And he knew she knew it.

"So, I now know that it's definitely true." Tiff propped her chin up and gazed out of the patio doors.

"I'm not having him threatening you like that though." Joe stroked her arm gently.

"He doesn't scare me. He's a completely delusional freak." She broke off and looked at Joe. "Actually, he did terrify me. Can't believe how brave I was. Yep – delusional freaks freak me out."

"Yes but those are the kind of weirdos who have totally lost their minds and could attack someone."

Tiff sighed and lifted her head. "Now you're being delusional – I don't think he's capable of attacking anyone. And..." The faint hum of Joe's mobile phone, vibrating in his pocket, caused Tiff to break off. She peered at him and forced a smile. "Going to see who it is?" she asked, a little too impatiently.

"Err... yeah." Reluctantly, Joe pulled the phone out and peered at the screen. "Ah, just missed it," he said, thumbing the screen.

"Who was it?"

"Just... nobody really."

Tiff frowned. "It can't have been nobody."

Letting out a chuckle, he looked up as he slid the phone back into his pocket. "No, of course not... it was only... Wayne."

"Wayne?"

"Yeah, golf... Saturday morning I'm guessing."

"Give him a call back." Tiff's mind was already working overtime.

Joe pulled himself up from the chair and headed for the kitchen. "I'll call him later – no problems."

It wasn't Wayne. That's what you always say. Tiff stared across the room at him. It was happening again. The raw emotions of distrust had resurfaced, no matter how much she tried to fight them back. Joe was useless at lying. His shifty gaze and edgy persona were no better covered up than Alvin's.

"Joe?"

"Yes, babe?" He swivelled on his heels to face her.

"Who was that call from really?"

His mouth dropped. "Wayne, I just told you."

"Then why do I find it hard to believe you?"

Joe laughed nervously. "I don't know babe – maybe this bloody Alvin/Jeremy business is getting to you."

"Maybe it is," Tiff began to backtrack, for fear of another big argument. "I'm sor..."

"Babe."

Tiff looked at him pleadingly.

"Don't start being sorry again – please. Now, do you want to show me your dress or have some tea first?"

Tiff smiled weakly. "I don't mind – you decide."

"Dinner it is then. I'm cooking again, so if you want to get a shower or bath, go and do it. And don't forget babe..."

"What?"

"I love you."

It was very odd that Joe should leave his phone lying on the dining table. He'd left for work some 30 minutes ago. Tiff tutted to herself. She didn't really have time to look through it and it wasn't even on anyway. She picked up her bag and jacket and left the house.

As she locked the front door, Tiff was aware of the door, to her left, opening. She turned and stared.

"Morning," chirped Georgie, a wide, lipstick grin across her face. Wearing a pale blue, cotton jacket, white top, white canvas trousers and *Cath Kidston,* floral canvas pumps, she looked fresh and pretty. Her hair was tied up in a ponytail and apart from her rose-pink lips, her eye make-up was subtle. "Off to work?"

Tiff pulled her key from the door and nodded. "Yes – you?"

"Oh – out and about for the day. Busy, busy, busy."

"You sound very cheerful," said Tiff, admiring Georgie's casual shoes.

Georgie locked her front door and walked down her pathway. "Got to be, I suppose." Her eyes met Tiff's. "Here," she said, beckoning to Tiff to move closer. "What were you doing last week – I saw you looking out of your window, with binoculars," she asked in a hushed voice. "See anything interesting out in the fields?"

Tiff cleared her throat. "Err... no not really. First time I've ever looked out there, to be honest. I... I wanted to get a closer look at the horses. I like horses."

Georgie eyed Tiff sharply. "Nice horses."

"Yes, not bad. So... sorry, where did you say you're going today?"

"Nowhere special – just out."

"Well, have a nice day. It's a beautiful one."

"I will." Georgie grinned. "Don't you work too hard. Especially as it is a beautiful one. Got to go now – bye." She waved a hand as she trotted off down her path, towards the gate.

Tiff didn't want to walk around the green with her, she had no intention of ever walking alongside Georgie, anywhere. She fumbled in her bag, pretending to look for something as Georgie headed out of her gate and walked across the green, towards Alvin's house. Then she disappeared around the corner and was gone.

Switching the Bluetooth on in her car, Tiff searched for Joe's work number. She pressed the call button on the dashboard's radio system and drove along steadily to work.

"Good morning, Ashdown Leisure Centre – how can I help you?" A woman's voice came through the radio speakers, after several rings.

"Hello, is that Carol?"

"No, Carol's not in today – can I take a message?"

"Tracey?"

"Yes, I'm Tracey."

"Gosh you sound just like Carol on the phone," said Tiff as she tried to concentrate on the road ahead. "Hi Tracey – it's Tiff."

"Oh, hello Tiff, how are you? I didn't recognise your voice either. Are you in a car? Sounds like it."

"Yes, driving into work. Is Joe there? I just need a quick word with him."

"Joe?"

Tiff giggled and slowed as she approached the usual, long queue of traffic, into town. "Yes, Joe – the manager. My boyfriend?"

"Sorry Tiff, I knew who you meant. He's not here."

"He left home quite some time ago – are you sure he's not there yet?"

There was a silent pause.

"Hello?" Tiff turned the dial up on the radio's volume.

"Yes, hi Tiff – still here."

"Could you check if he's arrived yet?"

"Tiff, Joe's not working today. He's got the day off."

Tiff's heart plummeted. "Oh," she spluttered. "But I thought... He left..." The traffic had come to a halt but she continued to grip the steering wheel tightly, with both hands. "Are you sure?"

"Yes," replied Tracey. "Dave's in. He's covering for him today."

First a burning flush filled her cheeks, then the swirly sensation hit her stomach. Queasy and hot, she attempted to backtrack, embarrassedly. "Oh yes! How stupid of me – I forgot he was having the day off." Tears began to sting her eyes. "Sorry Tracey, but thanks anyway. Have a nice day."

"You too, Tiff. Hope we might see you soon."

"Sure you will – bye."

"Bye."

This was the only day that she had ever been relieved to be stuck in the morning traffic. Giant tears fell from her eyes and almost fizzed and evaporated when they landed on her burning cheeks. *Where is he?* she thought, fretfully. Tears fell quicker now. She grabbed a tissue from the glove compartment and blew her nose, trying to make the sniffles go away. Peering up into the rear view mirror, she could see that her face was already turning red and blotchy. It always happened when she cried a lot. Luckily, her mascara was still in place, and as long as she didn't wipe her eyes at all, she would look OK, as soon as she could stop crying.

She had another ten minutes of her journey left. She had to try and sort herself out before she got to work. Crying, because your boyfriend had taken the day off work, was not a good enough reason to go into work with a wet, grief-stricken face. Because then she would have to let her colleagues know what was really going on. That was the biggest problem of all. She had no idea what was really going on, just that there was *something* going on. She couldn't get her head around any of it. One moment Joe was as loving as anyone could ever want their partner to be.

The next, he was elusive, vague or decidedly edgy. Then, in an instant, he'd become the caring, understanding boyfriend who could see that his partner had insecurity issues and want to help and be so supportive. Nothing made any sense.

She couldn't even call him. Joe had mysteriously left his phone at home. He'd gone out of the door, wearing his usual work attire, carrying his normal briefcase-style bag. He'd even made packed lunches for them both.

An image of Georgie, dressed beautifully in casual attire, entered her mind. Tiff felt a new surge of sickness rise into her throat. Where was *she* going today? She'd practically avoided the question of where she was off to and shrugged it off as unimportant. But maybe it was important. Perhaps it was all-important. Tiff tossed the idea away by shaking her head and then pulled into the studio car park. She turned into her usual parking bay and checked her face in the mirror. She looked OK-ish. She felt utterly rubbish though. If she didn't pull herself together before she went into the studio, she would burst into tears the moment anyone greeted her. How was she going to get through the day like this?

Chapter 28

Babe – don't know what to say. Sorry I didn't tell you I was having the day off. It was a little secret to be honest with you. Maybe it could still be? Wait until you get home, love Joe xxxx

Tiff had struggled through the morning, hardly eaten anything during lunchtime and now this, half way through the afternoon. It had better be a great big surprise if she was going to believe it. She discreetly thumbed a reply message on her phone.

Picked up your phone then? How did Tracey contact you, to tell you your phone was at home? Or have you been at home all day?

Wait and see when you get home, love you, Joe xxxx

Tiff threw her phone into her bag, angrily. She did not like 'little secrets' as Joe had stated. It was all too much. Sycamore Close seemed to be full of 'little secrets' and now her boyfriend was admitting that he was keeping them too.

She picked up another ornamental rabbit and began to buff the scumble from its back – two more trays and she was going home. She'd had an absolute rubbish day and hardly spoken a word to anyone in the studio. Using the excuse of, 'time of the month, she had scraped through the morning and lunchtime, by nodding her head here and there and smiling now and again. Her thoughts drifted backwards and forwards – *Georgie, Joe, hatred, despair, disbelief, secrets, lies, insecurity, jealousy...*

Hang on a minute, she wasn't much better herself. She had secrets, she had told lies. Wasn't it all getting a little out of hand? Was it really all in her head? Or were her worst thoughts really true and Joe was simply cunningly clever and highly deceitful? Backwards and forwards, forgiveness and accusations, Tiff struggled with all of it. It really had to stop. She was losing her mind.

The journey home had seemed much longer than normal, but Tiff guessed that it was because she was desperate to get back and see what this 'little secret' might be. It would have to be a really good one if she was going to believe anything that came out of Joe's mouth.

As she walked around the green she could just see Betty's head bobbing up and down, behind her fence. "Hello Betty, how are you?" said Tiff, peering over the fence. "And how is Cyril doing?"

"Hello Tiff, yes I'm very well thank you." She heaved herself up from the tiny stool she'd been sitting on. "Cyril's doing very well too – he'll be absolutely fine tomorrow."

"Why tomorrow?" Tiff peered at her puzzled.

Betty slapped a gloved hand to her mouth and then screwed up her face in disgust, as she realised she'd just covered her face in black soil. She spluttered and spat. "Silly, silly me," she said, between slobbering and spluttering, and brushing her mouth with her sleeve. "Ah, tomorrow, yes, we're going out for the first time, since..."

"Oh, I see," said Tiff, not wishing to pry further and rake up the memories of Cyril's unfortunate episode. "Say no more. I'm really pleased to hear it. Hope you'll have a lovely time, wherever you're going."

Betty grinned sweetly and then spat another tiny piece of black soil from her mouth. "Thank you, Tiff – I'm sure we will have a lovely time."

Tiff peeped over the fence. "They look nice – what are they?"

"Those are petunias," said Betty pointing to several tiny, flowering green bushes. "And those ones are pansies." She looked up and met Tiff's eye. "I have some spare ones if you'd like them."

"Oh no, I couldn't take any more from you. You've already given us more than enough."

"No, please, take them." She bent over and picked up the two trays. She counted the little plants, still left in their pods. "There are... six, seven, eight, nine there. They'd look nice in your garden, please take them." Betty smiled warmly and passed the trays over. "They'd give some colour to your back garden if you dotted them around. There you are."

Tiff took the trays, reluctantly. "Are you sure? I can't thank you enough for these. I would love to plant them over the weekend. Are you absolutely sure?"

Betty nodded her little curly head and grinned.

"Can I offer you some mon –"

"No, you can't," Betty chimed in.

"Well," said Tiff, peering down at the tiny plants, "thank you so much." She made a mental note to make a thank-you card for Betty. It was about time she started to repay her kind neighbours for the nice things they did – well, some of them anyway. She still needed to make a card for Cyril as well, although it seemed a bit pointless now that he was home from the hospital. Maybe she would make a card saying something like, 'So pleased to hear that you are back home recuperating'. "Right, I'd better get indoors – Joe will be wondering where I am."

"Fine young man, is Joe. You look after that one."

"Oh, I will Betty, don't you worry. Thank you again and have a nice day out tomorrow."

"Evening," Betty corrected.

"Oh, OK. Have a lovely evening. And please say hello to Cyril for us."

"I certainly will. Bye for now."

At first, the striking smell of paint hit Tiff's nose, followed by a subtler, sweet smell of flowers. She walked slowly into the dining room, not knowing quite what to expect. On the dining table, sat a tall vase, filled with colourful tulips in shades of pink, blue, yellow and orange. The whole room (including the kitchen) smelt and looked fresh, clean, spotless – immaculate in fact. Had Joe really taken the day off, secretly, just to clean the house and get some tulips and why could she smell paint? She placed the trays of plants on the floor next to the patio doors and turned to slyly admire Joe's efforts to make the place look so nice.

"Tiff – is that you?" Joe called from upstairs.

"Yes, who else would it be?"

"Come up here."

"Why?" Tiff didn't want to make it too easy. He had an uncanny knack of wooing her into bed at a moment's notice. She's couldn't resist his charms at the best of times but today, she wanted to be grumpy with him. Today she would make him suffer – just a little. Like she had suffered all day long. Why make it such a big secret to have a day off work, just to clean the house? Why clean the house anyway? Wasn't that her job at the weekends?

Grumpily, she walked back through the lounge to the staircase. "Why do I have to come up there?"

"Because I want you to," Joe replied. "Please, babe."

She climbed the stairs resentfully as the smell of fresh paint grew stronger. "Where are you?" she said, having reached the top. It was normal for her craft room door to be closed but every other door was closed too.

"In here," Joe called from the bedroom.

Tiff tutted to herself and stepped across the landing. She opened the bedroom door slowly and a waft of paint fumes filled her nose. "Oh my God, Joe."

"Do you like it?" Joe stood at the far side of the room, covered in speckles of white paint, beaming.

The room was much brighter than before. The old wardrobes had been replaced with new wider, white ones and the walls were satin-white, on two sides. Two new, white bedside cabinets sat either side of the bed, with small, white table lamps on the top. A neatly made, new, pastel pink and purple flowery quilt cover and pillowcases, with dainty butterflies speckled here and there, lie on the bed and, as Tiff stepped further into the room, she could see a beautiful, matching wallpaper on the opposite wall with a large, white filigree framed mirror in the centre. A luxurious, deep-pile, purple carpet lay at her feet and the window was adorned with brilliant white, vertical blinds and a pair of purple curtains, held against the sides of the window frame with dainty, butterfly tie-backs. Underneath the window was a small, white dressing table with matching stool. The padded seat of the stool was covered in a rich purple, plush fabric.

Tiff met Joe's eye and stared incredulously. "How?" She began to say before breaking off and scanning the room again. A beautiful, white lampshade with tiny butterfly stencils hung from the pendant in the centre of the room, which she hadn't noticed a moment ago, and matched the table lamps perfectly. "How have you done all of this – in a day?"

Joe walked around the bed and approached her with open arms. "With some careful planning and a bit of sneaking about. Sorry." He pulled her into his arms and kissed the top of her head. "You like it then?"

"I... I love it... but why?"

"I wanted to surprise you, babe. You deserve to have nice things. I've cleaned the whole house too."

"Why?"

"So you don't have to do it." Joe peered down at her. "Don't forget we're out tomorrow night, but apart from that, I want you to have a nice, relaxing weekend, with no worries of doing the housework – you deserve it."

"Do I?" whispered Tiff.

"Yes, you do." Joe smiled down at her sincerely. "Also, the weather's good all weekend, so we'll try out our new barbecue on Sunday."

"You've bought a barbecue as well?"

"Yes, why not? We can eat *al fresco* this weekend, what do you think?"

"I'm not sure what I think – I'm a bit overwhelmed by it all, to be honest."

"Ah babe," said Joe, pulling her closer and burying his face in the top of her head. "Your happiness is so worth this – all of this. I know how you've struggled lately." He reached down and took her hand. "Come on, I've made a chicken salad for tea – we'll eat it outside." He grinned cheekily. "We'll use the patio suite."

"Patio suite?"

"The *new* patio suite. Come and see and while you're trying out the new chairs, I'll crack open your favourite peach wine."

Tiff followed him out of the room, completely dazed by his actions. "I can't... I can't believe you've done all of this," she said, as she followed him down the stairs. "I've had a..."

"Terrible day?" He finished her sentence for her. "I know. I mean, I can imagine you have and I'm so sorry about that." He turned when he reached the bottom, placed his hands round Tiff's waist and picked her up from the third step. Turning around, he kissed her softly, while she was still held up, and then carefully lowered her to the ground. "That was the one mistake I made today – leaving my phone behind. I had so much going on in my head that I completely forgot to take it with me. I'm so sorry babe. I knew you would be thinking the worst of me all day."

"Where did you go this morning?"

"Nowhere." Joe sniggered. "I drove my car to the lay-by, back on Oakley Close, and waited for you to go."

"I can't believe you've done all of this in a day. Has anyone helped you?"

"Ah…" Joe pulled her through to the garden and around the corner, where he had hidden a grey, plastic whicker-style patio table and six chairs. "Just give me a hand to move this round – I didn't want you to see it when you came home, so we hid it."

"It's lovely," said Tiff, still dumbfounded by the amount of work and secrecy Joe had put into the day and all, it seemed, for her benefit. "So, who's 'we'?"

"Wayne."

"Really?" Tiff was more surprised by the fact that Joe had obviously formed more than just a casual, neighbourly/golf partner relationship with Wayne and they had actually become real friends.

"Yes – couldn't have done it all without him. He put the furniture together while I did the decorating."

Tiff shook her head disbelievingly, as they carried the table across to the patio and then returned to the corner to collect the chairs, one by one. "I am totally amazed by you, Joe Frey. I can't believe you've done all of this, just to surprise me."

"Full of surprises," said Joe, winking an eye, as he placed another chair at the table.

"This patio set is just what I would have chosen and the bedroom…"

"I know."

It suddenly hit her, like a gush of water smacking her in the face. He did know. He was more attentive than she'd ever given him credit for. Every tiny little detail of the bedroom, the tulips on the dining table, the patio set, the peach wine, the chicken salad, the *al fresco* dining, they were all things she'd mentioned at one point or another. All things she would like to have or to do, all her favourite things. Did she really deserve him?

It no longer mattered. Her jealousy was something she had to sort out on her own. It was obvious that her envious trait was completely unfounded. Perhaps the goings-on with Georgie and Alvin had really tainted Tiff's view of everything.

The smell of paint soon disappeared as they became accustomed to it. Butterflies danced above their heads as they made love, for hours, among the pastel pink and purple blooms.

The only thing he hadn't done, yesterday, was empty the bins around the house. She wouldn't expect him to do her craft bin and it wasn't a problem that he hadn't done the others either. She was completely enamoured of him, dazedly swoony, every time she thought about him. So emptying the bins really had no significance to the whole clean-up affair at all.

Until...

The snapped, beige coloured hairband sat at the bottom of the bathroom pedal-bin – broken blonde hairs wrapped around it. Hiding underneath a discarded empty toilet roll, the hairband was not meant to be seen.

Tiff picked it out and examined it as the familiar surge of sick hatred began to brew. Her knees buckled and she lowered herself to the floor, gripping the hairband tightly in her palm. There was no mistaking this hairband. Georgie wore beige ones to tie her hair back into a ponytail or a messy bun. There was absolutely no mistaking it at all. Georgie had been in the house since last week's ceremonial bin emptying, that was for sure. The worst part of it was – the woman must have been upstairs. She had to have been, otherwise, why would a hairband be in the bathroom bin? What had she been doing upstairs? In Tiff's house. She struggled to breathe. Pinned to the bathroom floor with an overwhelming jealousy, she shuddered as tears welled and stung her eyes before they fell on to her cheeks. How could he? How could Joe do this? It was plainly obvious why Georgie would have been upstairs. How could he? In their bed? Was it before the new bedding went on? Or after? Maybe it was *her* who helped him yesterday and not Wayne. How could Joe be so false? How could he make love to her so meaningfully when he must have been sleeping with Georgie too? Did he love the woman? Did he love them both? Tiff sobbed harder, still rooted to the floor. What should she do now? There was no way out of this one for Joe, although, she desperately searched for feasible ways that he could talk his way out of it. For the first time in her life, Tiff wanted to be irrationally jealous, she wanted to be the envious, insecure, paranoid girlfriend... who was utterly wrong.

Joe wouldn't be home for another couple of hours. He'd left early, to play golf, with Wayne or so he'd told Tiff. Was he really playing golf? The doubting and suspicion had risen tenfold. Could she believe anything that he told her? Could they ever get over this latest piece of the jigsaw? It was all adding up and an affair with Georgie, would explain a lot of strange things, a lot of Joe's odd behaviour. Yet, if he and Georgie were really together, did he have a split personality? He had played the doting, loving boyfriend very well, as far as Tiff was concerned. Did Georgie love him? How could she when she was also rollicking around in the woods with Alvin. Did Joe know about Georgie's other affairs? Tiff doubted it. Maybe he should know. Maybe he wouldn't want to be with *her* if he knew what she really got up to. Then Tiff could have him back and have him all to herself. Although it hurt considerably to think about it, she knew, deep in her heart that she would never want him back if he had been with her. It would be over, without a doubt.

With a thumping head, tired, sore eyes and a broken heart, she pulled her weary self up from the bathroom floor and trudged through to their newly decorated bedroom. The calming pinks and purples had a new feel about them. An unpleasant, morose feel. She climbed into bed and closed her eyes as saddened butterflies fluttered, half-heartedly, in circles, above her head. Round and round and round. Sleep was her only sanctuary. Her only means of escape from herself.

The sound of the front door clicking open, woke Tiff from her restless sleep. She opened her heavy, puffy eyelids and strained to see as the brightness of the afternoon sun lit up the room even more than usual. Peering at the clock on the new bedside table, she noted the time, 2.30pm – she'd been asleep for a couple of hours.

"Tiff?" Joe's voice broke into her awakening memories of why she had eyes which felt bruised and puffy and why she had been asleep for some time. "Babe – I'm home." His voice sounded cheery.

She lay still, not daring to move, in case the torturous recollections she was having were real.

Joe's footsteps faded as he walked through the living room and into the dining room.

The memories were real.

Then the sound of his feet, pounding across the carpets, grew louder. He reached the bottom of the staircase. "Tiff? Are you up there, babe?"

She held her breath. She didn't want to see him. She didn't know how to tell him. She almost felt sorry for him because he had been found out.

Joe bounded up the stairs. "Tiff? Are you OK?" he asked as he entered the bedroom.

Peeping over the top of the quilt, she stared at him desperately. He was gorgeous. She loved him. Still. Tears bubbled up again and she blinked them away.

"Babe, what's the..."

Pulling the quilt over her head, she began to sob. A hand touched her shoulder.

"What's the matter?"

Her sobbing grew in strength and she trembled. His big hand gently smoothed her hair.

"Tiff – talk to me – what's happened?" Joe pulled the quilt back and attempted to scoop her up into his arms. "Babe, please, tell me what's wrong."

She resisted his embrace and fell back on the pillow. Covering her face with her hands, she continued to cry, inconsolably. Reaching under the covers with one hand, she searched blindly for the hairband she had still been holding when she fell asleep. Found it. She drew it out from under the quilt and threw it into Joe's face. He flinched and then peered down at his lap.

"What's this?"

Drawing in a deep breath, she let it out slowly, trying to calm her shredded nerves.

"Tiff – what is this?"

Peeping between her fingers, she could see Joe holding the hairband up and examining it with a puzzled expression on his handsome face.

"Tiff, talk to me please. I have no idea what this is."

She watched as he twiddled it around with his fingers and stretched the elastic cord. "Where's this from? Is it yours?"

"Haven't got blonde hair."

"Babe, where did you get this?"

"Bathroom." Tiff lowered her hands as her face reddened with the heat of sobbing so much.

"OK. Well, I have no idea how it got there."

"It's... Georgie's." She sniffed and reached over to the bedside table for a tissue.

"Georgie's? Why have we got it then? I don't understand what's going on." Joe's cheery voice of earlier had turned to a wobbly, worried mutter.

"Found it in the bin... in the bathroom."

Joe shot a startled look from the hairband to Tiff and back again, shaking his head from side to side. "I... I don't know. Are you sure?"

Tiff pulled herself up to a sitting position. "Sure? Sure of what? That I found it in the bin? Or that it's Georgie's?" Her grief was turning to sheer anger.

"That it belongs to Georgie." Joe met her eye and stared sorrowfully. "I..." he shook his head again and lowered his eyes. "God – I know how this must look babe."

"Don't call me, babe. And yes, I'm pretty sure. After all, I don't have long blonde hair and *she* wears those all the time – you must have noticed."

"So do a million other women I'd imagine. Tiff... please. Why do you think it's a woman with *long*, blonde hair?"

Tiff snorted disdainfully. "For a start, she'd hardly need to put her hair up if it were short, would she? And the hair is blonde – do you get it?"

Joe nodded his head and reached a hand out towards hers.

"I want an honest answer Joe. No more of this skirting around the issues." She broke off and took a deep breath. "Are you seeing her?"

Joe shook his head once more and met her eye. "I'm not seeing anyone babe. I promise you. I don't know how that..." He pointed to the hairband, "got in the bin. Maybe Wayne put it there. He might know something."

Tiff feigned a roar of laughter. "Wayne? Does he wear those? Wrong colour hair anyway."

"Maybe he found it."

"Found it – where?" Tiff's anger had turned into cynical sarcasm. "Maybe here – in the bedroom?"

"I don't know, maybe he did – when we were laying the new carpet. I just don't know."

"I don't know, I don't know, I don't know. That's all you can answer to any of my questions. Why should I believe you?" Tiff snatched the hairband out of his hand and tossed it across the room. "That is just too much," she said, pointing a trembling finger towards the hairband, lying on the floor. "All the little signs. The things I find. Your secretive behaviour. The dodgy text messages. They all point to one thing, Joe." She paused and stared directly into his troubled eyes. "They point to you – having an affair – with *her*, next door."

Joe buried his face in his hands and sighed, loudly. He shook his head from side to side before lifting it again. "Tiff – it's not true. This has got to end. I don't know anything about that hairband – I promise you."

She gasped.

"I'll prove it..." He paused thoughtfully, "yes, I can prove it. Come out with me tonight and the first thing we'll do is talk to Wayne and get this all cleared up." Joe reached across for her hand again but she snatched it away.

"I don't feel like going out now..." She broke off. "But if I don't go..." She glared hard at Joe's face, "well, God knows what you'll get up to and... and you'd get a chance to forewarn Wayne anyway. He probably knows exactly what you're doing. I'm not stupid. He tried to cover up for you before – pretending that he'd sent you a message when he hadn't."

Joe stood up purposefully, peered down at her with a stern face and drew a deep breath in. "Please come with me tonight. I will prove it somehow. I don't want anyone else in my life – not Georgie – not anyone. I love you." He held a hand up and motioned to the bedroom. "Why do you think I've done all this for you?"

"Don't see why you had to be so secretive about it."

"I wanted to surprise you – to make you happy. I wanted to spoil you. You have no idea..." He broke off and sat back on the bed. He took hold of her hand and held it with both of his. "You have no idea how much I love you. Please, let's go tonight and you can ask Wayne anything you like. I won't go anywhere near him until you've spoken to him... and here," Joe pulled his phone from his pocket, "you can have this until we go, just so that I can't forewarn him."

Tiff flung the phone back on to his lap. "I don't want it. You keep it. You might get another one of those secretive text messages." She paused in thought as she pulled her hand slowly away from his. She was confused. She wanted to be angry. She wanted to hate him. It was so hard because she wanted to believe him so much. What possible explanation could Wayne have for the hairband, if any? "OK, I'll go, but I need answers if we are to continue our relationship. Someone put that hairband in our bin – and I know it wasn't me."

Joe slumped on the edge of the bed. He looked relieved, tired and stressed. "OK, just give me this one last chance. Make sure you speak to Wayne tonight. I'm as confused as you are."

Chapter 29

They'd hardly said two words to each other by the time Tiff was ready to go out. Wearing her new outfit, she sat at the dining table, drinking a glass of wine and planning what she would say to Wayne when she saw him. Because she was most definitely going to broach the subject. She had to. Too much had happened and been said between her and Joe, and things had to be sorted out one way or another. She was at the end of the line and by the way Joe's wistful expression had lingered all afternoon, she knew that he could be too.

She gulped nervously at her wine, while Joe was getting dressed upstairs. The alcohol was already having an effect, after just one glass. They'd had nothing to eat, as Joe had said there would be food before the charity disco started, so the wine was going straight to her head. She really didn't fancy the idea of going out tonight, let alone go to some fund-raising disco. Having said that, she was quite astonished at how nice she looked in her new, figure-hugging, low-cut, red dress. So maybe she should go out and flaunt her look, just for the sake of it. Especially if Georgie was going to be there – dishing out hot dogs or burgers, with a conceited smirk on her face. She made a mental note to thank her work colleagues, who had been spot-on with their suggestions for the perfect outfit. Tiff's long, brown hair twisted and tumbled down her back in wavy bands and she'd applied a little more eye make-up than usual, finishing her look off with a rich, red lipstick. She was dressed to kill – or thrill. Whichever came first.

Draining her wine glass, she listened as Joe thudded down the stairs. He appeared in the doorway, tall, broad and looking exceptionally handsome in his new grey suit. He swivelled the knot of his tie and smiled.

"Stand up," he said, "Let me see."

Tiff rolled her eyes and pulled herself up from the chair.

"Bloody hell – you look absolutely stunning babe." He took three steps towards her and rested his hands on her tiny waist. "Do you still care about me enough to kiss me?"

She turned her head away. "I've just put lipstick on."

"OK." Taking a step back, he looked down at his suit. "Does this look all right? You know, especially if we're going on to a casino later – got to dress right."

Tiff nodded nonchalantly. "Yeah – OK." She picked her empty glass up from the table. "Think I might have another one of these before we go. What time are we going over to Hayley and Wayne's?"

"We're meeting them there," said Joe, opening a can of beer and taking a long gulp. "I've booked a taxi for us – didn't think you'd want to walk there in those heels."

"Good," Tiff forced a smile. "I wasn't looking forward to walking there. Why have they left early, without us?"

"Not really sure. I think Hayley had something to sort out on the way."

A sadness swept over Tiff as she thought about the difficult situation they were in. If Wayne didn't come up with the right answer tonight, or she didn't believe him, she would be back to the same scenario as this afternoon. Then, how would the hairband be explained? What would she do next?

"Go easy on that wine, babe, we've got a long night ahead." Joe smiled warmly. "I'm only having this one, for now. Thought I'd wind it up a gear later on."

"I'll be fine," she replied, sipping at a fresh glass. "I'll slow down once we get there, although I feel like getting completely pissed actually."

"Why?"

She gave Joe a lingering glare. "Why do you think?"

"OK babe," he said, putting his hands up. "Speak to Wayne – we'll get this all sorted out."

"Oh, I will, most definitely."

Joe lifted his can of beer to his lips and gulped down the rest of the contents. "Aar..." he gasped as he crushed the can in his hand and then threw it in the bin.

"You can hardly moan at me when you knocked that back so quick."

"I wasn't moaning at you, babe, merely concerned. I know how you say wine goes to your head quickly. I just didn't want you feeling ill later or tired." He twitched a nervous smile. "I'm only having that one, for now. A bit of Dutch courage, I suppose."

"Why do you need Dutch courage? Am I going to hear something I don't want to?"

Joe tried to backtrack. "No... I didn't mean Dutch courage, I meant... well, you know..."

"No, I don't know what you mean anymore."

"Babe – it was a figure of speech – and in hindsight, probably the wrong one. Yes, I do feel a bit on edge but that's only because I'm worried about you."

"Don't need to worry about me. It's you I'm worried about." Tiff eyed him suspiciously.

"Me? Why?"

"We still haven't sorted things out have we?"

"We will babe – trust me. It will be sorted out. I'm sure Wayne must know something."

The short taxi ride to the community centre was in silence. Although Joe insisted that they hold hands in the car, no words were uttered between them. Joe was the only one who'd said anything and that was to the taxi driver.

Walking into the reception area of the community centre, Tiff noted a beautiful arrangement of tulips (just like the ones she had at home, but much bigger and with the addition of twisty curls and spirals of glittery plastic), sat on a table.

"That looks nice," said Joe, as they walked past, hand in hand.

Tiff was dumbfounded. He had never given a bunch of flowers a second glance, let alone comment on how nice they looked.

It was strangely quiet in the reception area. Tiff had been expecting a couple of the older folk to be milling around the reception room, welcoming people to the charity do. Yet, there was no one around at all. Not even any partygoers.

"Are you sure you've got the right night?" asked Tiff, in a whisper, as they paused outside the main hall door.

"Think so. I'm sure Wayne said it was here." Joe turned to her and let go of her hand. He peered into her eyes. "Babe," he said, cupping his hands around her face. "I love you – please don't ever forget it." Then he kissed her softly on the lips.

A rush of excitement hit her. She needed him to love her. She wanted to love him too. She did love him. It was just too hard to ignore the little things that were so wrong, so unmistakably telling. A tear welled in her eye.

"Babe," he whispered, "please don't cry." He kissed her lips again. "I love you so much. You've got to believe me." He smiled and brushed a strand of hair away from her face. "Come on, let's see if Wayne's here."

Tiff peered up at the ceiling and blinked the wetness away from her eyes, before it ruined her make-up. She looked down again and mustered up a half smile. She wanted to enjoy the evening. She wanted Wayne to say the right things. She wanted to find answers to everything. She wanted to believe.

Reaching down, Joe took hold of her hand and smiled. "Come on, we'll find Wayne first."

He opened the door. Pitch black, apart from a solitary spotlight which shone on the floor, directly in front of them. There was complete silence and darkness in the room. No party.

Tiff halted momentarily. "Joe," she whispered, as he continued to drag her into the room and under the spotlight.

A shuffling noise could be heard at the back of the room. Tiff held her breath. What was he doing, dragging her into a darkened room, it was more than spooky, it was utterly creepy and bizarre. Where were the partygoers? Where were Hayley and Wayne? The heat from the single spotlight warmed the top of her head.

Joe turned to face her and gave her a lingering look.

"What's going on?" she whispered.

Lowering himself down to the floor, Joe knelt on one knee, still holding her left hand. He peered up at her and smiled.

"Joe?" She looked down at him, her heart racing in her chest. Emotions surged through her body erratically. Fear, love, confusion and elation.

"Tiffany Cuthbert..." He squeezed her hand, his eyes fixed on hers. "Will you do me the honour..." He smiled so sweetly, an expectant look in his eyes, "of marrying me?"

Tiff clapped her free hand across her mouth and stared at him incredulously. Tears welled in her eyes instantly.

Time stood still for that moment. Under the warm spotlight, her head swam with images and conversations they'd had in the past. Now she was here... and he'd just asked her to marry him. Was he truly serious? She nodded her head, took her hand away from her mouth, as the tears fell on to her cheeks, and said, "Yes."

Joe pulled a tiny box from inside his jacket, opened it up and presented a shiny, gold ring, encrusted with three sparkling diamonds. He carefully removed the tiny ring from the box and gently slid it up her ring finger. It fitted snugly. Pulling himself up from the floor, he took both her hands in his and kissed her lips softly. "Thank you my beautiful babe," he whispered.

He was truly serious.

It was real.

A sudden vibration of energy and sound resonated around the room. People clapping and cheering.

The lights went on. Blindingly bright.

Tiff turned towards the back of the room, startled by the din. Her eyes took a moment to adjust to the glaring lights. Still holding onto Joe's hands, she swivelled her head from side to side along a crowd of people standing at the back of the room. They began to move forward slowly, still clapping, cheering, whistling and whooping. She stared at them incredulously. Trying to comprehend what was going on. Who these people were.

The first people Tiff recognised, once she'd become compos mentis, were Hayley and Wayne. They were clapping their hands together and smiling at one end of the crowd. And there was Lilly, dressed in a beautiful lime-green, flowery dress. She waved heartily. A huge crinkly grin filled her face.

Tiff looked back at Joe, who was still holding her hands. She stared deep into his eyes disbelievingly.

Turning back, she peered along the throng and then took a second look. Alex and Grant were there. They were clapping and grinning widely. Alex's eyes looked glassy. Was she crying? Emma (Joe's younger sister) and her new boyfriend, Andrew, stood alongside Grant and Alex. They all continued to clap and slowly move forward. Aaron (Joe's older brother) was there with an attractive young lady standing closely beside him. Letting go of Joe's hands, Tiff turned and faced the crowd, head on. There was Pat and the rest of her work colleagues, all smiling and slapping their hands together enthusiastically. Tiff recognised several faces from the rugby club – they were Joe's friends and their partners too. The staff from the leisure centre, where Joe worked. Carol, Lee, Dave and Tracey. She had only spoken to Tracey yesterday, on the phone. Tiff was speechless. She could only gape at the sea of familiar faces.

Continuing to scan along the lines of people, incredulously, Tiff could see Betty and Cyril at the far end... and there... at the very end of the line... Tiff gulped back overwhelming emotions. Her dad was standing tall and proud... alongside her mum. Her mum was here. She had travelled here. She was wiping a tissue under her eyes and smiling waveringly. Their eyes met before Tiff's mum began to weep on to her dad's shoulder. Tiff smiled and cried at the same time.

Huddled at the back, right in the corner of the room was Georgie, clapping along with everyone else, a broad, friendly smile across her face.

"Babe."

The sound of Joe's voice, filtered in over the raucous din. Tiff turned back and peered deeply into his eyes. He had asked her to marry him. He'd arranged for all these people to be here. He really, truly loved her. More tears fell from her eyes and he gently wiped them from her cheeks.

"Babe, you are my wife-to-be. I have so much to tell you... so much to explain to you."

Tiff gazed into his eyes, not knowing quite what to say. She glanced down at the sparkling ring on her hand and then looked up to see that everyone had now surrounded them both.

Some people, particularly Joe's friends from rugby, patted him on the back while others took hold of Tiff's left hand and gazed, admiringly at her new ring. Everyone seemed to be talking at once and Tiff struggled to comprehend anything. People congratulated her, hugged her, held her hand and looked at her ring. She was dumbfounded. Speechless. Bowled over by the scale of Joe's secrecy. Astounded by his intention.

"Ladies and gentlemen." A familiar voice of a man boomed through the room's ceiling speakers, jolting Tiff back from her bewildered state. "If you could all make your way towards the bar area, champagne will be served while we arrange the tables at this end of the room. Thank you."

Tiff began to search the sea of friendly faces, acknowledging, greeting, smiling and showing off her ring as she went, as if she was on automatic pilot. She eagerly looked for her mum and dad. Within seconds, she had been separated from Joe and slowly drifted away from him, on a tide of inspired guests.

"Congratulations Tiff." An unmistakable voice whispered in her ear, "I'm so happy for you both."

Tiff turned and almost touched noses with Georgie. Dressed in smart black trousers and a cream blouse, her attire was rather conservative.

"Thank you."

Georgie brushed a hand down her trousers, "I'm working here tonight – an invited guest as well. I'll catch up with you later, we really must have a proper chat." She grinned and winked an eye before walking off to the bar.

Tiff peered after her, stunned by her turn of character. She had just spoken to Tiff in a friendly, courteous manner. Or was Tiff seeing and hearing her properly for the first time?

A small hand touched Tiff's shoulder and she turned around. "Mum," she cried and threw her arms round her mum's shoulders. "You... how...?"

Mum wiped her eyes again, took Tiff's hand and looked down at the ring. "It's so beautiful." She sniffed. "We got here this afternoon."

Tiff peered incredulously. "By car?"

Mum nodded. "Your dad helped me. We did it in two stages. I told you a little white lie last week." She shrugged her shoulders and grinned as the tears continued to fall. "I've been seeing a counselor for several weeks now."

"Oh, Mum, I'm so proud of you." Tiff hugged her again and felt like she could burst into tears herself. She had to remain calm, keep focused. For the sake of her mascara, if nothing else.

"I'm so proud of you too Tiffany – look at you – you're going to be getting married."

The words hit Tiff between the eyes. She hadn't quite taken it all in. "Yes – oh my goodness – yes."

"Dad's just getting you and Joe a drink. He'll be over in a minute."

"Congratulations." Tiff turned to see Alex standing beside her, "I'm so excited for you both."

"Thank you," said Tiff, kindly. "I can't believe you're all here. Did you know about this when I saw you last?"

Alex nodded her head wittingly.

Tiff turned and beckoned to her mum. "Mum, this is..."

"Oh, I know who this is. She's your mum – well she had better be." Alex let out a burst of laughter.

"Sorry?"

"She'd better be your mum – she's been round my house all afternoon, drinking tea."

Tiff stared, disbelievingly. "You've been..."

Mum nodded her head and grinned. "Oh yes, we've met already. Your Joe has been pretty cunning behind your back.

Tiff shook her head, unable to get her thoughts around the extent of Joe's covert activities.

"Hello Tiff – welcome to the family – almost." Aaron bent down and pecked her on the cheek. "Can I introduce Jenny to you?"

"Hi, call me Jen, most people do." Jen offered a handshake. "Congratulations to you both. It's lovely to meet you."

"Thank you," replied Tiff. "It's nice to meet you too."

"Ooh, I'm so excited for you." Emma appeared from nowhere and flung her arms round Tiff's neck. "We'll be like sisters, when you two get hitched.

Tiff's eyes widened. It was really starting to dawn on her. She was engaged to Joe. He'd asked her to marry him. In front of so many people. They were going to get married.

"Meet Andrew..." Emma turned and introduced a tall, dark-haired man behind her, who was standing with his hands in his pockets. He smiled politely, mouthed a 'congratulations' and shook her hand.

"It's nice to meet you Andrew – I've heard a lot about you."

"All good I hope." Andrew smiled and placed a hand round Emma's waist.

"Yes, all good."

Dad appeared with a tray of drinks. "Champagne all round," he said, a wide beam of satisfaction spreading across his face. "Congratulations Tiffany. He'll make a fine husband, you know."

Everyone agreed and took a flute from the tray.

"Ladies and gentleman."

Tiff had gathered her thoughts together enough to realise that it was Charlie speaking over the microphone, from the stage.

"If you can have your drinks ready..."

Tiff could see Joe, over the throng, edging his way back through the crowd towards her.

"Ladies and gentlemen, I'm sure you will join me as I propose a toast to Joe and Tiffany. Congratulations to you both and we all look forward to the day you become Mr and Mrs Frey. To Joe and Tiffany." Charlie raised his own glass and the crowd of onlookers did the same.

A hubbub of voices repeated the words and the clinking of glasses resonated around the room like the peal of high-pitched church bells.

Joe slipped an arm round Tiff's waist and clinked his glass on to hers. "To us," he said, before taking a sip from the champagne flute. "Here's to our future."

Tiff gazed into his eyes, still stunned by the breadth of his surprises. She had no words to express her feelings or even to reply. Whatever had happened before, she knew that she loved him entirely. Nothing mattered anymore. She would become Mrs Joe Frey in the future and that was all that counted from now on.

Charlie, Peggy and several other members from the community centre voluntary staff were shifting tables from the back of the room and scattering them around. Georgie was busily adorning the tables with vases of tulips in an array of colours, while others placed chairs around. Peggy looked across the room and smiled at Tiff. Then she put the chair she was holding, under a table and walked towards her.

Several people were bringing trays and giant sized, serving plates, filled with buffet nibbles to one side of the stage and placing them on tables. On the other side of the stage, Tiff noticed a huge pile of wrapped presents and cards, neatly displayed on another table. She stared in awe at the glitzy ribbons and bows and the assortment of shapes and sizes of the presents. They were their engagement presents. Hers and Joe's. They were engaged. They were going to get married. She hadn't had a clue about any of it. She believed it. She was utterly astounded.

"Hello Tiffany," said Peggy as she approached her with an extended hand. "Pleased to meet you properly, at last."

Tiff took her hand and shook it gently.

"I'd like to congratulate you. Joe's a fine young man."

Tiff nodded. "Yes, he is. He's full of surprises too."

"I think I need to explain why I used to come and sit in your front garden." Peggy tutted and rolled her eyes. "It wasn't until Joe came here to talk to us about his engagement party that I realised you both lived there."

"Oh... OK," said Tiff, unsure of what to say.

"Dear old John, the man who lived there before you..."

"Oh, yes, I've heard of him."

"He used to let me have a sit down there when I was delivering the community centre leaflets."

"I see," said Tiff, politely.

"I'd seen a 'for sale' sign. I knew he'd gone – dear old soul. I didn't know you lived there though. Silly me. I live in a blinkered world."

"It's not a problem, really."

"Well, of course I stopped, just as soon as Joe told me his address." Peggy grinned. "He said that you recognised me at the quiz night. He was fretful that you might find out about his plans. But I could see by your pretty little face that you didn't have a clue about this tonight."

"No, I didn't know, but a lot of things are starting to become clearer now."

Up on the stage, a DJ had appeared from behind the curtains and was pulling his speakers and turntable forward, to the centre. He picked up his microphone, mumbled, '1...2...3...' and then the main lights dimmed and an assortment of colourful spotlights danced around the floor and shone out from the stage. "Just wanna congratulate Joe and his beautiful fiancée, Tiffany, before we get this party started," said the DJ, in a low, husky voice. "Heard a whisper that the buffet will be ready at nine o'clock... so let's set this off with one of Tiffany's favourite tunes."

Tiff looked up, surprised by the DJ's personal touch. She turned and smiled at Joe, who was slowly drifting away in a crowd of well-wishers, as her favourite song came pounding out of the giant speakers. Joe turned around and began to move back towards her.

"That's your cue to have a wonderful evening," said Peggy, smiling kindly before she turned to leave.

"Thank you, I know I will."

People began to move their hips and shoulders in rhythm to the song, *Clumsy* by *Fergie*. Tiff pulled Joe back towards her, before he could get sucked up by his group of friends and encouraged him to move his feet and dance alongside her to the up-tempo beat. Normally shy to be one of the first to dance at a party, she just couldn't help herself when she heard this song. Luckily, surrounded by a crowd of people, their dancing was not too noticeable. Then some of Tiff's work colleagues joined in and Joe's rugby friends stepped in beside Joe too.

Over at the back of the room, Tiff could see her parents grabbing some seats, next to Alex, Jenny and Emma. They'd claimed a neat little corner of three tables and were arranging the chairs to accommodate the men who were at the bar, getting more drinks. Emma looked over, lifted her shoulders and grinned. Then she bent down and whispered something in Jenny's ear before they both headed over to join Tiff on the dancefloor.

"You had absolutely no idea, did you?" shouted Emma, directly into Tiff's ear.

Tiff shook her head and grinned. "No – I thought I was coming to a charity do. Joe told me to dress up though, as we were going on to a casino later."

Emma giggled and jiggled alongside her. "We've known for weeks."

"Have you really?"

"Yep! Joe said you've been hard work." Emma laughed heartily and put an arm round Tiff's shoulder as the three girls danced together.

"Hard work?"

"Yeah – trying to keep it all a secret from you."

"Oh, I see," said Tiff, nodding her head agreeably. "Yes, I think I probably have been. I was starting to think he was having an affair."

Emma and Jenny laughed simultaneously.

Joe smirked at his sister, stepped away with a few cool dance moves and headed for the bar.

"Well, now you know," said Emma, winking an eye. "That's Joe for you – never does anything by half."

"He certainly doesn't."

Tiff came to a halt as the music stopped. "Phew," she breathed, "I do love that song but it's a fast-paced one to dance to." She smiled politely at Emma and Jenny. "I'd better go and thank everyone for coming. I'm just about landing back down on planet earth now."

"Catch up in a bit," said Emma, patting Tiff on the back. Then Emma began to jig around with Jenny as the next song started.

Chapter 30

The alcohol was going down swiftly, as it seemed that everyone wanted to buy Tiff and Joe a celebratory drink. They'd been separated for the last hour or more as they both worked their way around the guests, in different directions. Tiff knew she had to slow down on the drinks as she could feel her legs wobbling slightly as she went from one table to another, thanking people for coming, repeating the fact that she had no idea about Joe's intentions and generally making polite conversation.

"Hi Tiff – that fooled you. The look on your face when you realised what was going on." Hayley grinned. "We thought Wayne was going to get into trouble with you at one point."

Tiff took a seat next to Hayley and placed yet another wine spritzer on the table. "Wayne? Why?"

"He messed up a couple of weeks ago – about the text messages."

"Oh, OK. I get it. You know, I'm beginning to realise that Joe's odd behaviour lately is all because of this."

"It is," agreed Hayley. "It's been quite funny to hear what's been going on."

"I can imagine it has."

"Georgie thinks you hate her as well." Hayley laughed and pointed to the bar where Georgie was busily serving people with drinks.

"Does she?" Tiff concealed her true feelings, and feigned amusement. "Why?"

"Said you've been a bit off with her." Hayley smiled and sipped her drink. "Don't worry – she's cool with it. She said she was hoping to catch up with you and sort it all out."

"Oh, OK..."

"She's done so much though. Joe couldn't have done all of this without her."

Tiff picked up her glass and gulped at it.

"She did all the food – looks great doesn't it?"

"Err… yes, it does… I didn't know she'd helped out so much."

"Oh yes," Hayley said, "she's been a little star – bless her."

"I'm shocked."

"Well, if it hadn't been for her yesterday, Wayne and Joe wouldn't have got your bedroom finished either."

Tiff stared, wide-eyed and had to snap her fallen jaw shut. "Really? Why? What did she do?"

"Well, apart from chivvying them along and making them drinks, she also hung your curtains, put the lampshade up and built the two bedside cabinets. She said your bedroom must look gorgeous now it's finished." Hayley paused and looked over at the bar. "She's put in so much effort. She was so excited that you two were getting engaged, so she offered to do the buffet weeks ago."

Tiff sat perfectly still and speechless. Everything was beginning to add up.

"She can't wait for the wedding – she's already said to Joe that she wants an invite." Hayley giggled. "She wants to do a buffet for that too."

"I…" Tiff took another large gulp of her drink. "I can't believe she would do so much. I… well, we hardly know her."

"She does have an ulterior motive to be honest with you."

"Oh, does she?"

"Yes, she wants to go into catering – self-employed – she saw Joe as an opportunity to make a start. He was happy to give her the chance."

"Ah, OK."

"She needs a break to be honest. She's never had much going for her."

"Yes, I can see that now. I'd better… I should thank her later when she's less busy."

"Think she'd appreciate that. She's pretty worried that you hate her and she's had to hold her tongue a couple of times as she wanted to tell you things so that you'd understand."

Tiff stared incredulously. "I'll… I'll definitely talk to her later. Thanks for letting me know." She stood up and wiggled her dress down. "I'd better go and talk to some more people. Thank you so much for everything you and Wayne have done. Hopefully, I'll catch up with you again in a while. The girls from the studio, where I work, are sitting over there. They're as bad as the rest of you and have kept this very quiet at work. I can't get over the fact that everyone knew except me." Tiff grinned and waved her fingers as she walked away from Hayley, her wine spritzer, firmly in her other hand. It was becoming more and more apparent that she had been seeing certain things and certain people in an ultra-negative way.

"OK, guys and gals – gonna take a little break now as the buffet is officially open." The DJ put down the microphone, pulled the top from his bottle of water, and gulped it down as the main lights went on around the room.

Tiff had listened to her colleague's tales of how Joe had popped into the studio to deliver some invitations. He had happened to choose a day when Tiff had left work unexpectedly early. The girls in reception had to hide him under the desks until she had gone. Tiff had unknowingly, been the laughing stock of the studio as she hadn't noticed his car parked two along from her own, when she'd driven away that day.

Tiff heaved a contented sigh. "I don't know," she muttered, "I can't believe this has all gone on behind my back and I didn't see any of it coming."

The girls laughed and chattered around her.

"You are in your own world most of the time, Tiffy," said Pat, shaking her head. "You've been at your worst just lately."

"Yes, I know. I'm going to make a concerted effort to get my act together, be more attentive and pull my head out of the clouds." And Tiff's words had far more meaning than anyone else could imagine. She'd spent far too long obsessing over Georgie and the things that woman got up to, that she had to agree with everything her colleagues had said. "Right – shall we get some food?"

Joe was hanging out with his rugby friends and their partners, in one corner of the room, as Tiff walked towards the buffet tables. A queue was forming at one end so she joined the back of it, behind Betty and Cyril. "Cyril – how are you? You look so well. I'm so pleased you could come."

Cyril smiled. "Joe invited us just before the heart attack – I wasn't going to miss it."

"I told you we were going out tonight," interrupted Betty, a sly grin on her face.

"That's right, yes, you did. I never imagined it was here though." Tiff placed a hand on Betty's arm. "You're very sneaky," she said in jest. "I'll have to watch you in future."

"Poor Joe has been running around frantically, sorting all of this out. Have you seen the engagement cupcakes, up there?" Betty pointed to the end of the tables where a mountain of silver coloured cupcakes stood, each one with a sugar-work diamond ring on the top. The little cakes stood on a giant cake stand, which must have held at least 60 cakes. "I made those."

"Oh my goodness – they are totally amazing."

"And the tulip sprays."

"You put those together too?"

"Oh, yes," said Betty, beaming proudly.

"They are my favourite flowers..."

"I know they are. You've got some on your dining table, haven't you? Joe wanted some for your table at home as well. He said you'd love them."

"Yes," said Tiff, stunned, once again, by the magnitude of Joe's attention to detail. Yet she hadn't even mentioned the beautiful tulips at home, let alone thanked him for them, due to her obsession with him having an affair with Georgie. How wrong she'd been. How terribly wrong. This had to be a new start now. She felt incredibly foolish and unworthy. She'd made a big mistake and put Joe through so much misery when the crux of the matter was that she had been the one who was really hiding things. Things that had been going on around them that she had kept to herself and let them twist her mind into all kinds of wicked, malicious and unfoundedly jealous thoughts.

Scanning the bewildering array of tantalizing nibbles, Tiff was astonished by the complexity of the bite-sized food. Georgie had really made some effort to make and present the buffet. From tiny plaited sausage rolls to elaborate canapes and creative open-sandwiches in finger shapes. All of the guests were commenting on the skill and time it must have taken to create such a spread. Tiff picked up some of the miniature pieces of art, one by one, and placed them on her plate. As soon as Georgie was free, she would make a point of thanking her and try to have a harmonious chat with her. She had to do this and tonight was probably the best time, as she had an alcohol induced courage about her.

Aaron had sidled up to Joe and his band of merry men. Tiff could see and hear them all laughing together as she moved along the line with the rest of the hungry people. Joe's family were sitting in the corner with Tiff's mum and dad, nibbling away at their food. They all chatted contentedly, as if the two sets of parents had known each other for years. Tiff smiled as she watched her mum natter to Alex, Emma and Jenny. They all looked happy. Dad was even having an in-depth discussion with Grant, which worried Tiff a little. Her dad usually talked about lectures and mathematics, non-stop, which tended to bore most people, but Grant seemed to be responding in a positive manner, so maybe he wasn't doing a maths-overload speech. Maybe she needed to stop worrying so much about what others were doing and concentrate more on herself and Joe.

"Are you getting some food?" Tiff had wandered over to the rowdy group of men. "It's utterly amazing."

Joe turned and wrapped an arm round her shoulders. "Yes, my darling fiancée, I will be, in a minute." He pulled her into the circle and squeezed at her shoulder. "Here she is," said Joe, a little slurry. "My beautiful wife-to-be."

"Hope you're going to keep him in check," said one man, who Tiff recognised but couldn't, for the life of her, remember his name at all.

"Oh yes, I certainly will," she replied, mockingly. "He needs to get something to eat now, before he falls over – that's the first check."

Joe and the others laughed and the circle naturally broke as they began to wander off to the buffet tables.

"What do you think then?" said Joe, still holding her round the shoulders.

"I'm completely overwhelmed by it all."

"I knew you would be babe. Tomorrow, I will explain everything to you. Let's just enjoy tonight while it lasts. We have the rest of our lives to sort everything else out."

"I don't think you need to explain anything to me. I need to say one thing though."

"What's that?"

"I never thanked you for the tulips on our table, yesterday."

"You have now." Joe lowered his head and kissed her briefly.

Tiff smiled warmly. "Thank you for everything you've done."

"No," said Joe, softly, "thank *you*, for saying yes." He pecked her on the cheek and walked away to the side of the stage.

Tiff turned around to head back to the tables when she noticed Joe up on the stage, alongside the DJ.

"Ladies and gents… Can I have your attention for a minute?"

Tiff froze on the spot, wandering what on earth he was doing up there.

A hush flooded around the room and a sea of expectant faces peered up at the stage.

"I want to say a big thank-you to a few people before we carry on with the evening and I'm sure that I will be speaking on behalf of my beautiful fiancée, too." He pointed a finger towards Tiff. "First of all, I must congratulate Georgie on a spectacular spread this evening – please give her a round of applause."

A thunderous applause and an odd cheer, filled the room.

Georgie waved coyly from behind the bar.

"We will most certainly be using her services again, for the wedding, in the near future."

Near? Thought Tiff as a rush of tingly excitement darted around her body.

"If anyone has any catering requirements coming up, please don't hesitate to take a business card from the bar. Georgie would be more than happy to give you a quote." Joe peered over to the bar and smiled at a bashful Georgie.

Tiff also looked over to the bar and was a little surprised to see Georgie looking so coy. It wasn't her usual type of expression but she did seem to be portraying a far friendlier look. Or was it that Tiff had never really looked at her in any other way than with disdain? Maybe Tiff had never really seen her for who she really was.

"I'd also like to thank Betty, for the incredible cupcakes; Wayne and Hayley, for keeping me sane throughout this whole secret mission; all the volunteers, here in the community centre, and last but not least, thank-you to each and every one of you for the amazing amount of gifts and particularly, for successfully deceiving my future bride." Joe scanned the audience, smiling widely. "A toast to the future," he roared and lifted the microphone up in the air.

The guests grabbed the nearest glasses of alcohol and lifted them in the air, as a hubbub of voices echoed around the room. "To the future – To Joe and Tiff."

The evening had been such fun and everyone had appeared to enjoy themselves immensely – some more than others.

Poor Emma had been overly drunk when Andrew carted her away. The whole family, including Tiff's mum and dad, were staying in a quaint, countryside hotel, just two minutes away. Once again, Tiff had been astounded by the depth of Joe's rigorous planning, right down to the finest of details. She'd also learnt that they were all attending a barbecue at her home, tomorrow afternoon. That explained the clean-up, the new barbecue and the patio furniture.

As the guests began to dwindle down to the last few, the DJ packed away his equipment and the volunteers began to clear away the empty glasses and plates from the tables. Georgie was still behind the bar, tidying up and wiping down the tops. Joe was sitting down with Wayne, Hayley and the remaining family, namely Tiff's parents, Aaron and his girlfriend, Jenny.

Tiff had just seen her work colleagues to the door, after Joe had politely thanked them for coming and commented favourably on the generous number of gifts they had given. So now she had two choices as she wobbled back across the room and looked from one side to the other. Did she go and join Joe and co. or venture over to the bar and speak to Georgie? She had to do it. It would be better to do it tonight. Right now.

"Hello Georgie."

Georgie looked up from behind the bar and smiled. She placed the cloth she'd been holding, into a bucket behind her and leant over the bar. "Hello."

"I just want to say a massive thank-you to you. The food was utterly amazing."

"Thanks," said Georgie, lowering her gaze to the bar top. "I wanted it to look really good for you – I think it went OK."

"Oh, it did look really good and it tasted even better." Tiff pulled a stool over and sat down. "Look, I know I haven't been that friendly towards you. I want to apologise. It's just that..." Tiff broke off and averted her eyes.

"No need to apologise for anything. I suppose that from your point of view... well, it must have seemed a bit strange..."

"Strange?"

"Well, more Joe's behaviour, I suppose. He told me not to text him at home and... well, I forgot on a couple of occasions. I'm sorry it caused some upset."

Tiff shook her head incredulously. "It's like all the pieces of the jigsaw are coming together. Somehow, I knew it was you texting him but I... well, I had completely got the wrong end of the stick."

"I know. Joe did say that..." Georgie turned and grabbed the cloth from the bucket. She wrung it out and began to wipe the top again.

"What did he say?"

"Oh, only that you were a little suspicious of..." She let out a little awkward giggle. "He said you thought we were having an affair."

Tiff lowered her head, shamefully. "Yes, that's right."

"Tiff," she said, moving further over the bar, "I'm not like that. I would never dream of doing anything like that. I consider Joe to be a friendly neighbour who I was able to help – that's all."

"But..." Tiff replied, defensively, "I know what..."

"What?" Georgie leant even closer still. "What do you know? Please, tell me."

Tiff shook her head. "It's nothing – really."

Georgie shot a quizzical stare. "Is it..." She hesitated and looked across the room to where the remaining guests were huddled around the last few tables. "Is it anything to do with... I don't know how to say it."

"Please, just go ahead," said Tiff, curiously. "Whatever we say here, stays between me and you."

Georgie pulled up from the bar and straightened her back. "I just wondered what you meant when you said you know something."

"Look, Georgie, when we first moved here, I had no jealousy in me at all. It all began soon after we moved in. The things I saw..."

"Saw?" Georgie's eyes turned wide and fearful. "What did you see?"

"I can't believe I'm having this conversation with you. I only wanted to come and thank you... and hopefully be friendly neighbours in the future. It's just that..."

"It was the day I saw you in the window, wasn't it? With the binoculars?" Georgie's eyes were wider than ever and she met Tiff's eyes with a terrified gaze.

"What do you mean?" Tiff feigned ignorance.

Georgie buried her face in her hands. "Oh dear."

"Shall we talk about this another time?"

Nodding her head, Georgie continued to cover her face. She sniffed.

"Are you crying?" Tiff whispered, before turning her head to check that no one was around.

Peeping through her fingers, Georgie looked across the room before taking her hands away from her face. She blinked her watery eyes. "You know, don't you?"

"Know what?" Tiff looked at her deeply. "I've seen..." She broke off. She couldn't bring herself to say anything. It seemed too unreal now that she was standing face to face with Georgie.

"Can we talk sometime else? I've got to get this place cleared up before I go." Georgie casually brushed a finger under one eye and then the other. "Can we? On Monday? Just you and me? Have you told anyone else?" There was an unnerving desperation in her voice. "We really need to talk."

Tiff nodded her head. "Yes, we do and no one else knows, I promise you, not even Joe knows anything. I've really struggled with this. I can get the day off on Thursday. Is that any good for you?"

"Yes, Thursday is fine," Georgie replied with a wavering voice. "I'm sorry."

"What are you sorry for? You don't need to be sorry to me."

"No, I am... I never realised..." She froze as she stared across the room. "Joe's coming –"

Joe casually strolled over with his hands in his pockets.

"See you Thursday," whispered Tiff, just before he arrived at the bar.

"Babe, we're going to make a move in a minute," he said, sidling up to her and slipping an arm round her waist. "You all right Georgie?"

"Yes, fine thank you. Just finishing up here."

"Do you want a lift back, we've got a couple of taxis ordered, there are just so many presents."

"No, you go on. I'll get finished here. Charlie's going to run me home anyway." Georgie smiled falteringly. "Hope you all have a lovely barbecue tomorrow."

"Thanks, I'm sure we will. And thank you again, for everything you've done." Joe tutted and raised his eyebrows. "I have a lot of explaining to do when I get home."

"No you don't. It's fine." Tiff stood up, tugged her dress down and smiled. "Bye Georgie, and thanks again, for everything."

Chapter 31

Two trips back and forth, from the taxis in the lay-by, and Joe and Tiff's living room was filled with unopened gifts. They stood at the front door and waved the others off, before retreating to the comfort of their home. Their new home. It felt like a brand new home filled with a harmonious, cordial atmosphere.

Tiff kicked off her shoes, pulled Joe around, by his arm, and flung her own round his neck. "I can't believe you've done all of this," she said, gesturing to the assortment of sparkly boxes and packages, scattered around the floor. "And this..." She held her left hand up and admired her glimmering, diamond ring.

"How else could I have told you, I want you to be my wife?"

"Oh, Joe..." She kissed his lips softly, "I'm so sorry for doubting you. I've acted so terribly."

"You did have a point babe, I *was* deceiving you and you nearly found out. At one point, I wanted to tell you everything. The worst time was when you left and went to your mum and dad's. I had to practically chew my lip off, not to say anything to you on the phone."

Tiff looked down at her ring again and splayed her fingers out, twisting her hand around one way, then the other. "I'll never mistrust you again – I hope you'll forgive me in time."

"I'm over it babe, we're going to get married and that's all that matters now." He squeezed her close and kissed her softly. "Shall we open those tomorrow?" he gestured at the presents.

She nodded her head and pulled away from him. "Shall we have a coffee?"

"Yes – then bed, my fiancée."

Tiff slapped his behind and strolled, carefree, into the kitchen. "We'll have to get some food for the barbecue, in the morning."

"No we won't." Joe replied, following behind her. "It's all sorted."

"Really?"

"Yep – everyone's bringing food and I hid some other bits in the back of the fridge and the cupboards."

"Joe Frey – you are an endless source of astonishment."

"Well how's this for a surprise then? Would you do me the honour of getting married this year?"

"This year?" Tiff went giddy with excitement. "How can we affor…"

"I've got a couple of grand saved and our parents want to contribute hugely."

"You've spoken to them?"

"Yes." Joe raised his eyebrows and smirked. "You *could* have your dream, winter-themed wedding."

Tiff slumped back against the kitchen work top. "We'd never get everything done in time. What about *Battle Abbey School*?" She had a passion for historical buildings and towns but *Battle Abbey School,* in *Sussex* held a particular interest in her heart. Her parents had both lived in the area, before they married at the old school. When Tiff was a child, she'd spent many holidays in *Sussex* and had many trips to the school. She'd fallen in love with the place and vowed to get married there, herself, one day.

Joe smirked and folded his arms as he leant back against the worktop. "I have a provisional booking in December."

Pulling herself up straight, Tiff stared fixedly. "You… Joe… how?" she stuttered. Shaking her head, she continued to gaze, open-mouthed.

"If you want it – it's ours."

Tiff cupped her hands around her nose and mouth as tears welled in her eyes yet again. "I… I… can't believe you've done this," she spluttered, incredulously. "Oh, Joe." Rushing across the kitchen, she flung her arms round his neck.

Scooping her up from the ground, Joe hugged her tightly. "Only because it's you, babe." He laughed into her hair as she cried and giggled and cried some more. "Wouldn't have gone to these lengths for anyone else."

Considering it had been their first night of being half way to Mr and Mrs Frey, both Joe and Tiff had fallen into bed exhausted from their long day and night.

So much had happened yesterday and so much had changed. Tiff lay in the bed, staring at the ceiling, while Joe continued to sleep peacefully next to her. Sunlight filtered through the cotton curtains, willing her to get up. She wanted to get up and start her first day as Joe's fiancée but she also wanted to stay in bed and relive every single second of last night's party. Once she was up, she knew that she would be distracted by all matter of jobs-to-do, before the family arrived for the barbecue this afternoon, and then that beautiful, morning-after moment would be gone. She closed her eyes, shutting out the brightness in the room, and reflected upon the past, the present and the wonderful future she had to look forward to.

"Can't believe we've slept right through till eleven," said Joe, picking his cup of tea up from the worktop and carrying it out to the garden.

Tiff followed behind and joined him at the new patio table. She grinned, contentedly, without saying a word.

"You're quiet this morning babe." Joe sipped his tea, then smiled.

"Oh, I've been reliving last night. That's all. I'm still in a state of shock, I think." She glanced down at the ring on her finger. "We're engaged."

"Now, do you believe me when I say I'm not interested in anyone else?"

Tiff nodded her head. "Yes, I do and I feel so foolish."

"It's all in the past – we'll move on and start planning the wedding after this afternoon. What do you say?"

"Oh God, yes."

"Good, and before you ask, the family will probably want to discuss it, in length, this afternoon as well." Joe smirked before draining his mug of tea. "They're all so eager to get things rolling – even my dad, can you believe it?"

"Wow – it's all like a dream come true. You're so amazing Joe Frey."

Joe turned his mouth up, smugly. "Come on, drink up. We've got a lot of presents to open before three o'clock."

Tiff had almost forgotten about opening the presents. She'd passed them earlier and thought how beautifully wrapped they all looked. For just a fleeting moment, she'd wondered what was inside them, but it hadn't occurred to her that they would be opening them this morning. In her heightened state, she was quite content just to admire the wrapping paper – opening the goodies was something else entirely. Had she really deserved all of this?

Each and every gift was either something they needed, a replacement for something else, or something they'd both said they would like to have. After sitting on the floor together, unwrapping one after another and making a list of who gave them what, Joe confessed that he had given out a gift-list, or emailed one, to those who asked.

Yet another mind-blowing moment for Tiff.

"I've got so many thank-you cards to make."

"Thought you'd want to make them. I'll take over the housework if you want to get started this week."

"Deal," replied Tiff, admiring the new stainless-steel, wire fruit basket she had wanted for ages. It had a long arm rising up from the basket base, with a hook at the end, to hang bananas from. "I'll start tomorrow evening."

"Good. Right, let's get all this upstairs, out of the way, then we can get ready for the barbecue."

Joe hadn't been kidding when he said that the family, from both sides, would want to discuss the possibility of an upcoming wedding. They were all ecstatic when he told them that Tiff had agreed to go for the provisional December booking.

The women sat around the patio table, discussing the finer details of the wedding, like themes and colours; flowers and dresses; and who would be paying for what. While Joe, Grant, Tiff's dad, Andrew and Aaron stood around the barbecue, talking about rugby, football and golf. The men were unanimous in their decision to let the women deal with the finer details of the wedding as they would do a much better job of it.

It seemed that there would be little left for Joe and Tiff to pay, after both parents had generously put forward an amount that they would like to contribute towards the wedding. Tiff was, once again, overwhelmed by their generosity and eagerness to help in any way they could.

"You could be a bridesmaid," said Tiff, eyeing Emma, hopefully.

"Ooh – yes! I'd love to." Emma grinned tightly, "Joe – I'm going to be a bridesmaid. How do you feel about that little bruv?"

Joe looked over and shrugged. "Thought you'd be the first to jump in there somewhere."

"They love each other really," said Alex. "They've always been the same." She eyed Tiff's mum and smiled in amusement. "Making out they hate each other, yet, when it comes down to it, they'd do anything for each other."

"They are very alike," Tiff's mum smiled back, politely.

"Oh yes and very close too. Aaron's a bit more of a loner and Jack, well, you haven't met him yet – I do hope he'll be able to come over with his family in December."

"Then of course, there's Grandma..." Emma rolled her eyes upwards. "She couldn't come this weekend. Thank God." Emma mumbled the last two words under her breath.

"Emma!" Alex peered at her daughter with a critical eye. "Your grandma's had a tough time of late, you should be more understanding."

Emma sighed. "I am understanding Mum, but you have to admit, she is hard work – you have to agree with that."

"Well, yes, OK. But I don't think we should be giving Tiff's parents..." Alex turned and smiled awkwardly, "the wrong impression. She's just a muddled old lady, that's all."

"Please, don't get me wrong," said Emma. "I do love her to bits. She couldn't come this weekend because she's away for a couple of weeks – on one of these OAP cruise holidays."

"Sounds very nice," said Tiff's mum.

"She'll be well looked after, there's a whole group of them." Alex peered over to where Grant was standing with the others. "And it gives poor old Grant a bit of peace too," she added, in a hushed voice.

"Oh?" Tiff's mum enquired.

"They don't quite see eye to eye."

Emma giggled. "Not since the day he threw her into a lake, years ago – but that's another story."

"Oh dear," whispered Tiff's mum.

"Anyway," said Alex, getting up from her chair, "shall we get the rest of the food ready? Looks like they're nearly done with those skewers."

The family barbecue had been a success, Tiff and Joe's parents got on so well and everyone was now looking forward to a wedding in December. Tiff was still stunned by the transformation to her life, in just one weekend. Having said their goodbyes to both families, tidied up the last bits in the garden (both Tiff's and Joe's mum had insisted on doing most of the clearing up), and finding new homes for the countless gifts, Tiff climbed the stairs wearily.

Joe was already soaking away the smoky traces from the barbecue, in the bath. She smiled to herself as she passed the closed bathroom door, as she could hear him singing along, badly, to a song on the radio. She entered the craft room, with a fresh approach. It no longer seemed to matter about the view or the potentially disturbing goings-on in the distance. She was over it and the fact that she may well get an explanation, on Thursday, had put her mind at ease.

Checking that she had enough materials, and the right sort of embellishments that she would need to make all of the thank-you cards, Tiff ticked off a list in her mind as she searched through the drawers and boxes. She had enough of everything she needed. There was no need to go to the craft centre to stock up.

Looking up from the table, she naturally peered out across the fields. A flash of black caught her eye, on the left. Then again. Georgie's dog was bounding up and down the lane, in and out of the trees. Instinctively, Tiff reached for the binoculars, in the opened drawer. She couldn't stop herself. It was wrong but she had to see – to know. She stepped back, so as not to be seen, and slowly lifted them to her eyes.

Dreading what she might discover, she moved the binoculars and slowly scoured along the lane. Her heart jumped. There was Georgie, arms folded around her waist defensively and shaking her head from side to side as if she was angry. She was very slightly bent over and appeared to be shouting. And there *he* was. Alvin. Jeremy. Once again, wearing the same style *Speedos,* except these ones were black. He was nodding his head and pointing a finger, as if he was saying something like, *yes, you will.*

Tiff stepped back further in the room, holding her breath as she did. It felt even more wrong than it usually did, to be spying on Georgie and Alvin but she couldn't tear herself away. There was definitely not anything sexual and crude going on with the pair today. They appeared to be arguing. Then Georgie gestured towards Tiff's own house. Her craft room window.

Tiff froze.

Both Georgie and Alvin were looking straight at her window. Straight through it. Staring straight at her. Right through the binoculars.

Jerking the binoculars away from her face, Tiff felt a flush of heat redden her cheeks. She couldn't move. Her breathing had turned shallow. Were they arguing about her? Why would Georgie point to her house? To the window, in particular. Quietly and calmly, she lowered herself to the floor and tried to peep over the top of the table. She pulled the binoculars up to the table top and rested them there. Did she dare look again? Would they be staring right at her? As if they were actually there, in the room with her? Her curiosity grappled with her conscience. She wanted to look but feared seeing two pairs of eyes peering back through the binoculars.

The bathroom door opened.

Tiff slid the binoculars under a pile of cardstock on the table.

Thudding footsteps.

She bent over and shuffled under the table, on hands and knees. This had to stop. She was engaged now. She was turning out to be the liar, the secretive one in their relationship.

"Babe," Joe's voice spoke calmly, behind her. "What are you doing under there?"

"Oh, I..." Tiff reversed back out and sat back on her heels. "I was err... just looking. I dropped something."

"Looking?" Joe eyed her amusedly. "For what?"

"Dropped a... sorry, I mean I was looking for the binoculars actually. Can't seem to find them anywhere."

Joe laughed and stepped further into the room. "You mean those ones?" He pointed to the table top. "Under that pile of card?"

"Oh yes – there they are."

"I don't think they will help you find anything under the table babe. Wouldn't a magnifying glass be better?" He reached across the table and picked up her tabletop magnifier.

"Oh yes, thanks." Tiff took the magnifier and placed it against her eye as she scanned the carpet under the table."

"What have you lost?"

"It's only a pin. I didn't want to get it stuck in my foot at a later date. Silly me – can't imagine why I'd want to search for it using the silly binoculars."

"Because you're a nutcase?"

"Yes, something like that."

"OK, well there's a bath ready, when you've found it."

"Thanks," said Tiff, feigning interest in an elusive, make-believe pin.

"Looks like Georgie's out the back with her dog," Joe remarked, casually. "I'm sure that's her, two fields back." He peered through the window, squinting his eyes.

"Oh, really? Nice evening for a dog walk." She didn't know why, but Tiff could feel her heart galloping. Was he about to become embroiled in the clandestine affairs of the neighbours too?

"Yeah, maybe we should get a dog in the future. Found it yet?" He moved away from the window, towards the door.

"No," she replied, brushing a hand across the carpet. "Oh well, hopefully it won't end up inside my foot."

Joe smiled. "Come on, jump in the bath. I'll find a good film for us to watch. I'm thinking we should chill-out tonight and then start the wedding arrangements tomorrow. Don't know about you but I'm shattered after this weekend." He left the room and padded down the stairs.

Tiff stood up and peered out of the window again. How could she be so deceitful to her fiancé? How could she have ever condemned *him* in the past? She was worse than he was. She could just see Alvin darting out from the trees, across the back fields. He'd obviously left Georgie and by the length of his stride, he looked like he was in a rush to get somewhere. Or had he done something to her? Had they argued and he'd lashed out at her? Was Georgie all right? Tiff slid her hand under the cardstock and reached for the binoculars. Just one last time. She had to check. Make sure that Georgie was all right...

She was OK. Striding back along the path with her dog. She looked all right, if not a little disgruntled. Hopefully, all would be revealed on Thursday. It had to be – for Tiff's sake. For Joe's sake – unknowingly. Maybe even for Georgie's sake.

Chapter 32

Thursday couldn't come around quick enough. Tiff had worked solidly all week, to ensure that she would have time to escape the studio today. Dearest Joe had also kept to his word and done the cooking and clearing-up every evening so that she could get on with making the thank-you cards. One of the cards, would be Tiff's perfect excuse to call round to Georgie's house today.

She had been worrying during the week whether Georgie would still be so forthcoming as she seemed to be on Saturday night. Did she still want to have the meeting? Tiff had no idea and only hoped that they would still be able to chat about everything, rather than leaving it all up in the air, which was tormenting the life out of her. She'd struggled to stay focused in her craft room this week, as her binoculars kept calling out to her to pick them up. Just one peep. One little peep. Thankfully, she had managed to resist and get on with the task in hand – making thank-you cards for just about everyone she could think of.

A time hadn't been planned for Tiff's visit. When would be a good time to call on Georgie? This morning? Lunchtime? Or maybe this afternoon would be better. The problem with the afternoon was that, if they did end up having an in-depth conversation and the time ticked away unnoticed, there would be a risk that Joe may come home and discover her whereabouts. No – she would have to go there this morning.

She stood facing the long mirror in her bedroom, semi-naked. She hooked the straps of her bra over her shoulders and fastened it at the back. What could she wear? The bed was covered in tops and t-shirts, jeans, shorts, skirts and trousers. Anyone would have thought she was going for a job interview. Did it matter what she wore? She was only going next door to deliver a thank-you card – and hopefully get invited in for a chat. So, no, it did not matter at all. As usual, Tiff was getting herself in a flap about nothing. She picked up her jeans and a pastel pink top and proceeded to dress.

A faint knocking came from the front door. Tiff stopped still and listened intently. Who was that at her door? She moved over to the window and peered down. She could see a blonde head at the front door. It was Georgie.

Racing down the stairs, her heart thumping in her chest, she went to the door and opened it. "Georgie, I was..."

Georgie smiled shyly. "I wasn't sure if you were coming to mine or I was coming round here. Just thought I'd ask. Is it still OK? Is it convenient?" Wearing a pair of tatty, ripped jeans, a baggy, lilac t-shirt and flip-flops, Georgie's ruffled appearance was somehow, calming. She'd made no effort to impress or indeed, threaten, in any way.

Tiff stepped back from the door and beckoned to Georgie to come in. "Yes, of course it's still OK. Another ten minutes and I would have been round to you." She gave a short laugh. "I wasn't sure either, I mean, if I was supposed to come to yours or vice-versa. Or, if you still wanted to chat."

"Yes, I do." Georgie stepped inside and slid past Tiff uncomfortably.

"I'm pleased you're here – I have something for you."

"Oh?" said Georgie, turning around.

"Go through to the dining room. It's upstairs – I'll be back down in a minute."

Georgie smiled weakly and went through to the dining room as instructed.

Closing the front door, Tiff flew back up the stairs and into the craft room. She sieved through the mound of cards, already made, and found Georgie's. As she passed by the bathroom, she made a quick detour to the mirror to check she looked OK and then trotted back down the stairs satisfied with her appearance. "Phew," she said, upon arrival in the dining room. "Think I'm unfit – all that running up and down the stairs, has worn me out."

Georgie twitched her lips into a half smile and continued to sit, hunched up, on a chair.

"Can I get you a drink of anything?"

"Just water, thank you."

"Are you sure that's all you want? I'm making coffee if you'd like one. Or tea?"

Georgie shook her head. "No, thank you, water's fine."

It was odd, Tiff thought to herself, how all of a sudden, Georgie didn't appear to be this wanton, promiscuous woman anymore. She seemed quite vulnerable. Polite and lacking in confidence. Insecure. It was almost like she was the same type of person as Tiff was.

"OK, do you want ice?"

Georgie nodded. "Please, if you have some."

Tiff stretched a hand out towards Georgie. "Here's a card – I made it. Hope you'll like it."

"What's this?" Georgie took the envelope and looked at it puzzled.

"A very small way of saying thank you for everything you did on Saturday."

"I enjoyed doing it." Georgie paused thoughtfully. "It's what I'd like to do for a living, if I can get any orders."

"Well, if there's anything I can do to help, please let me know."

"That's very kind of you – thanks." Georgie looked genuinely surprised by Tiff's offer as she opened the envelope.

"Look," said Tiff, carrying a glass of icy water to the table. "I think we probably started off on the wrong foot. I know *I* did and I want to apologise for..." Tiff struggled to find the right words, "for judging you so harshly. It was my fault – not yours."

"It's lovely, thanks." Georgie held the card up and smiled. "I don't think anything is your fault. It takes me a while to trust people. I probably came across a bit... I don't know, maybe ignorant?"

"You seemed to hit it off with Joe from the start." Tiff bit her bottom lip, hoping her words wouldn't be taken offensively.

"Yes, I did." Georgie twisted her mouth to one side. "But you seemed to look at me like you hated me, the first time I met you," she added, awkwardly.

"I'm sorry for that." Tiff moved closer to the table. "Georgie..."

"Yes?"

"Can we talk about what has been going on?" Tiff pulled a chair out and sat down, her coffee could wait, this was far more important. "I... well, I've been worried about you. I think it's the reason why I took so badly to you when I first met you."

Georgie slumped down further on the chair and pulled a lock of hair across her lips.

"I just don't understand what's going on."

Georgie shook her head and kept the golden blonde tresses covering her mouth. It was as if she were hiding. Or stopping herself from talking. "I..." she mumbled through her hair, "I can't..." She stopped abruptly and pulled herself up straight. Her hair fell away from her mouth and she buried her face in her hands. "I can't take any more." She wiped her hands around her face and looked up momentarily, before her desperate gaze dropped and she stared down at the table.

"Any more of what?" Tiff spoke softly. "Let me help you, I know this is to do with Alvin, isn't it?"

Georgie looked up again, her terrified eyes fixed on Tiff's. "He'll... he'll have me killed if he finds out."

"Killed? If he finds out what?" Tiff gripped the edge of the table. This was turning into far more than she had expected.

"If he finds out I've been talking to you." Georgie chewed her bottom lip nervously. "I'll be killed."

"OK," said Tiff, putting her hands up. "Can we start at the beginning?"

Georgie nodded her head and took a sip from the glass of water in front of her.

"I'm going to make that coffee – are you sure you don't want one?"

"I'm sure – this water is enough, thank you."

Darting across to the kitchen, Tiff hurriedly prepared a mug of coffee and waited for the kettle to boil. She turned and smiled once or twice as erratic thoughts whirled around in her head. So Georgie was frightened of him. Petrified, it seemed. He had some hold over her and she had to find out what it was. By the sound of things, Georgie had no idea who Alvin really was either.

Tiff poured the water into her mug and carried it over to the table. "Right, where shall we start?"

"It's all my fault really..."

"What's your fault?"

"Why Alvin thinks he can do anything he wants." Georgie stared blankly, like a woman who had been robbed of her emotions.

"Can he do what he wants?" Tiff eyed her neighbour, puzzled.

"It's a deal we set up."

"What deal? Nothing you're saying makes any sense." Tiff frowned, desperately trying to fathom out what was going on. "Look, I've seen you and him out the back... in the fields. I hate to say this but... I've seen you both in your garden. Purely by accident. I get the feeling that you hate him, yet..." she paused, wondering how to tell Georgie exactly what she'd seen. "Well, you don't do those things with someone you hate."

Again, Georgie buried her face in her hands, ashamedly.

"Why are you doing this?" Tiff had decided it was all or nothing now. She had to clear the air. "Why are you degrading yourself by letting some filthy creep do this to you?" She sighed loudly. "Do you even know who he really is?"

Georgie looked up and brushed a tear from her cheek. She was sobbing like a child and her pitiful expression was one of deep sorrow. "I do," she muttered, waveringly. "He's a secret service agent..."

"No, he isn't," Tiff interrupted. "I have found out who he really is. He couldn't be any further away from being an intelligence expert, if he lived on the other side of the planet."

Georgie wiped her eyes and sniffed. She looked up and met Tiff's eye, incredulously. "How..."

"How do I know?"

Georgie nodded.

"Because, when I was away visiting my parents, I bumped into him," She slurped at her hot coffee, "at the place where he really works."

"In London?"

"No, not in London. He works in a supermarket. In Salisbury."

"He must have been under..."

"No." Tiff blurted. "He wasn't undercover. And his name isn't even Alvin."

Georgie peered quizzically. "Are you sure?"

"Positive. His real name is Jeremy – Jeremy Greene. You can check the name registered against his address if you like."

Georgie pulled her hair across her mouth again and held it with her lips. Her eyes darted around as if she was frantically thinking about a lot of things.

"I'm telling you the truth. He's worked at this supermarket for over 20 years."

"Oh my God. Are you sure?" said Georgie, whipping the hair away from her face. "Are you sure it was him?"

"Yes, I'm absolutely positive."

"So is that where he goes when he's away?"

Tiff nodded her head cheerlessly. "Yes, I'm afraid it is."

"I can't believe it. He's conned me. I..." Georgie broke off and crunched her brow together as her eyes narrowed angrily. "The bastard. He's lied to me all this time."

"So what's been going on with you and him?"

Georgie huffed and folded her arms across her waist. "He..." she faltered. "I was in a lot of debt a few years ago. He bailed me out when the bailiffs were constantly at my door."

"OK," said Tiff, encouragingly. "I suppose that was good of him."

"It was... at first. He said I could pay back just 100 pounds a month as I didn't have a job. He'd given me £4000 to clear the debts."

"Wow – a lot of money."

Georgie looked down. "Yes, it was... and for the first year he was happy with that repayment arrangement."

"So what went wrong?"

"He started demanding more money – he wanted it paid off quicker as he had to take some time off work to care for his sick, elderly mum."

"That figures."

"Oh?" Georgie's eyes widened.

"His mum *has* been ill, so I've been told. He lives with her, just outside Salisbury, when he's working at the shop."

"Oh God, really?" Georgie shook her head disbelievingly. "I have been such a fool."

"No you haven't. It was by pure chance that I came across him, otherwise we would have believed him too. Although we were slightly suspicious of him. But I think that was more to do with his jogging and the bird watching that he said he liked to do." Tiff smiled faintly. "Anyway, carry on."

"I couldn't pay any more money. I just didn't have it."

Tiff nodded sympathetically. "We've all been there Georgie. It's tough, especially when you're on your own."

"Yes, it is. Then I got sick. I was supposed to look after Betty and Cyril's birds while they were on holiday."

Tiff leant back in the chair. "OK, so what happened there?"

"I couldn't do it. I was so ill. Alvin..." Georgie stopped abruptly. "Or whatever his name is..."

"Jeremy. Jeremy Greene," Tiff reminded her.

"Well, he said he would look after the birds but I had to pay him the money I'd been given by Cyril. They'd given me £800 to look after their birds."

"OK. I know a little bit about this story. They mentioned it to me."

"He took it all."

Tiff shook her head disgustedly.

"It wasn't me. He killed them. A lot of Cyril's birds died and they blamed me for it. They demanded their money back as they would have to buy new birds."

Tiff nodded her head, knowingly. "Why didn't you tell them about Alvin?"

"He'd threatened me. He said I wasn't to tell them anything or he'd make sure that life became very difficult for me. He said he knew a lot of people in the underworld. He told me that my face could be rearranged. I knew what that meant."

"Oh dear me," said Tiff, rubbing her forehead with her hand.

"I got in such a state about it all. I was depressed and couldn't think straight. I couldn't pay back Alvin – let alone Cyril."

Tiff took a deep breath, knowing she had to ask the all-important question. "Georgie, why are you having sex with him if he has been treating you so horrendous like this?"

Georgie lowered her head. "Oh God, this is all such a mess."

"It sounds like it is – yes."

"It's like a payment-in-kind. That's what *he* said."

"Oh no." Tiff looked down, filled with abhorrence. "He's paying you?"

"No." Georgie let out a long sigh. "He knocks money off the debt – he gives me a receipt each time."

"Oh God, no. You can't do this."

"I hate doing it – I don't know what else to do. He's disgusting. Perverted. Sick in the head. He…" Georgie broke off and sighed again. "He treats me like a dog and it makes me feel sick." Her eyes watered over and she stared pleadingly, into Tiff's eyes.

Tiff shook her head and placed a hand across her mouth. She peered deep into Georgie's sorrowful eyes as the revelation turned over, sickeningly, in her head.

"I get £200 every time. It's knocked off the debt. And £50 when…" Georgie locked her fingers into a tightly clenched fist and placed them in her lap. She looked down at her hands and continued. "I have to undress at my bedroom window or in the garden sometimes… while he spies on me with his binoculars."

Everything was becoming so revoltingly clear.

"It's the only way…"

"No – it bloody well isn't Georgie."

Georgie looked up, taken aback by Tiff's abrupt outburst.

"Sorry, I didn't mean to sound so angry. But you can stop this. You should not be going through this. It's like a form of rape."

"But I consent to it."

"No, you don't really. You've been threatened by him and he is using the fact that you owe him money to practically rape and abuse you constantly. This can't happen."

Georgie shuddered, unlocked her fingers and placed her hands around opposite arms, as if she was hugging herself. "I need to pay the debt back. I'm scared he might send someone to kill me. What else can I do? It's not rape – I agree to it."

"Do you *want* to do it each time?"

Georgie shook her head frantically, her expression, a desperate picture of revulsion.

"Then it is. You're not going to go through this anymore." Tiff paused, thoughtfully. "We've got to stop this."

"But..."

Tiff met Georgie's eye, as an overwhelming revulsion and hatred for the man, known as Alvin, came over her, stronger and stronger. "No buts – we've got to stop this. He can't hurt you Georgie. He's no one. If we stand up against him, together..." She stopped and thought about what she was saying. "We'll turn this around, on him."

"But I still owe him £1250. He said that was only six more times and one striptease."

Tiff looked at her neighbour pityingly. "No more Georgie."

"He'll be mad if..."

"I don't care how mad he gets. He's no one and we can do this. We can turn it around and against him."

"I don't know how to."

"Well you've got me to help. We will sort this out together. You could have him arrested for something – I'm sure. There must be a crime here somewhere."

Georgie looked fearful. "No, please. I don't want any of this getting out. Have you told anyone? Does Joe know?"

"I haven't told a single person and no, Joe doesn't know. I think he'd go straight down to Alvin's – Jeremy's house and knock him out, if he knew."

"Please don't tell him or anyone else. Please."

"I'm not going to tell anyone – I promise. But I need you to promise me something."

"What?" Georgie stared, wide-eyed, her bottom lip clamped down painfully between her teeth.

"Promise me that you will see this through with me and we will stop it."

"Why are you doing this for me? Why would you want to help me?"

"Because it's all so wrong – you must see that."

"Yes, but..."

"And because I consider you to be a new friend. I cannot know about this going on and do nothing to stop it. I just can't. I couldn't live with myself."

Georgie peered, incredulously. Her eyes filled and tears fell over the rims and ran down both cheeks. "I..." she stumbled. "Thank you."

"No need to thank me for anything. When you've got yourself together, we'll go down to his house – we'll get this sorted out today."

Georgie sniffed and wiped her nose. "I'm scared."

"Don't be – he'll be the scared one when we've finished," said Tiff, boldly.

"As long as you're sure…" Georgie said in a wobbly voice.

"I'm sure. We have the upper hand here. He is not going to get away with it." Tiff drew in a long breath and held it momentarily before letting out a lengthy sigh. "There is one other thing."

"What's that?" asked Georgie, listening obediently.

"Would you explain what went on with the birds and apologise to Betty and Cyril?"

Georgie's mouth dropped.

"I don't mean tell them everything. Just explain that Alvin took their money from you and threatened you." Tiff peered at her newfound friend. "And promise to pay them back, as and when you can."

Georgie eyed her quizzically. "Why do you want me to do that?"

"Because they are good people and you could make a difference to their lives."

"They won't forgive me…"

"They will, I'm sure. Especially if I go with you."

Georgie nodded her head resignedly, wiped her nose again and mustered up a faint smile. "OK."

"Can I ask you something else?"

Georgie nodded her blonde head like a young child.

"Again, it was by accident, but my craft room is at the back of the house and… I saw you and Alvin, sorry Jeremy, having an argument out the back. Well, it looked like you were arguing."

"Yes, we were, he… he wants me to split you and Joe up."

"Oh God, really?"

Georgie nodded her head slightly. "He said I had to start flirting with Joe. I said, no way."

"Thank God for that. The man is sick. Can you see why we have to stop him?"

"Yes, I'm scared though."

"Don't be. He will be the scared one by the time I've finished with him. How dare he ask you to do something like that. I know that's not as bad as what you've been through but… well, I'm taking this personally now."

Chapter 33

Tiff was completely stunned by the discovery of her powerful aptitude for determination, courage and integrity. Never before had she felt so impassioned to help someone else to do the right thing. She was stunned by her sudden strength of character. Was this the new Tiffany Cuthbert?

They'd spent almost an hour, planning their veracious attack and Georgie had succumbed to the offer of coffee half way through as well.

"Right," said Tiff, setting her empty mug on the table a little too forcefully, "are you ready for this?"

Georgie met her eye with a menacing stare. "Yes, I am."

"Let's go then." Tiff swallowed hard as her nerves began to tingle with anticipation and her heart beat heavily in her chest. "Just remember that I am representing you and you don't have to speak at all, if you don't wish to."

Nodding her head, Georgie stood up and tugged her t-shirt down. "I'm nervous."

"Me too but this all ends, right here, right now... well, at Alvin-Jeremy's house, as soon as he opens the door." Tiff laughed nervously.

"I can't ever thank you enough for helping me like this."

"No need. I'm hardly doing anything, apart from opening my mouth to talk."

Georgie gave a genuinely warm smile and it was at that moment that Tiff realised just what a vulnerable, misunderstood person her new friend really was. "Remember, if anyone on the close stops us, we're popping round to Alvin's to sort out an issue with something he borrowed from you."

Georgie grimaced. "Oh, yes. Forgot that bit."

"Just leave it to me – I'll do all the talking." Tiff peered up at the clock on her kitchen wall. She knew she had about three and a half hours before Joe arrived home. This had to be cleared up by then. She wanted to make a fresh new start this coming weekend and the only way that could happen would be if there were no more lies, no more obsessive, sneaky spying on the neighbours and no more thoughts of Georgie being the wanton witch who lived next door. "Ready?"

Georgie nodded and followed her out of the house.

The brilliant sunshine of the morning, had faded to a hazy wash of orange and yellow. In the distance, dark grey clouds were bubbling up into vast, looming threats of a thunderstorm. The air was thick and heavy, creating an eerie silence around the close.

"It's going to rain," whispered Georgie as they walked around the path, towards number nine.

"Looks like it." Tiff eyed the gardens across the green, making sure that no one was around. She did not want to cause a scene at Alvin's house and have all the neighbours watching. No, in fact, her tactic would be a highly professional, passive-aggressive approach. There would be no shouting, no screaming and definitely no violence. She desperately hoped so anyway. Her saving grace was that she knew, for sure, that Hayley and Wayne weren't in. Hayley was on a long, late shift today and Wayne wouldn't get home until around the same time as Joe. Thankfully, neither Tiff or Georgie would have to explain anything to them. So, as far as Tiff was concerned, she would say her little, poorly rehearsed speech, give Alvin-Jeremy an evil, we-mean-business-so-don't-cross-us glare and casually walk away with her new friend, Georgie.

That was all there was to it – simple.

Except, after three rings of the grubby looking doorbell, several raps on the glass-fronted door and a casual peep through the bay window, both Tiff and Georgie resigned themselves to the fact that he wasn't at home.

"Damn," said Tiff, feeling the anticlimax of it all.

"He might be away – I never know when he's at home or away on a mission for a few days."

"Georgie," whispered Tiff, quite exasperated by it all, "he doesn't do missions – remember?"

"Oh – yes. I still can't get it into my head."

"The only mission he is ever likely to do is accept a customer's return and give them their money back."

Georgie let out a giggle and clapped a hand over her mouth.

"Well, there's no point waiting around here any longer," said Tiff, with a sigh. "Let's go back to mine."

"Oh, OK." Georgie's face dropped dramatically.

"Don't worry," Tiff added, "I have another plan."

"Plan B?" asked Georgie, her face softening into a smile.

"Yes – exactly! Plan B."

Dear...

Tiff stopped and put the end of the pen to her lips. She hated the idea of addressing Alvin-Jeremy with an endearing term like 'dear'.

"What's up?" asked Georgie, peering over her shoulder.

"Nothing – just thinking how to set it out."

"I'm no good at writing stuff. I'm so thankful to you for doing it."

"Don't start all that again. I'm doing this for both our sakes."

"Both?"

"Yes," said Tiff, "I couldn't live with myself, knowing what has been going on, if I didn't do something about it, and how dare he threaten mine and Joe's relationship."

"Oh, OK." Georgie pulled a chair up next to her and looked at the blank sheet of paper.

Dear Jeremy Greene...

"No – I can't do it," said Tiff, scribbling through the words on the page. She reached for another sheet of paper and started again.

To Jeremy Greene,

I am writing this letter to you on behalf of Georgie Ford. It has come to my attention that you have been mistreating this lady for quite some time now. It will stop as of today!

Georgie will NOT be paying you the rest of the money owed and should you have any concerns about this, you may take it up with myself or my fiancé, Joe.

Tiff hesitated. Should she involve Joe in this? Would Alvin-Jeremy approach him? Surely not, how could he have the nerve?

"Joe!" Georgie looked around at Tiff's face, questioningly. "I thought..."

"You thought right – he doesn't know. It sounds more serious though, don't you think? I'm sure that Alvin-Jeremy wouldn't want to get on the wrong side of Joe – he's a bit of a brute. I mean, Alvin couldn't exactly complain to Joe about the letter could he?"

Georgie shook her head. "As long as Joe doesn't find out."

"God help me if he does."

Alternatively, should you wish to do so, you can file a claim in a small claims court, however, I must warn you that this would lead to a counterclaim for sexual abuse or, at worst, countless rape charges.

"That'll get him," Tiff puffed her cheeks out and exhaled slowly as she read through the letter. Then she continued eagerly.

Georgie Ford is now well aware of your activity as a fraudulent, double-life sex-pest and will no longer be taking part in your illicit, degrading requests.

"What does that mean?" Georgie pointed to a word.

"Illicit? Means – unlawful or forbidden by law."

"OK." Georgie grinned. "You're good at writing letters."

"Thanks."

Should you find this letter a little threatening, please be assured that it is, and is only a reflection of your own affairs regarding the aforementioned, Georgie Ford.

"What's that?"

"Aforementioned? – talking about you before. Don't worry about it. It's just one of those big words that sounds official and helps to achieve the scare factor."

"OK – I'll say no more. You know what you're doing."

"I hope so." Tiff tapped the end of the pen on her chin for a moment and then carried on.

For now, we have agreed to keep this episode confidential and also your true identity, however, should you wish to take things further, we cannot guarantee that the confidentiality will remain intact. Please be aware that things could get out of hand if the residents of Sycamore Close were to find out, firstly, who you really are, and secondly, what you have been doing. I am sure that you would not wish to have any of this information divulged to your neighbours.

Also, please be assured that, under no circumstances, will it be acceptable to contact Miss Ford from this day forward. Doing so, will be considered a breach of the terms of this letter and hence the start of formal proceedings to have you prosecuted for the violations you inflicted upon this vulnerable young woman.

We trust that this letter has been clear and informative. Should you have any questions, please speak to Tiffany Cuthbert at, 4 Sycamore Close. She, and her fiancé, will be more than happy to go over the points raised with you. Alternatively, you could take it to your line-manager at Sainsbury's, as I am sure that he or she would be very interested in the content of this letter also, and may be able to offer you some helpful advice.

Before closing, I would like to take this opportunity to personally advise you of the repercussions, should you choose to continue your endeavor to 'split' myself and my fiancé's relationship up. It won't happen! It will never happen. Sadly, you are unable to comprehend what a true relationship is and the strength within it. Your feeble existence is no threat to a stable, loving connection between two people like myself and Joe. You are a failure. A sick individual who preys on the vulnerable, less fortunate people in this world. My greatest advice to you would be for you to leave Sycamore Close, forever.

Georgie laughed, heartily. "Can you image his face when he reads this?"

"I'd love to see it."

"Me too."

Yours sincere...

Tiff paused again, she didn't want to be sincere.

From Tiffany Cuthbert, on behalf of Georgie Ford – united against perverted losers.

Tiff read through the letter and held the pen to her lips, thoughtfully. She then added a postscript.

PS. I have one further piece of advice that may help you in the future, with regard to your alter ego, Alvin Snodgrass. Could I recommend that you don't use such a pathetic name in the future and also, try to go for a more believable profession (such as Customer Service Assistant). Lastly, please let me suggest a new name for your alter ego, should you chose to continue to use one. Both myself and Georgie think that the name Jogging-Jerk-Jeremy would be a far more suitable name.

Tiff put the pen down and giggled. "What do you think?"

"Amazing – I could never have done anything like that." Georgie grinned. "And that bit is so funny." She pointed to the postscript.

Tiff nodded and grinned. "Right, shall we post it? Perhaps we could call into Betty's on the way back."

"Oh no, I forgot about that bit." Georgie's smile turned down, into a grimace.

"Better to get it over and done with – then we can both move on and get on with our lives."

"Yes, I suppose so..." Georgie replied, waveringly. "Are you sure it'll be fine, not to pay Alvin the rest of his money?"

"I'm sure it will be just fine. When he reads the letter, he'll realise what he's been doing and I'm hoping he'll know how wrong it has been. I'm confident that he'll be so worried that he's going to get into big trouble that he'll... well, just vanish."

"Hope so," said Georgie, giving a little shrug of her shoulders.

"Come on, let's go and post this. Then visit Betty and Cyril on the way back. Your new life is just about to start."

Both Betty and Cyril were extraordinarily forgiving. Tiff got the distinct impression that it was like their one and only daughter had returned from a long absence. Betty, in particular, was elated to have Georgie back in her life and insisted that the momentous occasion should be celebrated with cake. On the downside, Betty and Cyril were shocked to hear of Alvin Snodgrass' part in the whole affair.

"We don't want you to pay back the money, Georgie." Betty stated quite adamantly. "What's done is done. It's all forgotten about now. The fact that you have come round here, explained what really happened and apologised, is enough for us."

"But..." spluttered Georgie.

"No buts," Cyril interrupted. "We'll forget about it now. It's good to have you back as a friendly neighbour."

"Yes," said Betty, smiling and shaking her head. "You did the right thing by coming round to apologise and explain exactly what went on."

"It's water under the bridge," added Cyril. "Water under the bridge."

Georgie mouthed a 'thank-you' and smiled awkwardly.

Tiff smirked and wondered if Georgie knew what Cyril had meant by, 'water under the bridge'. She wasn't the brightest of people. But that didn't matter. She was kind, thoughtful and caring and that was what really counted.

Leaving Betty's with a tummy full of cake and a plate loaded with three extra slices for Joe, Tiff strolled along the pathway with Georgie. "I'd better get indoors," she said, sluggishly. "Joe will be home soon."

"Do you want to swap mobile numbers?" Georgie smiled, expectantly.

"Yes, of course. I was going to say that if you hear from Alvin... or Jeremy, you might want to let me know. Or, indeed, if I hear anything I'll let *you* know." Tiff peered across the green to number nine. "I wonder when he'll be home."

Georgie shrugged. "Don't know. I'm a bit worried about what he's going to say or do though."

"He won't say or do anything. I've confronted him before and he backed away from me like the pathetic, shameful bully that he is. Tiff put the plate of cake on the ground and pulled out her mobile. "Give me your number and I'll ring you. Then you can contact me if you get worried about anything."

"Thanks."

As Georgie was adding Tiff's number to her phone, Tiff looked across the green and spotted a tall, darkly clothed figure emerging from the corner of number nine. The man raised a hand and smiled. Then he began to walk up the pathway. Straight past his house. Alvin-Jeremy was approaching.

"Georgie," Tiff muttered under her breath. "Say nothing."

Georgie looked up from her phone, startled by Tiff's words, and gasped.

"Evening Georgie," called Alvin-Jeremy. "How are you?"

Georgie sidled up next to Tiff and looked down at her phone.

As Alvin-Jeremy drew closer, he eyed Tiff with contempt.

"Don't come any closer Jeremy," said Tiff, sternly.

"Still piping on about that Jeremy business are you?" Alvin-Jeremy tutted. "Has she told you about that?" He peered suspiciously at Georgie, who was still looking down at her phone. "Bloody ridiculous."

"You should go home Jeremy. You have a gravely important letter waiting for you." Tiff picked the plate of cake up from the ground, grabbed Georgie by the arm and pulled her into her front garden. "Come on Georgie – come and have some tea with us tonight."

Georgie didn't lift her head at all, as she was dragged towards Tiff's front door.

Alvin-Jeremy stared after them incredulously. "Georgie," he said in a patronising voice, "you're being rather rude."

Tiff opened the front door and pulled her in.

"Sorry," Georgie called out as she went inside the house.

"Why did you say sorry? He's the one who should and will be sorry."

"Sorry," she said again.

"Don't keep saying sorry."

"Sorry – oops."

Tiff tutted and peered out of the living room window. "He's leaving and Joe's on his way up the path too."

"Oh no..."

"Don't worry. I'll say that we got chatting outside and... and then Betty came out... and then the truth came out about Alvin-Jeremy... and then I invited you in for a coffee. Got it?"

"Got it."

Tiff continued to watch as Joe and Alvin-Jeremy got closer to each other. They crossed paths and it seemed like they didn't say a word to each other. "Right, he's nearly here. Get in the kitchen, I'll make you a coffee."

Georgie hurriedly followed Tiff to the kitchen and sat down at the table. "Argh!" she spluttered.

Turning around from the kettle, Tiff looked at the piece of paper in Georgie's hand. The first piece. The one that had, *Dear Jeremy Greene*, scribbled out. "Give it to me," said Tiff, panicking and thrusting herself forward as the front door opened. She snatched the piece of paper out of Georgie's hand, scrunched it up and threw it in the bin as Joe walked into the dining room.

"Hello," he said, with a quizzical stare.

"Hi there – Georgie's popped in for a cuppa."

"Hello again." Georgie smiled sheepishly, avoiding Joe's eye. "I just bumped into Alvin down the path."

"Oh, did you?" Tiff grinned falsely.

"Yeah, miserable sod. Didn't even say hello."

"That's probably because we... err... upset him." Tiff smirked. "Sit down and we, or I..." Tiff flicked a reassuring gaze towards Georgie, "will tell you all about it and how Georgie now has the approval of Betty and Cyril again."

"Oh," said Joe, widening his eyes, "great news. I can't wait to hear it."

Chapter 34

3-bedroom semi-detached house for sale

Sycamore Close, Bashfield, Hampshire

Tenure: Freehold

£256,000

This end of terrace property, situated in a pleasant and quiet close in the heart of the countryside, boasts a spacious interior. It has 3 good-sized bedrooms and a bathroom to the first floor. The ground floor has a large kitchen/diner, a roomy living area and a large office/utility room. General repair and considerable decoration would be required to bring this property up to the standard of others in the area.

Outside, the property has a small garden to the front and a sizeable garden to the rear – both in need of some clearing. Parking facilities can be located on the lay-by, close to the property as a small green is situated in the centre of the close, preventing vehicle access directly to the property.

An early viewing is highly recommended as this property has the potential to become a beautiful, family home, should it fall into the right hands.

Contact Bashfield Estate Agents for more details:
01794 748119

Ref no. BEA/9SycCl-2675

***

No one ever saw him again. Jeremy Greene aka Alvin Snodgrass vanished overnight, just as Tiff had predicted. His house went up for sale, just three weeks after the letter had been posted. The gossip around the close was interesting to listen to as the residents speculated on his sudden disappearance and the 'For Sale' sign standing in his front garden.

There were only a few who really knew where he would be. Tiff, Georgie and Joe had a jolly good idea where the lecherous coward had gone. But only Tiff and Georgie could truly surmise as to what might happen to him in the future...

Once the second letter arrived at *Sainsbury's* in Salisbury.

***

Hello Georgie, Tiffy gave me your number. Hope you don't mind. I'm interested in getting a buffet quote from you, for a family wedding coming up this October. We also have another one next June. I should have taken your business card when I was at Joe and Tiffy's engagement party but I forgot. Would it be possible for you to contact me as I was very impressed with the buffet you provided for Joe and Tiffy? I've also passed your name on to a few of my friends. Kind regards Pat Slater (Tiffy's boss).

***

I'm sure it must have been you who got rid of that nasty man, at number nine. I've seen what's been going on there. It wasn't right and I think you knew all the time. I saw you with your binoculars. Thank you, dearie.

Tiff sat in her car and read the note again. She smiled to herself. The author of yet another mysterious note, left under her windscreen wiper. Except this time, that person had just given themselves away. She now knew exactly who it was. She knew who *she* was.

***

Booking Confirmation

Dear Mr J Frey,

We are pleased to confirm that your provisional wedding booking has been changed to a fixed booking for Saturday 8th December from 11:00am.

Please ensure that full payment reaches us, no later than 2nd September.

Please see the enclosed set of forms to be filled in and returned to us no later than 8th November.

We look forward to spending your very special day with you and are proud of our achievements in providing a smooth-running, memorable day for all our wedding clients.

Yours sincerely

Jennifer Tomby

Operations Manager

***

Tiff waited as the extension number rang.

"Hello, is that the manager?"

"It is madam. Mr Hardy, how can I help you?"

"My name is Titianna Frey – from the Social Security Office." Tiff's heart beat heavily in her chest. She smiled at Georgie and winked her eye.

"Hello – what can I do for you?"

"I'm investigating a fraudulent claim and wondered if you could tell me whether you have a Jeremy Greene still working in your employment."

"Absolutely not – he's been sacked."

Tiff's eyes widened. "Oh, really? Could you tell me when and why? Obviously, I need this information in order to speed the process of the investigation at our end."

"Yes, of course. We did some investigating of our own, once we'd received an anonymous letter regarding his activities on the south coast. He was given an instant dismissal just two weeks ago."

"I see..." Tiff grimaced and nodded her head to Georgie. "And are you able to confirm his whereabouts at present?"

"I have absolutely no idea, nor wish to. All I can tell you is – he won't ever be setting foot in this store again."

"Thank you for your time, Mr Hardy. You have been very helpful."

"You're welcome. Goodbye."

Neighbours

Good neighbours, bad neighbours
Some noisy, some quiet
Some peep through net curtains
Others friendly and polite

The Smiths down the road
like to party all night
And young Johnny Brown
picks a Saturday night fight

Old Mrs White
still gets quite a fright
When the kids enjoy kicking
a ball at her light

The Greens have a dog
that barks every day
While the boy at the end
has a drum kit to play

The Pennington-Smyths
like to travel abroad
But a day trip to Brighton
is all Jean can afford

Good neighbours, bad neighbours
Some noisy, some quiet
Some peep through net curtains
Others friendly and polite

Joan Stevens (2015)

I hope you have enjoyed this book
But even if you didn't
Please leave a review at Amazon
Hugely appreciated

Tara Ford

Printed in Poland
by Amazon Fulfillment
Poland Sp. z o.o., Wrocław